P9-DCM-575

1/9

EAT, DRINK, *and Be from* MISSISSIPPI

EAT, DRINK, *and Be from* MISSISSIPPI

A Novel

NANCI KINCAID

Little, Brown and Company
NEW YORK   BOSTON   LONDON

F
KIN

Little, Brown and Company
Hachette Book Group
237 Park Avenue, New York, NY 10017
Visit our Web site at www.HachetteBookGroup.com

First Edition: January 2009

Little, Brown and Company is a division of Hachette Book Group,
Inc. The Little, Brown name and logo are trademarks of
Hachette Book Group, Inc.

The characters and events in this book are fictitious.
Any similarity to real persons, living or dead, is coincidental
and not intended by the author.

Library of Congress Cataloging-in-Publication Data
Kincaid, Nanci.
    Eat, drink, and be from Mississippi : a novel / Nanci
Kincaid. — 1st ed.
        p. cm.
    ISBN 978-0-316-00915-7
        1. Domestic fiction. 2. Mississippi — Fiction. I. Title.
PS3561.I4253E18   2009
813'.54 — dc22   2008028506

10 9 8 7 6 5 4 3 2 1

RRD-IN

Book design by Brooke Koven

Printed in the United States of America

for my husband

After the feast comes the reckoning.

—PROVERB

MISSISSIPPI

One

HINDS COUNTY NEEDED RAIN. Heat rose to nearly a hundred degrees most afternoons. Already two boys had gone down, fallen to their knees, threatening to collapse of heat stroke. They'd been sent to sit under a sprawling shade tree with cups of ice chips to chew on. One spilled the ice on his head and rubbed it over his parched skull.

Truely had long ago sweat through his pads and jersey, adding a couple of pounds to his misery. It occurred to him that wearing a helmet in this kind of heat could cause your brain to fry. Still, drill after drill, he went at it full speed. Nobody on the field worked harder or complained less. According to his coach there was a certain genius to that. Truely liked pushing himself. He liked knowing that no matter how tough it got out there, he didn't quit. Nobody could make him.

Between series he glimpsed his daddy, Truely Sr., standing there, watching. He was easy to spot among the fathers huddled on the sideline en route home from work, mopping their brows with soiled handkerchiefs, squinting into the glare of the afternoon sun, spitting plugs of chewing tobacco to the ground, their trucks parked helter-skelter in the dry grass. On any given day there might be as many as twenty men gathered to watch their sons suffer through Hinds County football practice. A few suit wearers had abandoned their jackets midday and now loosened or lost their knotted neckties. The rest wore overalls or jeans — or like Truely's own daddy, a uniform of some kind. Some men were gray or losing their wispy hair altogether. A couple of older guys were of the flattops forever persuasion. One old man, a local recovering hippie, a veteran, had a stringy ponytail left over from his post-Vietnam rebellion. The men wore ball caps and bifocals and had biscuit bellies overlapping their sagging belts. To a man, all of them had dark underarm circles on their cotton shirts.

Truely Sr. was middle-aged like the others but he was thin and remained fit. He stood with his feet apart, arms folded across his chest, watching tirelessly as young Truely went at it play after play. Truely played corner. His job was to keep Mose Jones, the team's promising receiver, from catching the ball and waltzing it into the end zone. He succeeded in stopping him maybe forty percent of the time, which was nowhere near good enough.

Truely Sr. nodded when he caught his son's eye after he'd batted down a spiraling missile meant for Mose. It was a wordless conversation between them. Encouragement unspoken. Truely's daddy was tanned dark from working long hours in his garden or tinkering with his truck under the glaring sun. Once, when Truely was a young boy, a kid at school had asked him, "Is your old man I-talian or something?"

Truely had not liked the question. "No," he'd insisted. "Why?"

His daddy's hair was thick and brown, compliments of an unsubstantiated Indian ancestor he liked to claim. Truely had been told his daddy was a handsome man. That's what some people said—like his mother for example. Mostly her. His daddy wore his green JACKSON APPLIANCE coveralls with his name on the pocket and his leather work boots. The only things that betrayed his age were the deep lines carved into his square face and, if you knew him, his taste in nearly everything.

At one point that afternoon Truely saw his daddy speak to one of his teachers who had wandered out to the football practice field carrying a Coca-Cola in her hand. Another time he saw him share a word with one of the other fathers, a subsidized soybean farmer whose son, Lamont, a fat boy, played offensive line. Lamont made up in size whatever he lacked in talent. People in Hinds County respected that.

After practice, spent and sore, Truely showered with the others, threw on his jeans and wrinkled shirt, gathered his outdated, tattered books, and climbed into the sweltering cab of his daddy's truck. The sun was beginning to set, turning the sky the color of a bruise. Truely and his daddy rode the half-dozen or so miles home in relative silence as was their habit. At one point his daddy broke the spell and said, "I talked to your history teacher."

"Mrs. Seacrest?"

"She says you're doing good in her class. She says you understand the power of the past and that's unusual at your age."

Truely nodded absentmindedly. He was wishing he could put the radio on.

"What you guess she means by that?" his daddy asked.

Truely shrugged his shoulders, more bored than bewildered.

"Is she talking about the War Between the States or something?"

"Don't know."

His daddy drove as slow as Christmas. Truely doubted his daddy had any idea how fast his truck might actually go, since it would never occur to him to exceed the speed limit. He had never been a man in a hurry. "Guess that's just teacher talk," his daddy said.

"I guess." Truely hung his head out the window, letting the hot air slap his face.

They pulled off the highway and drove the gravel road out to the house. Truely saw his mother standing outside in the yard, wiping her hands on her apron. "There's Mama," he said.

His daddy glanced in her direction. "She don't look too happy, does she?"

They parked the truck in a sandy spot next to the carport and got out, slamming their doors in unison. It was obvious his mother had been crying. Her face was flushed and her eyes were swollen. Her once dark red hair was mostly gray now. It was damp around her neck, jutting out everywhere in little wet points. She walked toward them. "Courtney's home," she announced. "Her roommate drove her."

"Anything wrong?" his daddy asked.

"This." His mother reached into the pocket of her apron and pulled out a folded page from a magazine and handed it to his daddy.

"What is it?" he asked.

"Read it," she said.

"Let me get in the house where the light's better." He took the paper and walked toward the front door.

"She says she's quitting school and moving," his mother blurted.

"Moving where?" Truely asked.

"California."

"California?" Truely almost laughed. "No way."

"That's what she says," his mother insisted.

"We'll see about that, won't we?" His daddy slapped the paper across his leg.

"Don't get anything started, Truely John." His mother reached for his daddy's arm. "Not now. Let me get supper on the table first."

TRUELY'S SISTER, Courtney, first believed that if she could just graduate from high school and get away to college then her life would finally begin. She could live on her own, think uncensored thoughts, meet new people from distant hard-to-pronounce places, mingle with *the other* she had craved all her life and at last transform herself more nearly into who she was really supposed to be. But it hadn't happened that way. Now here she was, about to abandon her scholarship to Millsaps—something a lot of people would kill for—to do what, hitchhike across the country?

What was it about red-haired people? They were different from normal people. Truely believed that. "With two redheaded women in this house, me and you, we don't stand a chance." His daddy had said this when Truely was a boy and the two of them got run out of the house by the sheer womanness that overtook the place. They'd retreated outside to eat a sack of boiled peanuts or drop their cane poles into the small catfish pond. "If a

redheaded girl ever gets after you, son—you run, you hear?"
his daddy had teased. The pure absurdity of such a notion had
made young Truely laugh. It was his plan at the time to run from
all girls—red-haired or otherwise. He was glad to be a brown-
skinned, brown-haired boy—like his daddy.

A S S O O N A S they all sat down to supper Courtney kicked Truely
under the table and raised her eyebrows as a signal for help.

What? he mouthed silently.

She was wearing a Mississippi State T-shirt and a pair of cut-
off jeans. She'd clipped her hair up off her neck with a plastic
barrette. It was a mess of part-curl, part-frizz framing her pale,
fine-featured face, pink with heat. She swiped at a trickle of sweat
with her paper napkin. As always Courtney wore lots of black
mascara so her eyes would show up—that's what she said—and
some shiny stuff, Vaseline maybe, on her lips. She folded her
legs under her Indian-style in her chair—something his mother
didn't like—then rethought it and put her feet on the floor and
sat up straight.

As soon as the blessing was asked, before the first bite of food
was passed or eaten, Courtney said, "Daddy, you know I'm over
eighteen now. I'm legal. I've made up my mind to go out to California and you and Mama can't stop me."

"Damn, Court." Truely hated it when his sister disrespected
his parents.

"I'm sorry," she said. "But it's the truth."

"Start over," Truely told her.

"Just because you've never heard of it doesn't mean it isn't a
good school, Truely," she announced defensively. "Look." She
handed him the folded ad from the back of a fashion magazine.
"It says they'll help you find a job in your field while you work
toward your degree. See? Read the fine print." Truely looked at
the ad. It included a small picture of happy students, all of whom
looked—by Mississippi standards—foreign.

"I don't know," Truely said. "You sure about this?" It was a stupid question.

"You're not going anywhere, anytime soon," his daddy said flatly. "You're not ready."

"It's just that girls—you know, well-brought-up girls," his mother interrupted, clearing her throat, trying to keep the discussion on a civil keel, "can't just take off on their own. People get the wrong idea. They take advantage of young women out in the world. You've never been west of the Mississippi. It's different out there."

"I'm not joining the circus, Mama," Courtney insisted. "I'm going to school." She gripped her fork like it was a pitchfork, the way a child does.

"Not in California you're not," his daddy repeated. "That's final."

"I am going," Courtney said resolutely.

"Hell if you are." His daddy piled pinto beans on his plate as he spoke.

"They accepted me, Daddy. I've sent my deposit."

"You'll do as I tell you to do, young lady."

"No, Daddy. Not this time."

His daddy set the bowl of beans down on the table, the serving spoon clanking against it. "Don't back-talk me."

"I leave two weeks from Sunday," she said.

If looks could kill, Courtney was in the line of fire. "So you're planning to defy your mother and me. Is that what you're saying?"

"I've already got my bus ticket."

His daddy slapped his napkin down on the table and stood up abruptly, scraping his chair across the floor. His fork fell to the floor and bounced across the room. Truely saw his daddy's jaw flex and the anger flash across his face. He walked out the back door, letting the screen door slam behind him. It echoed like a gunshot.

"Can't you be happy for me, Daddy?" Courtney called out. "Just once?"

Minutes later his mother got up silently. She poured a cup of coffee, put a slice of pound cake on a saucer and took it outside to his daddy. Truely imagined his daddy standing outside by the pond, slinging rocks into the black water—his mother approaching him cautiously, bearing gifts.

"Man." Truely shook his head. "You're something, Court. You know that?"

"I'm trying to be an adult here, True," Courtney said. "Adults make decisions about how to live their lives. They don't just follow the path of least resistance."

"You have to blindside them with this kind of news?"

"There is never any good way to tell them the truth, True. They always hate the truth. You know that."

"Give me a break." He rolled his eyes.

"You think I like disappointing Mother and Daddy all the time, True?" Her voice quivered. "Well, believe me, I don't."

THAT NIGHT when Truely was trying to drift off to sleep in his hot bed, his body aching, his muscles cramped and sore, he remembered a conversation he had had with his sister the last time she was home. She was talking about California even then, calling it the most promising part of the promised land, a place generously littered with dreams and dreamers. She'd told Truely she imagined California as one huge lost and found where if you looked hard enough you could probably find whatever you needed.

He wasn't sure about that, but he was sure about this. Whatever he needed he expected to find right here in Hinds County, Mississippi.

HIS PARENTS spiraled into despair wondering where they'd gone wrong. It became their primary pastime—lamenting. His mother especially spent hours searching out the misstep that had brought them to this dark passage. Okay, so maybe Courtney would never marry a nice local boy and become a devout preacher's wife—the fondest dream of Mississippi parents—but did she need to move out to California, where there were no rules at all, no guarantee of good manners or good sense, where that free love movement got started and all those homosexuals were out of hiding, even marching in the streets unashamed, and drugs and gangs were taking over everything? Did Courtney think they were born yesterday? Did she think just because they lived in rural Mississippi they didn't know what was going on in the world? They watched the six o'clock news same as everybody else.

"Remember that freaky Charles Manson, who roamed California as evil as Satan himself? Remember how he talked all those creepy girls into performing obscene criminal acts?" His mother was washing dishes at the kitchen sink, directing her remarks to his daddy, who did not respond. He sat in his usual chair with the newspaper in his hand, trying to focus on the day's baseball scores. Truely thought he looked like a man who'd had a hard day on the job—and now had come home to an even harder night.

"Those wicked people are still locked up in some California prison to this day," his mother said. "Thank God for that." Truely's mother usually concluded her comments with a favorite rhetorical question. "I read where half the people out in California can't even speak English anyway, so even if you were screaming for help, who would come?"

ON THE DAY of Courtney's departure all the family got up and went to church together as though it were any ordinary Sunday. When they got home from church they sat down to Sunday dinner. His mother asked the blessing, embellished appropriately for the occasion at hand. Then they ate quietly, avoiding one another's gaze.

Afterward, while his mother cleared the dishes from the table, Courtney went to her room and dragged out her battered suitcase. The wear and tear had come from some previous, faceless owner. Days earlier his mother had made an impulse purchase at a garage sale over in Jackson. A good-bye gift of sorts. It passed as a peace offering.

Truely's daddy stood silently with his hands in his pockets, watching Courtney struggle with her heavy suitcase. He resisted the temptation to step in and carry it for her—so Truely did it. "What you got in here anyway?" he asked. "Rocks?"

"I love you, Daddy." Courtney kissed him. Truely's daddy stood fixed in the doorway. He took a deep breath, exhaled slowly, but said nothing. Truely's mother cried and slipped his sister five crisp one-hundred-dollar bills. At the time it was the most cash money Truely had ever seen.

He was the one who drove his sister to the bus station. He'd had his learner's permit less than a month, although he had been driving the country roads since he was fourteen. His parents had agreed that he, rather than they, should deliver his sister to the bus station in order to avoid any family drama, which would likely become the fodder of gossip. Nobody wanted the harsh local spotlight shining on Courtney as she boarded the Greyhound bus destined to set her on the path to ruin.

He made a dumb remark like, "This ought to give people around here something to talk about for a while." Which was true. All through school Courtney had had a knack for getting herself talked about—something Truely personally had never aspired to.

Truely didn't tell his sister he'd never admired anybody more. He wasn't even sure he'd told her he loved her. Surely she must know that, right? Until that moment in time he had never realized it was possible to leave the place you were born and move someplace far away and unfamiliar—just because you wanted to. Nobody had bothered to tell him that where you lived your life could be a choice you made yourself. Who knew the accident of birth had an expiration date?

Two

T RUELY LISTENED to his sister fall in love with Hastings long distance over the telephone. She called home nearly every week and before long was describing at great length the many quirks and wonders of this guy, Hastings Cabot Littleton.

Courtney had been in California less than a year when she met Hastings at a Grateful Dead concert at Berkeley. Some friends from art school had offered her an extra ticket when somebody backed out at the last minute. She took the bus out to the stadium when she got off work, with plans to meet up with the others, but there was mass confusion and she couldn't find them. She confessed later to Truely that she had been maybe slightly out of her element. The last concert she'd gone to was Charley Pride over in Jackson at the Civic Center. She'd gone with Truely and their daddy that time. When Charley crooned "Missin' Mississippi" he had the whole audience choked up with geographically inspired emotion—including the three of them. But this was totally different.

Out of all the guys in the throbbing concert mob she had chosen to ask him—Hastings—directions to the gate where she was supposed to meet her friends. Hastings didn't stand out really, she would insist later. He was a tallish, sort of handsome guy, with longish hair, a stubble of beard, wire-rimmed glasses, brown eyes and a quick but cautious smile. She told Truely that he had looked a little older and calmer than the others in the crowd. Maybe that was why. She explained to him—Hastings—that her ticket was confusing and it seemed that everywhere she went the gates were chained closed anyway. "I can't figure this out," she had said. "What's going on here?"

He claimed he had been so startled by the rawness of her accent that he couldn't understand a word she was saying. After he asked her to repeat the question three times—*What? What did you say? One more time?*—she became exasperated and walked away, calling him rude. Now, that might not have been such a big insult out in California—Truely wasn't sure at the time—but it was the ultimate insult that could be hurled your way on Mississippi soil. Hastings must have sensed that. He spent the rest of the night trying to talk to her, explain himself, apologize again, provide detailed directions pretty much anywhere else she might ever need to go. She avoided and ignored him—forcing him, naturally, to try harder. Avoiding him was pure instinct on her part. It was pure genius too. She would learn much later that Hastings was not a man used to being dismissed and ignored.

Toward the end of the night, the story went, Hastings was slightly crazed by the lost girl searching in vain for a familiar face. He didn't even know her name—this eccentric redhead, hot tempered, high strung and Mississippi exotic. When he finally heard her laugh it was all over. That's the way he would tell the story later. "That laugh. My God. I knew I was a goner." Somehow he managed to convince Courtney to leave the Grateful Dead and go have a late supper with him, which he still claimed to be his crowning achievement in the art of persuasion, a talent at which he considered himself—and in the future years would in fact prove himself—to always have excelled. "I know a place you'll like," he'd told her. "The people speak your language there—or close to it."

Courtney said she only agreed for two reasons: one, she never did find her friends and consequently had no ride home and not enough bus fare, and two, inhaling all the secondhand marijuana smoke was wearing down her defenses, besides making her ravenously hungry. It was really the thought of a cheeseburger, she said, that was irresistible.

At the time she was going to art school nights and had a part-time job at an art gallery downtown on Geary Street. She took the bus into the city four days a week and one day out of every weekend. Her boss liked her and paid her well enough, even helped her sell three modestly notable pieces of her own work, but still her money was always running low and she struggled to keep herself afloat. So she was not too proud to let an apologetic man express his regrets by buying her dinner.

They drove to Fat Daddy's, a hole-in-the-wall all-night diner in Oakland that Hastings knew about. It played nonstop blues on scratched 45 records on a temperamental old jukebox. It was in what Hastings called an iffy neighborhood, but it specialized in Southern food and that was the lure. They were the only white people in the restaurant, a commonplace occurrence back in Mississippi, and Courtney's comfort zone for sure. She guessed, according to Hastings' definition of iffy, that she must hail from an extremely iffy homeland. The sights, sounds and smells at Fat Daddy's helped put her at ease, which was good, since she was uncharacteristically nervous. She ordered a cheeseburger with Vidalia onions, watermelon rind pickles and a side of greens with pepper sauce. Hastings ordered the same, hold the onions.

While they waited for their food he said, "Anybody ever tell you your freckles are great?"

"Everybody," she said. "Of course, most people are lying."

"I'm not," he said.

"Back home people are all about tans, you know? Freckles are not the thing down there."

"I think they're spectacular."

"That's a good start then." She smiled. "So, what else do you like about me? I mean, so far? Let's make a list, okay? How about my eyes? Do you love the way they sparkle and dance with light? Do you see your very soul when you look into the depths of my eyes?"

He laughed. "Do I detect a tinge of sarcasm here?"

"When I'm nervous I can get a little sarcastic I guess." She was sipping sweet tea through a paper straw.

"Good. I like that," he said. "So does that happen a lot with you? Men gazing into those liquid pools of yours in search of their souls?"

"Pretty much always," she said. "Are you surprised?"

"Ask me later," he said, "after we see if my soul makes an appearance."

"Fair enough." She leaned toward him. "Are you going to eat that slice of white bread?"

"Help yourself." He passed her the red plastic bread basket.

"People in California don't eat much white bread, do they? That's what my roommate says. It's not healthy, right? But in Mississippi we love it. Sunbeam is our favorite. Sometimes we fry it in a skillet with lots of butter and mayonnaise. That's how Elvis liked his white bread."

He watched her spread butter on her bread, fold it in half, and eat it daintily.

"Down in Mississippi we're actually quite famous for our bad habits. Maybe you've heard?"

He nodded almost absentmindedly, staring at her so intently that she was slightly uneasy. "You're staring," she said.

"Sorry." He smiled.

"Don't stare."

"You're right. I'm sorry."

"It's rude."

"Of course. Rude. Twice in one night. Damn," he teased.

"So let's try this again," she said. "We're aiming for a little pleasant conversation here. Help me out, okay?" She smiled her hundred-watt smile. "I take it you're a Grateful Dead fan?"

"You could say so, I guess. I mean, I haven't sold everything I own to follow them around the country in a stolen van or anything."

"But maybe you wish you could?"

"Never," he said. "You know how you hear people say, Oh, music is my life. I'm ready to die for the band or the art—or whatever. Well, I like music, but it's not my life. What about you?"

"I mostly listen to country music." She mimicked playing a fiddle for emphasis. "You know, I like a lot of different things, but when I'm alone in a car I nearly always go straight to the country music station."

"Really?"

"Really."

"I always wondered who was out there listening to that stuff."

"Well, it was probably me. My mother and daddy too. My brother—his name is Truely—he thinks he's black, so he mostly listens to R&B, blues, Motown—you know."

"Country music, huh? That's what you like?"

"That's right. Why? Do I lose points for that?"

"I'd say you leave me no choice but to deduct a couple of points."

She laughed and wiped her mouth with a paper napkin. "I'd say we might need to broaden your horizons a little, mister."

"I like the sound of that," he said.

"You're flirting."

"I am," he agreed.

"Well, on behalf of country music just let me say this. It is some of the finest organic art produced in this country."

"Organic?"

"Untaught. You know, spontaneous, spirit-inspired, naturally evolving."

"And that makes it good? That it springs from musical ignorance?"

"I can see you don't have proper respect for ignorance. Ignorance inspires great courage and free thinking—if you must know. The purest form of artistic expression is born of what you are calling ignorance. You can educate yourself right out of having even an ounce of artistic creativity left. I've seen that happen."

"So you're in favor of ignorance and against education?"

"No." She smiled. "I'm in favor of both."

A fat man carried two plates heaped with food and more or less slung them down on the table in front of them. "Hot," he said. "Ya'll need anything else?"

"More sweet tea?" Courtney rattled her empty glass.

The man nodded and walked away.

"Looks good," she said. "I love a good hamburger."

Hastings began to laugh.

"What?" she said. "What's so funny?"

"I like you."

"Already? Just wait until you get to know me." She picked up her cheeseburger with both hands. "You'll be out of your mind."

"I believe you," he said.

Courtney bit into her cheeseburger with what she later described to Truely as a swooning gesture, eyes closed. It was a messy venture too, onions and pickles sliding, sauce dripping. "You're doing it again," she told him.

"Staring?" He laughed. "Sorry."

She returned the unwieldy cheeseburger to her plate and wiped her mouth with her napkin. "So let's talk about you, okay? Tell me something interesting."

So far Hastings had not touched his food. "How interesting exactly?"

"Not earthshaking. Just, you know, reasonably interesting."

"Well, I don't know how interesting you'll find this, but I own a business. I'm one of those geeky guys who actually like to get up and go to work every day. I might be a little overeducated by your standards, but I'm hoping you can overlook that."

"What kind of business?"

"I buy failing properties, reinvent them and sell them. Sort of like real estate rehabilitation. Littleton Properties. It's my baby, you could say."

"You're Littleton Properties?"

"I am."

"I've seen some of your signs down on Geary Street where I work. That's you? Aren't you a little young—you know, to be Littleton Properties?"

"Not really."

"How old are you exactly? By the way, it is not rude to ask a perfect stranger how old he is when he has lured you off the beaten path like this."

"Perfect? I guess we're off to a good start here."

"Just answer the question, please."

"I'm old enough to know better," he said. "Turned thirty in January. How about you?"

"Nowhere near old enough to know better. I'm twenty."

"Twenty? My God. You're a baby. You look older."

"I'm an old soul—if that counts."

"Wise beyond your years?"

"Definitely."

"Me too," he said.

WHILE THEY ATE, with Smokey Robinson and Muddy Waters crooning in the background, Courtney learned some things about Hastings Littleton. He was originally from Connecticut—a man she might have fondly referred to as a Yankee back in Mississippi—but he had come west to college and claimed the West Coast had won him over entirely.

He was an only child born to older parents. His dad had died of a heart attack when Hastings was twenty-four. His mother had been diagnosed with dementia shortly afterward and had died two years ago from an overdose of medication. Hastings never knew whether she ingested a lethal dosage to stave off the inevitable or whether in a state of confusion she continued to retake her medicines because she was unable to remember having already done so. She'd lost her short-term memory almost entirely—remembered her father but not her husband, her childhood but not her child. It was heartbreaking the way Hastings explained it. "She wasn't the sort of woman who would want to live wearing a diaper, not knowing who she was or where she was," he said. "Sometimes death is merciful."

"That's sad," Courtney said. "So there is just you now?"

"Some distant cousins somewhere," he said.

"Are you lonely?"

"Wow. Now there's a question."

"You don't have to answer," she told him.

TRUELY KNEW all the details of this first meeting because Courtney called home and talked to him at length—reported and repeated the significant events of her new, foreign life. "True," she'd said on this occasion, "I met this interesting guy."

"Good." He was only half interested.

"No, True. This guy is different. We had this really delicious conversation. The words just came," she said. "They flowed, True. Before we knew it dinner evolved into breakfast." That image stayed with Truely—his skinny sister with her big appetite, nourished by a mouthwatering conversation.

"Fried eggs and grits later the sun was coming up," she'd said.

TRUELY MISSED Courtney more than he'd expected he would after she left for art school. The house was eerily quiet without her. He had come to look forward to her Sunday-night phone calls just to break the spell of serenity or—on a couple of rare occasions—the lack of serenity. Her calls came late, when the rates were low and his parents were asleep. "You'll never believe this, True, but..." and she updated him on her new and improved life, relayed the conversations and struggles of her worldly new friends—or opened briefly the windows to her own surging soul. Nearly everything Truely thought he knew about women—however little—he felt he'd learned from his sister's late-night revelatory and unrestrained phone conversations. She trusted him. And he appreciated being connected somehow to the world beyond Hinds County.

Whenever Courtney asked him about his own life, as she often did, he replied with nonanswers. "Nothing much going on," he might say. "No news here."

Sometimes it made her furious. "True, you really scare me. You need to get a real life." It didn't bother him to be perceived as boring. He took comfort in it.

"How's Tay-Ann?" Courtney routinely asked.

"Fine," he always said.

"You two still going out?"

"Yep."

Courtney sighed loudly into the phone and said, "Okay then,

Mr. Excitement, gotta go. You be good. Don't you do anything I wouldn't do."

"I didn't think there was anything you wouldn't do, Court."

"Ha, ha," she said. "Love you, little brother."

"Me too," he told her.

THERE WAS ONE SPELL when Truely was disturbed by Courtney's calls home. It was a period of maybe three or four weeks when she seemed distant and emotional when they talked. He thought at first that something had gone wrong between Hastings and her—but she insisted nothing had. "Hastings is great," she said.

"Then what is it, Court?" he'd asked her. "You don't sound like yourself."

"I am myself." Her voice cracked. "That's the trouble."

"Tell me what's wrong then."

"I just wonder sometimes, True, if I've made too many mistakes." She began to cry. "Sometimes I feel, you know, lost out here."

He held the phone to his ear and listened to her cry. Her voice broke into small desperate sobs. It was all Truely could do not to panic a little. "Why don't you come back home, Court?"

"I can't," she insisted.

"You can always come home, Court," he argued.

"I wish it was that easy," she said.

In time her sadness seemed to dissipate and she returned to her more exuberant self with a new stash of anecdotes to report. Whatever caused her dark second thoughts seemed to have worked itself out. She was happy again.

COURTNEY MOVED in with Hastings when she was barely twenty-one and Hastings was thirty-one. Like clockwork, just as Truely's parents had predicted—Courtney's moral collapse was fully under way.

His mother had her own ways of dealing with humiliation. One was to pray long and hard. Ordinarily she implored the Baptist Women to join her in prayer. "Where two or more are gathered," she said to Truely. But in this situation, she was not about to explain to others why their prayers were needed. So she went it alone. She played a spiritual game that she had invented herself which brought her comfort and peace of mind. It consisted of closing her eyes and opening her Bible to a random page, then reading that particular page aloud in search of whatever perfect message awaited her there. So far it had never failed her.

Her other technique was to cook. On the occasion of discovering that Courtney was living in sin with a virtual stranger she began with a pot of vegetable soup and a skillet of cornbread. Next she made a big dish of macaroni and cheese—and nearly ruined it by adding a few pink hot dogs cut bite size and stirred in. Next a pan of brownies with pecans. And a pot of pinto beans with fatback. At this point Truely and his daddy became nervous and began exchanging knowing looks.

She made two lemon icebox pies using cans of frozen lemonade and one prune cake using jars of baby food. She baked a ham one day, cooked smothered chicken and barbecue pork chops the next, and country fried steak the day after. There were twice-baked potatoes, collards, butter beans, green bean casserole and creamed corn.

When the three of them sat down to eat, his mother ate heartily. "Nerves," she explained when it became clear she had out-eaten both Truely and his daddy.

Truely's mother's cooking binges triggered his daddy's loss of appetite. He tried to eat enough to please her. Truely could see that. But his daddy was never a man of excesses. Excess of any kind made him uncomfortable. Besides his daddy had long suffered stomach trouble. He had rarely consulted a doctor about it, but he self-medicated with buttermilk, milk of magnesia tablets, and bottles of Pepto-Bismol. He didn't complain much either.

Nonetheless his mother took his daddy's refusal to eat as a personal insult, some sort of negative comment on her deficient coping technique. She began to prod him, to put servings of food on his plate which he had no hope of eating. She did the same to

Truely. It was like a test. Usually Truely passed the test, but his daddy rarely did. "Stop shoving food at me, Linda," he snapped at her. "I'm not a child."

This time the scene ended with his mother storming to the bedroom close to tears, leaving Truely and his daddy to clean the kitchen and put the leftover food away, which they did without discussing the matter much. "She blames herself," his daddy said, "for whatever Courtney does."

"I don't get that," Truely said.

"She's a mother," his daddy said listlessly. "They see things different."

His daddy set aside some of the leftover food, wrapped it in aluminum foil, placed it in a large paper sack, and walked the quarter mile over to Fontaine Burroughs' house and gave it to his mother, who he knew would be happy to get it. When he got back home that evening—Truely heard the screen door slam and the coffeepot rattle—his daddy poured himself a cup of lukewarm coffee and sat alone out on the back steps for a long time.

The next day Truely's mother gave his daddy and him her modified version of the silent treatment. This had always been one of Courtney's specialties too. Truely wasn't sure whether she'd learned it from his mother or been the one to teach it to her. His sister and his mother were as different as night and day, but in some ways they were the same. Courtney had his mother's Irish good looks—pale skin, dark red hair, green eyes—although his mother was on the short side and Courtney was tall and lean like her daddy. Almost as long as Truely could remember, Courtney had pretty much been a head turner—in spite of her self-consciousness. Maybe his mother had turned heads too when she was younger. His daddy said that when he met her she was the prettiest girl he'd ever seen. Now her hair had faded and thinned. She was slightly plump, her body soft as a marshmallow. His mother spent less and less time studying herself in the mirror—sometimes haphazardly powdering her face in the car en route to her destination, not even bothering to consult the rearview mirror.

Truely never understood why Courtney couldn't do like most every other free-spirited college girl at the time and simply fail to mention the specific details of her living arrangements. It was a dumb move on her part—the confession, and maybe the cohabitation too—and he told her so. "So, let me get this straight, Court. You feel compelled to tell Mother and Daddy the truth when you decide to move in with a guy almost twice your age that they consider a total stranger?"

"This is too big to lie about, True. Don't you see?" She spoke as if he were the dense one. "This is not some trivial detail. This is my actual life."

He wasn't sure whether this was something he'd learned from watching Courtney's messy techniques or not, but Truely personally made it a point to let his parents know as little as possible about the details of his own life. They seemed to really appreciate it too.

IT TOOK HIS PARENTS a while to accept the fact of Courtney's lost innocence. Their suffering only began to subside because even a fool could tell how crazy happy Courtney was with Hastings. She sometimes forced Hastings onto the phone to say hello to her parents or to Truely. It was awkward for everybody, but Hastings did it. Whenever there was something Hastings could do to make Courtney happy, it was done—pronto, no questions asked. Truely thought Hastings' love for Courtney was embarrassing in its intensity and magnitude. It was certainly nothing Truely ever aspired to, the humiliating depths of excess. Losing one's dignity to love.

TRUELY DIDN'T KNOW the exact moment that Courtney found out Hastings was rich. He remembered clearly the way she had warned him before she brought Hastings home to Mississippi the first time. "Hastings is begging to come to Mississippi," she'd said. "He really wants to meet you all."

"Good," Truely said.

"You think so, True? Really?"

"Why not?"

"Maybe it's too soon."

"The sooner the better," Truely said. "Bring him on. What? You afraid we'll scare him off or something?"

"Look, True, I need to tell you something about Hastings. It's important for you to know before you meet him."

"Shoot," Truely said.

"You can't hold it against him, Truely. Promise me."

Truely scanned the possibilities. Maybe the guy was black. She'd had a crush on a black boy when she was in high school—it had been a poorly kept secret too. He remembered the day his daddy had gotten wind of it. Maybe this guy was Asian. Or Moslem. Was he blind? Wheelchair bound? Did he have a criminal record? Or was he a crazy artist—Lord knows, Courtney liked that type. Maybe he was going through a messy divorce. Or worse, was still married.

"He's rich."

"Rich? What do you mean rich?"

"He has money, T. Lots of it."

"What kind of money?"

"Family money," she said.

"He inherited it?"

"Sort of. I mean, yes. But he works hard to make his own money too. He owns his own company. I told you that, didn't I? He's not just sitting around counting his daddy's money or anything."

"Okay," Truely said.

"You won't hold it against him, right?"

"Maybe just a twinge of envy. Is that allowed?"

"Don't tell Mother and Daddy. They don't need to know until the time is right."

"All right," he agreed.

"Just act like he's a normal person, True. Because he is—basically."

"Got it."

"Why am I being so apologetic?"

"You tell me."

"I just want you all to give him a chance."

"How about you give us country bumpkins the benefit of the doubt, Court."

"You're right. I'm sorry, True. You're right."

"One more thing."

"What?"

"Have you explained to him that we have our own thing going on down here in Hinds County? Family not-money."

"See?" she said. "That's exactly what I mean."

HASTINGS' FIRST VISIT to Hinds County was not a total success. He and Courtney had been living together for months by then, their romance in full bloom. Nonetheless, Truely's parents would not allow Courtney and Hastings to stay together unmarried under their roof. That was understood. It went without saying. So Hastings rented himself a hotel room at the best hotel in downtown Jackson.

"I told him I could fix up the sofa in the living room," Truely's mother said. "But nooooo. Mr. California has to check into the most expensive hotel in Jackson."

"His name is Hastings, Mama."

"Who is he trying to impress?"

Courtney and Hastings drove out to the Noonan place for supper the first night. Their high hopes were painfully apparent. Truely's mother's nervousness caused her to talk too much. His daddy's resentment made him silent.

It was Truely who finally invited Hastings outside to walk the property—a ritual his daddy usually conducted when company came. His daddy took pride in pointing out the vegetable garden, the fruit trees, the catfish pond where they'd spent endless hours watching corks bob, the old shed turned woodworking shop, the woodpile ready for winter, the antique John Deere tractor he had spent a couple of decades working on, the pen where he once kept chickens, the bird feeders he built himself, the deer lick at the edge of the pond, the stream that ran along the property boundary, the spot where he might like to build a smokehouse someday to cure his own venison there. Truely could give the tour as well as his daddy did but was offering it mostly to diffuse the tensions in the house.

Hastings was walking beside Truely, trying to listen to his explanation of the surrounding terrain. "I get the feeling your father would like to take me behind that woodshed over there and beat the hell out of me with a slat of that timber."

"Probably would," Truely said.

"Courtney told me they equate California with hell," he said. Truely tried to laugh. "Pretty much."

"So what does that make me — Satan?"

"Pretty much."

YOU DIDN'T HAVE to be Sherlock Holmes to know that nights after she thought the family was asleep Courtney snuck out of her girlhood room, started her mother's old station wagon and drove to Jackson, where she stayed with Hastings until the early morning hours, when everybody in the house could hear her pull up into the side yard in the dark, get out of the car and sneak back into the house before daybreak.

"You're acting like a jerk," Truely told her as she crept in the second morning. "Two days of abstinence is going to kill you? Is that right?"

"My God, True, you think this is about sex?"

"Isn't it?"

"It's about seeing the world differently from the way they see it — living my life differently from the way they live theirs. Don't you ever get tired of marching to the beat of Mother and Daddy's drummer, True?"

"Dammit, Court, this is their house. When in Rome. Would that kill you?"

"The good news is I'll be gone tomorrow, True. But you know what? I hope I'm never as passive as you are."

"God forbid," he said. "I hope I'm never such a selfish pain in the ass."

HASTINGS CAME by the house the next afternoon in his rental car to pick up Courtney for the airport. Truely had a few minutes alone with Hastings as he loaded Courtney's luggage in the trunk of the car. Hastings seemed miserable.

"Courtney is pretty upset."

"You can be sure if Courtney is upset, everybody is upset."

"None of this is her fault," Hastings said. "I was the one who wanted to come down here and meet her family. She tried to talk me out of it."

"Let me ask you something, Hastings." Truely folded his arms and leaned against the rental car. "You planning to marry my sister?"

"We talk about it. When the time is right."

"I'm not telling you how to live your life or anything," Truely said. "But I'd hold off on coming back down here until you put a ring on my sister's finger, man."

"That's the way it is?"

"My parents just want what they believe is right for Courtney."

"I understand."

Truely smiled. "One more thing."

"What?"

"How invested are you in that ponytail?"

"The ponytail stays," Hastings said.

"Right," Truely said. "Just asking."

Three

FOR HIS SEVENTEENTH BIRTHDAY Courtney and Hastings sent Truely a plane ticket to fly out to visit them. It was far beyond anything he'd thought to wish for. His parents briefly discussed insisting that he send it back—claiming it was excessive. But Truely talked them out of that—with the long-distance assistance of Courtney. First they'd learned that Hastings had plenty of money. Now they learned that he wasn't the least bit stingy. Knowing the second thing made it much easier to tolerate the first thing.

Before meeting Hastings neither Truely nor Courtney had ever known anything at all about money or the people who had it. Like most Mississippi kids they had dreamed dreams that had little or no significant financial dimensions to them. They thought of money the same as they did weather—necessary in some form, unpredictable, volatile enough to wipe you off the map of the world at any given time. It would have been fair to say Truely and Courtney had little interest in money, people with it, or ways to get it. Truely thought that might be what Hastings had found so irresistible about his sister. She liked him in spite of his family money. She forgave him his wealth.

Truely's trip to California was the first time he had ever flown—and he'd been plenty scared. He'd never prayed that much at one sitting before. By the time he landed the third time that day—Jackson to Atlanta, Atlanta to Chicago, Chicago to San Francisco—and saw Courtney and Hastings waving to him at the gate, he felt like a veteran traveler—and closer to God too, his prayers answered. He was visibly relieved to have arrived mostly intact.

They all squeezed into Hastings' small sports car with the top down and drove headfirst into the luminous city. Truely thought about *Star Wars*—the way he had felt the first time he saw the movie and had actually considered the possibility that there might be other worlds out there somewhere, incredible places waiting to be discovered by the best and boldest. San Francisco gave him the *Star Wars* feeling.

"What do you think, True?" Courtney watched him scan the horizon, crouched down in the tiny back space of the speeding car.

"We're not in Kansas anymore, Toto," he said.

By the time they got to Hastings' apartment Truely felt he had traveled beyond the known galaxy. Hastings' apartment was on the eighteenth floor and had a view of the bay, which he would not see fully until the following morning. But what Truely liked even more were the endless city lights in all directions sparkling like a million fireflies as far as he could see.

The actual apartment was the nicest place Truely had ever been. It was small, even by Mississippi standards. It was modern too, with sleek furniture, glass tables and what his mother would have referred to as "genuine oriental rugs." There were abstract paintings on the walls. Large canvases. Two he recognized as Courtney's work. There were fresh flowers, of course. Hadn't their mother taught them that you always welcomed visitors with a vase of fresh cut flowers—or in the winter months in Mississippi, holly berries, nandina or a stem of magnolia leaves? Both tiny bedrooms in the apartment had beds low to the floor on wooden platforms. Truely had never slept low before—unless he was camping someplace out in the woods. In Hinds County people liked their beds high off the floor so you had to climb up into the bed and could store Lord knows what underneath it. Here everything was simple and sparse. Truely might have said the rooms were mostly empty. Courtney called them minimalist modern. "In California," she explained, "less is more."

Back in Mississippi Truely had never learned less-is-more or any of that. He was pretty sure less-is-more was some indulgent concept only a rich person would think up. Down in Hinds County less was less and more was more and everybody knew the difference. What he liked most were the floor-to-ceiling windows and the sights beyond. Two weeks visiting Courtney and Hastings was more than enough to dazzle Truely Noonan, son of the South. Afterward he had gone home to Mississippi changed.

It was clear to Truely's parents that he had taken to California same as Courtney had and come down with a serious case of California dreaming that would keep him feverish all the next year. Not long after his trip he sat at the kitchen table and filled out a small stack of college applications, among them an application to San Jose State. "San Joe's?" his mother said when she looked over his shoulder. "What kind of school is that?"

"It's a good school," Truely said.

Courtney and Hastings wanted him to apply to Berkeley and Stanford instead, because as they put it, "a degree from there will open doors for you the rest of your life." Hastings was a Berkeley man himself. He liked to make that known too.

It would have been a long shot, but maybe Truely could have gotten in those schools since he was near the top of his class in Hinds County and had blown the lid off the SAT, which was somewhat of an embarrassment to him back in Mississippi, where an excess of brains was generally frowned upon. But when Courtney had taken him to look at both schools he decided that neither one was a real fit for him. The glut of privilege and money was hard for a Mississippi boy to embrace. Unlike Hastings, he didn't have the prerequisite sense of entitlement. In Mississippi they might forgive you for being smart, but never for *acting* smart.

A few days later, while they were shoveling a load of manure over tilled garden soil, his daddy broke the silence, saying, "Son, I'm not against college, you know that, right? But I hope you don't set out to try to be something you're not."

Truely paused, bare-chested, shovel in hand, his ball cap sweat-soaked to his head. His daddy had never said such a thing to him before. It didn't set right. He took off his ball cap and slapped it against a fence post, a spray of sweat flying out. "I don't know what you're getting at."

"Too many books can change a man—and not for the best sometimes."

"What's your point?" Truely slung a heap of pungent manure over the newly dug soil and tried to stir it in with the blade of the shovel like he had watched his daddy do so many times before.

"A man's got to know who he is. He's got to accept what he knows." His daddy was going over the spot Truely was working, rearranging the soil with his hoe.

Truely stabbed his shovel into the dirt. Anger crept over him like a swarm of fire ants.

UNLIKE SOME OF HIS BUDDIES, Truely had never been afraid of books. Following his daddy's example, he had read the newspaper every day of his life since sixth grade, starting with the sports page. He had a vague idea what was going on in the world. It was true that Truely could generally nail a test, took a certain pride in it, but he was also a guy who liked to dance all night to throbbing music in makeshift clubs off unlit country roads. He liked to drink a cold beer on a hot day, maybe a flask of Jack Daniel's on special occasions. He wore his baseball cap backwards, his jeans ripped and torn—because they were old and practically worn-out, not because he bought them that way. His hair was a little too long, his boots a little too big, his aspirations modest. He preferred listening to talking—and wasn't all that great at either. He liked barbecue joints more than restaurants. Catfish and hush puppies or hot dogs burned black over a campfire were his favorites. He preferred simple food dished out in large helpings. He liked to serve himself and go for seconds.

Truely got a rush out of seeing geese flying in V formation, every kind of dog—but especially a hound on a scent—hard-hitting defensive football, explosive tackles, athletes with suddenness, tan-legged girls in bare feet, girls with guts and gumption who spoke up and got heard, guys who didn't talk too much, who only lied when it was the right thing to do, great teachers who made you rethink things, and true stories of every kind. He was partial to old people, old trucks and old stories he'd heard a thousand times. None of this was going to change because he went off to college. Not if he could help it. He'd gone to church nearly all his life, but had never considered himself religious. If he'd actually had a religion he guessed it would have been familiarity—he worshipped the familiar.

He was exactly like his daddy that way, wasn't he? They both liked things that actually were what they appeared to be. People especially. Truely liked mothers who looked like mothers and fathers who looked like fathers. He cringed when he saw those too-thin mothers trying to pour themselves into tight-fitting jeans and wearing their hair like a teenager. He'd felt bad for guys with mothers like that. Truely generally felt lucky to have his own mother with her dated hairstyle, which she referred to as "a body wave." Truely liked his mother's sensible shoes just fine, her pear shape in her polyester JCPenney's pantsuits, all the little lines around her eyes, and the way she insisted on putting powder on whenever she left the house so her face didn't shine with heat. He could tell from the wedding photo that sat on her bedroom dresser that she had once been young and pretty. It was okay with him if she didn't stay that way forever. He didn't notice his daddy complaining either—not exactly. He loved the way she insisted on hanging wet clothes outside on the line, letting them bake in the fresh air, even though she had a clothes dryer out in the carport that worked just fine. He admired the way most of the messages put out by the modern world were wasted on his mother. He counted on that.

His daddy too. Every morning his daddy was up early, dressed in his work coveralls, drinking his black coffee when Truely came stumbling to the table for breakfast. His daddy worked repairing large household appliances, refrigerators, washing machines, stoves, for Jackson Home Appliance and he was good at it—was made manager of the repair department a few years earlier. Sometimes he brought home an abandoned appliance and repaired it in his spare time and then sold it on the side. Or sometimes he just gave it away to somebody he thought might need it.

Truely liked the way he'd come to know what his daddy would say before he said it—like he had memorized the short script that constituted the basic dialogue of his daddy's small life. It comforted Truely in its predictability.

To this day there was not much he loved more than hunting with his daddy, sitting silently for hours cramped in the deer stand in the dark, damp, early morning listening to each other breathe and shiver—never speaking a word. They had gotten a buck the last three years he was home, the third one six points. All three bucks still hung on the garage wall, two looking left and one looking right. He was proud of them too, even though his mother had refused to allow them to hang over the fireplace in their den where he thought they actually belonged.

When he was a kid he had loved to sit out by the pond and fish with his daddy too. For hours on end the two of them sat in the shadiest spot they could find, eating sandwiches they'd made themselves, sharing an RC Cola and believing they had all the time in the world ahead of them. Even though he didn't get around to it much anymore, he still liked to fish. You could think when you fished. That was the thing. It was like doing something and doing nothing all at the same time. If more people fished, then fewer people would need to pay psychiatrists. He believed that. If he was part redneck, the way Courtney had lovingly introduced him to her California friends on occasion, then he was okay with that. Maybe he was even proud of it.

Maybe some of Truely's Mississippi buddies spent their days wired to sound systems or watching the mind-numbing tube, but not Truely. He liked to wander down to Snake Creek by himself and throw his line in the slow current. Sometimes he took a tattered notepad with him in case something came to mind that he thought he needed to jot down. It wasn't a journal. Girls kept journals. It was just a notebook that helped him keep track of his thoughts. He hid it from his mother the same way he used to hide dirty magazines when he was a kid—in the same place too, inside an old sleeping bag rolled up on the floor of his closet.

Truely Noonan knew who he was. Hell yes. He knew who he was and where he came from—and he was mostly at peace with all of it. He'd swear he'd never spent a minute of his life trying to be somebody he wasn't.

EVENTUALLY they sent photos, of course, the two of them on the windy beach in Santa Cruz, on a cold day, surrounded by smiling friends, jackets slung over their shoulders, lifting glasses of champagne. Courtney's newly blackened hair was flying across her porcelain face like dark, wet seaweed. Hastings' hair was slicked back in a tight ponytail, his lone earring almost indiscernible to the naked eye. The expression of pure adoration on his face was more than endearing to Truely's parents. And there was no mistaking the certainty in Courtney's eyes. She looked perfectly beautiful to them, in that pale, half-starved way of hers. His parents wept when the photos arrived in the mail. Their daughter was married. A legal wife. Her virtue was restored.

Truely always wondered how, of all the guys in California, Courtney had known that Hastings was the one most likely to transform her life into the masterpiece she had always imagined.

TRUELY HAD BEEN going out with Tay-Ann Rogers for nearly two years. She was a pretty girl, dark-haired, book smart and ambitious. She dreamed of being a doctor someday, maybe doing mission work in Africa or South America as a testament to her love for Jesus Christ. He didn't know a single person who didn't like her. His mother and daddy, for example, claimed they loved her and he believed they did.

Tay-Ann was a great dancer—which was how things had got started in the first place that night out at Lester's off Highway 18.

The girl might have Jesus in her heart, but she had music in her blood. He really loved a girl who could dance—and would. Truely had seen Tay-Ann at school a thousand times and never really noticed her. It wasn't until two summers ago, when he had gone out to Lester's with some football buddies and Tay-Ann was there, sweat drenched, wet-haired and dancing barefoot, that he had not been able to take his eyes off her. She wore a short white sundress pasted to her tanned skin. Her dark hair was curled around her damp face and her mascara was smeared. The movement of her hips was hypnotic. She bit her bottom lip as she danced, concentrating on the pulsing music with her eyes closed. Truely was done. It was over.

He never technically asked her to dance. He just made his way through the crowd to where she was swaying with some half-coordinated guy, caught her eye and began to dance beside her. She smiled. The place caught fire. That's the way Truely remembered it.

Lots of nights now, he picked up Tay-Ann in his daddy's truck and they drove the back roads of Hinds County. She was easy to talk to. She had plenty to say even when Truely was at a loss for words. Her daddy owned some significant tracts of land and Tay-Ann had keys to all the locked gates on his property. Some nights they parked on dark dead-end roads in the woods and made each other promises, whispering their way to perfect silence. He lost his virginity to her on a blanket laid out in the back of the truck, the two of them stark naked under a pale fingernail moon.

TRUELY AND HIS DADDY were sitting in tattered lawn chairs in the yard, facing the pond, watching a pair of bullfrogs leap at the water's edge, finishing up bowls of chili and saltines, when Truely handed his daddy his acceptance letter to San Jose State. "This came," he said.

His daddy read the letter with anything but enthusiasm. Afterward he folded it carefully and dropped it into his lap. "Why?" he asked.

"I'm not trying to follow in Courtney's footsteps if that's what you think."

"What's right for your sister is not necessarily right for you."

"I know that, Daddy." Truely leaned forward in his chair, annoyed. "This is not about Courtney."

"What's this about then?"

"I've been in Hinds County all my life. Maybe I want to try something else for a while. I like California. I got this scholarship out there."

"Is that some kind of Mexican college?"

"San Jose State? No. It's not Mexican, Daddy."

"Sounds Mexican."

"It's a good school. Maybe you'll come west and see it sometime. Bring Mama. Do some sightseeing out there."

"They got a football team?"

"Yes."

"Any good?"

"They beat Stanford practically every year."

"Stanford?"

"Pac-10 team."

His daddy shook his head. "You're going to break your mama's heart with this news."

Truely had to swallow hard to keep from saying something he might regret. In matters of breaking his mother's heart he didn't think he was in danger of being the primary offender. He bit his tongue. "I'll write y'all," he said. "I'll call."

"It's not the same."

"I'll come home at Christmas, Daddy. It'll be like old times. The four of us—well, the five now. We'll decorate the house and everything like always."

"Courtney wants your mama and me to fly out to her place for Christmas this year," he said. "She's sending us tickets."

"Okay then," Truely said. "Good. Even better."

"I don't understand why you're doing this, son." His daddy looked away from him then. He cleared his throat. "Is it because—"

"No." Truely didn't want the conversation to take the turn his daddy was hinting at. He'd promised himself never to allow it.

"Anything you might need to ask me?"

"No." Truely's tone was abrupt.

His daddy looked at him then, saw that the subject was closed. He looked away a minute, as if rethinking something. "This is not how your mama and me thought things would go, you know? Courtney out there with..."

"Hastings?"

"Yes."

"She's real happy, Daddy."

"That's what your mama says."

"You don't believe it?"

"I don't like it—that's all. My daughter so far off. Now you leaving too. Makes me wonder what we should have done that we didn't."

"Nothing," Truely said.

"Look." His daddy pointed across the pond. "There's that doe again. See her over there?" In the thick brush on the bank of the pond where his daddy had put out a salt lick stood a fearless doe. His daddy made his hand into an imaginary gun, aimed it and pretended to pull the trigger. "Bam," he whispered.

The doe looked up momentarily then went back to grazing.

His daddy sat still a minute, then swatted a gnat on his forearm. "Okay then." He returned Truely's letter. "Congratulations are in order, I guess."

Truely took the letter, folded it and put it in his pocket.

"How about let's get these chili bowls washed up and put away before your mama gets home. You know how much she likes to come home to a clean kitchen."

Truely grabbed his empty bowl and followed his daddy to the kitchen.

"When you planning to tell your mama what you've decided?"

"Not yet," Truely said.

"You told Tay-Ann yet?"

"Yes."

"What'd she say?"

"She thinks she can change my mind."

"Can she?"

"No. I don't think so."

His daddy held the screen door open for Truely, nodding for him to step into the kitchen. "It's decided then," his daddy said mostly to himself.

Four

THE SUMMER AFTER GRADUATION Truely loaded his primitive, outdated home computer, hopped-up stereo equipment
and goldmine of CDs and old LPs, along with his clothes—three
pairs of jeans, some T-shirts, sweatpants, shorts and one brand-
new pair of khakis his mother had bought him, along with a basic
navy sport coat with brass buttons exactly like every one he had
ever owned and two less-than-notable neckties his mother had
chosen for events unknown—into the used pickup truck he
and his daddy had negotiated for as a graduation present. It
wasn't a bribe exactly, more like an unspoken thank-you for Truely's maturity in exercising restraint and demonstrating loyalty
to his daddy in ways that would remain unmentioned by both of
them all the rest of their lives.

Truely didn't like secrets—knowing them or keeping them.
The fact that he had found himself an involuntary steward to a
handful of secrets belonging mostly to other people was no small
part of his decision to leave Mississippi and the weight of such
knowing. He hoped distance would free him. California seemed
like a place that would let him forgive and forget, which was
nearly always his instinct.

He drove himself across country to California, taking back
roads, listening to Al Green, Percy Sledge and the Temptations—
pretty much the same stuff his daddy and most everybody
else in Mississippi listened to. He had come to like Willie, old
Hank Williams stuff and Don Williams too. All the mellow
country guys. When it came to music Truely liked his vocals

strong and his instrumentation simple. Driving along with a sack of sandwiches and peanut butter cookies his mother had packed him, an old map of his daddy's, the open road and the freedom to take his own sweet time, he was pretty close to perfectly happy. At the time, he was convinced that happiness had something to do with freedom.

Back in Hinds County he had left Tay-Ann Rogers if not heart-broken then at least heart-bruised. He felt bad about that. As far as he knew he had never made a girl cry before. Tay-Ann Rogers was a special girl by all accounts. Saying good-bye to her had been harder than saying good-bye to his mother. A few months earlier he had even found a way to tell Tay-Ann he loved her, which he believed he did. Just not enough to give up his California dream. He had imagined he could house her in some pleasant waiting room in the back of his mind until the time was right to merge her life with his—if the time ever was actually right. He hadn't expected her to refuse to cooperate. Once it was clear to her that he was leaving Mississippi she turned to someone who was staying—some guy she had met at Ole Miss, where she was headed in the fall.

The irony wasn't wasted on Truely when at one point his daddy took him aside and said, "Son, sometimes the thing you go searching everywhere for is sitting right under your nose. You need to think twice before you let Tay-Ann get away."

But he had already let her get away. Their last night together they had parked under a stand of old oaks in the middle of a slop-ing cow pasture. You could see the glow from Jackson city lights from there. "Nothing has to change," he said.

"Don't lie to me," Tay-Ann said angrily. "I'm as smart as you are, True. I know whether or not things have to change."

"Maybe you can come to California sometime," he offered.

"I don't want to come to California," she said. "That's your dream—not mine."

She looked so pretty sitting beside him in the dark, wearing a tight white T-shirt and a pair of white jeans. She had kicked her shoes off in the floor of the truck. Her dark hair was curling in the humidity, her skin smelled sweet. How could he think of actually leaving her?

"Once you leave Hinds County, True," she said, "I don't want to hear from you again. No letters, no phone calls."

"You don't mean that," he said.

"Yes I do," she insisted. "Why prolong the inevitable? What would be the point?"

And because Truely couldn't think of a response to that—he agreed.

TRUELY FOUND a way to ignore the heartbreak his parents seemed to suffer at his too going so far away. "I don't see why you need to go out to California for college," his mother said more than once. "What's wrong with Ole Miss? A lot of smart people go to Ole Miss." He hadn't argued the point.

On the night before he left Mississippi his mother came to his bedroom and slipped him an envelope of money. "I don't need it," he'd told her, which was a lie. "You keep it."

"Take it," she insisted. "I'll worry if you don't."

He thanked her and put the envelope in his notebook with his scholarship information and his road maps.

"You know I love your sister with all my heart," his mother said. "I always will."

"I know," he said.

"But you"—she touched his face—"you'll always be my baby."

HE TOLD HIMSELF that his parents' slumped posture and sudden pallor was the traditional demeanor of parents parting with their youngest—and easiest—child and facing the impending silence of the empty nest. He didn't feel guilty.

TRUELY FELT at home in San Jose almost from the start. It wasn't San Francisco, but San Francisco belonged to Courtney and he wanted a place of his own. San Jose was perfect. Close, but not too close. He liked being a stranger among strangers. In

Hinds County he felt he had known and been known by nearly everybody. This was better. He had slept in his truck the first few nights after he arrived. But eventually he bought a copy of the *San Jose Mercury News,* scanned the classifieds like his daddy told him to, and rented the cheapest place he could find. It was a modest one-room apartment with a small closet converted into a substandard bathroom. It was located downtown in San Pedro Square over a low-budget Mexican restaurant with no name, just a sign that read MEXICAN FOOD. His landlord was a guy named Ernesto Pena. He and his wife, Maria, ran the small restaurant with the help of a constantly changing assortment of non-English-speaking relatives passing through San Jose on their way to destinations elsewhere. Besides selling tacos three for a dollar, Ernesto was also known for offering unsolicited advice to his regular customers at no extra charge. He was the first to warn Truely, "Not the safe neighborhood. You lock your truck. Don't cause nobody the trouble."

Every night Truely walked down the back alley, climbed a set of fire-escape stairs to get to his modest un-air-conditioned room, which he entered by stepping through a large window that doubled as a door. But he liked his tiny apartment just fine. It was like living in a small oven, reminiscent of his boyhood room in Mississippi. As a bonus, he was able to pick up part-time hours waiting tables at the restaurant downstairs—sometimes Ernesto paid him in meals, which was okay with him. He'd taken some Spanish in high school. He had a naturally lazy tongue to go with it. So after a while he'd managed all right.

IT WAS AT MEXICAN FOOD that he first met Jaxon, a nice-looking guy, big and blond, who made Truely think of a Nebraska farm boy except for his devotion to tacos, which he ate by the half-dozens. It turned out he was a California semicowboy who grew up on a commercial farm over in Fresno. Like Truely, Jaxon had some country boy in him too—cowboy boots, shaggy hair, a hearty appetite for which he was famous and a fondness for loud music. He was a couple of years ahead of Truely at San Jose

State, an unlikely computer programming major who was always game to drink a few beers and hang out at some of the low-rent neighborhood clubs where there was live music and women of all persuasions could be glimpsed. Truely's first year in San Jose he must have danced with a hundred different women. Jaxon, more of a slow-dance kind of guy, had danced with a few girls too. They weren't guys looking for love exactly—just two guys looking to find their way in the world and have a good time trying.

They became friends by default. Jaxon used to joke, "Just how many people do you actually meet eating three meals a day at Mexican Food? Before you showed up Ernesto and Maria were the only friends I had."

Truely and Jaxon had more in common than love of the land and love of pretty women who were quick to laugh and willing to slow-dance. They had a fascination with computers and the untested possibilities that loomed. Jaxon taught Truely about collecting data, designing spreadsheets, and letting the computer do some of your thinking for you. Truely was a fast learner.

In time the two would go into a small start-up business together—a couple of young guys who'd started out just fooling around with search engines—and had as an unanticipated result attained a degree of financial security that far exceeded their original modest aspirations and left them as connected as blood brothers. But more important than any of that, it was Jaxon who introduced Truely to Jesse.

Five

JESSE WAS CRYING the first time Truely saw her. Her eyes were swollen into tiny zippers. Her nose ran and she carried a dishcloth in her hand which she periodically swiped across her entire face in surges of despair. Jaxon had mentioned her before, this girl, his buddy Jess. "She's cool," he'd said. "But too damn serious. You know the type. Out to save the world."

Now they were standing in the parking lot outside her apartment on Seventh Street. She had called Jaxon to come over because she said something awful had happened and she needed his help. "They've taken him," she sobbed.

"Who?" Jaxon asked.

"Rubio."

"Who's Rubio?"

"He needs to know none of this is his fault. I need to tell him that." She bent over and covered her face with the dishcloth. Truely stepped toward her with his hands out, ready to catch her because her grief frightened him and he thought she might collapse. She reached out unconsciously and took his hand—the hand of a stranger. She looked right into his eyes. "This is awful." Her hand was small and strong in Truely's. He didn't let go until she did.

"Who's Rubio?" Jaxon asked again.

"Remember? From the park. He had that cast on his arm. You signed it."

"The kid?"

"Social services took him away from his parents. They won't tell me where he is. I'm not family, so they won't tell me. I tried to make them understand that I'm one of his student teachers." She turned to face Truely then. "A student teacher is still a teacher," she said, as if she were expecting him to argue with her. She was nervously slapping at her leg with the dishcloth. "They're punishing him when they should be punishing his father. If you can call a creep like that a father. His mother is just as bad. She doesn't do anything, Jax. She lets it happen."

"What was it this time?" Jaxon asked.

"His dad is a monster. You know that. He gets drugged up and takes his rage out on little Rubio. He beats up a second grader, Jax. A grown man. He beats him up. Precious Rubio." She swiped the cloth across her contorted face. "He didn't come to school the last few days so I made some calls, right? When I finally got a call back they told me he was taken to the hospital over the weekend. His neighbors called the police when they heard his father go at it again. I really hate that man. I went to see Rubio at the hospital after school today, but when I got there they said he'd been discharged to a temporary foster family."

"Shit," Jaxon said.

"He's shy, Jax. He'll be afraid." She put her hands over her face and caught her breath. "Somebody needs to kill that man, Jax. Really. I would kill him if I could. He doesn't deserve to live. What good is he?"

"You want us to kill him, Jess? Is that it?" Jaxon sounded dead serious.

"Of course not," she said. "It's just that Rubio doesn't have anybody else. Just me. Just the school. We're all he's got."

Even before the three of them piled in Jaxon's truck to try to get to the social services office before it closed at five, Truely thought he might already be falling in love with Jesse. Jaxon had never mentioned that this girl was gorgeous—in a messy sort of way. Her hair was a noncolor brown. She had pulled it back into a sloppy ponytail, but wisps had come loose and hung in her face. She kept pushing them away. She had big beautiful eyes, hazel—or maybe green—that flashed with anger one minute and compassion the next. He had never witnessed such overt passion in his life. Love radiated off this girl. When she spoke he was mesmerized by her mouth, her full lips and big white teeth—the way the movement of her mouth forced you to pay attention to what she was saying. He would swear to himself later that meeting her was like a sort of religious experience for him, like she was as near to Jesus as he might ever come. Someday he planned to tell her that.

Truely never took his eyes off Jesse even for a second that first day. He noticed her jagged, chewed fingernails—she bit them when she was nervous, he guessed. He noticed that when she smiled her dimples cut into her face just perfectly. She had a Band-Aid on her big toe—well, it was half on, half off. She needed to shave her legs, the blond hair on her legs catching the sunlight. A loose thread was hanging from the unraveling hem of her dress. It all came together just right. She transcended every notion he'd ever had about what made a woman attractive. He was tongue-tied for maybe the first time ever. He wanted her to like him, girls usually did—but for some reason he was afraid that this girl might not. It was the first time he remembered fearing being dismissed as inconsequential.

From listening to her he found out she was an elementary education major, the disrespected curriculum people liked to make fun of. "Isn't that where lots of girls major in drawing Snoopy posters?" He'd heard that sort of remark from other students. But they didn't know this girl. He could barely breathe in her presence. She felt called to work with children, she told him. She wanted to be a teacher the way other people wanted to be president of the United States—or wanted to make millions of dollars selling something useless that nobody needed. "Teachers sell the future," she told him. "With certain kids that takes the greatest salesmanship in the world. It's a daunting task, but it's worth it because it's something everybody needs, right? A future?"

Truely was speechless.

She had always wanted to be a teacher, she said—since the day she was born. When other little girls were playing Barbie, she was scouring the school Dumpster looking for school supplies teachers had discarded. Her parents wanted her to aim higher, she told him, maybe be a lawyer or a pharmacist, which made her furious. "You can't aim higher," she had explained to them again and again. She and her parents had had lots of arguments about her financial future. "They'll come around," she'd said confidently. "They have no choice, really."

Truely listened to this story and others she told and was riveted. He had never laid eyes on her before, but he felt oddly connected to her, like maybe he had known her in some other life. She was a strange mix of the hypnotic *other* and the painfully familiar. His own mother had wanted to be a teacher too. He remembered her saying wistfully, "I always wanted to be a schoolteacher. I think I might have made a good teacher, don't you, True?"

"My mother wanted to be a teacher." Truely blurted this as they drove toward the San Jose Department of Social Services. He knew he sounded like an idiot, even to himself.

"What stopped her?" Jesse was sitting in the truck cab between Jaxon and Truely. She had on a sleeveless cotton dress that buttoned down the front, and it was soft and wrinkled in a nice way. He couldn't even tell exactly what color it was, but only that it was the best dress he had ever seen a woman wear. She had insisted she needed to get her purse before they left. It was worn leather, the size of a knapsack. "They might want my ID or something," she'd said. Now her thigh was pressed against his, and even though Truely was sure she had not noticed, he definitely had. He found it nearly impossible to believe that she didn't feel the stinging heat they generated from accidentally touching.

"My mother didn't go to college." Truely cleared his throat.

"Why not?" she said. "If you don't mind my asking."

"No money," he said. "Plus, I don't think my daddy wanted her to. He came back from the service and just wanted to get married and start their lives together. Keep things simple, you know."

"Oh." She looked at him curiously. "Too bad."

"It's okay," he said. "They were happy." He wanted to kick himself. Why was he saying this? What was wrong with him?

"Good then," she said. "Happy parents make a big difference. But, you know, not everybody, I mean—then there are kids like Rubio."

"Right." Truely went silent.

The ride to social services was a wild goose chase. The office was closing when they got there and it was nowhere even near five o'clock yet. The secretary was turning off the lights and locking up. She told them to come back tomorrow. But Jesse persisted. Sat in a chair in the waiting room and refused to budge until she finally persuaded the secretary to give her the number of Mrs. Leong, Rubio's social worker. It was the only chance the secretary had of getting Jesse to leave the office voluntarily. She was not a girl who took no for an answer. Truely noted that.

Afterward Jaxon invited Jesse to stop at Mexican Food or someplace and have some cheap sort of supper with them, but she declined. "I've got papers to grade," she said. "I've got things to worry about. I can't eat when I'm worried. But thanks anyway." So they dropped her off at her apartment.

As they drove off, Truely punched Jax in the arm. "Damn, man, you been holding out on me. You never told me your buddy Jess was so crazy beautiful."

Jaxon laughed. He looked over at Truely, who was still watching her in his side mirror. "Jess? Beautiful? You're kidding, right?"

BY THE TIME she finally tracked Rubio down several days had passed. Jesse had spoken with Mrs. Leong, who had agreed to bring Rubio to Naglee Park, not far from his old school. He'd been forced to move to a school across town. This disturbed Jesse no end. "They're afraid his mother will come and snatch him," she explained. "The sad thing is I doubt she would bother."

Jesse invited Jaxon and Truely to come with her to meet Rubio and Mrs. Leong at the park. Jesse had put together a new backpack for Rubio, filled it with notebooks, papers, pencils and markers. But also jelly beans and chocolate-covered raisins. She put two new T-shirts in it—one SJSU and one Forty-niners. She gave him a list of phone numbers to call if he needed anything. One was her apartment phone number, one was her parents' home phone, one was Mrs. Leong's number and one was the police station. She put in some toy Hot Wheels and some sugarless gum and a twenty-dollar bill in an envelope. She wrote him a card he would probably be unable to read. It said, *Rubio, you are a special boy. You will grow up to have a good life. Always remember that. God will bless you and watch over you. I promise.* She signed it *Miss Chase, your teacher.* She had struggled for what to say. Even when she sealed the envelope she was not satisfied with the note.

"Here I am promising him God will watch over him."

"God will," Truely said. It was a Mississippi thing to say.

"Well, so far he hasn't," Jesse reminded him.

It was not a point either Jaxon or Truely was equipped to debate.

"Mrs. Leong says they might send Rubio to live with his paternal grandmother down in So Cal," Jesse said. "I'm totally against it. How can the woman who raised someone like Rubio's dad be good for Rubio?"

"They're his family, I guess," Truely volunteered. It all ran together in his mind after a while—the stupid things he said, the odd sound of his own voice.

"Family, family, family," she snapped. "Families can be overrated sometimes. I guess the only thing worse than a family—is no family." Truely had never heard anybody say such a thing.

Little Rubio came to meet them wearing new shorts and tennis shoes and a little red muscle shirt with BATMAN on it. He had a shy smile, but a smile nonetheless. He was missing one of his front teeth. When Jesse hugged him she nearly cried, but Rubio didn't. He noticed the backpack immediately. She handed it to him and he unzipped it like a kid on Christmas morning who had not expected that Santa would ever find his house. He was cautious though. He kept looking at Jesse and Mrs. Leong to make sure he wasn't doing anything wrong, his eyes darting from their faces to the backpack. He saw the gum first thing and his eyes lit up. "For you," Jesse said. They watched him slowly unwrap the gum and fold a piece into his mouth.

Mrs. Leong asked to speak to Jesse alone. Jaxon and Truely took Rubio over to play on the climbing equipment, but he was still sore from his beating. Bruises on his thin legs were obvious. What appeared to be seeping cigarette burns dotted his neck and arms. He had trouble moving with ease like a little boy should. "Damn," Jaxon said, "the kid is hurting."

Rubio had liked the swing and the slide and being carried around on Truely's shoulders. He laughed when Truely ran and bounced him up and down, his head bobbing back and forth, his small fists gripping Truely's hair. The sound of Rubio's laughter was beautiful to Truely. Jesse was right. Rubio needed to know that nothing that happened to him was his fault. He deserved a happy life if any kid ever did.

Later that afternoon, after saying good-bye to Rubio, watching him walk away with Mrs. Leong, his new backpack on his small shoulders, his obedient wave to them, Jesse managed to stay surprisingly composed. But Truely didn't. He wiped his eyes with his hands and cursed under his breath. "Damn," he muttered. "This ain't right."

That night he lay sweating in his matchbox of a room, listening to business as usual downstairs in Mexican Food. He could hear Ernesto shouting out orders to the kitchen help. Truely was reliving the day's events for the hundredth time. This was new to him. Until he laid eyes on Jesse he had never met a woman that made him flash forward this way. He had never looked at a woman before and seen the mother of his unborn children. He didn't think like that. Ever. Now here he was obsessing about Jesse, and the houseful of kids he suddenly, for the first time in his life, imagined having. He looked at her and saw himself as a father and a husband. It was scary as hell.

The way the story should have gone was that Truely had asked

Jesse out right then, that day at the park, and they immediately got busy falling in love. But for reasons he didn't understand nearly a month went by and Truely never called her. He didn't know why. Goodness knows he thought about her day and night. He thought of her hair pulled back into a messy ponytail, her strong tan legs, her flip-flops and toenails with the chipped polish. He thought of the way she had hugged Rubio, the note she had written him, the money she had hidden in the envelope. Truely obsessed over Jesse's pure emotion and raw strength. He took to driving by her apartment two or three times a day. Only once he thought he glimpsed her, walking up the stairs with a bag of groceries. He fished for news of her from Jaxon whenever he could. But Jaxon had met a girl himself—Melissa. She played on the San Jose State women's water polo team. So Jaxon wasn't much good anymore. "Jess? Yeah. She's doing okay. Why? Who's asking?"

THE NIGHT Jesse wandered into Mexican Food Truely had no idea she was there looking for him. It actually occurred to him that she was lost or had stopped by to get three tacos for a dollar. He saw her speak to Ernesto, who motioned her inside, and pointed to the back. Truely was waiting tables in the back. Just the sight of Jesse standing there in her jeans and Spartan T-shirt, her hair long and loose on her shoulders, made his blood surge. When she saw him she waved nervously and made her way to the back of the small restaurant. Truely stood, watching her, waiting. "Hi," she said. "Jaxon told me you worked here."

"Guilty." He smiled.

"I was wondering if I could talk to you?" She seemed jumpy and fiddled with the hem of her T-shirt as she spoke. "You know, maybe when you get off work?" She had the slightest perspiration above her top lip. She was definitely nervous. It was definitely attractive.

"We can talk now. Why not?" He took off his apron with the carne asada stains and the spilled beer on it and laid it on an empty table. He reached for her hand and led her through the

NANCI KINCAID

tiny, hot kitchen, where Maria and some of her relatives were shouting at each other in Mexican slang. They usually kept the kitchen door open to the alley in hopes that maybe some air might stir. Truely led Jesse out into the alley and closed the kitchen door to the loud complaints of the kitchen help. It was dark in the alley except for a dim streetlight down on the corner. Jesse's hand was sweaty in his. "I guess you must wonder..." she started to explain.

On instinct Truely stepped nearer her, pressing her body against the kitchen wall with his own, touching first her face, then her cool, tangled hair. He began kissing her. At first she seemed startled, even resistant for a moment, as if she might bolt and run. But the moment passed and she leaned into Truely, pulling him close. Truely had kissed plenty of girls. But this was not the same. This was something else entirely. For a couple of seconds she pulled away and looked at him. "Why didn't you call me?" She sounded genuinely bewildered.

"I'm an idiot," he said.

This was an experience Truely had only ever heard about from dead poets and awful cornball movies that made him cry no matter how hard he tried not to. He had dismissed both as foolish. But being near Jesse this way made him want to surrender his soul, to plead guilty to something he could never take back. He was ready to change his mind about any vague plans he'd ever had before touching this woman. Truely felt his future ricochet out before him in small shock waves. He knew his life was about to unfold in some new direction, but was too distracted by the warmth of her body to care.

Maria pushed the kitchen door open, saying, "Arriba, arriba. Está más caliente en la cocina."

The door flew open and banged hard against Truely's back, nearly knocking the two of them to the ground. Truely barely noticed. But it embarrassed Jesse, Maria standing there in her soiled apron, wagging her finger, scolding them. Jesse began to laugh.

"Bad timing, Maria," Truely said. "Muy mal."

"Bastante." She waved her hand as if to dismiss him, then wiped her hands on the dirty apron and said, "Come eat now, niño. Bring the girl. We close up soon."

"You hungry?" Truely asked Jesse.

"I guess so," she said.

"I hope you like tacos."

And as luck would have it, she did.

THEY'D BEEN TOGETHER a few months when Truely invited Jesse to his sister's house for the holidays. He was a little nervous about it. If he'd had his way maybe he'd have preferred to take her home to Mississippi, but his parents had spent the last two Christmases at Courtney's house. It was the new Noonan family Christmas tradition—his mother and daddy, Hastings and Courtney's special guests, not required to lift a finger. Back home in Hinds County his daddy didn't even climb on the roof anymore and string flashing lights around the eaves of the house, or strap that old plastic Santa to the chimney like he used to. His mother said she was glad, since she worried he might slip and fall off the roof and break a bone. "We don't need all those decorations anymore anyway, just the two of us, out on a county road like that," she said. "Your daddy puts up a little tree in the den and I bake a little bit. We're content with that."

Truely felt a twinge of regret. He had loved those Christmases back home. It was different at Courtney's house. A million times nicer in every way. But somehow not quite as good. Maybe it was just a matter of growing up—of having to. "This is almost too perfect," Jesse had whispered when they walked into Courtney's fabulously decorated house. "Like life inside a Christmas card."

Truely would later feel that witnessing Courtney's life had helped Jesse fall in love with him—that she began to imagine that they could have the same sort of happiness and prosperity, live the same sort of gentle and generous life that his sister did. He didn't really care what it was that had made Jesse love him. He was just so damn happy about it that he didn't want to ask a lot of questions and risk ruining things.

Hastings had hit dozens of home runs in real estate and Courtney was his living proof. They'd bought acreage in Monte Soreno and built a handsome stone house on a hillside. Truely had been as dazzled as anybody. He'd never seen anything like it. Here, Courtney showcased Hastings' success and good taste—especially at the holidays. Courtney always went all out for the holidays. She'd learned that from their mother and daddy. Jesse got into it too in an appreciative way, like an audience member at a great theatrical performance.

Their first holiday together was great. Food, frolic and festivity. Gifts and gratitude. Roaring fires and candlelight dinners, mornings walking Courtney's dogs through the woods, afternoons in town dropping big bills into the Salvation Army buckets, four childless adults scoping out the Toys "R" Us and hauling the loot over to the Toys for Tots bins.

His parents arrived from Mississippi two days before Christmas Eve bringing homemade divinity sweating in aluminum foil, fresh shelled pecans to butter and roast, and deer sausage his daddy had had especially ground. They brought modest gifts for everyone wrapped in inexpensive Christmas paper with stick-on bows—socks, underwear, mimeographed recipe books put out by the women from the Hinds County Baptist Church, a sack of bulbs for the garden, Christmas tree ornaments made out of pine cones sprayed silver with red ribbons hand tied—and were happily embarrassed by the elaborate gifts Courtney had waiting for them under the tree—a leather jacket for his daddy, diamond earrings for his mother. Truely appreciated seeing his parents spoiled a little. He loved Courtney for going to the trouble and Hastings for encouraging her.

He and Jesse, newly in love, projected forward to the lives that awaited them full of holidays just like this—only with lots of kids and pets and socially responsible giving and elves and reindeer and all of the wonders of believing in miracles and living a purposeful life.

IT WAS JESSE who proposed to Truely. He had been waiting until the time was perfect, plotting some sort of magical moment they would always cherish, when one afternoon when Truely picked Jesse up after school where she was teaching fourth grade, she got in the car, dropped her satchel to the floor and said, "True, let's get married. You want to?"

He married her in her parents' backyard. It was a small, simple wedding, just family and a few significant friends. His parents had flown out and been quiet and gracious. He was proud of them. He knew they didn't like being in even a small sea of strangers—something that rarely ever happened back home in Hinds County. Courtney bought his daddy a new black suit—and he let her. She helped her mother chose a beige dress and took her to have her hair done. To Truely's surprise his mother liked being fussed over. Anything Courtney suggested—earrings, perfume, manicure—his mother agreed to and enjoyed. His parents stayed with Courtney and Hastings, something they seemed to have become comfortable doing.

Truely's wedding day was a blur, really. At one point Jaxon, after a bit too much champagne, had put his arm around Truely and said, "Man, if Jesse messes this up, that's it for her. I mean it. I've forgiven Jesse a lot, but I won't forgive her if she breaks my guy's heart. She needs to get it right this time." Truely had never heard Jaxon talk this way about Jesse. He was stunned and irritated, but Melissa came and scolded him for drinking too much and led him away—and so he let it go. Jaxon was a beer drinker. He needed to stay away from the hard stuff.

Naturally Jesse looked beautiful on their wedding day. Courtney talked her into getting her makeup done professionally for the occasion. He hadn't wanted her to do it, but Courtney convinced her that the wedding photos would be better if she was professionally made up. Jesse wore her mother's yellowing wedding dress and flowers in her hair. She started her period the night before, unexpectedly, at the rehearsal dinner. Her skin broke out a little too. Then on the day of the wedding she cried when she saw that the wedding cake was not exactly what they had ordered.

"It doesn't matter," he told her. "It doesn't matter. It doesn't matter." It was like the refrain of a song he was singing.

"Jitters, I guess," she explained to Truely. "You only get married once, you know. You want everything right."

"Everything is right," he said.

"Of course. Yes, everything really is right." She put her arms around him and rested her head on his shoulder. "You're right, True. I know that. I'm sorry."

"A woman should never be sorry on her wedding day," he teased.

Other than those two conversations he didn't remember much. He couldn't tell you much about their vows, or who came, or what they wore or ate or said. If they didn't have an album of photos he would hardly remember a thing. All he knew was it was the happiest, most significant day of his life.

AFTER HE AND JESSE were married the holiday rituals continued. Well, actually they improved. Hastings and Courtney moved a couple of times, their houses constantly upgraded. Some of the holiday traditions were fine-tuned too. Courtney and Jesse combined their philanthropic passions and began more elaborate Christmas shopping rituals for needy kids. Days of dumping random gifts in the Toys for Tots bins were over. They shopped for the poorer kids in Jesse's classroom now, as always, but they also got lists of wishes and sizes from Mrs. Leong at the Department of Social Services over in San Jose and every merchant Angel Tree in town and set out to buy every item on every list. These invisible children with troubled lives became the primary focus of the holidays, overshadowing Christmas dinner or the opening of gifts or midnight church service — or anything.

Courtney and Jesse threw themselves into it wholeheartedly.

They sat in the kitchen and plotted for hours, baked cookies in the shapes of snowflakes and bells, stuffed the turkey with cornbread and pecans, wrapped gifts and more gifts, addressed last-minute cards, sipped wine, whispered and laughed. That was the real music of the season, their contagious laughter.

Six

RUELY MADE PREDICTABILITY into a lucrative career. He respected predictability—he didn't apologize for that. Before they were even out of college he and Jaxon, his partner at TuBros Inc., had engineered a computer programming service that enabled people—and later businesses—to access vast amounts of public information relative to their existing or potential customers: what kind of cars they drove, what sort of items they bought regularly, restaurants they frequented, places they traveled, causes they donated to, names and ages of their children. It had begun innocently enough. Jaxon's divorced mother was dating some guy he didn't like and he set out to discover what he could about the dubious suitor. He called it a security check. Sure enough the guy was trouble—although to Jaxon's dismay the bad news did not deter his lonely mother.

It was unbelievable what you could find out about a person. It was just for kicks at first, to see if they could do it, tap into the public domain online. Less than eight years later, when they sold their company, Snoop.com, for millions of dollars, no one was more amazed than Truely. He was twenty-eight at the time and would never have to work again. Except he really liked to work.

He and Jaxon had since formed a new start-up, and at this very moment they had an offer on the table to buy them out again, which they had no interest in accepting. This time they had designed an ergodynamic chair with a computer and all manner of technologically induced comfort installed in the actual structure of the furniture. You could work without a desk, sitting in perfect lumbar position, get a push-button massage, or a heat pack if you liked, flip your laptop out of the chair arm, and go to work. There was a cup holder that would keep your coffee hot or your water cold. The first round of prototypes was exciting.

The idea had come from Truely watching the way Jesse set up to do her schoolwork at night. She never sat at a desk. Instead she had a big comfortable chair that folded into assorted positions—and reclined for napping. She had it rigged up with her heating pad for when she had cramps, a car massage thing she had gotten for Christmas, her laptop, a pouch full of paperwork, and a snap-on cup holder where she kept her bottled water. She claimed to hate the chair because it was so ugly, but she couldn't bring herself to part with it. She sat there nearly every night grading papers and preparing for the next day. Truely thought if it worked for her—this recliner/workstation—then maybe it would work for other people.

They consulted a chiropractor and a young high-tech furniture designer. The collaboration had been pretty wild. A long shot at best. In the beginning they had advertised their first clumsy attempt at the chair on TV, an amateurish infomercial. Within a year they had sold thousands of these high-tech chairs and were invited to debut at a prestigious tech show in Las Vegas. Now they were improving the product, diversifying it, paying homage to the high art of good design. Who said you needed to sit upright at a desk to be productive anyway? Not in the new, casual, free-thinking, high-tech world. People were looking for ways to be comfortable while they worked. To reduce strain on their necks and backs, to eliminate carpal tunnel syndrome and chronic stress. It wasn't hard to figure out what people needed next. They were people.

Truely hadn't expected his career to skyrocket this way. His success was based on accessing and selling predictability in one form or another. He was the idea man. Jaxon made things happen. But money didn't buy happiness in all realms. This wasn't a news flash. Truely didn't consider himself a guy who needed to learn this lesson since he felt he'd been born already knowing it.

It seemed a lesson better suited to other guys, who were inclined to be slow learners. And yet, here he was, beginning to prove what he had been born knowing.

For example, when his daddy got sick it didn't matter how much money was in Truely's bank account, he couldn't buy his daddy's way back to health. Instead he bought him a riding lawn-mower, which he accepted and appreciated. He also tried to buy his daddy a new truck. He had never had a new truck in his life, always a used one he bought cheap out of a classified ad and had to rebuild and coax into running—but he refused to accept it. "I don't need a truck," he said. "I got a truck."

He and Jesse took a cue from his daddy. Even after the Snoop .com buyout they continued living their simple lives in the same downtown loft. Jesse continued to teach in the public schools. Truely got up and threw on some jeans every morning and headed to his downtown office on Mariposa Street in the warehouse dis-trict on the bay, and once or twice a week drove over to San Jose to their Silicon Valley high-rise offices there. Of course, he and Jesse traveled and vacationed at a new level, she bought some nicer things for their loft, he got himself the pickup truck of his dreams—even if his daddy didn't want one, he did—although he rarely took it out of the garage. They helped out Jesse's family a little, paid her brother's college tuition, endowed the library at Jesse's elementary school, gave money to good causes. Truely had taken advice from Hastings and invested in real estate—some office buildings and two small apartment complexes, a couple of large plots of undeveloped acreage. They'd had some medi-cal expenses too—a luxury of sorts—but otherwise success had not changed their lives that much. As Jaxon liked to say, "Money doesn't cure you of worry—it just changes what you worry about."

Seven

HIS DADDY HAD BEEN OUT of the hospital several weeks and was doing a lot better. Truely had spoken to his mother only two days before and it sounded to him like some of the music had come back into her voice. She recounted all that his daddy had eaten that day. "His appetite is back," she announced.

She went on to describe the two of them sitting together out in the yard that afternoon watching as a flock of wild geese landed in the pond. Earlier in the week his daddy had felt well enough to go to church. That same afternoon, after lunch, he'd gotten on his new riding lawnmower and driven himself around the yard, pausing to pick up any fallen twigs or paper litter that had blown into the yard, sort of cleaning things up. "He likes that riding lawnmower you got him," his mother told Truely.

When she called days later to say his daddy had taken a turn for the worse and Truely and Jesse needed to come home to Mississippi right away—just as quick as they could—it caught him by surprise.

THE DAY OF HIS DADDY'S FUNERAL, Courtney gave Truely a couple of her Valium. "Stay by Mother's side," she told him. "She needs you." He was at his best when he had a specific assignment and knew exactly what was expected of him. He flourished inside those parameters. He didn't know how, but Courtney and he both made it through the service and burial without falling apart. It didn't hurt that Jesse and Hastings were watching them like hawks, ready to rescue them anytime rescue was required. That helped. They'd miraculously managed to be appropriately gracious and grateful to the friends and neighbors who came to mourn their daddy's death with them.

This included Mrs. Seacrest, his old American history teacher, an attractive, middle-aged woman, and the only person in all of Hinds County and maybe the world that Truely had ever really hated. She had been a good teacher who made him work for his grade. She'd made history seem relevant and America seem destined for greatness — two things he'd liked believing. He struggled for a B in her class. He'd actually respected her then. His hatred had come later, after Courtney had moved to California, when he had inadvertently witnessed a hateful aspect of Mrs. Seacrest's own personal history that repulsed him. He'd ended up in a virtual fistfight with his daddy over it too. He had despised the woman ever since — and made it no secret.

When later she had left Hinds County suddenly, he had considered it good riddance. He'd heard she married some schmuck of a guy in Tupelo. There's a sucker born every minute. But less than two years later she'd come back to Hinds County, divorced, with a young daughter named Mae. And he'd despised her all over again.

Maybe he hated her slightly less seeing her sitting in the back pew at his daddy's funeral service, head bowed, hypocritically clutching her small Bible, but appearing to sincerely grieve the death of his father, one good man in what Truely assumed to be her lonely life of lesser men. Her daughter, junior high age now, sat beside her mother and looked essentially bored by the funeral proceedings. How could she be made to understand the wonder of a simple man who'd lived a simple life? Truely had been late coming to understand it himself. How could Mrs. Seacrest even begin to try to explain the complexity of Truely John Noonan to her disinterested daughter, Mae, who sat beside her mother, distracted, shredding a tissue, letting the pieces drop to the floor.

A day earlier, Mrs. Seacrest had brought a three-bean salad by their house, leaving a note of condolence. It only reinforced Truely's belief that the woman had impaired judgment. *Truely Junior, your daddy was a good man in an imperfect world,* the note said. *God bless your family.* Luckily Truely had intercepted the note before the others saw it. He crumpled it in his fist and threw it in the kitchen trash with the coffee grounds and tomato peels.

SEVERAL TIMES the day of the funeral Jesse asked Truely if he thought his old girlfriend, Tay-Ann Rogers, would come to pay respects to his father. He told her he didn't know. He doubted it. But Tay-Ann did come by the house after the service and brought her two brown-eyed children and total stranger of a husband. Truely didn't even catch her new last name. She was prettier than she had been in high school. She was full-bodied now and had a calmer demeanor than he remembered. She told him she worked as an RN over at a hospital in Jackson. She squeezed his hand and said, "Lord, Truely, you're looking more and more like your daddy."

"Thank you," he said numbly.

"You know your daddy is the one who gave me the cuttings that got my garden started. I wish you could see my yard, Truely. It's beautiful—thanks to Truely Senior. He was special. My kids loved him too." Truely had looked at her as though she had never existed until this moment. No particular memories presented themselves, just some vague blur of sweet recognition. "Thank you," he said a second time.

SOME OF HIS OLD BOYHOOD BUDDIES from out around Highway 18 showed up wet-haired and over-cologned in ill-fitting sport coats and bright neckties. They were loud and sincere in their affection for Truely and he was genuinely happy to see them. These were the guys he used to roam the woods with when he was a boy, building forts from pine logs and saplings they chopped down with dulled hatchets. They'd spent hours catching snakes, turtles, raccoons and the occasional wild dog; shooting at squirrels and birds with BB guns, slingshots and badly aimed rocks; swimming stark naked in the muddy red clay waters of Snake

Creek and claiming to be part redskin afterward—Creek, Cherokee, or maybe Crow.

Later these same guys were the ones Truely camped and fished with who had first introduced him to the comforts of Southern Comfort and all manner of spirits—home brewed and store-bought. They used to pump loud country music into the night by rigging their truck stereos to big box amps, sit around a dwindling campfire, not doing much, just sipping brew, swatting mosquitoes, swapping lies, and if Billy Bishop was with them, maybe passing a joint when the liquor was gone, finally passing out cold in the early morning hours, sleeping facedown on the damp ground. It was where Truely first learned brotherhood. "Man church," Fontaine Burroughs had once called it. Where a guy learned to love his fellow man.

Seeing Fontaine come in with his shy young wife to pay respects touched Truely. Fontaine had grown up poor on the red dirt road about half a mile off the gravel two-lane behind Truely's house. Fontaine's daddy always had a hard time keeping a job. His mother sold eggs and homegrown tomatoes when she could. But there were times in the winter months when you could go weeks and not see smoke in their chimney.

Fontaine missed a lot of school as a kid. Some mornings old Mr. West, the bus driver, would sit in the road an extra ten minutes sounding his horn two or three loud times trying to rouse Fontaine, remind him that it was a school day and everybody was waiting on him, hoping he would see fit to join the rest of them in their eager pursuit of education and the better life that was supposed to lurk on the other side of that education. "Anybody know if Fontaine is going to honor us with his presence today?" Mr. West would holler out to nobody in particular. Truely remembered that bus of ragtag kids, himself included, with their runny noses and sack lunches in hand, waiting silently, secretly hoping Fontaine would hear the school bus horn and come running, wild-haired and repentant with his books under his arm. Truely remembered times when the kids on the bus actually clapped when they saw Fontaine come running up the road, kicking up a small cloud of dust.

Some evenings Fontaine and his starved excuse for a dog paced the back edges of the Noonans' land. It was before Truely's daddy planted the fruit trees. Truely's mother would see Fontaine out there, sometimes with no jacket, sometimes with no shoes. "Go get Fontaine," she would tell Truely. "Tell him to come eat supper with us." Fontaine never refused their invitation either. It didn't matter whether they were having fried chicken, fresh vegetables or tired leftovers the second day running, he was glad to get it. Fontaine would eat until there was hardly a scrap of food left on the table. He was so skinny Truely's mother swore he must have a tapeworm. After Fontaine had eaten his fill, Truely's mother wrapped up what she could in aluminum foil to send home with him. At the time neither they nor anyone else had high hopes for Fontaine's future. .

Nobody was ever sure whether Fontaine's daddy was killed in a car wreck up in Tennessee or whether he just yielded to his destiny and disappeared from their lives. Rumor had it that after Fontaine's daddy vanished there were nights his mother loaded Fontaine into the secondhand pickup truck with that loud muffler and drove out to a local nightspot where she would drink and dance and try to quell her sadness with some unsavory types she would be sure to encounter there. Meanwhile young Fontaine worried himself to sleep wrapped in an old quilt in the locked truck cab. On more than one occasion when the sheriff's department was called to deal with an eruption of drunken tempers, they discovered Fontaine just barely big enough to peer over the steering wheel of his mother's truck, big-eyed and brave.

Years later, when Fontaine's mother died of a broken heart and a broken spirit, Fontaine, her only child, inherited the small plot of land. Right away he sold off an acre of timber and replanted it. Then he bulldozed the old family home, which was caving in on itself, had been for years, and put money down on a nice double-wide trailer, fully furnished. He selected Mediterranean-style. It was all the rage in Jackson at the time. Fontaine had dropped out of high school years earlier and gotten a job washing cars out at the Ford dealership. Later he ran their detail department, supervising a staff of twenty guys a lot like himself. He was doing okay. After he married he had added a wraparound porch to his trailer and put latticework around the underside, making it look less like a trailer and more like an actual house. He expanded the modest garden his mother had started and built a patio with a brick barbecue grill out back. A few years ago he'd put in a swing set in the side yard for his twin daughters.

Seeing Fontaine again reminded Truely that there are things right with the world — even with something as seriously wrong as his daddy's death at hand. Here was Fontaine, beating the odds, finding a way, living a decent life when nobody had much hope that he ever would. Including Truely. Fontaine had let go of Truely almost completely when it got to be clear Truely would be a college boy someday and he would be a tenth-grade dropout with a fifty-fifty chance at a minimum-wage life. Now he walked across the room and hugged Truely, and both men fought the surge of emotion they felt in remembering themselves as a couple of wild young boys, roaming the woods as if that was where all the answers were hidden. Fontaine's wife's name was Tiffany. She was the size of a child herself.

"Who is that man?" Jesse had asked.

"That's Fontaine," Truely said. "We were kids together."

"He's handsome," she said. "He has such beautiful black hair."

It made Truely happy to think that Fontaine's miserable boyhood hadn't defeated him. According to Jesse it had not kept his hair from being gloriously thick and shiny and full of natural curl. On this day Fontaine was maybe the best-looking man in the room and as content with his life as anybody there. Truely took note of that too.

Other guys from Truely's past showed up on and off during the day. A number of guys who had played high school football with him came by with their wives whose names Truely couldn't remember. Like Truely these guys had loved the game then and loved remembering it now. Their coach had made it clear to them that a football player needed a lot more than just talent. "Talent is the easy part," his coach had said. "Either God gives you that or he doesn't." He told the team that a football player needed great heart, a work ethic and a mind-set that could trump talent in the long run and serve a boy well all his life. They had liked that way of thinking. Truely knew for sure he did. He had never been afraid of hard work. Football taught him that. Goal setting, getting stronger, never quitting, never blaming, never whining, being part of something bigger than himself, all of it, had made sense to him. Truely bought in completely and by his senior year had earned a spot as second-string corner and got at least a little playing time in every home game that year. He wouldn't trade that experience for anything he had ever done. His daddy had never missed a game either—and hardly a practice. Truely could still tell you the score of every game he ever played and what the key plays were that won or lost it.

When he saw Mose Jones come in the house alone, the only black guy there, his heart actually jumped a little. It was Mose who had been with him that night when they first spotted his daddy's truck at that motor court near Meridian. Mose had never brought up the events of that night to Truely afterward—not ever. That alone was reason enough to love him.

Mose and Truely had become unlikely friends off the field. Several times they went up to Memphis together and twice down to New Orleans just to hear some music and see what sort of trouble such places had to offer two small-town, small-minded boys. Nobody in Hinds County ever knew anything about it either. Even the time the cops stopped them for speeding outside New Orleans they managed to use their fake IDs and pay their fines in hard-earned cash without having Truely's parents called. They'd been thrown out of more than one seedy place for the crime of being underage, but they had never committed any real sort of misdeed. They just looked to hear some good music and dance with any wild and willing women they could find.

As much as Truely's daddy had loved watching Mose on the football field and admired him as an athlete, he would never allow Mose to eat supper or stay overnight at their house. He was old school like that. It had been a sore point with Truely, who was embarrassed by his daddy's overt, church-sanctioned racism. And Mose was ashamed of the little shotgun house he lived in with his toothless grandmother and impaired uncle and would never have thought of inviting Truely or anybody else to come over there and bear witness to his actual life.

So they lied to their families, borrowed Truely's mother's station wagon, and set out for weekends in the bigger worlds of Memphis and New Orleans about which they had heard tales which they'd decided to believe. They assumed possibilities existed in the big cities that never did in Hinds County—or even a town like Jackson. They'd imagined a place where beautiful black girls would line up to dance with a white boy like Truely and beautiful white girls would line up to dance with a black boy like Mose. It never actually happened the way they imagined. But they had some stories to last them the rest of their lives.

Straight out of high school Mose had gotten a scholarship to Ole Miss amid great public hoopla. He was as good as a local movie star. Truely would have traded places with him in a heartbeat. Anybody would. Mose's college career was the stuff of legends. Four years later he was drafted by the New Orleans Saints in the second round and signed a contract for more money than anybody had ever heard of at the time. Truely remembered calling him, saying, "Well, I guess it's the only way anybody would ever get away with calling Mose Jones a saint!" Truely was proud of Mose. Mose had set out to do it and he had done it. There was nothing to do but be happy for him.

Of course shit happens. His sixth year with the Saints he blew his knee out and was sidelined. Two surgeries later and a free-agent trade to Atlanta and his career was virtually over.

Mose, still a striking figure, had grown into a mature version of himself in recent years. He was slightly heavier now, square-jawed, and his hair was beginning to gray at the temples. Truely was a little bit surprised to see Mose at his daddy's service and later even more surprised to see him come to the house where he had never been made welcome. With his daddy dead Truely guessed Mose wasn't worried about being turned away at the door. The last time Truely'd seen Mose was when he had come out to San Francisco and stayed with Truely and Jesse because his agent got him a tryout with the Raiders, which in the end didn't work out either. He had stayed for almost a month before giving up completely on city life and city women — whom he had attracted like mosquitoes — and heading back to Jackson.

Back at home he opened a health club — Jackson's Gem (Gym). Mose was a high-dollar personal trainer now, with an upscale clientele who came from afar to work with him. He'd assembled a staff of high-profile trainers from among NFL remainders such as himself. He claimed it was easy to attract people to Jackson because the cost of living made the good life a steal. Recently he'd expanded Jackson's Gem to include full spa services and a weight-loss clinic. It had become a bit of a celebrity destination too, with well-known actors trying to get in shape for film roles, or trying to reclaim their health and fitness after a bout with drugs or divorce or some other form of defeat.

A rush of memories flooded Truely when Mose approached. It was like being transported back in time. They came together in an embrace, locker-room-style. "Sorry about your old man," Mose said.

"Thanks for coming, man," Truely managed to say. "I know my daddy never..."

"Look, I never did hold nothing against your old man," Mose said. "He was a old dog. I know can't a old dog learn no new tricks. I'm good with that." He slapped Truely's outstretched hand, and the recollections, both sweet and bitter, rushed them. It was not the only time Truely found himself choked up that day, but seeing Mose standing there in his daddy's house he came dangerously close to losing his composure.

He draped his arm over Mose's shoulder. "I hear you're the mayor of Jackson these days."

"Sheeeee." Mose laughed. "I hear you still out there on the West Coast. Story is you struck it rich out there, son. It's about time for you to come on home where you belong, ain't it? Where is your girl, Jesse? You ain't run her off, have you?"

Mose reverted to the Hines County dialect when he was among friends, but he could switch the dial to standard English, what Mississippians referred to as "the King's English," at will, and well enough to do commentary on network TV. He was a Mississippi Renaissance man and Truely admired him for that. But he admired even more his ability to keep a confidence and to forgive those who trespassed against him.

"Jess, look who's here." Truely waved Jesse over. "What, old timer, you still can't get a girl to marry you? You still way too pretty for them?"

"Can't get no volunteers," Mose teased. "You know how it is, man."

"Shoot I say." Truely laughed.

Jesse came across the room and hugged Mose. "Hey, handsome."

"You looking good, Jess," he said. "But you still hanging with this old guy? I thought you'd come to your senses by now."

Truely loved hearing Jesse's answer. "What can I say, Mose? I'm addicted to this guy."

In high school Mose and Truely had always imagined themselves to be ladies' men in the making, with great potential as lovers. Mose had proven it to be true in his case. But Truely was the one who'd scored Jesse, so in his mind that made him the real winner.

HASTINGS HAD DONE his part to make the day go well. He introduced himself to strangers and said, "Truely Senior was a good man. I couldn't have asked for a better father-in-law." Anyone who heard him say this would have believed it. Truely did. Hastings received callers, condolences and casseroles. He hand-delivered Courtney to nearly forgotten friends who came by expressly asking to see her. He kept her well oiled with sugary iced tea or when necessary orange juice with vodka. Whenever she signaled him he came, escorted her away from the mourners until she was ready to be among them again.

Their mother was like a spiritual vapor, floating through their daddy's funeral more angel from on high than earthbound woman. Truely got strength from her seeming weightlessness. She had been composed, reaching for Truely's hand when she needed to. He held on to her to keep her from drifting away, drifting heavenward, where she believed their daddy was hovering, waiting and whispering her name.

TRUELY MENTIONED it to no one, but immediately after the funeral services his daddy's lawyer, a man Truely Sr. had evidently met at the Elks Club, asked Truely to come by his office early the next day—and to come alone for reasons he would explain. Truely agreed. The following morning he made some excuse about needing to make a trip to the drugstore to get something for a headache and drove into Jackson to the small, renovated house turned law office out near the mall.

The nature of the conversation that day, the disclosures made, were painful to Truely but not altogether a surprise. In his father's effort to do the right thing—at his death if not before—he put Truely in an awkward position. His father's modest will could not be read, his small estate settled and divided, without his mother and sister learning the truth of Mrs. Seacrest. So Truely made the decision to protect them from any news that might cause them to doubt the character of his father or the love he had felt for them. Truely had a substantial bank account by this point. He was in a position to settle this problem with a personal check. And he did. He wrote a check to the lawyer for one-third of the estimated value of his father's meager estate. The funds would be delivered to Mae Seacrest by his father's attorney, and Truely hoped to God the matter would be closed forever.

AS TRUELY DROVE HOME from the lawyer's office he thought of Mose telling him that there was a new club out from town a ways and that they had a girl singer as good as Erma Thompson out there. "I ain't lying, man," he'd said. He wanted Truely and Jesse to go over there with him one night and hear the girl. "She can flat sang," he'd said. "You ain't gon believe her." And Fontaine had asked him to come by for supper, meet his little twin girls, see what he had done with his mother's old place. Some of his other buddies had issued him invites of similar sorts and several girls had said, "We sure hope we'll see you and your wife at church on Sunday." For whatever reason, he had understood all along that he would do none of those things.

"It will be good to get back home to California," Jesse said. They had decided to get a flight out of Jackson earlier rather than wait until the end of the week like they had originally planned. Jesse was busy catching up their laundry, packing their suitcases and labeling Tupperware containers of food to be put out in the garage in the deep freeze. "It will be good to get back to our real lives," she said.

Truely agreed. His real life was with Jesse. And Jesse lived in California. It had become as simple as that.

COURTNEY AND HASTINGS agreed to stay on in Mississippi after the funeral until the end of the week, when Hastings would need to leave the foreign terrain of his wife's people, which he claimed to find charming and amusing, if a little peculiar, and return to the real world and earning the big bucks in California real estate. Courtney would stay longer, just as long as her mother needed her to stay.

Two nights after his daddy was buried, his last night in Mississippi for a long time to come, Truely made quiet love to his wife in the small single bed of his boyhood room with the old cowboy bedspread they had pulled out of the closet, knots and lassos everywhere. Afterward they had fallen asleep slowly, tangled in a hot, cramped embrace.

OVER THE YEARS his visits home became rarer and rarer. His father's illness had forced him home, and then a few years later his mother's burial brought him home again. In the long absences Mississippi became less and less a real place to him. He noted the small changes, of course, a new shopping area, a building torn down, a small sea of new houses cropping up in what was once pastureland, the county road widened to four lanes and then six, a red light installed. Individually these edits seemed small to him. But collectively it all worked together to make Hinds County, Mississippi, illusive in his selective and skittish recollection, a place that rose in his memory like waves of heat off the hot asphalt highway weaving lazily through the barbwired landscape in his mind. Time stood still there.

CALIFORNIA

Eight

I N HIS RECURRING DREAM Jesse is walking away from him in a heavy fog. At first he isn't sure it's Jesse. He doesn't recognize her gait or the coat she's wearing. She's dragging a large sack. It's obviously heavy and she's struggling to pull it behind her. "Jesse," he calls. But his voice is lost in the shroud of fog. He shouts again, louder, but still she doesn't hear him. Soon he's hurrying toward her, screaming her name. At one point she turns and looks in his direction. She looks at him with such disdain that he is momentarily paralyzed. She's evil. He's sure of it. She turns her back and continues walking away. Truely runs after her and breathlessly overtakes her. He grabs the sack from her clenched fists and tries to open it, but she fights him, scratching him with her ragged fingernails. When he finally gets the sack open he reaches inside and pulls out what he thinks is a doll. Jesse snatches the doll away from him and it begins to cry. *A baby,* he thinks. He's overcome with panic. Blood races through his body. The sack is full of babies. Each one Truely touches begins to wail. This makes Jesse laugh hysterically. Truely wakes up in a cold sweat.

It had been four years now since Jesse had left Truely—not that he was still counting. The dream came less often than it had in the beginning. Sometimes now when it began he would recognize it and could ward it off by waking himself up. He would walk to the kitchen and get a drink of water or turn the TV on.

Still there were those very rare mornings when Truely woke up startled to find himself alone, when he had to slap himself, symbolically speaking, and remind himself that just because his marriage was over didn't mean his life was. Over time he had become easier to convince. His life was plenty good. More than good.

His on-and-off girlfriend, Shauna, helped him keep perspective, for one thing. She was a self-taught designer who worked out of her home. Jesse had hired her first to design and install some library shelves in the loft, which had been overtaken by books stacked all over the floor. Shauna had designed the shelves on industrial wheels and Jesse had loved the concept. Next Shauna had redone their guest bath using copper metallic tiles. Her last project was to help Jesse plan a nursery, which as it turned out, they never actually needed. Truely remembered writing Shauna a hefty check for her consulting services. Many months later, when he ran into her at the gym, he didn't recognize her until she asked how the nursery project had turned out. In an uncharacteristic moment, he had told her everything.

Two days later she called to see if he wanted to go with her to an Oakland A's game. A client had given her tickets. He said yes. The thing that had impressed him was that Shauna liked baseball, had every intention of watching the game like a devoted fan. She was not on a fact-gathering mission where he was concerned. No personal questions. No pressure for him to spill his gut. They ate hot dogs, drank beer, relaxed and enjoyed the game. They'd been more or less together ever since.

Truely had spent a fair amount of time with Shauna's family down in San Diego. Less than a year ago her family had all gathered to give her baby brother, Gordo, a great send-off. The kid was headed over to Iraq. He had joined the army without consulting any members of the family. Shauna was more than upset. But the deed was done. No amount of crying or begging could change it. All three of his older sisters had given it their best shot. Even his old man, Jerry, had resorted to tears.

Only a couple of months earlier they had all gathered to celebrate Gordo's nineteenth birthday. What a weekend that had been. Truely and Gordo had worn themselves out playing pickup basketball over at the park. Truely had a height advantage over Gordo. But Gordo—a strong-looking, brown-skinned guy with dark eyes like his Mexican mother and light-colored hair like his Irish daddy—had a surprising vertical jump and knew how to use his elbows too. Besides, he had youth on his side.

Afterward they ate enchiladas and drank beer and Gordo lectured Truely like the devoted younger brother he was. He liked to remind Truely how lucky he was to have Shauna in his life. "Man, you lucked out. You know how many guys would kill for my sister to give them the time of day? And she picks you, man. What's up with that?"

Truely got a kick out of Gordo. He was sort of like the brother Truely never had. He was proud of Gordo too, enlisting and going over to Iraq. The kid was calling the shots in his own life—and that was to be admired, wasn't it? Maybe Gordo hadn't convinced Shauna—but he had convinced Truely.

Truely would be forty-one years old on his next birthday. He was single, in good health, financially blessed and more successful than he'd imagined possible. He had a low-maintenance girlfriend who shared her family with him. It could be worse. You wouldn't catch him whining.

TRUELY STILL COULDN'T GO to Courtney's house without remembering Jesse—and the way it used to be. In recent years he had tried taking Shauna Mackey to Courtney's for the holidays in hopes of duplicating those good times. Instead he'd found himself trying to keep things short and sweet. He'd carved the turkey, decked the halls, smiled for the photos and gone home a day early—relieved to go. Shauna hadn't hit it off with Courtney. She wasn't as awed by Courtney and Hastings' large lifestyle and commitment to gracious living. She was a little bit older and wiser than Jesse, maybe, but she was perfectly easy to get along with if you made the effort. Courtney should have gone that second mile if she really believed in second miles the way she claimed to. She had been polite enough, but somehow her efforts had not come across as genuine. If Truely had noticed it, then Lord knows, Shauna had too.

After the disappointment of those occasions Truely had willingly spent at least part of most recent holidays with Shauna's family down in Southern California. He had come to believe that his ex, Jesse, was the one who had made things right between his sister and him and that without her the best they could do was pretend. Luckily, the high art of pretending was deeply embedded in their gene pool, a talent that rarely failed either of them.

OUT OF THE WILD BLUE Courtney called and asked if he could come down to Saratoga for the weekend. It caught him off guard. It wasn't Thanksgiving. It wasn't Christmas. He loved his sister—always had—but in recent years they'd streamlined their relationship so that it fit neatly into one faux-family Thanksgiving dinner and a semifestive Christmas gift exchange, occasions which, to be honest, he'd missed more than a couple of times. Truely's social life might not have amounted to much since his ex-wife, Jesse, left him, but on occasion he was still lucky enough to get the odd holiday invitation that was impossible to turn down. What his sister liked to refer to as "a better offer." In spite of his knack for occasionally disappointing his sister on the holidays she still invited him every year anyway, like clockwork, and for the most part he tried to go if he could. Why not? At this point Courtney and her husband, Hastings, were pretty much all the family Truely had left.

Truely and his sister had both lived in the Bay Area for years now—a couple of Mississippi kids who'd set out to seek their fortunes and ended up an hour apart in cool, foggy Northern California living their separate versions of the good life on a major fault line. Both their parents were dead and buried. Mississippi might as well be a million miles away—something they'd outgrown, like a pair of favorite shoes or a bad haircut.

HIS SISTER HAD never called him to come for the weekend just for no reason at all like this. "What's up, Court?" he'd asked her more than once. "What's going on?"

"Hastings is off on a golf trip," she said. "Some business in London. Then three weeks of golf in Scotland with some clients. So it will just be you and me. I thought we could catch up, you know?"

"Is everything okay?" he asked.

"Does something have to be wrong for me to call my baby brother to come for the weekend?"

"I guess there's a first time for everything," he said. "It's just that you've never invited me before — you know, for no particular occasion." It sounded like an accusation but that wasn't how he meant it.

"You're right," Courtney said. "I'm a terrible sister. I should call you more. After all, you're the only brother I've got and I almost never see you."

He was pretty sure she didn't think she was a terrible sister. He didn't think so either. He thought that when it came to her baby brother, the current version, she didn't have all that much to work with.

"So what do you say, little bro? I'll cook. I'll make you a good Mississippi-style supper," she said. "I've already bought the Velveeta."

"You always were good at dishing out the bribes," he said. "But look, Court, I'm not walking into an ambush, am I? You aren't going to take another stab at saving my soul, are you?"

"Truely?" Her voice lifted as if she were scolding him for something. She'd done that ever since their mother died.

"I'm just asking," he said.

"No sermons," she said. "I promise."

About the time his daddy first got sick, everything began to unravel. Courtney and Hastings got born again, and when Courtney and Hastings did something, they *really* did it. Truely figured

Courtney suddenly realized—maybe for the first time in her life—that she was helpless in the face of impending death. And their mother was too. Neither woman took to being helpless. Not at all. They talked on the phone every day. Courtney flew back and forth to Mississippi. She tried to talk their mother into bringing their daddy out to Saratoga, staying in the new guesthouse Hastings had just built. Courtney said she would hire around-the-clock nurses, get their daddy the best Stanford doctors.

But their mother wouldn't do it. She insisted their daddy needed to die at home in Mississippi in the house where Courtney and Truely grew up, with his vegetable garden in the backyard and the fruit trees he'd planted himself and his half acre of manicured front lawn with the two caught-in-the-headlight concrete deer he had hand-painted himself. She wanted him to be able to look out the window and see the bird feeders he'd built and the blue jays and wrens and crows—and even the renegade squirrels—vying for the handful of birdseed she religiously put out first thing every morning. If their mother couldn't pray their daddy's way to a total healing, then she wanted him to die surrounded by his lifelong friends and everything else familiar to him.

Naturally, Hastings had seized the moment to become a hero. He hired a lawn service when it was clear their daddy's riding lawnmower days were over. He paid for a local woman to come in and clean and cook so that their mother could sit by their daddy's bedside day and night and give him sips of water, read him the Bible, and wait for him to leave her for the dirt roads of heaven all graveled in gold.

Witnessing all this had torn Truely up. He swore that if it weren't for Jesse he couldn't have lived through it. He'd started thinking he needed to abandon the niche he'd made for himself in California and move home to Jackson. He'd started thinking he'd made a terrible mistake moving to the West Coast in the first place, abandoning his roots. Suddenly he'd felt like he was a total fake on the verge of being found out. "You are your father's *son*," Jesse told him a hundred times. "You are *not* your father."

She was right, of course. But for the first time ever Truely had looked at his daddy's homemade, do-it-yourself life and he was just in awe of it. It was like discovering a masterpiece right under his nose — a work of art he had dismissed as the most amateurish, run-of-the-mill, uninspired sort of paint-by-number. How had he been such an idiot? His sudden admiration for the way his daddy had lived just hit him like a bullet in the heart. A lot of men might have made some different choices if they found themselves in his daddy's place. He saw clearly for the first time that his daddy was a great man in his own humble way. You could be great without being perfect. His daddy's simple life — his joy in simple pleasures, his devotion to their mother, mostly, despite distraction and temptation, and to his five-acre plot of land, and his belief that no matter what happened, how many mistakes he made, how far away his children moved, that Jesus always loved them all, forgave them when forgiveness was needed, and just generally watched out for them — that was enough. Truely saw the pure genius of it.

The last days of his life Truely's daddy was mostly unconscious. Anything unsaid would remain unsaid forever. Truely sat by his daddy's bed some nights, drinking Jack Daniel's in a coffee cup, holding his daddy's calloused hand and sobbing his eyes out like a little kid. Jesse would have to come in and get him. "You're upsetting your mother," she would say. "You're breaking her heart crying like this."

AFTER HIS DADDY DIED his mother came out to California and stayed with Courtney and Hastings for months at a time. She made cornbread and biscuits for their friends and joined Courtney's exuberant Bible study. Courtney took her to the farmers' market in Los Gatos every week. Sometimes she brought her into the city for the international farmers' market down on Fisherman's Wharf, which their mother loved. "I've traveled the world today without even getting a passport," she liked to say.

Afterward she often stayed on until Truely and Jesse got off work. They had tried to wine and dine her — only the very best for his mother. She wanted to appreciate their efforts, they knew, but she hated all the "swankiness," as she called it. What she liked was to come over to Truely's loft and do his laundry—wash, dry, fold and—if she was lucky—darn a sock or two. She had never believed it was necessary to throw away an old sock just because it had become threadbare and begun to unravel. Jesse didn't mind her searching through their drawers with her needle and thread in hand. In an odd way, he thought, Jesse understood his mother. Even if not, she got a kick out of her. For example, his mother could not understand why two nice people with more than decent jobs would want to live in a converted warehouse loft. She thought they needed a yard with a couple of good shade trees and a sprinkler system. "You can afford it," she was fond of telling them.

Goodness knows she thought they needed some interior walls—lots of them. "What do Californians have against walls?" she'd asked. "You don't even know where the kitchen stops and the bedroom starts.".

"That's the whole idea, Mama," Truely explained. "It's an integrated living space."

"Well, I like to know where I am in a house," she insisted. "I don't like to be everywhere at once."

She never would spend the night with them because she said she did not want to look at them lying in bed, man and wife, every time she opened her eyes—and she did not want them looking at her either in her hairnet, Pond's cold cream and pink sleeveless nylon nightgown. Even if they hung sheets to create a private space for her she would have none of it. They always had to drive his mother back to Saratoga after supper so she could sleep in Courtney's well-appointed guesthouse with curtains she could draw closed and doors she could lock.

She died less than two years later—suddenly and quietly. When Courtney found her she was lying in bed with her eyes wide open and a smile on her face. Courtney and Hastings both swore his mother was smiling. He'd loved hearing that. He'd needed to hear it. Her funeral wasn't nearly as hard as his daddy's since they all believed she was happy to go, glad to be reunited with their daddy and not made to suffer any long-drawn-out illness.

SOMEWHERE AT THE BEGINNING of all this death and dying Hastings and Courtney had dedicated their lives to Christ. Well, actually Courtney had rededicated hers since she had walked the aisle for Jesus several times in Jackson back when she was in high school. She could never resist the call to witness. So getting born again was sort of born again-again for her. The difference was she took Hastings with her this time. He took to religion like a duck to water. It surprised everybody. He had never seemed the type. As sick as their daddy was when Hastings got saved Truely didn't think he'd ever quite believed it. "Daddy," Courtney would whisper to him, "Hastings has turned his life over to Christ. He has accepted Jesus as his Lord and Savior. Isn't that wonderful?"

About all their daddy could do at the time was shift his gaze to Hastings and blink at him in a way that Truely thought meant he didn't believe it for a minute. Hastings just nodded *yes, yes,* like he was a truly happy man now that, along with everything else, he could lay claim to everlasting life.

Truely was a Mississippi boy still. He didn't have a thing against religion, especially in the gentle hands of somebody like his daddy—or his mother either. But he wasn't too much persuaded when salvation was fired out of a double-barrel shotgun aimed point-blank at his skull. Courtney and Hastings were formidable enough as sinners, but as born-again Christians they were hell on wheels. No lie.

Add to that the fact that Courtney had taken Truely's divorce personally, which as far as he was concerned, she had no right to do. She had aimed the Bible at him like a machine gun and then just proceeded to mow him down with scripture. She called it loving him. It was a collision of catastrophic events leaving them both seriously altered, Courtney feeling significantly empowered by Jesus' love and Truely feeling significantly diminished by loss of Jesse's.

He'd never explained to Courtney what happened between Jesse and him—and he never would. For one thing Courtney assumed she knew and he had never bothered to correct her. Besides, technically speaking, it was none of her business. He had resolved never to discuss it with anyone. Period. It was his fault. He had made the personal decision to operate on that premise. It was what any gentleman would do.

Besides Courtney pretty much operated on that premise too on instinct alone. She'd sent him daily Bible messages about *cleaving*—and warnings about living a godless life. It wasn't much comfort. He hadn't been shy about pointing that out. Afterward he'd kept his distance. For one thing he was pretty torn up about Jesse. For another, he didn't like to have his tormented and resistant soul put on conspicuous display like that, like a target hung in the zealous line of fire of his exuberant born again-again sister and her husband and earthly personal savior.

SO A WEEKEND alone with his sister was not Truely's idea of a great time. Courtney always meant well—even when she was driving him crazy. Hastings could be a jerk sometimes, but what the hell. His sister loved him. She was happy and Hastings was good to her. No kids, which was tough on them, he thought. But they lived a clean life. A *big* clean life. Hastings was a real estate genius—flipping houses, developing strip malls over in San Jose, building planned communities that were pretty damn nice, even if theoretically maybe Truely was not totally sold on that concept.

Hastings and Courtney had just built their third showplace house, this one the nicest so far, smaller, less pretentious, and probably three times as expensive. Courtney had a real knack for it—making a house a home. Truely had always thought she would have been a great mother to some damn lucky kids. But it wasn't in the stars, he guessed. His sister was a big part of the secret to Hastings' success though. Everybody who knew them thought so. She had an artist's eye and great taste. He didn't know where she got it either. It was fair to say their parents never had any style—and Lord knows, he didn't think he had much.

Lately, Truely's idea of a good weekend was to call some-body—well, usually it was to call Shauna—on Friday night and grab something to eat, some sort of ethnic takeout. He had a vir-tual United Nations at his doorstep, food from the far corners. Maybe put in a DVD at home. A feel-good chick flick if that was what Shauna wanted. Just chill. Saturday they could sleep in, take her dogs for a run, catch a ballgame on the tube—the San Jose State Spartans were hard to find on TV so he would have to settle for Cal or Stanford, one of the local pretty-boy teams, although he still preferred Ole Miss whenever he could get a Rebels game. Then they could get a good workout at the gym, maybe a nap.

Shauna prided herself on being fit. She worked at it—even when she wasn't in the mood. That inspired Truely to do the same. Jesse had never been much of an athlete. She had never devoted herself to fitness and exercise, and had been even less interested in beauty and fashion. Jesse was just naturally great-looking—at least Truely, for one, used to think so. But Shauna was different. She took a lot of pride in her appearance, taking care of her nat-urally tan complexion with what she called a skin regime. She got facials and massages and all manner of exotic wraps and scrubs and peels and waxes regularly. She kept her thick straight dark hair well trimmed and glossy. She displayed her muscular arms and legs in sleeveless tops and short skirts. She soaked and mois-turized and tweezed and exfoliated and steamed and who knows what else. Truely had never seen anything quite like it—not up close. But when Shauna dressed in her simple tight-fitting clothes she left no doubt about the fact that all the effort she put into herself was well worth it.

Truely thought their arrangement was nearly perfect. Shauna was high-maintenance—okay—but only to herself, not to him. All the time and energy Shauna required for her intense self-preservation and upkeep freed up lots of time where Truely was left to his own lazy devices. He appreciated that too.

It was actually Shauna who had taught Truely that the best

plan for a weekend was no plan. She had made a believer out of him.

Another thing. Shauna was the kind of woman who didn't pressure him for a lot of jumping through hoops. She didn't wish Truely could read her mind the way so many women did—the way Jesse used to—and then punish him because he didn't always know what she was thinking. "I guess I was absent the day they taught mind reading," he used to say to Jesse. "Or maybe I just flat-out flunked it." But Shauna didn't test him that way. She never said, "Guess what I'm thinking." She didn't try to read his mind either, which was more than a little relief to him. If Shauna wanted to know something, she asked. If she had something she wanted to do, she went and did it, left him out of it. Like lately on lots of Friday nights or Sunday mornings she went alone to mass to light a candle and pray for Gordo. She didn't insist that Truely come along, although he would have been willing. Sometimes on Saturday nights they might cook something. Well, she sort of cooked it. He sort of cleaned up afterward. It sounded like nothing, he knew. But he prized his weekends. He prized a couple of days without having to try hard to please anybody. But this was his sister calling. She'd never asked much of him—especially not since Jesse'd left him.

"Okay," he said. "Leave the porch light on. I'll drive over Friday after work." That was what their mother used to say when she knew they were coming home to Mississippi, *I'll leave the porch light on.*

"Perfect," Courtney said.

Truely had no idea what this was really about, but he knew his sister's voice. She always kicked up the good cheer in her voice when she was upset. She tried to kill with kindness. It was a Mississippi thing. Just because a woman was grinning ear to ear and had sing-song music in her voice didn't mean she was happy. Usually it meant she wasn't.

TRUELY THREW A SPORT COAT and a tie into his bag. He was thinking Courtney would want him to go to church with her on

Sunday before he drove back to the city. She'd made it clear she liked to display her sporadically churchgoing single brother, just in case there were any women "who would be perfect" for him scouting the pews for eligible men. He used to sort of like going to church, a bunch of people getting together wishing they were better people than they were, vowing to try harder, himself included. It made him remember their mother, the way she had clutched a tissue throughout the service ready for whatever sentence the preacher might speak, or lyric the choir might sing, that would bring on the tears and cleanse her for the coming week. For all he knew church might even do him some good.

Truely was still living downtown in the same loft where he and Jesse had started out. He had great views of the bay. The loft was a great investment too. If he moved today he would double—maybe triple—his money. Sometimes he toyed with the idea of moving to Santa Cruz, living on the beach, working out of home. He could do it. He didn't know what stopped him.

He called Shauna to tell her that he'd be away for the weekend. If she minded she didn't let on. He loved that about Shauna. Her best quality was that she could take him or leave him. She didn't waste any time trying to make sure he loved her—and maybe that was why he wasn't sure he did. But he did love that she didn't seem to overneed him either and didn't pretend to. "Truely," she said once when he drank himself into some sort of stupid confessional mode, "your issues belong to you. I'm not really interested." Pretty damn hard to find a woman who thought like that. Jesse had been so high maintenance she'd left him skittish and worn out. So he felt lucky to have an easygoing woman like Shauna. Had no intention to mess things up.

FRIDAY AFTERNOON he waited out the traffic a little while, then left the office and took 280 over to Saratoga. He always liked the drive. It was a good route for thinking—green, peaceful, not exactly the Mississippi landscape, but beautiful still in that semirural way he used to love as a kid.

He wouldn't say he was uneasy exactly—but he had that feeling like lightning bugs were loose in his gut. It's when you sensed that something was going to happen—but you didn't have any idea what. His mother used to say, "Oh, Truely, baby, something is fixing to happen. I got a belly full of lightning bugs."

He thought about his mother and daddy, buried a million miles away down in Hinds County, but still sort of alive out here in California, a place they'd never had much use for. It crossed his mind that he ought to make a trip back down to Mississippi and put some flowers on their graves, make sure people were keeping things nice out at the cemetery. Some cemeteries would let things go if the families didn't stay after them.

Truely took the Saratoga exit off 280 and made his way through the Friday traffic out to the village and then wound through the hills, past upscale homes tucked into the hillsides, until he came to the stone gate to Courtney's house. It was designed to look like it'd been there forever. He punched in the code. It was Courtney's birth date, easy to remember. Through the thick of trees he could see the porch light on up the drive. So he took the winding road toward the light.

Courtney was waiting for him. He saw her shadow through the open door as he pulled around in the circular drive. She waved. Courtney knew how to make you feel welcome. She'd learned that from their mother too. You didn't ever have to wonder whether or not Courtney was glad to see you. He grabbed his overnight bag out of the backseat and a bottle of good wine he'd brought. He was nearly to the front steps before he got a good look at Courtney, her arms open wide, ready to call out, "Hey, baby brother!" and give him her trademark welcome home kiss. When he saw her face in the dim light he stopped dead in his tracks. Both her eyes were puffed and purple and protruded like somebody had stitched golf balls under her skin. Her face was ballooned to twice its normal size and she had a gooey-looking gauze bandage wrapped around her head. "Damn, Court," he said. "What the hell?"

"It's okay," she said.

"What the hell happened to you?"

"Come give your big sister a big hug." She stepped toward him. He dropped his bag, swung his arms around her, slamming the bottle of wine into the small of her back.

"My God, Court." She felt breakable in his arms, like when he was a kid and caught a bird with a broken wing and feared crushing it in his clumsy effort to keep it safe. It was the same exuberant sister-hug she always gave him, only prolonged this time, her thin arms tight around his neck for a few extra heartbeats. When she pulled away she managed her lightning-strike smile. "It's not as bad as it looks."

"Either Hastings beat the fool out of you or you've been run over by a truck."

"Wrong," she said. "Get your bag. Come in. I'll get you a drink."

He followed her inside. She looped her arm through his and led him toward the kitchen. "I had work done," she whispered. "A face-lift." She spoke quietly, as if there might be somebody in her house that she wouldn't want to overhear her. "Three days ago. You are witnessing my recovery here."

"A face-lift? You don't need a face-lift! My God, Court, does Mona Lisa need a face-lift?" He was practically shouting. He didn't know why.

"Shhhhhh . . ." She kissed his face.

In the kitchen light he studied his sister, her lean, soft build, white skin that used to freckle in the Mississippi sun but had turned porcelain over the years with the help of sunscreen and a couple of celebrity dermatologists. He had always liked the lines around Courtney's eyes and mouth. Now she stood before him like the victim of some self-inflicted unnatural disaster.

"Why, Court?" he asked. "I don't get it. Since when do you tamper with perfection?" His sister had always been an unconventional beauty, a self-conscious red-haired child who'd become a raven-haired woman. When all the other girls were slathering themselves in Crisco and heading for the beach at Gulfport,

Courtney had kept herself covered, mostly out of embarrassment, not liking her freckles or her snow-white skin. But it had paid off. She had taken a cue from Elvis, discovered ebony hair dye, and become a striking woman. Not leathery-looking and bleached like so many of her friends.

"Beauty has its price." She took the wine from his hand and fished through a drawer for the opener. He watched her uncork the bottle—an art fine-tuned when you lived at the edge of the wine country. He stared at her deft, capable hands, small square fingers, pale nail polish.

"You scared the hell out of me," he said. "How about a little warning before you surprise somebody like that."

"Sorry." She smiled.

"I suppose you've been told you bear a striking resemblance to E.T.?"

She laughed a loud, hearty laugh. His sister had a great laugh. She'd saved many a stalled social occasion, many a near-death family moment, with that laugh. She poured the wine, which technically speaking he should have been doing. She walked over and opened one of the ovens, glanced in, and closed it. "Dinner in thirty minutes," she said.

"Does it involve cream of mushroom soup, I hope?"

"Mother's famous chicken supreme—your favorite—sherry and mushroom soup. And green bean casserole—with more mushroom soup. Plus—just to round things out—macaroni and cheese with extra Velveeta. And for dessert, banana pudding with vanilla wafers."

"I've died and gone to heaven," he said.

Courtney raised her wineglass as if to toast him. "To the good old days!"

"Lord, how in the world did we live to become adults," he said.

"Oh, to hell with it all." She raised the glass again. "Eat, drink, and be from Mississippi."

"I know you didn't just say hell, Court." He laughed. "Wait a minute. You aren't really Courtney, are you? Oh my God, E.T., what have you done with my sister?"

"New face, new vocabulary." She winked, her swollen goose egg of an eye struggling to perform the task. "New is in, True. New is everything. Haven't you heard?" Courtney took his hand and he followed her to the study at the back of the house, where she had a great push-button fire going and where from the wall of windows you overlooked downtown Saratoga in modest lights. He thought it was a perfect room. Dark green enamel walls, bookshelves full of books Courtney and Hastings had actually read, pictures of friends and family—some notable, some not—that they actually loved or at least liked. Including, he was happy to see, a few residual photos of the good old days, Jesse and him caught in assorted hugs, beaming like they really believed *forever* was a word meant for them. For some reason he was touched that Courtney had not gotten rid of those outdated photos. A lesser sister might have tried to keep the family tree amended and up-to-date. It was oddly comforting to Truely to look over and see Jesse holding on to him, smiling.

Courtney folded herself into the overstuffed sofa like a cat in a warm windowsill. Firelight flickered across her carved pumpkin of a face. It was unnerving to see her so raw and wounded. Truely sat in Hastings' chair, put his feet up on the ottoman and took a big sip of wine. It occurred to him that he was glad to be here, alone with his surgically altered sister on this chilly night. He didn't miss Hastings. He realized how rare were the occasions when he had Courtney all to himself—no superstar brother-in-law to accommodate. He realized that with Hastings gone this house seemed more like Courtney's house. And Courtney's house felt a little bit like his house too. It was as near to a real home as he had. And he loved his sister for always trying to make him feel that he belonged here.

"Okay," she said. "Ask me questions."

He hardly knew where to begin. What do you say to a person who has just allowed someone—well, actually paid someone—to carve up her face with a knife? Lord knows how much that must hurt. "Are you on drugs...or what?" he said.

She laughed. "You mean at the moment...or leading up to this?"

"What made you do it?"

"I needed a change."

"What? A vacation wouldn't do? A new haircut? Maybe a day at the spa?"

"Very funny."

"It's not like you, Court, to resort to knives and scalpels."

"It's exactly like me," she said. "And since when did you become so conservative and condescending?"

"Sorry," he said. "I'm not trying to be judgmental here, I swear. It's just a little unsettling to see my beautiful sister stitched together and bandaged like a...a willing victim of some kind." This was coming out wrong and he knew it. Why couldn't he say what she needed to hear? That was why she'd invited him to come over, wasn't it, so he could say the right thing? "What does Hastings say about this?" He tried to pass his own ineptitude off on Hastings. "He didn't put you up to this, did he?"

"Hastings doesn't know."

"What do you mean he doesn't know? Shouldn't a man know when his wife submits her face to medical science?"

"I didn't tell him. He's in Scotland on a *so-called* golf trip. I told you that. He'll be gone nearly a month. That was all the time I really needed."

"A *so-called* golf trip?" he asked. *"So-called?"*

"Good ear, brother. You always did hear what wasn't said."

"It's the Southern in me," he said. "Good home training."

"I think it's the girl in you." She smiled, her black eyes sealing closed in a sluggish, terrible-looking way.

"The girl?"

"Your feminine side. You weren't a mama's boy for nothing." She slapped her linen cocktail napkin at him.

"Shoot," he said. "Mama's boy my hind foot. So why didn't you tell our boy Hasty Pudding about your surgery?"

"He hates it when you call him that."

"Doesn't he have a right to know his wife is going under the knife, getting her face rearranged?"

"He has his secrets. I have mine."

"I don't like the sound of that." Truely gulped down a swig of wine. "Both me *and* my feminine side hate the sound of that."

"Are you asking me a question?" Courtney looked at him head-on, her eyes like a couple of dimmed headlights.

"I'd say, Court, if you know Hastings has a secret, that you also know what that secret is."

"Meghan Morehead."

"Shit," he said.

"My sentiments exactly, little brother."

"Go on." He waved his wineglass like a checkered flag.

"She's with him in Scotland. He thinks I don't know."

"A big golfer, is she?"

"A personal assistant. She's on his company payroll."

"Lo, isn't that a little too obvious? Just how personal is this personal assistant?"

"You met her," Courtney said. "You and Shauna both. Last year at Christmas dinner."

"She didn't stand out," Truely said. "She doesn't spring to mind."

"You want to see a picture of her?" Courtney asked.

"Do you want me to?" The question was unnecessary.

"It might jog your memory. Wait right here." Courtney handed him her wine and unfolded in that catlike way of hers and headed down the hall in her sock feet.

He stood up and walked over to the windows. Below them, Saratoga was twinkling like a tiny town on a Christmas Card. He knew people of means were sitting in small, cozy restaurants, whispering and laughing and uncorking good wine. He knew that someplace down there amid the couples falling in love—or trying to—was at least one couple falling out of love, out of touch, out of luck. It happened. He sure as hell never thought it would happen to his sister and her husband. He would have put his money on their making it to the finish line—and maybe they still would. Born-again types didn't let affairs get in the way of their marriages, did they? They forgave, didn't they? Didn't a divorce cancel out your born-againness? Didn't you have to start all over after a situation like that? For Courtney, if this thing led where it might, she would have to be born again-again-again. Next thing you know she would be going for the world's record for salvation.

Courtney came back with a stack of photos in her hand. "Here she is." She pointed to the photo on top. "The brunette beside Hastings, see?"

"Yeah," he said. "I remember her vaguely. Quiet. Doesn't make much impact."

"Well, not on you and me maybe. But Hastings is smitten."

"Smitten? Define smitten."

"He thinks he loves her." Courtney dropped to the sofa without taking her eyes off Truely. "He told me so." Courtney shuffled through the photos until she found a particular one. "Here, look at this."

It was a shot of Hastings standing between Courtney and Meghan Morehead in their holiday finery. He had his arms around their shoulders. All three were smiling for the camera.

"What do you see?" Courtney tapped the photo with her finger. "Read the body language."

"Come on now, Court."

"Look," she insisted. "His arms are around both of us, but his hand is relaxed on my shoulder, right? His fingers are loose. Now look at his right hand. See? It's not limp. He's gripping her shoulder."

"Is this a metaphor you've got going here? I sure hope not."

"I'm serious, Truely. Can't you see it? Look, his head is cocked toward her too—not toward me. If he tilted his head any more in her direction his glasses would fall off."

"I don't know, Court. We might be taking our feminine sides to new heights here. I just see a happy guy with his arms around two happy women."

"You just see what you want to see then."

"Couldn't it be that *you're* the one doing that?" he said. But he knew better. It wasn't the first time he'd been accused of refusing to see something because he didn't like it. Jesse used to say he was devoted to ignoring the obvious. She was probably right too. He guessed you could say she more or less proved it.

"There are psychologists who do nothing but study personal dynamics using family photographs," Courtney said. "Photographs don't lie, Truely. Photographs can be extremely revealing."

"If they were both naked, maybe," he tried to joke. "Look, Court, I hope your suspicions are based on more than holiday photos."

"The photos are just a clue," Courtney said. "There've been lots of clues. I ignored them as long as I could, but I can't ignore Hastings' confession, can I?"

"And is it all those ignored clues that led you to the plastic surgeon?"

"Something like that," she said. "Come on, let's talk in the kitchen. I'll put supper on the table."

"Great." He picked up her wineglass and his. "I'll pour us more wine. I'm pretty sure we're going to need it."

COURTNEY HAD SET the keeping room table with their mother's old detergent box dishes complete with the jelly jar drinking glasses. She had designed this house with a fireplace in nearly every room and had another push-button fire roaring at tableside for perfect ambience. Their mother had never been a great cook—but they hadn't known it really. She had always worked magic with canned soup and Velveeta and they would have sworn growing up that her Cool Whip fruit salads were the best in town.

Truely watched Courtney move about the kitchen the same way he had often watched his mother when he was a boy, always a hungry boy, always ready to bow his head and mumble the blessing and shovel food—food exactly like this—onto his plate. They didn't eat like this anymore, Courtney or him, wouldn't be right now if Hastings were with them. But damn, he was happy about it. He hadn't felt this hungry in a long, long time. He was crazy hungry. "This is great, Court," he said. "Man, I'm loving this."

"You can wash up in the powder room," Courtney said. "I'm going to slice a tomato and we're ready."

When they sat down, Courtney took his hand. "Let's say grace, Truely. You don't mind, do you?"

"Sure." He bowed his head and waited.

She squeezed his hand. "You."

Public praying was not his strong suit. Never had been. But under the circumstances he thought he ought to try to come through for Courtney, his surgically altered, maritally challenged sister, in any way he could. *"Dear God, we thank you for this great supper before us. We thank you for this time together and I thank you for blessing me with the greatest sister a guy could have. I don't deserve her, but I'm grateful. Let Hastings travel safely. And let Courtney's surgery heal fast and let her be happy with the result. In Jesus' name we pray. Amen."*

"Amen," Courtney echoed. "Nice prayer."

"It's like riding a bike," he said. "You never forget how."

"Mother would be proud." She smiled.

"Well, it never took much to make Mother proud, did it?" he said.

"I never could do it." Courtney scooped green bean casserole onto his plate. Sitting close to her like this Truely could see the bruising around her face, the collision of tiny blue veins and black stitches around her eyes and in front of her ears. She saw him studying her.

"They put staples in my head," she said.

"No way."

"Yes," she said. "Underneath this bandage. Industrial-strength staples. They used a staple gun. I'll show you after supper if you want to see."

"No thanks." He was busy helping himself to chicken supreme. He watched as Courtney served herself the tiniest portions, then stabbed at them daintily with her fork. "That's not enough to keep a bird alive," he said.

"I don't have much appetite—pumped full of painkillers."

"Well, you can take my word for it then, you hit a home run with this chicken supreme."

"I'm glad you came tonight, Truely." Courtney's tone was so nakedly earnest he turned to look at her. "I was afraid you wouldn't. You know. After everything."

"Everything?"

"Truely, I know Hastings and I acted awful when you and Jesse split up. It must have seemed to you like we were practically hateful."

"You were self-righteous assholes, all right." He tried to smile.

"We thought we were doing the right thing, Truely. We thought we had Jesus on our side, I guess. The Bible is clear about divorce."

"So I've been told."

"Do you hate me for that?"

"I'm over it."

"You're not," she said. "You're not over our Christian exuberance—it's so ironic now, isn't it?" She shook her head. "We were well-meaning, Truely, I hope you know that at least. And you're not over Jesse either. You still miss her, don't you?"

"Jesse is a married woman," he said, not welcoming this subject but not wanting to protest too much for fear of proving Courtney's point. "*Happily* married this time. There's another baby on the way, I hear."

"I'm happy that Jesse is happy. I just wish you were too."

"I'm doing fine," he said. "Look at me. Fine. See? How about some of that macaroni and cheese?" Courtney passed him the macaroni and he took a helping.

"You should have a family too," Courtney said. "You'd make a great dad."

"Jesse didn't think so."

"Jesse was wrong."

"I'd settle for being the greatest uncle in the world."

"Too late." Courtney stabbed at her food. "By the time Hastings and I decided that the time was right—we were ready—it was too late. I couldn't get pregnant. We tried for years. We saw specialists."

"I didn't know," he said.

"I wanted to adopt. But Hastings didn't."

He nodded to let her know he was listening. It didn't seem to be something he should comment on. It might tempt him to reveal his own history of unrequited parenthood. He didn't want to say anything he would regret saying.

"Hastings insisted he had heard horror stories about adopted kids," Courtney went on. "Some adopted kid he grew up with went nuts, bludgeoned his parents to death or something. It affected him. 'Good grief, Hastings,' I said. 'How many kids who are not adopted have bludgeoned their parents to death? Too many to count.' He worried that maybe he couldn't love somebody else's child the way he could love his own. 'But it wouldn't be somebody else's child,' I said. 'It would be ours.' We went around and around. He feels guilty now. My time ran out while he was thinking things over, you know. It was too late for me. You know he built that after-school club in south San Jose? It was his project. All his philanthropy involves kids. Guilt. That's why."

"Hastings has done a lot of good. That's for sure."

"That's the irony," Courtney said. "Meghan Morehead has two children—boys. He's crazy about them. You should see him."

"So he's decided he likes kids after all. Can't blame him for that, can you?"

"If Hastings leaves me—he swears he's not going to—'No divorce,' he said. 'I won't let it go that far, Court. Trust me'—but if he does leave me, the first thing I'm going to do is adopt as a single parent. You think I'm too old?"

"Don't get ahead of yourself here," Truely said. "You just said Hastings didn't want a divorce."

"He says not. He swears he'll never ask me for a divorce. He says he just needs some time to explore this relationship with

Meghan. He believes God sent her into his life for a reason—and he needs to understand what that is. He says they have a soul connection and it's different from what he has with me—you know, a history. 'When you meet your soul mate, you can't turn away, can you?' he said. 'I hate the timing of all this, Courtney, I swear. But there is no such thing as pure coincidence. You're the one that taught me that. Everything happens for a reason, right?' "

"Damn, Court."

"I know."

"What is he going to think when he comes home—sees your new face?"

"I didn't have this surgery for Hastings." She patted the side of her ballooned face. "It's for me—in case I am about to start my life all over—alone."

"You won't be alone long, Court, if you don't want to be."

"Why not?" she asked. "You are."

"I'm not exactly... *alone*," he said.

"Why? Because sometimes Shauna spends the night on weekends? That's alone, Truely. That's sad and alone."

"Do I sense a sermon coming on here?"

Courtney shook her head and covered her face with her hands for a minute. "Sorry. I'm hardly the one to preach, am I?"

"You've always been the one to preach, Court." He faked a laugh, but it was sour.

"Maybe that's why Hastings likes Meghan. Maybe she doesn't preach."

"Maybe this is not really about you, Court. Or Meghan either. Maybe this is all about Hastings."

"Something tells me you've been watching *Oprah* again." She tried to smile. "I thought you swore off." She was referring to his postdivorce depression, when he was working from his home office and every day precisely at three o'clock he halted everything, lay down on the couch in the fetal position and watched *Oprah*. For all he knew it did him some good. But Courtney was newly resaved and saw it as something to worry about. She took to calling him over and over again during the show, to distract him, make him get up off the sofa, confess to his unmanly, unhealthy pastime. But he never picked up the phone. He let it ring non-stop. He got over it eventually and went back to work at his Mariposa office. Started seeing a therapist. But Courtney still saw it as his futile attempt at secular healing when, as she liked to put it, "It's God you need, Truely. Not Oprah."

"Maybe Oprah is one of God's mysterious ways, Court. You ever think of that?" He remembered saying that. He remembered believing it too. Oprah was from Mississippi after all. She knew firsthand some of the same stuff he knew. He thought if they ever ran into each other at Winn-Dixie late at night—or Hardee's early in the morning in pursuit of a chicken biscuit—they would have something meaningful to say to each other. Or at least they would have a solid starting place. He liked Oprah. She comforted him somehow.

"What do you think, Court—that I didn't pay attention to all my postdivorce counseling? I paid attention. I got my money's worth. You better believe it."

"Oh Truely," she sighed. "We're such a pair, aren't we?"

"Damn straight. All that hype about kids from broken homes—shoot," he said. "They don't tell you that being raised by happily married parents who adore you and each other—well, that can totally fuck you up in the long run."

"You need your mouth washed out with soap," she said.

"All I'm saying is 'no guarantees,' sister." He reached to tousle her hair but she flinched and he remembered her stapled scalp and stopped himself.

"You know how I found out Meghan went with Hastings to Scotland?" Courtney picked up her fork and tapped it against her plate, *tap, tap, tap*. It was distracting. "I called her house." She shrugged. "There was a time when such a thing would never have crossed my mind." *Tap. Tap.*

"Go on." He put his hand on hers to stop her tapping at her dinner plate.

"Sorry." She set her fork down. "Meghan's mother answered the phone. I told her I was Courtney, a friend of Meghan's. I said, 'Oh I bet you remember me.' And she tried to, then she just pretended to. She told me she was babysitting the boys because Meghan was out of town — 'on business,' she said. 'Oh,' I said, 'that's right, the trip to Scotland.' I was fishing, right? 'Yes,' her mother said, 'Scotland. Meghan was asked to make the trip. It's a great opportunity.' "

"Sounds like an understatement to me," Truely said.

Courtney looked away and rubbed the sides of her head where her skin was stitched together. "Before he left, I had asked Hastings point-blank if Meghan was going to Scotland with him. He denied it. Looked me in the eye and denied it."

"Very Christian of him."

"Christians are just people, Truely. None of us claim to be perfect. Least of all Hastings."

It was Truely's instinct to argue the point, but he didn't.

"This is awful, Truely. Isn't it? Why is this happening?"

"Bad things happen to good people sometimes." He sounded like a fortune cookie. "You'll get this resolved." He almost added, "like I did," but stopped short of that since he was pretty sure that comparing her plight to his would do little to cheer her up.

"I'm just thankful Mother and Daddy aren't here to see this happen," Courtney said. "They never really liked Hastings to start with. Especially Daddy. He never approved."

"I don't know about that, Court."

"Yes you do. You know Daddy always thought Hastings was too...too...*privileged*. Too much given to him. Not enough earned. Whatever. But Daddy was wrong about that, Truely. Hastings works really hard. He's ambitious and driven. So what if he was born to comfortable parents?"

"Comfortable? Is that the way you see it, Court? Comfortable?"

"Daddy shouldn't have held that against him."

"Daddy never expressed any of that to me. As long as you were happy, Court. I think that's all Daddy really cared about."

"Well, he'd be pretty disappointed about now, wouldn't he? He'd be thinking he was right all along, that I never had any business moving away from Hinds County in the first place."

"You know how Daddy was, Court. He probably thought you'd grow up to be more like Mother—and marry somebody more like him."

"Maybe I should have." She reached for her glass then as if to punctuate the moment, but her fingers hit it clumsily and it bounced across the table and flew off the edge, splashing red wine on both of them and shattering when it hit the tile floor. They looked a little blood-splattered, but neither of them made a move to address the mess. Courtney put her head on the table and he thought she might be crying. He put his arm on her shoulder, a futile gesture. Neither of them spoke.

It made him think of years ago, when they were young and secretly afraid of the world and Courtney had cried because one of her classmates' fathers had been arrested for molesting the girl. They had not known before then that such things could happen—especially not to people that they knew and went to church with. The girl was sent away to live with distant relatives and the father's life was forever ruined in Jackson. Courtney had whispered the story to Truely. Later she would spend days trying to write a letter to the girl—that she read him drafts of and which, in the end, she never sent.

"I'm okay." Courtney lifted her head and looked at him. "Really, I am. I shouldn't be drinking wine—not while I'm taking all these pain meds. It makes me dopey and I'm getting an awful headache. That's all."

"You really look tired, Court," he said.

"When Hastings is out of town I never sleep well. Every noise, you know?"

He convinced her to go to bed, leaving him to clean up the kitchen. She didn't argue, which was a pleasant surprise. She kissed him and said, "Thanks, Truely. You're a good brother."

He watched his tipsy sister make her way to the master bedroom at the back of the house. He loved her so completely watching her weave her way along, awkwardly touching the furniture and the walls as she went. At that moment he would have leaped in front of a speeding train or a stray bullet to save her from whatever disappointment might lie in wait for her.

TRUELY LIKED being left alone in Courtney's kitchen. He liked opening drawers and cabinets, loading the dishwasher, sponging off the counter. At his place it was a chore—the kitchen. Here it was an odd sort of entertainment. When he got the place pretty well spit-shined and had swept the floor just for good measure, he should have headed off to the guesthouse to get ready for bed. But it didn't take him long to realize that sleep would be elusive. He wasn't worried, really. His sister was a strong woman. It was more like his mind was swirling, his life intersecting hers at so many points, and he had this odd feeling of powerful connectedness—and total powerlessness too. He started thinking that it was true what they said about blood and water. Blood is blood. Always. What happened to him happened to her in some way. And what happened to her, well, it mattered to him and he knew that for sure and he was grateful to know it.

HE REMEMBERED the Mississippi version of Courtney—young and barefoot with a bandana tied on her red hair, out in the carport making some kind of big mess that she referred to as *art*. He guessed some of it was still there, stuffed in the rafters of the storage room.

After his mother's death Truely had been the one to go back home to put the old house and surrounding acreage up for sale. After a few days of sleeping in his boyhood room, walking around the yard, drinking his morning coffee on the back steps—he changed his mind and put up a FOR RENT sign.

Twice that same week Truely had gone out to hear music with Mose and some of his buddies. Mose had brought his current girlfriend along—Jennifer Shipley—a white girl they had gone to high school with. She had been under the radar back then, not a part of any of their distinct memories, but later had got herself together in such a way that it was hard not to notice. She worked for Mose now, teaching yoga at Jackson's Gem.

It was Jennifer who found a renter for Truely. Her sister, Beverly, whose husband, Ralph, had a horticulture degree from Mississippi State and wanted to try his hand at organic farming. They agreed to a fair rent, shook hands, and it was done. According to Fontaine, Ralph's effort was only moderately successful. "He's charging too much roadside," Fontaine insisted. "People around here not going to overpay just because he puts up a sign saying ORGANIC."

Once Ralph sent Truely a photo of the house decorated for Christmas—it looked like a collision of flashing lights, as if a red-and-green spaceship had crashed to earth. It made Truely remember the way he and his daddy—urged on and closely supervised by Courtney—had gone to work slinging Christmas lights on the eaves of the house and carport, on shrubs, tree saplings, fence posts and toolsheds. His daddy had had an obsolete-looking old Santa with a broken neck, surgically repaired with duct tape, which he perched on the roof every year with Truely's help—tied him to the chimney with fishing line. From a distance it had looked spectacular.

Back in those days Courtney had made Christmas tree ornaments by the bushel basket too—tiny yarn stockings, Dixie-cup bells, tinfoil icicles, paper plate snowflakes, glittered pecans, cotton-ball Santas. Where was all that stuff now? He hoped nobody had thrown it out. He realized all of a sudden that it meant something to him.

Truely wandered to the back of the house to see if Courtney was asleep. Her bedroom door was closed and there was no light escaping beneath the door, no sounds of the TV muttering away in the darkness. Probably she had taken something and gone right to sleep. He hoped so.

He was wide-awake and not ready for bed. It crossed his mind to call Shauna, but he decided against it. He didn't really have too much to say to Shauna right now and he would definitely not want to call only to find out that she wasn't even home. That was always a possibility.

He walked to the study, his favorite room. It was something he'd done regularly in recent years, at Courtney's house late at night when everybody else was asleep and he was sneaking around like a thief. It was like he had developed an addiction to Courtney's photo albums. He knew where she kept them. They looked like leather-bound ledgers or something. Not your regular garish photo albums or those cardboard photo boxes with everything dumped into them. These were engraved with Hastings' gold initials. He made a stop at the kitchen for one last glass of wine, then headed for the study and closed the door. He knew the albums he was after. The ones with all their childhood photos — black-and-white shots of life in Mississippi, then color Polaroids. Shots of his mother and daddy in their last years. He started there.

But what he really was after were the albums with the Jesse and Truely photos. All the holidays they'd spent at Courtney's houses. The special-occasion shots — their engagement party, their wedding, the surprise birthday party when he turned thirty-five, shots where Jesse began to look really thin and her smile was forced. He only noticed that now. He never noticed it when it was happening — when it might have mattered to notice.

He didn't gnash his teeth in regret. He liked remembering. There was no real harm in that. Courtney was so sure that he still loved Jesse, that he might never recover from their breakup, might never accept the fact that Jesse had moved on, to a new husband — some guy who had been assistant principal at her school and was as dedicated as she was to saving the world one child at a time. She hadn't married him until their baby was a year old — and now a second baby was coming, another girl, he'd heard. Her husband was principal of his own school now. She was a stay-at-home mom. They lived out at Silver Creek on the golf course. The Jesse he used to know would never live out there where everything was so big and brand-new. She was more a Rose Garden sort of girl, downtown San Jose, everything old, well planted and well tended. She was more understated then. Her dreams were traditional and — he had believed then — manageable. But he was the one who changed that. He was the one who turned her into a well-to-do woman living a well-to-do life. If anybody asked him, and nobody ever did, he'd say he didn't really miss Jesse — especially not the new updated Jesse, whom he didn't know at all. What he missed was the old Truely. The person he thought he was when he thought she loved him.

He remembered the night Jesse had told him she was pregnant. The first time. Long after he thought they had stopped trying. He had gotten swept up in the unexpected news, happier than he could ever have predicted because by then he had pretty much let go of the dream of fatherhood. He had practically talked himself out of even wanting a child because he thought his not-wanting would make things easier for Jesse. She had become so fraught with the pursuit of motherhood.

He remembered the look on her face when he came home from work that particular night. He couldn't tell whether she was happy or sad. She looked scared. He had never seen that look before. She met him in the hallway with a pregnancy test in her hand, saying, "Oh my God, True," then dissolving into a flood of tears that was almost frightening. He had taken her in his arms and held her for the longest time, mistaking her tears for joy. Because his were. It was an honest mistake.

Three delirious months later the blood came and washed away their hopes. Blood of my blood. Wasn't that in the Bible? The blood of their blood — gone. Despite the advice of her friends, Jesse had already bought the crib and set up a small white sanctuary in anticipation of their answered prayer. They had loved worshipping at the shrine of their firstborn. When the bleeding began it was terrifying. He had driven Jesse to the hospital and they had sedated her. A few days later she had gone back for a D&C. A silence had set in between them then that Truely was never fully able to exorcise. Jesse had gone to stay at her mother's house while Truely dismantled the baby furniture and donated it to the battered woman's shelter per Jesse's instructions. When she came home the loss was slightly less pronounced, like something you couldn't really prove since all the evidence was gone. It was almost like it had never really happened at all.

"WHAT ARE YOU DOING?" Courtney had cracked the study door and was staring in at him. "Can't you sleep?"

"Just cruising memory lane," he confessed.

She nodded, then stood in the doorway swaying like she was frozen there.

"Court?" he said. "Court, you okay?"

"Tell me what to do, Truely," she said. "I don't know what to do." Her voice had such a tone to it, like she was choking on a submerged wail that she refused to unleash, but he heard it. No more missed clues for him. He dropped the photo album and went to where she stood. She fell into his clumsy arms like a leaf falling off the highest branch of the family tree.

Nine

BY MORNING they were both exhausted from a restless night. But sunlight had the power to shrink the monstrous questions that loom at night to insect-sized pests in the morning. He had learned that for himself. Courtney confessed that she had gone to bed hoping to hear from Hastings, but he had not called. Usually, she said, when he traveled he made a point to call her several times a day—for no reason—*just because*. But her phone never rang. And when she tried to dial him—according to the travel itinerary he left—he had either not checked in yet or had just checked out. Or his cell was turned off or out of range. At night her inability to reach him was terrifying to her. By morning it was merely annoying.

They made coffee and took cups with them on a slow walk around the property. Saratoga was beautiful this time of year. Cool and fragrant, the leaves doing their modest best at fall colors—not nearly as pretentious and bold as Mississippi, but oddly calming in their subtlety. Somewhere along the path, most of which they walked in silence, Courtney announced to him, "I want to go into Saratoga today for lunch."

"You feel up to that?" he asked.

"I can't just hide out here and worry."

"I could go into town and bring something home," he suggested. He was thinking she probably wouldn't want to make an appearance with her eggplant eyes and blood-caked stitches and matted hair. He was thinking she wasn't thinking.

"No," she said. "I need to get into town, walk the streets, sit in a well-lit restaurant, see people—some I know, some I don't. If any-body asks me a question, I'll say, *Yes, I just had a face-lift.* If they ask me where Hastings is, I'll say, *He's in Scotland with Meghan, his per-sonal assistant.* I won't lie. Do you believe me, Truely? I won't lie."

"I think you might want to think this over," he said. "You're entitled to your privacy, Court."

"You don't understand," she said. And she was right. He didn't.

By noon they were dressed and getting in his car to go into town to lunch. Courtney had dressed in slacks and a sweater. She had pulled her unwashed hair and stapled scalp back from her face and covered it with a scarf. But her bare face was raw and wounded and she had not made any attempt to soften the shock of it with makeup or sunglasses. Truely was worried that she was not in her right mind exactly, what with all her meds and the recent anesthesia. Some people reacted badly to anesthesia, right? It messed them up. He had heard of that. Add to that the emotional upheaval of Hastings' recent revelations, his untimely discovery of a soul mate, when for almost twenty years Courtney had perceived herself as exactly that. Now she had been reas-signed to the role of a woman with whom he "had history."

If Truely were a better brother would he refuse to drive his sister into town, refuse to allow her to walk the streets freshly carved upon, freshly nipped and tucked and theoretically and artificially rejuvenated? Would she thank him later if he put his foot down and insisted she stay hidden at home until she healed? Isn't that what women did when they got work done? If he went through with this misguided lunch idea was she going to blame him later for his lapse in protecting her from herself?

He started the car and eased slowly down the winding drive-way. He looked at her for some sign that she was rethinking this plan, but she seemed relaxed and calm and more than happy to be on her way to a pleasant lunch. She even managed to smile at him. When they were maybe halfway to the restaurant she touched his arm and asked, "If Hastings does leave me, Truely, will you hate him?"

He was not expecting the question. If there was a right answer he didn't know what it was. If she was hoping he would say something to make her feel better, then he hoped so too, although he had no idea what that might be. "No," he said, finally. "I won't hate Hastings." It was the truth too, he wouldn't.

"Really?" She seemed amused. "Why not?"

"I don't know," he said. "I guess I've known him too long to hate him."

"Yes," she said. "Me too."

THEY PULLED INTO THE PARKING LOT behind the Plumed Horse, one of Courtney's favorite restaurants. He had parked as near to the door as possible and was walking around to open Courtney's door for her when her cell phone rang. It played "When the Saints Go Marching In," which he had once found oddly appropriate. She fumbled through her purse to answer it. He saw the way her hands shook. "Hello." She spoke in what he thought was a childlike voice. He stood beside the open car door, waiting. "Hastings," she said. "My God, it's you." She glanced at Truely with such a vulnerable expression, the relief and the pain of the call made apparent. Truely nodded and stepped away from the car. He would let her have this conversation privately. He would wait it out. It was the sort of moment when you might wish you smoked, so you could busy yourself with lighting a cigarette and standing idly by while you smoked it. It would feel like something to do, when there was really nothing to do but wait.

HE WATCHED COURTNEY GESTURE with her hands while she talked. He watched her bow her head and go silent. He watched her laugh out loud, a fake laugh that was sickening to him, the garishness of it. He watched her squirm in her seat and rub her hand over her bandages and over her eyes. He watched her shake her head no, no, no. He watched every move his sister made, sitting there in the car speaking to the husband who was making her so miserable, and he instinctively understood the nature of the call without ever hearing a word of it. They spoke for maybe ten minutes. It seemed a long time to Truely. When Courtney hung up she went limp, and rested her head in her hands.

"Everything okay?" he asked stupidly.

She nodded yes, but she obviously meant no.

Truely fished in his pocket for a handkerchief. It was wrinkled and worn, but it was clean. His mother had taught him to always carry a handkerchief—*A gentleman always carries a clean handkerchief,* she had said—and now he was the only guy he knew anymore who actually did. "Here." He handed it to her.

"I can't do lunch, True," she whispered. "Can you just take me back home?"

"Sure thing," he said.

He drove her back to her place, listening to her breathe in suppressed sobs. She would not let herself full-out cry, which made him want to.

When they got home Courtney didn't want to talk. She took a sleeping pill and went to bed. Truely was worried about her so he sat in a chair in the sitting area of her bedroom and pretended to read the paper. Her sadness scared him in a way his own never had.

HE THOUGHT OF JESSE, and the way he had lost her to a sadness too heavy for her to bear alone—and too secretive for him to help her bear. It wasn't until she became pregnant for the second time that he'd understood the depths of her anguish. He had suspected and dismissed the possibility that she might be pregnant because he heard her vomiting in the early mornings the same way she had done before. But he was afraid to mention it because the truth had the potential to destroy him. He would wait it out. Then, when she was ready, Jesse told him, yes, she was pregnant again. "I hope you can forgive me, True." Truely understood without further explanation. The baby she was carrying was not his. It couldn't be, since they had not made love since her miscarriage five months earlier.

Jesse would become a mother. But he would not become a father.

*   *   *

MAYBE there was something wrong with him. He had not come through for his daddy when he needed him. How much would it have meant to his daddy if Truely'd been around to mow the grass and feed the birds? Would it have been so hard to visit his widowed mother down in Hinds County more often? Instead he'd just lobbed onto her visits to Courtney and Hastings. It was less trouble that way—and he was ashamed of that now. He hadn't even been there when Courtney found their mother dead with a smile on her face. Now he was thinking of ways to escape the potential effects of the collapse of his sister's nearly perfect life. Did he just hate having anybody need him? He had an almost violent urge to run to the guesthouse and call Shauna and tell her he loved her. He imagined himself saying things like, "Shauna, you can count on me. I'll never let you down."

Then he imagined Shauna's response. Would she laugh? Would she think he'd been drinking and hang up in his face? Would she say, "Better late than never, I guess," and be happy? He had no idea how Shauna would respond. And that was partly what kept him from ever doing anything impulsive. There was no guarantee. Unfortunately, at this point in his life, he was a man who needed a guarantee.

Truely went to the kitchen and made a modest supper for Courtney. Hot soup from a Whole Foods carton and a tuna fish sandwich. He carried it to her on a tray the way their mother had done when they were small and one of them stayed home from school, sick. She had had a way of making feeling bad something special—almost better than feeling good.

"Wake up, E.T.," he said.

Courtney opened her purple, bloodshot eyes and sat up. "Thank you," she said. She nibbled at the sandwich and sipped the soup. Truely watched her eat and offered her a full range of services. "Do you want me to open the blinds? Here, let me put this pillow behind you. Are you cold? Should I start a fire? You want the paper? You want to catch the news on TV?" Courtney declined his offers.

"Truely, I know you want to know about my conversation with Hastings. But I can't talk about it now. I'll tell you tomorrow. Okay?"

"Sure," he said. "Whatever."

She blew him a small, clumsy sister-kiss before thanking him again and going back to sleep.

COURTNEY WAS FEELING better Sunday morning. She was up and dressed before Truely was and brought a hot cup of coffee out to him in the guesthouse. "Rise and shine," she sang. While he showered she went to the kitchen to make breakfast, waffles for him, dry toast for herself. By the time he made his way to the kitchen she was sitting at the table nursing her cup of coffee and eating her toast. She appeared rested and oddly composed considering the state she had been in yesterday. He pulled out a chair and sat beside her. "You didn't have to make waffles," he said, pleased that she had.

"It's the least I could do." She smiled.

"Looks like you're feeling better." Even he thought he heard the raw hopefulness in his voice.

"You'll go to church with me today, Truely. Right? Before you head back to the city?"

"Sure," he said. "I brought a sport coat. Got plenty of sins to offer up too."

She smiled. "I want to go. It'll do me good. It always does. We'll leave at ten. They have coffee and doughnuts in the fellowship hall."

"Coffee and doughnuts it is," he said.

"Hastings put Meghan on the phone yesterday."

"What?"

"Her mother told her that a Courtney had called. I'm the only Courtney she knows."

"Right."

"She asked me to forgive her."

"For what?" He swirled a forkful of waffle in a sea of sticky syrup.

"For falling in love with my husband."

"Wow."

"She cried."

"Well…that's one approach."

"She sounded sort of hysterical. Hastings had to take the phone from her."

"That's a lot of drama for one phone call, Court."

"I think they're suffering too, Truely—you know—in their own way."

"It's called guilt," he said. "Must be contagious. An epidemic maybe."

"So I thought church today would be good for me. Sometimes the minister says exactly the thing I need to hear. It's like he's speaking directly to me without even realizing it. Prayer is powerful too, Truely. Really. I've seen prayer work miracles."

He looked at his sister and nodded. "Of course."

"This is not a sermon," she said. "If that's what you're worried about."

"I'm just worried about you, Court. That's all. I hate for you to go through all this. Especially now."

"Why is now worse than any other time?"

"I don't know. Mother and Daddy aren't around, you know, to be there for you."

"But you are, Truely."

"Poor substitute for sure." He smiled. "And you just had your face done and all. You haven't healed yet."

"They're taking the staples out Tuesday," she said.

"That's not what I mean, Court."

"I know what you mean. You think it's like I'm going to church stark naked, my face a big mess, my not-secret out there for everybody to see."

"You are, Court. You're stark naked here. Should I try to talk you out of this? Damn if I know. I don't know about these things, Court. I wish I did."

"You're here, Truely. That's enough. That's everything." She stood and ran her fingers through his wet hair, messing it up. "I'll get my purse and meet you at the car."

"Okay," he said. "Got to make a quick call first." When Courtney left the room Truely took out his cell phone and fast-dialed
Shauna. Shauna was number one on his fast-dial. He let the
phone ring a long time. Why the hell didn't her machine pick
up? He felt a pang of panic, like a small fish darting around in
his blood.

COURTNEY WAS RAW-FACED and pale. Her hair was tied back in
a sloppy knot. She wore a pantsuit and a turtleneck sweater with
some noticeable jewelry that Truely remembered Hastings giving
her Christmases past. She was neither smiling nor sullen. He had
no read on her mood or her thoughts. They drove in silence to
the church and parked in the gravel parking lot. He opened the
door for his sister like they were on a date or something, courting
each other Mississippi-style. His good manners, instilled in ado-
lescence, still served him well in times of uncertainty.

When they entered the fellowship hall all eyes turned to Courtney. Truely thought he detected a moment of paralysis among
the people gathered in restrained clusters, a pause in the sen-
tences being exchanged, a few decibels dropped in the reverent
volume of the place. Courtney seemed not to notice. She entered
the room as a woman whose habit it was to conquer—both good
people and bad situations. Truely knew that no matter how sure
Courtney appeared, she was very unsure. It occurred to him how
rare a person she must be not to require certainty—not to insist
upon it, falsely fabricating it if necessary. She moved forward
without it the way he should have done in his life—the way he
wished he could do now.

People—some of them were friends of hers he recognized—
smiled, nodded acknowledgment, gave a silent wave. No one
rushed to her with questions. No one asked, "What the hell happened to you?" Two of Courtney's women friends that Truely
had met before, but whose names escaped him momentarily,
approached her with confident smiles of their own and timid
questions in their eyes.

Truely made his way to the coffee urn and poured two Styrofoam cups of hot black liquid. It neither smelled nor tasted like
coffee—more like muddy water. Truely understood that the idea
of coffee was the thing on an occasion like this. Sometimes the
idea supporting the reality was more important than the reality
itself. This had always seemed especially true to him at church.
The idea of blood was more important than the sip of wine—or
in Mississippi, the sip of grape juice—on communion Sunday.
The idea of Jesus' body was more important than the tasteless
wafers or the dry bread crusts. Maybe the idea of coffee fit into
these rituals in some way too.

He carried the cups of coffee over to Courtney—his black,
hers with a packet of Splenda. He watched her talk with her
friends, using her hands, her charm bracelet rattling as she spoke,
each charm meaningful, most of them gifts from Hastings, a
trip taken, a birthday celebrated, a plateau reached, an apology
accepted. Courtney's hand motions made him think of an accident victim filing a police report, explaining how the crash happened, the insane speed, the reckless man at the wheel, how she
had been thrown from her moving luxury vehicle of a life.

"Here you go." He handed her the coffee.

She took the coffee from him, her charm bracelet making its
distracting semimusical sound. "Truely, you remember Steel and
Angie, don't you? From the Christmas party last year?"

"Sure." He nodded.

"I was just giving them the *Reader's Digest* version of my
surgery."

"Don't forget to mention the staples." He smiled. "She says
they stapled her skull together," he told the women, "with a gun."
They laughed knowingly, the way women often do when a man
tries to enter an arena where they've had the experience whereas
he has simply read the book—if that. "Well, don't want to stop
you from this play-by-play. I think I'll get a doughnut. Can I bring
anybody one?"

They said no, of course, and he made his escape to the refresh-
ment table like an awkward teenage boy at a dance.

Originally, Jesse had been the one to teach him the evils of sugar and fat. She had introduced him to sprouts and every sort of bitter lettuce and bland unfamiliar vegetable. At the time he had been a willing learner. She had even tried to convince him of the superiority of the unseasoned steamed vegetable — but she had failed miserably. To his way of thinking there was not a vegetable in all of California that stood up against the squash and green beans of Mississippi — those genius dabs of bacon fat and cane sugar, that dash of hot pepper sauce. Now there was pure love in food like that. He had given it up, not because he didn't still love those overcooked, well-seasoned Mississippi vegetables, but because he simply couldn't get anything that came anywhere near it in California. Jesse used to tell him that people who gave up fattening foods would live longer — but he always wondered, *Why would they want to?* Since Jesse was no longer around policing his food he had his occasional lapses into the vast arena of comfort foods that had sustained him as a boy. On the list of sins he needed to be forgiven for, this seemed a small one. He ate first a glazed doughnut and then, what the hell, a jelly-filled with sprinkles.

He was glad when Courtney signaled to him that she was ready to go into the service. Otherwise he might have downed Lord knows how many of the artery-clogging, heart-stopping temptations in his futile effort to distract himself from the moment. Or maybe he was simply trying to neutralize that sour void that always seemed to flare in his belly whenever he went to church, reminding him that something important was probably missing from his life. He was relatively sure of it.

He escorted his sister into the sanctuary, where a smattering of worshippers sat in the pews, some with bowed heads and prayerful poses and others visiting quietly, touching each other on the arms, whispering greetings. It was like nearly any church service he had ever attended, except for the flush of dizziness he felt. He had worried that Courtney might collapse in an onslaught of emotion, but instead he felt unsteady himself, swaying a little, his knees threatening to buckle beneath him. He thought of his parents, church people, like angels now, both dead and yet still very alive, maybe even floating above, looking down on him — on them both — right at this moment. He wished for them and felt the flutter of their presence, which came to him in scraps of memory.

Truely followed Courtney down the aisle and took a seat beside her on the second pew from the front. He felt oddly exposed. He had always preferred to sit in the back, where he could slip out easily when the service was over and get on with his life in a hurry. He felt the eyes of others on Courtney. These people were her friends, her partners in faith. She had nothing to fear from them, right? Courtney sat up straight and stared ahead. She appeared calm.

Truely did not know what would happen today. He felt both dread and anticipation. He didn't really understand his sister — or himself. Maybe he had never fully understood anything in his life. He buried his face in his hands and tried to be grateful for everything good that had ever happened to him. He thought of Shauna smiling at him, waving as she left his loft to go home, her dogs tugging on their leashes. He hoped that if, as some people insisted, every life had a specific purpose, that he had not, in ignorance, strayed too far from his. If indeed his life had purpose he wanted to know exactly what it was. He wanted to cooperate fully and do his part. And he could too, he felt sure — if only it would become clear to him.

He sat in the pew slightly slumped with a hymnal in his hand. It was what he always did at church, hold the hymnal in his lap and flip the pages, waiting for the page numbers to be announced and the singing to begin. He never took much interest in the program spelling out these details. Beside him Courtney bowed her head and whispered quietly an inaudible prayer. He looked at her closed eyes, her moving lips, her strange cut-and-paste face. Seeing his sister pray made him think of their mother and her unyielding faith in things unseen.

Truely began to imagine the long-unseen Jesse walking into this church on this day, looking for him. They had been here a number of times together before everything. He imagined she might be wearing a simple dress and low heels because that was what she had worn before. His imagination steered Jesse to this very pew and watched her nudge her way in and take a seat beside him. It felt good to imagine this. It felt excellent.

At first his imagination wanted her to say, *I should never have left you, Truely.* This was a scenario he had rehearsed for months after she left, when he was trying to trick himself into falling asleep at night. But now he didn't want her to say anything she didn't mean. He just wanted to hear what she had come to say—whatever it might be. She took his hand. He felt the jolt of disbelief that accompanied a wish coming true.

"Truely, are you okay?" It was Courtney. She was squeezing his hand.

"Sure," he said. "I'm okay."

"Listen," she said. "No matter what happens with Hastings and me, I want you to know, I'm going to forgive Hastings for everything. It's the only thing to do."

"Good," he mumbled.

"If you can forgive Jesse the way you have, then I can forgive Hastings."

Something was caught in Truely's throat, a speck of dust or lint maybe. He began to cough. It was like he was choking on a fish bone, the sounds in his throat becoming embarrassingly harsh and vulgar. In seconds his cough turned into a loud, nasty-sounding hack-cough. He felt like one of those wizened old die-hard smokers who could not get his breath and just gagged his life away gasping for air. In something short of panic Truely reached for the handkerchief he always carried in his pocket. He covered his mouth but could not stop the spasms of loud, desperate coughing. Courtney was fishing through her bag. "I've got a throat lozenge in here somewhere," she said.

Truely stood up in the midst of this fit of grotesque coughing and with his head down made a hurried exit from the church, nearly breaking into a run before he reached the open doors. The coughing did not cease until he made his way through the church courtyard and out into the gravel parking lot where his car was parked. Even then he was wheezing and his eyes were watering, making him look like a man weeping for the ages. For a split second it actually occurred to him that he might die an untimely, freakish death.

He sat in his car and tried to compose himself. He turned on the radio and listened to some soothing, uninspired music and waited until he was sure the coughing had stopped and his irrational panic had subsided. When he was sure he was breathing normally again he fast-dialed Shauna on his cell phone. She didn't answer. He remembered her kid brother, Gordo, telling him once, "One of these days my sister is going to come to her senses—and you're going to be history, man. I don't know what's kept her hanging on this long." Truely had believed Gordo was half kidding, but now it crossed his mind that maybe he hadn't been. He dialed Shauna's number again. No answer. He intended to press redial until she did. Shauna had never been one to play hard to get.

When Courtney found him after church he was still sitting slumped over in his car in the parking lot with his cell phone pressed to his ear. His head was bowed and his eyes were closed. Anyone who didn't know him might think he was praying.

BEFORE TRUELY LEFT that afternoon to drive back to the city, Courtney said, "Too bad you can't stay for the unveiling on Tuesday."

"You got somebody to go with you?" he asked.

"Myra said she would," Courtney said.

Myra was Courtney's maid and to a certain degree her paid amiga as well. Hastings had originally hired her to come Monday through Friday for general all-around housecleaning, but Courtney was so hands-on, do-it-herself, such an over-the-top perfectionist, that over time she gave Myra enough days off that she could probably have taken on a second job.

"I really prefer to change my own sheets," Truely had heard Courtney say. "I like to clean my own kitchen too. Anyway, how much of a mess can a house be with only two adult neat freaks living in it?" Sometimes Myra would go to the farmers' market with Courtney, comb through all the produce in every booth, make an event out of it. Or they'd go to cooking classes with Courtney's idle friends — Thai, Indian, Italian, or French. Or wine tastings, which would leave Courtney tipsy and happy and Myra less so because she would be the one to drive them home with a cargo of selected wine in cases in the backseat. They had planted gardens together — a few vegetables, but mostly flowers. They had taken flower arranging classes together too — suppressed their urges to be anything but simple, maybe even stark.

Over the years in Courtney's employ Myra had become almost a mind reader. She had learned Courtney's various houses and with each move hauled away a truckload of high-end discarded furniture. Myra knew exactly how to cook the Thanksgiving turkey with the pecan and cornbread dressing, how to decorate the Christmas tree so it was perfect but never overdone, never gaudy. She knew how to wrap gifts so the wrapping was a gift in itself. She knew how to select gifts too, choose fresh vegetables, fold fitted sheets so they looked like flat sheets and arrange them in the linen closet in neat ensembles. She knew how to keep fresh flowers (from the yard whenever possible) in the public rooms and Courtney and Hastings' bedroom and bath and on occasion the guest room too. Myra had one hell of a good job. That was the way Truely saw it.

MAYBE TRUELY should have stayed until Tuesday, been there for the removal of staples from Courtney's skull. Lord. It would have been a loving gesture and he could have managed it.

"I haven't been able to get in touch with Shauna — and to tell you the truth it has me a little spooked." Truely was gathering his things to take to the car.

"You're worried?" Courtney said.

"She hasn't called me all weekend. Usually she checks in."

"Maybe she's just trying to give you some space," Courtney said. "Isn't that one of your personal themes of late?"

"Used to be," he said. "Right now I am not feeling like space is the real answer."

"You *are* worried," Courtney said.

"Got a wild imagination, I guess. Maybe I been watching too much six o'clock news or something."

"You don't think she's off with somebody else, do you?"

"I hope not. But it might be better than some of the scenarios I've been conjuring up."

Courtney walked Truely out to his car carrying a sack of home-made peanut butter cookies for the road. She probably sensed his sudden hurry to leave, watching him sling his overnight bag in the backseat. "Here," she said. "Just like Mama used to make."

He hugged his sister, careful not to touch her wounded face. "You're the best, Court."

"Thanks for coming," she said. "Just some time with you…it gives me perspective."

"Everything will work out," he said. It was short of a promise.

"You mean…even if it doesn't?" She smiled.

"I love you," he said.

"Love you too, little brother."

He waved to her as he started down the long drive. He knew he couldn't have been completely in his right mind on the drive back because he didn't touch the cookies Courtney gave him—which wasn't natural. Ordinarily he would have put away a few of them for medicinal purposes if nothing else.

Ten

SHAUNA HAD A SMALL WALK-UP STUDIO at the outer edge of Nob Hill where she worked as a freelance designer for insecure women with more money than taste. She paid too much for the apartment because she had to buy the big address along with the tiny space—but it was pretty nice. It was not an accident that Shauna had created a career for herself as a designer, self-taught. She'd made the substandard space feel roomy and fresh by painting the walls in strong colors and furnishing it with sparse, clean white slip-covered pieces. It was that California less-is-more thing again. In Mississippi less still was and always had been less and he never came across anybody who wanted to claim it was more.

When he turned onto Shauna's street he saw her car was parked at the curb. His heart took a little leap. She was home, then. Okay. Good. It was never easy to find street parking in her neighborhood, but he found a place almost big enough and fit his car into the tight space by leaving the back bumper protruding into the street.

Once almost two years ago Shauna had given him a key to her place. But he hadn't been ready for that at the time, so he had given it back. She had never offered it again. Maybe she was waiting for him to ask for it. He was such a damn fool sometimes. He'd love to have that key now. What kind of man refuses the key to a woman's place when she offers it? What did he think, that it was the key to misery? The key to forever?

Now he stood at the entrance and punched the buzzer to her unit. This was where she was supposed to answer his call. *Hey,*

True. Come on up. But she didn't. So he buzzed again. And again. He sat on the front stoop and tried to get a grip on this thing akin to fear that was slowly overtaking him. Then he remembered the cookies and made a run to the car and then sat again on the stoop and went to work on the cookies to ease the unbearable strain of waiting and not knowing.

He had been planted there less than an hour when he heard Foxie and Fred—Shauna's dogs—bark at the corner. They always started to bark when their house came into view after a walk. He straightened up and looked down the street only to see Doug Vu holding their leashes along with Rocket's, his own dog's. Doug Vu had not noticed him at first, sitting slumped over like one of the vagrants that frequented the neighborhood, his face in a sack of cookies. But Foxie and Fred saw him now and they began to jump and bark and dance—their welcome ritual. It warmed his heart too. "Hey, man," he yelled to Doug.

Doug saw him and nodded and was practically dragged up the walk by the rambunctious dogs. "How'd you end up with dog duty?" Truely asked.

"I owe Shauna," he said. "But you don't walk three dogs, man. Three dogs walk you."

"So where's Shauna?" There it was—the real question.

"She had to leave town. An emergency. Got a flight home to San Diego on Friday afternoon."

"What kind of emergency?"

"You didn't hear?" Doug was looking at Truely almost suspiciously. "Her brother, man. Shit. He got messed up by a car bomb over there. Her mother called to tell her. The kid got busted up bad. Lost one leg and both his feet. It's bad, man. They were flying him to Germany. Not sure he's even going to make it."

Truely felt his stomach churn. It was like someone had come at him slinging a tire iron and got him dead-on in the gut. Gordo was just a kid. "More kid than soldier no matter what the U.S. Army says"—Truely remembered Shauna saying that. And he had tried to tell her different.

Gordo had been the surprise child in the family, ten years

younger than the other three—and the only boy. He was not even twenty yet—a baby really—but he'd insisted to Truely that he was well educated in the school of hard knocks. That's what he used to say when Shauna tried to talk to him about college too. "I don't need college. I already got my degree from the school of hard knocks." Truely had actually chuckled when he said that.

Truely thought of the hours the two of them had spent shooting hoops when Truely had gone home with Shauna. It gave him something to do besides try to make impossible conversation with her two sisters and their husbands. He loved heading over to the basketball court for pickup games with Gordo's buddies. The hours had flown. Truely was the oldest guy on the court and, Lord knows, he suffered near-death experiences more than once, but he had loved it. It was the main thing that had made visiting Shauna's family manageable for him.

It was Gordo who told Truely that Shauna had instructed her family not to refer to him or introduce him as her boyfriend. Just call him my *friend,* she had told them. "What, you're not into my sister?" Gordo had asked with obvious disapproval, holding the basketball like some sort of weapon in case Truely's response was lacking.

"No, man," Truely had insisted. "It's not like that. Your sister is the best. They don't make them any better than Shauna. She deserves one hell of a lot better than me." Gordo had agreed totally and they went on shooting baskets until it got too dark to see.

At the time Gordo had been enrolled at a community college, but it was a waste, he'd said. He wasn't what he disdainfully referred to as *a college boy.* "My sisters, they think everybody has got to go to college," he told Truely. "They got my old man thinking the same thing. Shoot. He never finished college and he's doing okay."

The next time he and Shauna saw Gordo he had enlisted. Truely figured the army was his way to get Shauna and his sisters off his back, but it had had the opposite effect. Shauna was especially upset. There had been a surge of crying and arguing among the family members. But Gordo had made his decision and signed the papers. It was done. It was odd, but Truely remembered feeling as prideful as an old uncle when he shook his hand and wished him well. Gordo got a family send-off like nothing Truely had ever seen. Tears and kisses were second only to food and drink and toasts to his heroism and patriotism. All the family was there and half the neighborhood too. There was dancing and singing and at least two distressed would-be girlfriends weeping off to the side.

Before the party began Shauna's father, Jerry, had declared a truce in the family uproar and basically announced that as of this day Gordo was a grown man. He ordered everyone to be proud of Gordo, which came easy to all of them. They had always been proud of Gordo. He was a smart kid, so much potential they said, and a heart of gold. So the praisefest had begun. The prayers too.

Shauna had been happy when Gordo got an assignment in food services, which embarrassed and disappointed him as much as it pleased his sisters. Food services. That would be safe, right? His parents hung an American flag on their front porch the day he left and pledged not to take it down until he arrived home again — safe. Lord, they must be going crazy right now. Shauna must be a wreck. He needed to be there with her. "I been calling Shauna for three days," Truely said. "She's not answering her phone."

"I don't think she has it," Doug said. "It's been ringing off the hook in her place. I can hear it. Thin walls in this building. She left in such a panic I think she forgot it."

"You got a key?" Truely asked.

"Somewhere," he said. "She gave me one when she needed somebody to let the cable guy in. Don't know if I can lay my hands on it. Let's take the dogs in, I'll look for it."

Truely found himself hugging Foxie and Fred, making them go wild at the attention. He wanted them to know that he loved them, just in case over the years he had never made that completely clear.

Doug couldn't find Shauna's key the way a person can never

find the thing under his nose when there is urgency to the search. "It's here somewhere," he kept saying. By now the dogs were all going nuts, sensing something wrong, Truely thought, sensing trouble. Doug had to lock them in the bedroom to calm them down.

"You got a screwdriver or something?" Truely asked. "Maybe we can pick the lock somehow." As it turned out Doug was pretty good with the credit card break-and-enter method. With a few minutes of effort they were in Shauna's place and found her cell phone in the tangle of linens on her unmade bed. Truely grabbed it. "I'll take it to her," he said.

HE DROVE TO SFO without even going home first. No clean underwear. No fresh shirt. He would buy whatever he needed once he got to San Diego, and he wanted to get there as fast as possible. He kept thinking of Gordo, a soldier—a young, untraveled guy working the makeshift mess halls on the other side of the world, in the hot as hell desert full of angry and frightened people who both loved and hated him and his kind. He pictured Gordo doling out breakfast, lunch and dinner to the other soldiers before they went out on patrol, some of them as young and naive as he was. How the hell did a kitchen guy get blown up like this? He kept flashing to the TV news, all the nameless soldiers he saw nightly in desperate situations. The confident guys who led the way, shouting orders, danger be damned, and the nervous guys who obeyed and followed and hoped for the best. Heroes all in Truely's eyes. And now one of those nameless guys had a name, Gordo Mackey, shooter of basketballs, question asker, truth teller, beloved little brother and only son, young man willing to do his part, a volunteer. Truely prayed to God Gordo would not die, had not died already. It choked him up to even think the thought.

The flight to San Diego seemed unusually long to Truely. He drank a whiskey—and then a second whiskey—and tried to imagine what he would find when he found Shauna. Unlike Gordo, he didn't have much hero in him, but he hoped he could rise to the occasion for Shauna's sake.

It was late when they touched down in San Diego. By the time he stood in line for his rental car and got out on the road it was past a decent hour to drop in on anybody—but in this case he doubted anybody would be going to bed or sleeping at all even if they did. He thought of Shauna's mother. She was a small Mexican-American woman named Suleeta, who, according to Shauna, had surrendered her womanhood to early motherhood. Truely thought she maintained the residue of a formerly pretty girl. She had married Shauna's Scotch-Irish dad, eight years older than she was, right out of high school. Already Shauna's dad had had his own small construction business. He'd started out pouring patios and building decks for people in the neighborhood, but over time the jobs expanded to building entire houses from the ground up. Mackey's Construction. He had done well for himself and his family.

When they finally had a son, years after Shauna's dad had given up hoping for one, he had insisted that the baby's given name be the same as his. But it was Suleeta who had given Gordo his *real* name. Shauna's dad, Gordon Gerald Mackey, went by Jerry, and so when he named his son Gordon Gerald Jr. it was decided that the boy would go by Gordon. Suleeta had her own way of pronouncing Gordon where the *n* became silent and people mistook her Latino pronunciation of Gordon as Gordo. And so it was. Baby Gordon quickly became Gordo and stayed that way.

It was after midnight when Truely pulled up in front of Shauna's parents' house. The porch light was on and the hopefulness of that small gesture touched Truely with a quiver of sympathy. The outdoor landscape lights along the walkway to the front door presented themselves quietly but did little to illuminate the path to the house. Truely parked his car on the street out front. He glanced at the windows for signs of life, but saw none. He was beginning to wonder if he had made a mistake in coming, if the hour was all wrong and maybe his motives questionable too. Then he saw a lone figure up on the terrace, just the silhouette of a man, Jerry probably, pacing back and forth, maybe talking on his cell phone. It was hard to tell. Truely got out of the car, slamming the door as a way of announcing himself, and walked toward the house, cut across the yard's steep slope of grass and beds of agapanthus up toward the raised terrace. "Jerry," he called out. "That you?"

The figure stopped pacing and looked out into the dark. "Who's there?"

"It's Truely Noonan," he said. "Shauna's friend." He noticed his reluctance, even now, to introduce himself as anything more. *Shauna's boyfriend. Shauna's lover.* Maybe in time, *Shauna's fiancé.* "I know it's late," he said. "Just got word about Gordo. Got the first flight out of San Francisco."

"Come around to the front," Jerry said. "I'll open the door."

"No need," Truely said. "I can scale the wall—I mean, unless you'd rather I didn't."

"No," he said. "Come on."

So Truely propelled himself over the waist-high wall and found himself standing face-to-face with Shauna's dad, self-made man, builder of sturdy things, proud American, father of a fallen soldier. They shook hands almost as if they had never met before. "I hated like hell to hear about Gordo," Truely said.

"Thanks." Jerry looked away then, focusing his gaze on the surrounding darkness. Truely saw that Jerry was holding a drink in his hand. He could smell the liquor on his breath. "Can I get you a drink?" Jerry asked him.

"Better not," Truely said. "I threw back a few on the plane."

"One more won't hurt you," Jerry said. "I don't like to drink alone."

"Sure then," Truely said. "Pour me one." He waited while Jerry walked to the outdoor grill area, where a small refrigerator was set into the rock wall. He watched him grab a fistful of ice, throw it in a plastic cup, and walk back to where Truely stood beside a small metal table with a bottle of bourbon on it. Jerry filled his cup nearly full. "Heads up." He handed him the booze.

"To Gordo." Truely raised his glass.

"Hell, yes." Jerry tapped his glass. "To the best son a man

could ever have." They both drank to that and then offered up a moment of silence while Jerry composed himself, wiping his eyes with his paper napkin. "The others have gone to bed," Jerry said, clearing his throat. "They took those Ambien pills Suleeta got when she had her hysterectomy. But not me. I can't sleep. I don't want to sleep."

"I understand," Truely said.

"This is hell. Waiting."

"I can imagine." Truely shook his head. "It's tough. How's Shauna doing?"

"This thing has torn her up," Jerry said. "You know how she dotes on Gordo. She helped raise him—about like a second mother. She got her crying done early on—her sisters, you know, they can't see straight they're still crying so bad. You can't hardly say anything to them without them starting up again. But you know, Shauna, she was on the phone to DC, getting information and making travel plans. We got a flight out to Germany tomorrow night. Shauna is going with me. Suleeta hates flying and she wouldn't do Gordo much good as upset as she is. She wants to stay here and light candles and pray. It's her way and I respect that. But Shauna, no way to keep Shauna from going. I need her too," he said. "I don't mind admitting it."

For a second Truely thought he heard a subtle accusation. *I don't mind admitting that I need Shauna, unlike you, you asshole, who can't or won't admit it.* But Truely was being too sensitive. He and his deficient ways were the last thing on Jerry's mind. "Yes," he said. "Shauna is strong."

"In a time of trouble, you want Shauna on your team," Jerry said. "Becca and Shelly, they're more like their mother. I told their husbands to take them back home, but they wouldn't go. They want to do their crying here, all together. Shauna is more like me. We got to see things through. We got to know how things stand."

"Anything I can do?" Truely asked. "I'd like to help out some way, Jerry."

"Thanks," Jerry said. "I appreciate that."

The two of them stood there a minute looking out over the

dimly lit neighborhood, a nervous dog yapping somewhere in the distance, the thumping sound of too loud music a few streets over. "Gordo has got to live," Jerry said mostly to himself. He closed his eyes and took a long drink of liquor and shook his glass, rattling the ice. "We can find a way to deal with . . . the rest."

"That's right," Truely said.

"We can deal with whatever we have to deal with."

"You can." Truely nodded.

Then the men went silent again, just the ice melting in their glasses and the doves in the treetops cooing brokenheartedly. "You don't have kids," Jerry said.

"No."

"If you ever do, you'll know."

"I guess so."

"I was too hard on Gordo. I see that now." Jerry shook his glass again as if he were sounding an alarm. "Like every kid, Gordo got in his share of trouble, you know, did some stupid things. But he was a kid, right? I bet you did some stupid shit when you were a kid."

"For sure," Truely agreed.

"I came down on Gordo too hard. I just didn't want him to go in the wrong direction, see? One wrong move and you can lose a kid to the streets. I've seen it happen. I didn't want Gordo to get started down the wrong path. Right? Suleeta told me I was too hard on Gordo. She warned me he'd rebel if I didn't back off."

"He became an American soldier," Truely reminded him. "Takes a lot of courage to enlist—especially these days. You got to be proud of that, Jerry."

"I pushed him," he said. "Made him feel like he had something to prove—you know. But I never meant for him to join the military. The army was his idea. Still, I should have tried to talk him out of it, made him wait a few years."

"Easy to blame yourself," Truely said. "But Gordo wouldn't want that. Gordo has a mind of his own. Makes his own decisions."

Jerry finished his drink and walked over to pour himself another one. "I feel so damn helpless."

Truely wondered if his dad had suffered this way over every heartache he and Courtney had endured, but he doubted it because, looking back, he thought they hadn't really endured much heartache — certainly nothing close to this. Maybe that was some small part of Truely's passivity now, the fact that as a boy he was not sufficiently strengthened by catastrophe or disaster of any kind. Maybe a too easy life was not always the blessing it was perceived to be. Maybe the good life could never really be appreciated without the contrast of crisis to make you grateful.

"What time you leave for Germany tomorrow?" Truely asked. "I want to see Shauna before she goes."

"I'll wake her up now if you like. You want me to?"

"No," Truely said. "I guess not. Let her sleep if she can. I'll come back in the morning."

"I'll tell her," Jerry said.

"I can stay a while longer, Jerry, you know, if you need some company, but I don't want to intrude."

"I'm okay," he said. "Just because I can't sleep doesn't mean you shouldn't."

Truely patted him on the shoulder and briefly considered hugging him, but only completed a portion of the gesture before pulling away. "Night then."

Jerry nodded. Truely put his barely touched drink down on the table and swung his legs over the terrace wall, jumped to the damp ground and started toward his car. For some reason he thought of crickets, the absence of them here, the hollowness of dark nights without their pulsating chorus.

He was in his car, ready to start the engine, when a light came on inside the house and he paused and tried to see who might be stirring. Seconds later the front door flung open and he saw Shauna bound down the stone steps, leap the lighted path and run across the grassy yard toward his car. She was wearing white cotton pajamas and her brown hair was in a ponytail on top of her head. His heart pounded at the sight of her hurrying toward him. He got out, called her name, and met her in an awkward embrace. They both wavered on the edge of the unspoken.

Truely buried his face in Shauna's neck. "God, Shauna," he said. "You didn't call me."

"I know," she whispered.

"Doug told me. I came as soon as I could."

"It's awful," she said.

"I'm so sorry, Shauna." He kissed the top of her head. "What can I do?"

"You came," she said.

It bothered Truely that she sounded surprised. "Let's talk in the car." He led her across the small space of wet grass.

Truely wanted to take her inside the house, lie down with her on the single bed in her girlhood room with the shelf of soccer trophies and the photos of her dressed for proms wearing corsages on her wrists. He would like to have held her through the night and to have watched her sleep. He wanted his to be the first face she saw when she awoke. But Shauna's parents were what Shauna referred to as *from the old country*. There was no old country actually. Her mom was a good Catholic who did not allow her daughters any sleeping together—literally or figuratively—under her Catholic roof without that permission slip from God known as the marriage license. Shauna had made that clear to him on his first visit to her family, never mind that she was not a girl anymore, but a grown woman with a very real, very adult history. He had booked them a random room in Hotel Circle then and every time since. It was not something that could be negotiated—especially tonight with Gordo air-vaced to the army hospital in Germany, his future reduced to a series of unanswered questions.

They sat in the car facing each other with the aid of a fog-shrouded moon. Truely liked the night-look of Shauna—her wrinkled pajamas that he had never seen her wear before. But he felt the tension too, the worry that flickered in her swollen eyes and her nervous hands that she busied touching first the buttons on his shirt, then those on her pajamas, at a loss for words—or for the energy it would have taken to speak them. "We leave for Germany tomorrow," she finally said.

"Jerry told me."

"I called and told them to tell Gordo that we're coming. I think if he knows we're on our way, you know, he can hold on. I don't want him to wonder."

"Gordo is a strong guy, Shauna." She nodded and fell silent. Truely reached for her hand. It was sweaty. "I'm putting my money on Gordo," he said.

"These are his pajamas." Shauna tugged at them. "Becca gave them to him for Christmas a couple of years ago. He was horrified, you know. Not a pajama man. 'I'll save them for my next trip to the hospital,' he joked. He never even put them on. I found them in his drawer and got them out to wear tonight."

"That's good," Truely said. "I like that."

"Mother has candles lit all over the house. Gordo's room. Her bedroom. She's got their bedroom so lit up back there Daddy can't sleep. It's spooky."

"Listen. What if I came with you to Germany? I could arrange it."

"No," she said. "Thanks. But it's better if it's just Daddy and me."

"You sure?"

"Yes. No offense, Truely. Okay?"

"None taken," he said. But he was not sure he meant it. He wanted to help Shauna through this. He wanted her to need him to.

Shauna leaned against Truely, her face next to his. "I hate this stupid war."

Truely put his arms around her and pulled her closer. He could feel her heartbeat, the sweatiness of her skin. He felt like a teenager again, parked late at night with a girl whom he longed for and feared.

"Pray for Gordo," Shauna whispered.

LESS THAN AN HOUR LATER Shauna went back into the house to lie in Gordo's bed and try again to sleep in the candlelight. Truely drove over to the Town and Country and got a room. He was asleep as soon as he hit the bed, but it was not the good kind of sleep. He kept waking with a sudden jolt and having to remind himself where he was. The next morning he awoke to find the day had started without him. It was after ten a.m. He almost never slept late. He was immediately irritated with himself. He forced himself up and into the shower and plied himself with black coffee to shake off his drowsiness.

On the way to Shauna's parents' house he stopped for corn tamales and beans and rice at a little homegrown restaurant he knew Shauna's family liked. He bought enough for them to freeze some for later. It was pretty hard to spend a hundred and fifty bucks on tamales and beans and rice. Next he stopped at a Circle K for a case of cold beer and a couple of gallons of diet green tea, Shauna's favorite. When he pulled up in front of the house this time there were cars parked everywhere. He was glad he had the food to carry in—two trips at least. He liked having a self-assigned chore, a good deed even. He read once that love was an action verb and he meant to try to prove it today if he could—partly to himself, but mostly to Shauna.

A man he didn't know answered the door. "Hey," Truely said. The room was full of people he had never seen before.

"How's it going?" the man said.

"Shauna around?" Truely asked stupidly, carrying sacks of hot Styrofoam-encased food.

"The kitchen." The man nodded in the direction of the kitchen, but Truely didn't need the clue. He had spent many hours in the Mackey kitchen.

When Shauna saw him she hurried over. "Truely, what's all this?"

"Nourishment," he said. "Got to keep your strength up."

"Let me help you." She took one of the sacks from his arms. "Mother," Shauna called to Suleeta. "Truely's here. He brought tamales."

Suleeta came toward him. He struggled to set all the food on the kitchen table and free his arms to hug her. "Gracias for coming." Suleeta's face was swollen. There were dark circles under her eyes. Her chin quivered when she spoke.

"Gordo was my man, Suleeta. You know that. Mi hombre."
Was? Why the hell did he say *was?*

Suleeta patted Truely's arm. "You bring too much food."

"Gordo's friends like to eat," he said. "I know that."

"Yes." She laughed a flat laugh.

"We'll put this food out," Shauna told him. "Gordo's buddies are out on the terrace, Truely. You should join them."

"Got one more load in the car," he said. "I'll be right back." He took his time going out to the car, grabbing the rest of the stuff and bringing it inside. He felt nervous. Probably just the grief of the occasion at work, he told himself. He brought in the rest of the food and lingered around the crowded kitchen watching Shauna and Suleeta put the tamales on a platter and scoop the rice and beans into bowls. The dining room table was already full. Someone had brought a couple of rotisserie chickens and a wok of tofu fried rice and a coconut cake and a huge platter of raw vegetables and hunks of ripe cheeses and crackers and a tray of sushi. And now the tamales. Already they had a deluxe buffet shaping up in honor of Gordo.

Truely thought of his father's funeral, when the kitchen table was covered with fried chicken, glazed ham, potato salad, baked beans, green beans, butter beans, Jell-O salads of every color with fruit cocktail, nuts, Cool Whip, cream cheese and who knows what else suspended in them, quivering, and cornbread and hot buttered biscuits—everything good. But that was totally different. His father had died. Gordo had lived—was living. His life was something to celebrate. Truely helped himself to a soft drink out of the cooler on the kitchen floor. He was thinking of asking Shauna for a couple of aspirin to ward off the headache he felt coming on. But before he said anything, she called to him, "True, wait a minute. I need to talk to you about something." He saw Shauna look at her mother. He saw Suleeta raise her eyebrows in something less than an approving gesture.

"Sure." Truely popped the top off his soda.

Shauna walked down the back hall toward her room and he followed her. Shauna's room was a reminder of the young girl she had once been. Truely would have liked to have known her then. In pictures she had short, unruly curls everywhere, but since Truely had known her her hair was straight and thoroughly tamed. She had bordered on being plump in high school, despite having been an athlete. Now she was thinner—what he sometimes thought of as slightly shrunken, but in a very nice way. "Sit down." She patted the bed beside her. Suleeta had not changed the room's bedspread since Shauna left home. Shauna had told him so, but he would have guessed it anyway. It was a room frozen in time, Suleeta's attempt to honor and hang on to her children, who grew up in spite of her best resistance.

"What's up?" Truely sat beside Shauna.

"Look," she said. "Pablo is here."

"Pablo?" he asked. "*The* Pablo?"

"I thought you should know."

"Did you call him?" It was a terrible question because at the heart of it was his own insecurity, *Did you call Pablo, but not me?*

"I guess I did. Maybe."

"Maybe?"

"Look, Truely, Pablo was close to Gordo. When we were together he took Gordo to ball games and fishing trips—all sorts of things. He wanted Gordo to be his best man in our wedding—you know, when we were planning the wedding. Gordo looked up to Pablo."

"The guy who broke his sister's heart? The guy who nearly bankrupted her with lies?"

"Gordo doesn't know exactly what happened. What was the point? Besides, Pablo has changed. He's not the same way he used to be. He's maturing, Truely."

"Better late than never, I guess."

"That's all in the past anyway," Shauna said. "I'm over it."

"That's a new verse to an old song, isn't it?" Why was he sounding so annoyed?

"I don't want to rehash what happened with Pablo. I just want you to know he's here. I'll introduce you. It would be strange not to."

"Sure," Truely said. "Introduce away."

"If it's any consolation, Truely, it was Daddy's idea. He wanted me to call Gordo's friends. 'What about Pablo?' he said. 'You should call him.'"

"And so you called. I get it. No problem."

"Really?"

"I'm glad he's here. He should be."

"He lives near here now. He's practically a neighbor. You live hundreds of miles away in San Francisco, True."

"I know where I live, Shauna."

"He could jump in the car and come right over—right away. You were visiting your sister in Saratoga. I hated to..."

"So it was a purely geographically based decision. I understand."

"Truely, don't."

He kissed Shauna's forehead. "Come on," he said. "Pablo is a friend of the family. Of course you should call him. Of course he would come immediately. You don't need to explain, Shauna."

"I did it for Gordo."

"And it was the right thing to do too. I'd like to meet the guy. Really."

"Mother was worried. She thought I should give you a heads-up."

"The last thing you and Suleeta need to worry about is me, God knows. I'm a big boy, Shauna."

Before they left the room she whispered, "Thanks."

"You're something." He kissed her forehead. "You know that?"

SHAUNA RETURNED to phone duty in the kitchen. Truely headed out to the terrace, partly for fresh air, partly because it seemed to be the location of choice for Gordo's single buddies, a few of whom Truely knew. They were huddled around the outdoor grill in relative silence. He saw Marcel and Marcus immediately, two brothers he and Gordo had played basketball with on a half-dozen occasions, and a couple of other guys whose faces he remembered but whose names he did not. They were mostly Gordo's age. Young. Too young to confront the reality of the occasion. The possibility of death engulfed them like a collective hangover. If Gordo could look death in the face before he was even twenty-one years old, then God knows—they could too. Shit happens. It happens to good people same as bad. They don't tell you that when they're trying to convince you to be good.

Marcel and Marcus acknowledged Truely silently with somber handshakes. "Man," Marcel finally said. "This ain't right."

Truely agreed.

"Me and Marcus got to get back to work," Marcel said. "We're working for Gordo's old man these days. Jerry put us on his construction crews on a trial basis. We just came by to see Mrs. M. Pay our respects."

Truely nodded.

"Man, look who the cat dragged in," Marcus interrupted. "How long it been since you laid eyes on him?"

"You know who that is, don't you?" Marcel asked Truely, nodding in the direction of a sullen young black kid, sitting off to himself, wearing large—Truely assumed fake—diamond earrings. He was a good-looking kid in a would-be gangster sort of way. A do-rag around his neck. Short braids poking out under his ball cap. He had a handsome angular face. It looked like if you dressed him in khakis and a polo shirt he could probably pull it off just fine. Not that he would want to.

"Don't know him," Truely said.

"That's Arnold Carter," Marcel said. "He was like Gordo's shadow, man. He made all-conference safety his sophomore year. They wrote him up in all the papers. Looked like maybe he was going to have a future."

"What happened?" Truely asked.

"He blew it."

"Blew it how?"

"I know you don't got to ask me that, man. How you think?"

Truely watched Marcus and Marcel make their exit, pausing to shake hands with the moody-looking kid. "Good to see you, Arnold," Marcus said. "Everything going be okay, man. Gordo gon beat this thing."

"Yeah. It is what it is." Marcel shrugged.

After Marcel and Marcus left, Truely found himself walking over to the terrace bench near where this young guy, Arnold, sat slumped over, staring at his shoes, lost in thought. Truely was really trying to get someplace quiet where he wouldn't have to talk. This guy looked angry and silent enough to be a safe bet. Truely's headache was getting pretty bad. He reached in his pocket and got his cell phone to check his messages. Three from Courtney. He'd call her back later.

"Man, you got a cigarette?" Arnold was looking at him.

"No." Truely was thinking this kid was too young to smoke.

"It's all right. I don't really smoke. Just something to do."

"I know what you mean." Truely put out his hand. "I'm Truely Noonan."

"Arnold Carter." The kid stood and shook Truely's hand. "You the guy that goes with Shauna?"

"Right," Truely said. "And you?"

"Me and Gordo grew up together—he's a few years ahead of me. We started out over in Sunnyland Park, you know, before his old man hit the big time and they moved over to Crystal Lakes, long time before they moved on over here. Gordo's old man got them going upwardly mobile, you might say, about the time my old man bottomed out."

"What happened?" Truely was not particularly curious.

"He went and got hisself shot. His own brother killed him."

"That's rough," Truely said.

"According to my mama it was just a matter of time before somebody bound to get a gun and shoot him."

"Pretty cold," Truely said.

"My old man, he wasn't no prize. Nobody ever tried to tell me different."

"That the way you remember him?"

"I was too scared of him to remember much. He used to beat on my mama bad—slap me across the room if I cried about it. He was mean. I remember that."

"Sorry," Truely said.

"None of us gets to pick out our old man — just the luck of the draw. Me — I drew a losing hand."

It looked like Truely was wrong about Arnold. Arnold was turning out to be a talker. Truely really needed to get something for his splitting headache.

"After my old man kicked off, Mama and my sister, they moved into public housing over in Bay Vista. Mrs. M. — Suleeta — she let me stay with Gordo most of that next school year. I been staying with them on and off pretty much ever since. Gordo is older and all, but he always got my back. We like brothers."

"I didn't know you used to live with the Mackeys." It struck Truely as odd that he had never heard this story before.

"Yeah, man. This like my second home over here. All my life I been thinking, damn, man, Gordo is one lucky dude. Everything go right for Gordo. Jerry, he's a hard-ass, but he look out for Gordo. I seen that. And his mama — she the mama everybody wish they got."

"What about your own mother?"

"She's messed up, man. I never could expect nothing from her — no help or nothing. After my old man got hisself killed she started looking to me to help her out. I was just a kid — but she didn't have nobody else to look to. I don't hold it against her. Everybody got issues, right?"

"I guess so."

"When I hear the news about Gordo getting caught in that bombing, man, I can't believe it. Nothing bad ain't supposed to happen to Gordo. He's supposed to be the lucky one." Arnold stuck both his hands deep into his low-slung pants pockets and shook his head in disbelief. "Me and Gordo, we went down to the army recruiter together. We was both going to join up."

"What happened?"

"I spent time in juvenile, so that kicked me out. Besides, I told them I was almost eighteen. I looked as grown as Gordo, but I wasn't but fifteen."

"Guess you're glad about that about now."

"Naw, man. I wish we was both over there together. I always wanted to go in the military. My uncle is a career guy. He's got a good life too."

"So, what are you doing these days?"

"Trying to finish school. I got behind, you know?"

"How's it going?"

"I ain't cut out for school. That school is worthless anyway— pretty much everybody drop out. Suleeta make Gordo finish high school. Now she want me to finish too. I promised her, even though that school ain't nothing but a hell hole. Suleeta want me to get away from here when I get done—go up to Sacramento or someplace. They got plenty of work up there. But now this mess happened to Gordo I don't want to leave. I told Suleeta when Gordo comes home if he needs somebody to help lift him out the bed, or into his wheelchair or the bathtub or what have you—well, I sure would like to have that job. I think maybe we work it out."

"Good." Truely patted Arnold's shoulder. "Sorry, man, but I got to go find some aspirin or something. Got a bad headache."

"Suleeta keep some aspirin in the cabinet over top the kitchen sink," he said. "She got her own little pharmacy in there."

"Thanks. Good to talk to you." Truely should have said good to listen to you since Arnold had done most of the talking. Truely was not lying though, his head was about to bust open. He made his way back to the kitchen. He couldn't remember the last time he'd had a headache like this.

TWO EXTRA STRENGTH EXCEDRIN later Truely was standing in the den listening to Jerry talk about what he was going to take to Germany with him that might help lift Gordo's spirits—CDs, a photo album of favorite old shots and recent ones, a batch of Suleeta's homemade Mexican wedding cookies—his favorite—a couple of *Playboy* magazines which Jerry would have to sneak in and not let Suleeta see, a Chargers press guide and jersey, hand-written notes from his buddies, a video of today with personalized messages from all the people who loved him. The list was long. Jerry had already gathered most of it. It was good, Shauna said, because it kept him busy. Her father was a goal-oriented man, she explained—he liked to have a plan and to execute it.

When Pablo walked over to them Truely understood by instinct alone who he was—a lean, muscular man, not too tall, with square features and an easy smile. "How's it going, old man?" He slapped Jerry's back affectionately. It was Jerry who introduced Truely. It was the inevitable moment when Shauna's past collided with her present. But was her past also colliding with her future? That was the unspoken question. Truely noticed Jerry's unremarkable introduction. "Pablo, meet Truely Noonan. Truely, this is Pablo Sullivan." The two men shook hands. "What's up?" they said in near unison.

"I know you're putting together some things for Gordo," Pablo said to Jerry. "I got the Chargers highlight film—if you can call that Chinese fire drill highlights—from last season. Gordo might like it. He's got a little DVD player over there, right?"

"I got him a new one." Jerry took the DVD from Pablo and put it in his jacket pocket. "I need to get both you guys on video," he said. "Wait right here. Let me get my camera." Like that, Jerry was off on the continuation of his mission.

"So." Pablo was the first to think of something to say. "Shauna tells me you got a real nice place in San Fran. Got one hell of a good view, she says." So Shauna had mentioned Truely and Pablo was letting him know that.

"I like it. It's not decorated to Shauna's standards, of course," he joked. "The location is a lot nicer than the actual building. Building needs some renovation."

"I'm thinking about buying a condo from Jerry. You seen that development he's got over near La Mesa?"

"No," Truely said.

"It's nice. A little pricey. It'd be a stretch, but I been renting too damn long. A man needs to own something. Just got to throw caution to the wind and dive in. I just never liked the idea of a mortgage hanging over my head."

"Yeah," Truely said, "a mortgage can keep a guy sober for

sure." He wished he'd phrased that differently, but there was no sign Pablo took offense.

Pablo cracked his knuckles and glanced around. "This is a damn shame, man. Gordo is one hell of a good guy."

"He is," Truely agreed.

"Thing about Gordo is—you know—he really wanted to do something with his life. This wasn't just some fool thing he did on a lark, to get out of going to college like Shauna thinks. Gordo joined the army because he really wanted to stand up and be counted, do something that mattered. He was disappointed as hell when he got that damn kitchen assignment. He had his heart set on being a soldier in the field. He saw himself doing something to make a difference—being a true hero. It sounds sort of corny but that was Gordo, man."

"Every kid that ships out to Iraq is a hero—that's the way I see it," Truely said.

"Hard for Shauna to see that right now. She wishes he'd never signed up."

"What's happened to him—it's everybody's worst nightmare, I guess."

"Gordo's got to pull through. The rest—whatever it is—we'll take it. Just as long as he lives to come home."

"Amen," Truely said. "You wish you could do something."

"I'll tell you one thing. Gordo is a fighter—like Shauna. Those two—you can't make those two say uncle."

"Okay, guys," Jerry called from across the room. "One at a time. I want to get you on camera."

"You go ahead," Truely said.

"Okay, man. Good to meet you." Pablo slapped Truely on the back and made his way across the room to where Jerry waited with his camera pressed to his face.

Truely wandered into the dining room and took a paper plate from the stack. He dished up a couple of tamales and was headed back out to the terrace to sit among the strangers and eat something. He had not eaten all day and hunger was beginning to gnaw at him. That was probably what brought on his headache in the first place—hunger. He saw Shauna in the kitchen on the phone, fielding yet another condolence call. She blew him a kiss.

He would like to be locked away with Shauna—maybe in his room at Town and Country, just the two of them—grieving privately. Saying prayers of their own—together. Lighting a few candles and watching them flicker in the darkness. Maybe they could talk. He would be a good listener and comfort her to the best of his ability. He remembered how Jesse had come through for him when his father died—and later his mother. He could not even think about their deaths without thinking of Jesse too. He could do that for Shauna, he thought. He wanted to try.

It was hard to think of someone as high-octane as Gordo dying—impossible really. But Gordo would certainly be seriously changed—damaged—and the battle to recovery would be the greatest battle of his life, maybe even dwarfing the war itself. Recovery would be slow and discouraging at the very least. Maybe Truely could help most by being there for Gordo after he got home. Maybe he could lend a hand in some part of his rehab, same as the kid out on the terrace, Arnold, wanted to. But until then he wanted to lie down with Shauna and let her sleep in his arms.

Shauna caught his eye across the room. She was still talking on the phone, waving her free hand to get his attention. She mouthed the word *Mama* and pointed down the hall, where Truely could see Suleeta standing in her bedroom doorway. He nodded that he understood. When he passed Shauna in the kitchen she reached out and squeezed his hand.

Truely walked down the hall carrying his plate of tamales. Suleeta stood with her back to him, her shoulders rounded, her hair messy, as though she had been lying down and was startled awake. He spoke her name and put his arm around her. "Can I get you to share a couple of tamales with me?"

"Oh, True." She called him that because Shauna did. "Hey, niño." She laid her head against his shoulder and took a deep breath.

"How you doing, Suleeta?" Truely had never really stood this close to Shauna's mother before. He could smell the slightly sweaty odor of grief in her hair. He could hear the heaviness in her voice when she spoke and see the fluidity of hope in her red-rimmed eyes. "You're a good mother, Suleeta," he said quietly. "You make me miss my own mother. Gordo is lucky to have you here praying for him."

"All these candles," Suleeta said. "I keep them burning for Gordo."

"A mother's prayers are the most powerful of all." Truely believed it because his own mother had been known to bring on small miracles with her insistent prayers. He had witnessed it for himself.

"I want to show you something," Suleeta said. "Come here. I want you to see this." She led Truely into the bedroom and closed the door. "Did you see today's paper?"

"Not yet." He had bought a paper that morning but it was in his car waiting to be read on his late flight back to San Francisco.

"You need to read this," she said. "A sign from God."

"Another write-up on Gordo?" He had seen the one that came out two days ago, a big picture and an article on Gordo's courage and the injuries sustained. According to the article he was driving a truck transporting food supplies from the airstrip back to the mess hall and a parked car blew up just as his truck pulled along-side it, stopping to let another car pass which—coincidently or intentionally—trapped his truck. Wham! Before anybody could think. Gordo's two feet gone and most of one leg. Fingers missing on his right hand. The soldier riding shotgun was killed.

Suleeta took his plate and motioned him to sit down in the chaise. She went to her dresser and picked up the newspaper there. "You believe in signs, yes, True?"

"Sometimes." He did not say that he worried that he missed more signs than he intercepted—that his life might be a series of missed signs, so well or poorly camouflaged that they passed him unnoticed, unheeded and unhelpful.

"Look at this." Suleeta handed him the paper. "First I see it on TV. I went to my knees, saying a Hail Mary. Then I look in the paper to see if they say anything about it and look, here it is. See?" She tapped a photo. "It's the president."

Truely studied the photo. It was a shot of President Bush jogging with a soldier who had lost both his legs in the war, one from the knee down, one from the thigh down. It showed the soldier jogging on springy metal devices—not fake legs, but metal attachments that seemed to put enough bounce in his step to allow him to simulate running. He was handsome too, the soldier—like Gordo. Strong-looking.

"Wow," Truely mumbled.

"Maybe they make these legs for Gordo? Yes?"

Truely pictured Gordo bouncing along on metal legs. He imagined him playing basketball, the added bounce enabling him to dunk the ball and hang from the rim that perfect few seconds. "I don't see why not," Truely said.

"This boy, he keeping right up with the president. See there?"

"Looks that way," Truely said.

"Jerry should take this picture to show Gordo, yes? Tell Gordo never mind, he going to walk again."

"Sure," Truely said.

"God, he gives signs," Suleeta insisted.

Truely nodded in agreement, although this was not his comfort zone, neither signs nor God. But he respected Suleeta's spiritual certainty the same way he had respected his parents' variation on the same.

"Gordo does not hate the president like Jerry do," Suleeta said. "A soldier cannot afford to hate the man he's fighting for. It mess up his mind too much. Gordo write me a letter one time and say so."

"He's probably right," Truely said. "Good to stay positive."

"The president do his best," Suleeta said quietly. "I know that." Before Truely could respond she said, "You never go to the military, no?"

"Never did." Truely felt almost apologetic admitting it. No, he had never had his feet blown off and his mind and body jolted into a near-death state. "My dad was in Vietnam," he said. "He told me some stories."

"Very hard to be a hero," Suleeta said.

"Yes," Truely agreed.

Suleeta took the newspaper article out of his hand and put it back on the dresser. Her mood had shifted. "Good you could come see about Shauna. She appreciate you for coming."

Suleeta was dark-haired like Shauna, only her hair was cut short and was still curly. Truely felt a new tenderness for this woman in her own right—a person. It seemed he had never fully noticed her before today. She was naive by conscious decision, he thought, a characteristic he was more than familiar with growing up in Mississippi. It was not something he admired really, but he accepted it with the perfect ease of the familiar. Normally life experience would not allow a woman of Suleeta's age to remain so innocent unless she willed it with great determination. Suleeta was a woman who had chosen to believe only certain things despite all the evidence to the contrary. He didn't know how she managed it. Even his own mother had been forced, on occasion, to yield to reality, although never for long.

Truely had always gotten along well with Shauna's mother. He found her accepting and kind. But before he had much chance to express that, Becca and Shelly opened the door.

"Mama, you okay back here?"

"Just talking to True." Suleeta touched his arm, a gesture he appreciated.

"Hey, Truely," Shelly said. "It's good you came. We don't want Shauna to be alone at a time like this."

"Of course not," he said.

"Mama, the priest is here. He's waiting in the kitchen."

"Okay," Suleeta said. "Very good then."

Truely picked up his plate of now cold tamales and excused himself. He had never been sure what Shauna's sisters thought of him. He always felt like they were disappointed in him, that they had hoped that after what Shauna had been through with Pablo the next guy—him—would do better by her, have the guts to make a commitment and marry Shauna. Nothing less would suit them. He sensed that they had given up on him, tolerated him now as an impotent, harmless fixture in Shauna's substandard life.

It was clear to Truely that once you had deeply disappointed one woman you found yourself disappointing others without even trying—maybe without even knowing it. It became an involuntary habit. Now he knew that if you disappointed a good woman with your inertia, then you disappointed her sisters too, and her friends, and probably more than anyone else her mother, although Suleeta had never let on. Truely was pretty sure that at this point Shauna's family looked at him and saw only a ghost of a man committed only to haunting Shauna's lonely life.

Eleven

B Y SIX O'CLOCK that evening nearly everyone had gone
home. Jerry was loading the car with his and Shauna's luggage. The plan was for Becca and her husband to drive them to
the airport on their way home. Truely lucked out with a few last
minutes alone with Shauna. They sat together on the bed in her
room. She had crashed earlier, free-falling into the savage reality of it all. He was thankful for the chance to hold her while she
cried.

Afterward Shauna had gotten herself together. She dressed
in a black easy-wear travel suit that he had seen her wear many
times. She brushed her hair up on her head and put a clip in it.
She was quiet, busy organizing her purse and the notebook she
carried with all their pertinent information, lists, phone numbers, addresses and assorted folded papers she had paper-clipped
everywhere. Truely sat on the bed, just watching her, glad to be in
her presence — glad to bear witness to her life and her strength.

"Truely, do you believe in God?"

The question had come out of nowhere. He wasn't expecting
it. "I guess," he answered without conviction.

"You guess? You're not sure?"

"I mean, I can't prove God exists. Nobody can, right? But
that there is a God makes more sense to me than that there isn't
one."

"I prayed for Gordo every day he was gone," Shauna said.

"You think God didn't listen?"

"I don't understand how God could let this happen."

"The enemies' sisters are praying too, I guess."

"Truely, I'm serious."

"I don't know what to say, Shauna. Lots of things happen that shouldn't happen. Maybe God can't stop it. Maybe we expect too much from God."

"That doesn't sound like a believer talking, Truely."

"Maybe not."

"I need you to believe in God, Truely. If God can't help Gordo get through this—then who will?"

"We will."

"No." Shauna zipped her purse closed and slung it on her shoulder. "We're not enough."

TRUELY WISHED he could replay those last minutes. Shauna was what he thought of as a backsliding Catholic, same as he was a backsliding Baptist turned occasional semi-Episcopalian or something under Courtney's tutelage. The best he could tell, God conducted his business in this world with little or no regard to who believed in him and who didn't. Right now Truely believed in Gordo. Right now Truely had faith in Gordo's will to live, in the healing power of modern medicine when mixed with equal parts love and luck.

Normally a man who watched the woman he loves drive off to take flight to the other side of the orbiting earth might call out, "I love you," or "I'll miss you, Baby. Hurry back." Something. But Truely's last sentence to Shauna was, "I may not have all the answers, Shauna, but I'm not an atheist." As she and Jerry pulled out of the driveway Truely had called out to her like an idiot. That was the last thing he said before watching Shauna and Jerry drive off to the airport, absentmindedly waving to him where he stood alone in the street.

Truely noticed that Pablo pulled out of the driveway seconds later, as though he were following them. But that was paranoid. Hadn't Shauna told him that Pablo lived in an apartment nearby? Hadn't his car been blocked in the driveway? He was probably just damn glad this day was over, happy to be going home.

Truely had planned to fly back to SFO that night, but his relentless headache was only getting worse so instead he went back to the Town and Country and took a couple more Extra Strength Excedrin Suleeta had given him, stripped down, and went to bed with hopes of sleep. His body was restless and his mind wandered, but mostly it was his racing heart that kept him worried and bolting awake. He was overcome with a sense of loss—Gordo's mostly. But also his own.

It is odd how a man senses loss. He cannot always name what it is that is gone, or soon will be gone. He cannot point to the exact moment the unnamed thing was lost forever, but he knows with relative certainty that it is no longer his, whatever it was or ever had been or might have become. He would try not to know it, of course, for as long as it took him to accept the inevitable. There was plenty of loss to go around—enough for everybody. What he had lost would become clear to him in time. He dreaded the revelation.

THE FOLLOWING MORNING Truely stopped by Suleeta's for a cup of coffee before heading to the airport. Shauna's sister Shelly was there. Her husband, Trey, had had to go home and return to work, but Suleeta wanted Shelly to stay with her longer so she wouldn't be alone in the house.

The unlikely trio sat at the kitchen island and drank strong black coffee. Truely had set out several of his business cards on the counter. "I want to make sure you know how to get in touch with me, Suleeta," Truely said. "If there is any news, call me. Anytime. Please."

"Gracias." Suleeta seemed tired.

Truely wasn't even sure she'd heard what he said. But he was determined to push on, try to make his point. It had come to him in the sleeplessness of night that this was what he should do.

"Shauna promised to post e-mails every day, Truely." Shelly was eating toast. "You shouldn't count on Mama to keep you in the loop. Don't take it personally. You know Shauna won't have time to call everybody individually. She'll have her hands full with Daddy. Believe me. Crisis management is not Daddy's strong suit."

"That is wrong to say, Shelly." Suleeta clanked her spoon on the countertop. "Your daddy is very good with trouble. But this is Gordo this time. This is different."

"Shauna will take good care of him," Truely said. "Both of them."

"Good ole Shauna." Shelly stopped midsentence but her sarcasm was clear.

"Hush," Suleeta said. "You talk right about your sister."

Shelly looked ready to explain her comment, but her cell phone rang. When she left the kitchen to take the call in privacy Truely took the opportunity to speak frankly with Suleeta. "Look, if Shauna calls you, please ask her to call me. It's important, Suleeta. I need to hear from her." Truely tapped his business card for emphasis.

"Probably Shauna will call you," Suleeta said. "Don't worry."

"I don't know. She didn't call about Gordo."

Suleeta looked genuinely surprised. "Why you think not?"

"I'm asking myself that."

"You two still friends, yes?"

"I hope so, Suleeta. The last thing I ever want to do is let her down."

"Why you think you let her down?"

"I'm not saying I did. I hope to God I didn't. That's why I need to talk to her. To make sure. You know what I'm saying?"

"If you love Shauna, then she understand the rest."

"I guess."

"Do you love her?" Suleeta asked.

"God, Suleeta. I think she's the greatest. I respect her. I admire her..."

"But do you love her?"

"Sure I do."

"Why you don't say it then?" Suleeta asked.

"She knows it."

"How she know it if you never say it?"

"Mama, don't harass Truely." Shelly returned to the kitchen, snapped her cell phone closed and held it in her hand like a grenade. "Don't try to make him say anything he doesn't mean."

"It's not that I don't mean it," Truely insisted.

"When you love somebody, Truely, you aren't afraid to say so. In fact, you can't stop saying so. That's how it works." Shelly looked at Suleeta. "Isn't that right, Mama?"

"If you don't love Shauna, then you let her go, Truely." Suleeta had never spoken to him this way before. "Shauna need a man who wants to marry and make a nice family."

Lord, Truely thought, how did they get off on this tangent? He hated to think of letting Shauna go, then finding out she'd met some other guy, married him, had lots of beautiful babies and a house in the suburbs—reducing him to just a name on her Christmas card list to whom she would send a happy family photo once a year with the words *Peace on Earth* printed on it. "I love Shauna," Truely said. "You know that, Suleeta."

Suleeta and Shelly looked at him as though he had just said the opposite of what he had actually said. "I do," he said defensively.

When Truely excused himself to wash up before heading to the airport he overheard Shelly say to Suleeta, "Shauna needs to break it off with Truely, Mama. I told you. Truely's not right for her. He's wasting her time. She needs to find somebody else."

"Shhhhhh," Suleeta said. "He hear you."

Twelve

WHEN TRUELY GOT HOME to San Francisco he found that Courtney had e-mailed him three photos of her unbandaged head. If he had just casually glanced at them he might have thought he was looking at the mug shot of a battered Asian woman. He winced at the misplaced smile on Courtney's face. In one shot she was giving the peace sign — or maybe it was V for victory.

Truely called to assure her that she was a testament to the wonders of modern medicine. Myra answered the phone. "Hey, Myra," he said. "You think my sister has gone off the deep end? You couldn't talk some sense to her?"

"She like to be beautiful," Myra said.

"Did you think Courtney needed to get her face fixed, Myra?"

"It worth it to her, I guess."

"How's she doing?"

"She sleeping now. The doctor give her some sleeping pill, said stay off her feet so she don't swell up too much."

"Well then, tell her I called. I'll call back tomorrow. How about you? How are you doing?"

"Okay. Just watching TV is all."

"Lola okay?"

"She doing good."

"All right then, you take care."

"You also."

Truely hung up and switched on the TV. He would unpack tomorrow. Right now he just wanted to go for a long run, grind his way up a few hills. Then maybe he would get some Thai take-out and plant himself in front of the TV for the night until it—or he—finally went off the air.

TRUELY MISSED THE FIRST CALL from Shauna when it came three days later. He came home to find her message on his house phone. "Hey, True. Just checking in. It's rough. Gordo is being kept unconscious. He opens his eyes sometimes but we can't tell if he really sees us. He doesn't answer when we talk to him. Daddy is having a hard time, but he'll toughen up—he has to. It's just a shock to see Gordo like this. We can barely recognize him. Pray for him, True. Please. Sorry I missed you. Take care."

He had been at the gym when the call came, his cell phone in his locker. He cursed himself. Shauna left no number where she could be reached. She didn't mention the name of their hotel. There was no way for him to call her back. That fact alone made Truely uneasy. It was unlike Shauna to overlook such crucial details. For that reason he concluded that it was not an oversight.

He had called Suleeta several times and she had had very little real news. "They taking it one day at a time," she said once. "Gordo need your prayers," she said another time.

At home Truely kept his TV going around the clock, with the misguided notion that he might glimpse Gordo on the screen, maybe bear witness to his accident after the fact—proving to him that this nightmare was no nightmare. The television was as near as Truely could come to the terror. All Truely understood was that it wasn't right that he should be able to turn this tragedy on and off with his remote control when Gordo couldn't.

AT WORK Truely had instructed his secretary to take messages if his sister called, which she had been doing almost daily. But he had instructed his secretary to track him down if a call came in from Shauna—even if he was away from the office she was not to let him miss the call. He had started going straight to the gym from work, keeping his cell phone in his pocket. He needed the distraction of a workout and to be made exhausted by something other than pure worry.

At night Truely fell asleep with the news on. He channel surfed for news of Iraq, hoping he might get a glimpse of Gordo's accident — maybe they might rerun the footage weeks later for people like him who needed to see the thing actually happen in order to really believe it. Maybe he would see Shauna and Jerry, the fear in their eyes, as they rushed across the rocky streets, dodging burned-out cars and bombed buildings. Of course, they weren't even in Iraq. They were in a hotel in Germany, but he felt connected to them only by the television and not much else. He listened for Gordo's name, shuddered when he saw the aftermath of an explosion or the rantings of an angry mob. Every young soldier who ran across the screen or stood nervously, gun in hand, poised for an interview, became Gordo. Truely couldn't sleep more than a few hours at a time without waking with a start, wondering if Gordo had died.

Thirteen

WHEN TRUELY HEARD the buzzer he ignored it at first. It was late, after ten p.m., time for the local news, which he planned to watch as he always did, already dressed for bed in his old T-shirt and sweatpants. But the buzzer was so insistent that he became irritated—then curious. "What?" he yelled into the intercom. "Who is it?"

"I need to talk to you, Truely. It's Hastings."

"Hastings?"

"Buzz me in."

He did. He was annoyed and surprised to hear the insistent voice of his brother-in-law. It swept over him like sudden fatigue. When Hastings got upstairs to his doorway Truely was waiting. "What the hell?"

"Thanks for seeing me, Truely."

"Aren't you supposed to be in Scotland?"

"I'm back early."

"I can see that."

"Can I come in? Can we talk?"

Truely gestured Hastings to come inside. He noticed Hastings' agitation and felt a small moment of triumph on Courtney's behalf. "You want a drink or something?" Truely asked.

"You got any Diet Coke?"

Truely walked over and turned down the sound on the TV, then into the kitchen space where he kept his meager stash of cold beverages. He poured Hastings a glass of Diet Coke and one for himself too. What the hell. He got a fistful of ice and dropped the cubes into the two glasses. Hastings was standing in the middle of the room, still wearing his coat. "Here," Truely said. "Take your coat off. Sit down."

Hastings peeled off his coat and sat on Truely's couch the way Truely had never seen him do—as if he were falling into it rather than sitting upright on the edge ready to dart from the room at the first opportunity. Hastings had never been known for his ability to relax and kick back. He took the Diet Coke from Truely absentmindedly. "Look, Truely, let's don't pretend here. Courtney said she told you the whole damn thing. It's one hell of a mess."

Truely wanted to ask, *So where have you stowed the little home wrecker?* But instead he simply said, "Where is she?" He imagined her waiting it out in a parked car someplace, shivering in the cold, ashamed and sorry.

"Meghan? She's at the St. Gregory. We'll go home tomorrow, face the music. She insisted we come home early. She's pretty upset."

"Lot of that going around."

"Look, Truely, if you hate my guts, then I accept that. I know you hate to see Courtney hurt. God knows, so do I."

"Why come to me, Hastings? How can I help you?"

"Like it or not, little brother, you're my family." Hastings had taken to calling him little brother in recent years—the same way Courtney did. It was a term of endearment, he knew, but he had never really liked it. "You're pretty much all the family I've got. I mean I've got those cousins on the East Coast, but they're old enough to be my parents—and their kids, well, I hardly know them, never really see them—don't really like them much anyway."

"Process of elimination then," Truely said.

"I guess." Hastings took a sip of his drink.

It occurred to Truely that Hastings might actually cry. He hoped not. That would be more than he could deal with. "Say what you need to say then. I'm listening."

"I love her, man."

"Her?"

"Meghan."

Truely felt a kick in the gut. He wanted to pounce on Hastings and slam his fist into Hastings' arrogant face. "And Courtney— your wife? My sister? What about her?"

"You know I love Courtney. I've always loved her and I still do. I've always been good to her too. But, you know, this thing with Meghan is totally different."

"Dare I ask?"

"Court is a great lady. A great companion. I mean it. She plays a good game of golf. She loves to snow ski. She can throw a party or a fund-raiser like nobody's business. She's a talented artist. She's smart as hell. She's as beautiful as ever. There is nothing wrong with Courtney. You know that. I see her the same way you do. She's like the sister I never had."

"Don't go there, man. That's bullshit."

"You're right. You're right. Look, Courtney is special and none of that has changed."

"But...?" Truely asked.

"I guess I've changed. Courtney would be a perfect partner to grow old with. But I'm not ready to grow old. I'm not ready to settle for predictable—no matter how good it looks from the outside."

"I guess Meghan helped you realize this."

"She doesn't hold a candle to Courtney in a lot of ways—we both know that. She's not well educated really. She lacks confidence sometimes. But she's sweet, Truely. She's oddly naive and a little unsophisticated—and I don't know—I find it all really charming. She's a single mom who has struggled long and hard and done a damn good job raising two great boys. I know it sounds corny, like some cliché garbage, but she makes me feel excited about life. We stop at the store to get some milk and a loaf of bread and I start thinking, man, how cool is this, the two of us buying some groceries. Every little thing—it all feels new and full of possibilities."

"And Courtney makes you feel old and bored with life? Come on, Hastings. You're not that much of a simpleton."

"Sometimes things end, Truely. You know that better than most people. There are no guarantees. Isn't that what Jesse said when you guys broke up?"

"This is not about me," Truely said. "Besides, as I recall, you and Jesus took issue with her point of view."

"Okay, maybe I was a jackass. But I think I've apologized for that. I was caught up in—look, I've tried to explain this—I thought the Holy Spirit was speaking through me. And maybe it was. But I've apologized for all that."

"Not really."

"Is that what you want, Truely? Another apology? I'm sorry I was such a self-righteous jerk. I glimpsed salvation, maybe for the first time in my life. A thing like that changes a man. I wanted you on board. Is that a crime? I was trying to reach out to you."

"Let's get back to the reason you came." Truely had long believed he wanted an apology from Hastings, a confession of the trouble Hastings had added to the trouble already in place in Truely's disintegrating marriage at the time. But now that he'd heard Hastings speak the words *I'm sorry,* it was just as inadequate as the lack of an apology had been.

"Look, we had a good run, Courtney and me," Hastings continued. "We've pretty much been there and done that, Truely. No real surprises left."

That's what you think, Truely thought. He imagined Courtney's lifted and stitched face awaiting him in Saratoga. "Look," Truely said. "I don't need to hear all this. I don't want to hear it. You've screwed over my sister and nothing you can say will make that okay with me."

"I don't know how this will all play out, Truely. But I need to know that you'll be there for Courtney. I know you like to keep your distance, you know, since the divorce and everything, but you're her brother, man—her only real family. She loves you. I don't want this to play out like some insipid triangle, two against one. If it's over for us, I'll do right by Courtney. I swear to you. You can be sure of that. The house... whatever...."

"You need to save this discussion."

"Right."

"If you've made up your mind, Hastings," Truely said, "Courtney doesn't need to be the last to know."

"If I follow my heart, I'm gone. I have to go." He took a drink of his Diet Coke like it was straight-up whiskey and he was drowning his sorrows.

"And if you follow your head and act like a mature adult—then what?"

"My head says stay. My finances say stay. My friends, when they find out, will want me to stay. Hell, even my lawyer says stay."

"You've already spoken to your lawyer?"

"He works for me, Truely. You know that. He's on the Littleton payroll."

"One thing I want to say, Hastings."

"Of course. God knows I need you to say something."

"Don't lie to Courtney. I mean it. Don't jerk her around. No false hope. No more broken promises. Tell her the God's honest truth. You hear me?"

"Done," he said.

"I ought to kick your sorry butt."

"I almost wish you would."

"When Courtney married you I always thought she could do a hell of a lot better."

Hastings actually laughed. "I know."

"And I was right."

"I guess you were."

"Shit, man."

"Can I count on you to come though for Court, Truely? She's got Myra, but she'll need you."

"Fuck you, Hastings."

"I know. You're right."

Before Hastings finished his drink and left, his mood noticeably worsened, he said, "One more thing, Truely."

"What is it?"

"Meghan needs me. Her boys do too. You know how it feels to be needed?"

"Courtney doesn't need you? That's what you're saying?" True-ly wasn't going to let himself think about the question. How much sleep had he lost asking himself how he had come to need Jesse so badly—and now Shauna—and they had seemed not to need him. Despite his clumsy efforts in that general direction he had no real experience with being needed. "Courtney doesn't need you. Is that what you're telling yourself? Is that your out?"

"Your sister never has needed me. I used to love that about her too. She was always independent—a free spirit. It was a turn-on." Hastings shook his head like a man only now realizing how fun-damentally wrong he had been about something so basic as the need to be needed.

"You're messed up, man," Truely said. "You know that, right?"

"This is not easy, Truely. I was counting on you—of every-body—to understand that."

"I think you're making a big mistake," Truely said. "You're going to regret all this."

"Maybe," Hastings said. "But it's gone too far now. I need to see this thing to the end."

"To the end, then." Truely raised his glass of Diet Coke. "So be it."

AFTER HASTINGS LEFT his apartment, Truely turned up the volume on the TV again. Rumsfeld was holding a press confer-ence, taking a defensive stance, a replay from earlier in the day, but Truely didn't want to listen to any more talking heads of any persuasion. He switched the channels until he found a news sta-tion with actual soldiers in the streets of Iraq, young heroes going about their business. He wanted to spot Gordo driving along in a U.S. Army food service truck before the detonating bomb ripped off both his feet and most of one leg. Truely wanted to warn him, to scream, *Gordo, no, man. Turn back! Turn back!*

IT DIDN'T SEEM that long ago that Courtney's happiness was the most important thing to Hastings. He had allowed himself to suffer an assortment of small humiliations at the hands of her family because he had loved her so much. And then, over time, something had happened. Something had gone wrong. Now his own happiness was as important to Hastings as Courtney's was. And he was not apologizing for that either.

Truely's daddy had never understood Courtney really. Her dramatic tendencies always embarrassed him, her high-spiritedness, her irritating independent streak, her awkward courage in the face of pain or disappointment, but still Truely always thought that in his own way his daddy had admired Courtney. In time he had tired of trying to change her into the daughter he had assumed she should be, that he assumed he deserved. He had, in the end, allowed her not to fit his idea of who she should be, who she should marry, where and how she should live her unpredictable life. Truely saw that letting go as a great act of love on his daddy's part. The present situation with Hastings would not have surprised his daddy. Considering Mrs. Seacrest, how could it? It would disturb him—but he would have quietly stepped aside and allowed it to play out without offering any remedies or advice, without saying, "I told you so."

Truely's mother, though—although she had found Courtney to be a handful at times—had eventually come to love the surprising ways that Courtney lived and the way Courtney had drawn her into unknown realms. California, gracious living, big money, fine food and wine, art, travel, prosperity and philanthropy—all were totally foreign to their mother, but intriguing. His mother had been grateful for all the vicarious thrills Courtney provided her in her late life. His mother would know just what to do to help Courtney now too. She would know the things to say. At the very least she could bake a sugar-drizzled prune cake, Courtney's favorite, with jars of baby food and a box of confectioners' sugar. Maybe his mother had lived the sort of boxed life that Courtney refused to live, but the best Truely could tell she had never seemed to resent it.

Fourteen

WHEN THE CALL from Shauna finally came Truely was almost giddy with gratitude. She had left several short messages on his home machine in recent weeks, all disturbing in detail and lack thereof. All disappointing in the impersonal nature in which they were delivered. She sounded weary, as if she could be speaking to almost anyone on her list of obligatory calls.

"It's you, Shauna. Thank God." He was practically shouting.

"Hey True."

"I've been out of my mind with worry. I'm afraid to leave my house for fear of missing another call."

"I'm sorry."

"Don't be sorry, Shauna. Just talk to me. What's going on?"

"Well . . . Daddy is drinking."

He wasn't sure he'd understood her. "Did you say drinking?"

"Sometimes he doesn't come back to the hotel until nearly morning. I don't even know where he's been. He sleeps most of the day. He doesn't even go to the hospital with me anymore. He is so angry he scares me, True."

"Damn, Shauna. I hate to hear that." Truely had never known Jerry to be anything but a take-charge kingpin sort of guy.

"I tried to get him to go back home to San Diego, let me stay here and deal with things, but he won't listen. His heart is broken. You can just see it in his face. It's not just Gordo, you know. It's all the soldiers they keep bringing in, their faces burned, their limbs gone, the fear in their eyes—or the courage. It's too much for him. He's not strong enough to stand it. Nobody is."

"But you are?" Truely asked.

"Somebody has to be, True. In my family, that's me."

"I can fly over, Shauna. I could be there tomorrow."

"No, True. I don't want you to come. I'm just tired. I haven't been sleeping. Gordo is not showing much progress. They want to schedule him to come back to the States. They're saying Walter Reed first and later maybe San Antonio. But they need to get him stabilized enough to travel. He's still in ICU. It's awful. You wouldn't recognize him, True."

"You shouldn't be going through this alone, Shauna."

"It's changed me, True. You should know that. I'm not the same. I don't know if I can ever go back to who I used to be."

"I understand that," he said. "Just know this, Shauna—whoever you are I'm with you. I'm in your corner. I just wish I could help you."

"Well, there is one thing you could do, True."

"Anything," he said. "Name it. It's done."

"It's the dogs. They're driving Doug crazy."

"The dogs?"

"They probably think I've deserted them." She paused as if she might cry. "You know?"

Truely waited for her to continue. His mind was racing.

"Do you think you could go over to Doug's and get them and maybe drive them down to San Diego? Mother said she'd keep them for me until I get back. And if she had the dogs, then maybe she would let Shelly go back home. Mother doesn't like to be alone at night. She gets scared. The dogs would be good company."

The request took Truely by surprise.

"True, are you there?"

"Yes, sure. I'm here."

"Do you think you could do that? Take the dogs to Mother. I hate to ask."

"No problem," he said. "I'll call Doug. I'll drive them down this weekend."

"Thanks, Truely. I knew I could count on you." Her voice was soft and distant. "Miss you, True."

"I miss you too," he said.

After he hung up the distance between them began to ricochet at an even higher frequency. It was one of the most unsatisfactory conversations of Truely's life. It left him agitated.

HE CALLED JAXON, to meet him at the gym. It was not because he needed somebody to talk to, but because he and Jaxon had developed a ritual where on an as-needed basis they would meet at the gym, no questions asked, and compete like madmen for an hour or two to see who could do the most reps on the weights circuit before reaching exhaustion. There was not much talking involved. It was the pursuit of exhaustion that was compelling.

On this night Jaxon was no match for Truely. For an hour and forty-five minutes Truely was a freak of nature. "Damn," Jaxon said. "What are you on?"

"Nothing," Truely said.

"Okay. Either you're in love and you've got it bad — or you've just been kicked to the curb."

"What? Now you're a psychic?"

Afterward, they went out to a hole-in-the-wall bar not far from the gym for a couple of icy beers. It was Truely's idea. He didn't really want to talk. He simply didn't want to go home.

"You okay, man?" Jaxon asked him.

"Never better."

ON FRIDAY NIGHT Truely swung by Doug's place after work to pick up Foxie and Fred. When they went into a barking frenzy he couldn't tell if they were actually glad to see him or just totally confused. Foxie ran in circles chasing her own nub of a tail. Doug was obviously relieved to see Shauna's dogs go, although he was appropriately apologetic for his blatant sense of relief. He had the dog cages from Shauna's apartment ready to go. He and Truely carried them out and loaded them in the back of Truely's car. Then they carried Foxie and Fred out and put them in their respective cages. It was like putting a couple of genies back in their bottles. The dogs always rode in their cages whether they liked it or not because otherwise they tended to leap nonstop from front seat to back barking hysterically and generally threatening to cause a major accident. "Thanks, man." Truely shook Doug's hand when the mission was accomplished.

"Have a safe trip, guys," Doug called out as Truely and the dogs drove away.

Truely's plan was to take the dogs back to his place for the night, then get up early on Saturday morning and make the trip down to San Diego, spend one night, and drive back on Sunday. Now that the trip was inevitable Truely was almost looking forward to it. He did some of his best thinking while driving long distances alone, listening to music. He could use the distraction.

Back at his own building he got both dogs on their leashes, no easy task, and took the elevator up to his loft, where—to his surprise—a couple of uninvited guests paced outside his door. "Truely," Courtney called to him. "Thank goodness you're home."

The dogs began to bark and strain against their leashes.

"This is a surprise," he said. He saw that Myra was waiting for him to unlock the door, carrying what looked like a heavy overnight bag.

"Myra and I just decided we needed to get away for the weekend," Courtney said, "so we thought we'd surprise you. Come up here and try a little city life."

"Let me get these dogs inside." He fumbled to unlock the door. Foxie was jumping all over Myra, who seemed oblivious. "You guys come on in."

"You're not mad are you?" Courtney asked. "I know we should have called."

"Actually," he said, "I can use all the help I can get. It may take all three of us to keep the lid on Foxie and Fred here."

Courtney and Myra followed him inside. He took the dogs to the bathroom and closed them in there and turned off the light. Shauna had taught him this trick when she used to bring them with her for the weekend. It settled them down almost instantly. Truely returned to Courtney and Myra, hugged them both properly and brought their bags inside. While he poured wine for everybody he got his first good look at Courtney's new face-in-progress. "Nice," he said. "You're practically healed."

"Just a little swelling still." She touched her hand to her face.

"So you're happy?" he asked.

"I feel great," she said.

"Mr. Hastings tell her she look great too," Myra spoke up.

"So Hastings liked the big reveal?"

"Well, *great* was not what he actually said," Courtney corrected. "What he said was that I look ten years younger. So, you know, I'll take that as practically *great*."

"Mr. Hastings move his things out the house this weekend," Myra explained. "We get out his way."

"Hastings is moving out?" Truely had an annoying way of asking the obvious.

"He's rented an apartment in San Jose. I'm about to be a free woman!" Courtney waved her hands in mock celebration.

"Well, look out world." Truely knew he sounded falsely happy. "Here's to being a free woman!" He raised his wineglass and they joined him.

"To be free," Myra said.

"I was the wind beneath his wings!" Courtney sang sarcastically. "And next thing you know damn if he didn't fly off." Then she laughed her fabulous laugh and Truely and Myra laughed with her. They couldn't help it.

"Courtney keep the sense of humor," Myra said.

"God bless her," Truely said.

"So we can spend a couple of nights here with you, True?" Courtney asked. "Maybe you could wine and dine Myra and me a little. Lord knows, we need it." He studied Courtney's expression the best he could without being obvious, but saw no real warning signs of high distress or anguish.

"Sorry, ladies. I'm driving down to San Diego tomorrow," he said. "Taking Shauna's dogs—whom you just met—down to her mother's house. You guys can have the place all to yourselves. Knock yourselves out."

"We'll have a pajama party, Myra," Courtney said.

"I need some dinner," Myra said. "That's what I need."

TRUELY TOOK THEM DOWNTOWN to dinner at Scala's, one of Courtney's favorite spots. It was there that she announced, "I want to go with you tomorrow, True. Okay? I'd love to meet Shauna's mother. I could help you with the dogs."

"What about Myra?" he asked.

"I stay at your place," she said. "Maybe I call Lola to come too. We make a little vacation."

"Perfect," Courtney said.

"Also we clean your place a little too."

"No need," Truely said. "The place is clean. It's fine, really. You guys just relax and have fun."

"First we clean," Myra said. "Then maybe we relax. Your apartment get away from you. You a bachelor now. A bachelor always think his house is clean. It's like bachelors—they go blind."

"If it makes you happy, Myra, you can paint the damn place," Truely teased.

They ordered more food than any three people could eat. It was a habit Truely had acquired since his divorce to always order more food than necessary so there would be some to take home and eat the next day or two. Now at least Myra would have sustenance if she wanted it. If she disapproved of the dust in his apartment he expected her to doubly disapprove of the meager contents of his refrigerator and his basically bare cabinets. He didn't actually keep a stocked kitchen these days. He didn't get that much drop-in company.

They ordered a second bottle of wine and drank just enough to keep them away from the subject at hand. Hastings had told Courtney he was moving out, that when she got back home on Monday morning he would be gone—maybe for good.

Myra was the only one who seemed unafraid to speak Hastings' name. "Mr. Hastings come back to his senses after while," she said. "I tell Courtney, Mens, they go loco sometimes. He just scared he getting too old."

Courtney didn't respond, but Truely thought he saw a pained expression move across her Botoxed eyes.

WHEN THEY GOT HOME Truely dug into his linen closet for some clean sheets for his bed. It took him a few minutes to find a matching top and bottom, which he knew in this instance might matter. His sheets had seen better days. "I remember these," Courtney said. "See?" She pointed out the monogram, TJN. "I gave you and Jess these for your wedding. Remember?" Truely cringed. How old were these damn sheets anyway? Why hadn't he ever thrown them out? After Jess left, taking with her whatever she wanted, he had just kept the rest without even paying attention to what it was.

"We need to go shopping, True-baby."

"If you're looking for a project, big sister, I ain't it."

"You're giving me an idea." She laughed. "A woman in my fragile state of transition needs the distraction of a project."

"Just don't get any ideas that concern me," Truely said. "I mean it, Court. Besides these are just for sleeping—in the dark, with the lights off. Doesn't matter what they look like. Right? We're not making a statement here."

"Of course you are," Courtney said.

"Courtney believe everything make a statement," Myra said. "Give me them sheets and let me get this bed fixed. I'm tired. I never stay up this late no more."

Courtney and Myra slept in Truely's king-sized bed on his shabby monogrammed sheets with a worn but well-loved quilt his mother had made him. He bunked on the sofa with another set of his frayed mismatched sheets and a faded old blanket. When did everything get so ragged? He hadn't really noticed before Courtney and Myra showed up unexpectedly and more or less pointed it out. It wasn't that it embarrassed him. It was that his failure to notice was annoying.

* * *

THE DOGS WERE QUIET until the sun came up. The minute day broke they seemed to sense the journey at hand. He and Shauna had made this same trip with Foxie and Fred many times before. They had their rituals now, dog biscuits as needed, favorite stops along the way for water and running around. Leisurely travel was the only option. No hurry was possible. That was one of the good things about traveling with dogs. It was almost easy to load them into their crates in the backseat of his car. Foxie was actually whining with excitement the way she used to when Shauna was around.

Myra saw them off, saying, "As soon as you two get on your way, and out of my way, I'm gon to take this kitchen apart."

Oh shit, Truely thought.

TRUELY COULDN'T REMEMBER the last time he'd made a car trip with his sister. Nearest thing he could recall was one of their rare so-called family vacations years ago, when they had set out in the overpacked station wagon with their there's-no-place-like-home parents to visit a distant cousin over in Meridian or down in Phenix City, Alabama, or best of all, their cool bachelor uncle who lived in a beach condo down in Panama City, Florida.

Courtney was a surprise. She seemed to really enjoy the dogs, rationing out their biscuits and chewy treats, talking to them, sensing when one of them needed a bathroom break. She was patient and relaxed, ready to stop a dozen times for dog reasons real and imagined. She got Truely and herself bottled vitamin waters or cranberry juices while he walked laps in the grass with the dogs. Twice she got hamburgers and fed the meat to the dogs, making them friends for life. Truely didn't tell her that Shauna would not approve.

They were several hundred miles into the trip when Truely realized that Courtney didn't seem to want to dissect her relationship with Hastings, which was what he had expected. They hadn't avoided the subject altogether. She had shared a few details with him. "Hastings is seeing a therapist," she said. "It was Meghan's idea evidently."

"I'm surprised," Truely said. "Hastings has never seemed like the therapy type."

"Well, it's not an ordinary secular counselor, True. He's seeing a Christian therapist. He's really well known nationally. He's written some books and all. He specializes in prayer counseling. They say he doesn't take that many clients anymore."

"But he took Hastings. Why doesn't that surprise me?"

"Hastings is in his *permission-seeking* phase," Courtney said.

"His what?"

"I've been reading some books. We all seek permission from some real or imagined authority when we set out to make changes in our lives."

"So these books? They keep you one step ahead of him?"

"Not really. They just help keep me sane. More or less. Like my own do-it-yourself therapy I guess."

"Does it bother you?"

"That Hastings wants change or that he's in therapy?"

"Either one."

"I guess I think if he suddenly believes therapy is the answer, then maybe we should have gone to therapy together before things got to this point. Maybe I should have suggested it."

"You always do that, Court."

"What?"

"Take responsibility for Hastings' behavior—good or bad."

"I do?"

"You do."

"Then I need to stop."

"Yes, you need to stop."

BY THE TIME THEY PULLED into Suleeta's driveway it was dark. The dogs realized where they were and began to yap and whine. Foxie chased her own tail in circles in her crate, urinating on herself. Courtney struggled to get the leashes on the dogs but they were so frenzied it was impossible. Truely had to take them out one at a time and grip their necks with a near stranglehold while Courtney snapped their leashes on. Suleeta heard the dogs' frantic barking and came outside. "There they are," she called out, inciting a near riot. They strained to get to her, jumping at her, barking as if they might bite. Truely had to yank their leashes to keep them from knocking Suleeta down.

"They glad to see me." Suleeta knelt to embrace the dogs. They sniffed her shoes and the hem of her slacks and began to tremble with recognition. Suleeta bowed her head over them and Truely saw tears in her eyes. The quivering dogs were silent then, licking Suleeta's face and hands, waiting for her tremor of grief to pass.

"Oh God," Courtney whispered, watching.

For the rest of the evening the dogs sat at Suleeta's feet. If she tried to walk across the room for a glass of water they circled her so nervously that she could barely take a step. Before bed Truely volunteered to take them out for a long walk, to help them tire enough to sleep. Suleeta had set out two dog beds in her bedroom, but at this point the dogs were too wound up to even think of sleeping. Truely was actually glad for the excuse to get out into the late-night air, and Foxie and Fred seemed more than willing to go with him. An hour's walk easily turned into two hours.

When he got back to the house he went in quietly through the kitchen and took the exhausted dogs down the hallway, back to Suleeta's bedroom, where their new beds awaited them. True-ly tried to make them lie down. Minutes later he turned off the light, a signal they understood, and closed the door behind him and they were silent.

Truely walked back to the den, where he found Suleeta and Courtney huddled on the sofa, drinking hot tea, speaking in quiet voices, almost whispers, he thought. He didn't like it. He looked closer and wasn't sure, but he thought maybe Courtney was crying. It frightened him a little. "Is everything okay in here?"

"Everything fine," Suleeta said.

"Courtney?" he asked.

She nodded as if agreeing. Now it was clear that she had been crying.

Truely took a couple of steps in her direction but Suleeta said, "Oh no, True. You go on ahead to bed now. I got Gordo's room ready for you. Clean sheets on the bed and good towels on his chair. You make yourself at home. Me and your sister, me and Courtney, we just sit up and talk little bit longer. Okay? You go ahead to bed now. You tired after your long drive."

It was like she was delivering an ultimatum. He resented being sent to bed like a child. When was the last time anyone had told him that it was his bedtime? Even his mother had not bossed him that way.

"Courtney?" he asked.

"It's okay," she said.

"You're sure?"

"We're having a good talk, True. That's all."

He left the room reluctantly. Suleeta was right about one thing, he was tired.

He walked down the hall to Gordo's bedroom and looked inside. It was just like he remembered it except that Suleeta had put an imposing photo of Gordo on the bedside table. He was wearing his army uniform. His shaggy hair was shaved short and he had what Truely would call a nervous smile. Gordo was a good-looking kid. He was open-faced and clean-cut. Truely turned the photo so it faced the wall. He didn't think he wanted to sleep with Gordo staring at him all night. He stripped down to his boxers, then remembered the pajamas Shauna had worn last time he was here. He fumbled through a couple of Gordo's drawers until he found them, folded neatly. Even though he wasn't a pajama man he stepped into the pajama bottoms and crawled into Gordo's bed, where the clean sheets awaited him. It was a small gesture, sleeping in something belonging to Gordo. That was all.

THE NEXT MORNING Truely was up before Courtney or Suleeta. It was still cool and dark outside. He decided to go for an early run while they slept. He hadn't had the best night of rest. He had tossed and turned, looking around Gordo's room in the dark, almost seeing him there, fooling with his stereo system or getting a clean shirt from his closet. The room even smelled like Gordo—part sneakers and socks, part Obsession cologne that a would-be girlfriend had given him, part stale enchiladas, any number of which had doubtless been eaten there. Truely got dressed in his running gear and turned the photo of Gordo face front again. "Morning, Gord," he mumbled.

By the time Truely got back from his run Suleeta was in the yard in her housecoat with Foxie and Fred on their leashes. He noticed the dark circles under Suleeta's puffy eyes. Her face looked drawn, as though maybe she hadn't slept all night. The dogs were sniffing around the flower beds with great agitation. They must have known on some level that they were home again. On the other hand they must have wondered where Shauna was and whether or not she was ever coming back.

"Morning, Suleeta." Truely was winded. He needed to walk a while to cool down. "You're going to have your hands full with those two."

"They keep me company," she said. "It's good."

When he went in the house he found Courtney dressed and drinking coffee in the kitchen. She had her wet hair tied up in a scarf, no makeup. It occurred to him that she looked clean and young. "Morning, Sleeping Beauty," he said. "What time did you night owls get to bed last night?"

"It was nearly morning before we shut it down, True."

"Who knew you two would have so much to talk about?"

"I know that makes you nervous, huh?" If she was making fun of him he didn't much like it.

Truely poured himself some coffee. Suleeta came in the house and took the dogs off their leashes so they could race from one end of the hall to the other. Truely could see that Shauna was right about one thing, the dogs would be good for Suleeta. It was clear they would keep her annoyingly busy and distracted and maybe pleasantly exhausted too. It wouldn't surprise him if they slept in the bed with her at night and she took to hand-feeding them from her own plate.

Truely showered and dressed and threw their overnight bags in the backseat of the car. Suleeta still had not dressed. Instead she'd made toast and sat feeding small bites to the dogs as they circled the island. Truely thought she seemed unusually distracted. He wondered if it was sadness overtaking her—or fear of being alone in the house again, just the dogs to keep her safe and distracted from her dark thoughts. He and Courtney hugged her good-bye and they were in the car and on the road while dew was still on the grass.

They wove their way through the sparse early traffic over to the San Diego Freeway. Without the dog crates and the nervous dogs in the backseat the car seemed empty. Courtney was unnaturally quiet. He noticed, but thought maybe the late hour the night before had left her wordless and tired.

At one point he did aim to make a little harmless conversation. "What did you and Suleeta talk about so long last night?" he asked. He hoped he didn't sound curious. He wanted to sound casual.

"Everything."

"Everything?"

"Everything."

"Well, no wonder it took so long then."

Courtney smiled and waved her hand dismissively. She left the music selection to Truely and curled down in her seat as if she were going to sleep. Only she didn't sleep. Truely saw that her eyes were open where her head rested against the passenger window. She was watching the world go by as he drove along.

He didn't recognize this mood. He didn't question it either.

They stopped near La Costa for a late breakfast. Courtney had been to the spa there and knew a home cooking place nearby, where the spa-goers sometimes escaped to eat themselves into a rebellious stupor. The food was good. Courtney was absentmindedly nibbling at her egg white omelet when she asked, "True, how do you feel about the truth?"

"What truth?"

"I mean do you think you're better off knowing the truth or not having to know it?"

"That depends, I guess."

"So does that mean you only want to know the truth if it's good, but not if it's bad?"

"I didn't say that."

"Okay, look. There are two ways to look at this. Either a person loves you so much they are compelled to tell you the truth, always. They honor you that way, you know. It's a show of respect and high regard, right? Or else they love you so much they would go to great lengths to spare you the truth. They want to protect you from having to know anything that might cause you any hurt or pain. That's love too, right? So, to respect you with the truth or to protect you from the truth — which is it? Which do you think is best?"

"What is this, philosophy 101?"

"Can you just answer the question?"

"I don't know, Court. I don't like to go looking for trouble — or causing it either. But do I think people are better off living a lie? Who knows? The thing about lies, you know, is that they don't last forever. Eventually they wear out. Like a set of retreads — eventually, with enough wear, they just unravel and fly all over the place."

"That's downright poetic, True," Courtney teased.

Truely thought of the lengths he had gone to to hide the truth of Mrs. Seacrest from his mother — and from Courtney too. If they had asked him about it point-blank, he thought, he probably would have looked them in the eye and lied about it. At the time he was sure he would have. Now, he didn't know. At this point in his life it seemed that lies were of a fragile nature. The ones he told, the ones told to him. Lies had expiration dates — he believed that. It was just a matter of time before they betrayed you. So maybe it would spare everybody a lot of wear and tear just to speak the truth from the beginning and deal with the backlash at the front end. Because the best he could tell, you would deal with it in the end — no matter what.

While Courtney made a run to the ladies' room, Truely got a paper cup of hot coffee for the road, a couple of newspapers, and paid their bill. They got back in the car where again Courtney half pretended to sleep, with her eyes wide open. Truely ignored her and kept the music going. He played it loud the same as he would do if he were alone and Courtney wasn't even in the car. Sometimes he sang along too, snapped his fingers, played drums on the steering wheel.

IT WAS HOURS LATER when at last they hit the outskirts of San Francisco. Courtney finally seemed ready to talk. "True," she said. "There's something I need to tell you."

"Okay," he said. "Shoot."

"You're not going to like it."

"Try me."

"Suleeta thinks you need to break it off with Shauna."

"She said that?"

"She did. That and more."

"Shauna needs a man who wants to marry her and have kids. Right? And that guy is not me. Is that it?"

"Something like that."

"I'm listening."

"It's not just that you're not right for Shauna, True."

"What else?"

"Shauna is not right for you either."

"Who says?"

"Suleeta."

"Excuse me, Court, but maybe Shauna's mother doesn't really know what's best for me."

"I think she's right, True."

"You and Suleeta think you know what I need better than I do?"

"Maybe."

"And how did the two of you come to this conclusion, if you don't mind my asking?"

"You know how you've hardly heard from Shauna since every-thing happened."

"What about it?"

"There is a reason why."

"And that reason would be...?"

"She is not alone over there, True."

"No. Jerry is there with her."

"And so is Pablo."

"Pablo?"

"He's been there all along. He flew over there with them."

"Pablo?"

"Suleeta told me. She thinks Shauna is wrong not to tell you herself."

"Pablo as in Pablo? Former fiancé, heartbreaker and all-around jerk?"

"One and the same."

"Damn."

"I'm so sorry, Truely."

"Pablo?"

"I know."

WHEN TRUELY WAS A YOUNGER MAN he might have turned to a bottle of Jack Daniel's to help him face the truth. It had seemed to work back in high school when he was trying to deal with Mrs. Seacrest. He and Mose had drunk her into oblivion on more than one occasion. But liquor didn't soothe him now like it had then. He couldn't remember the last time he had gotten drunk.

He and Courtney had returned to his loft only to find the place cleaned, his furniture slightly rearranged, his rugs laid at angles, his closets and cabinets reorganized and six large trash bags of what Myra referred to as "stuff for the Goodwill." He hadn't even bothered to look and see what she was giving away. He simply trusted her on the matter. He wrote checks to Myra and Lola for their labor of love even if he considered it to be just as annoying as it was helpful. He kissed all the women good-bye, watched them leave and rejoiced in being home. Alone.

Truely's response to losing Shauna surprised him—in its absence. He wanted to honor her with some degree of heartbreak and suffering, and so he waited for those feelings to present. Meanwhile, he went on with his life feeling oddly accepting of this inevitable turn of events.

Fifteen

WHEN ARNOLD'S PHONE CALL CAME Truely had forgotten who Arnold was. "Who?" he repeated.

"Remember man, at Suleeta's. We was talking."

"Suleeta's?"

"She give me your number. Said call you when I get here. Maybe you can come down here and get me?"

"Get you? Where are you?"

"Down here at the bus station."

"I don't understand," Truely said. "What are you doing here?"

"I'm gon stay in Shauna's place, you know, until she get back. She got me hooked up with a job at a furniture store. Delivery man."

"What does that have to do with me?"

"You the only dude I know up here, man. The only friend I got."

The word *friend*, falsely used, echoed in Truely's mind. He did not know Arnold. But he did know that he and Arnold were not friends. Either the kid was naive — or else he was playing Truely for a fool.

"You don't remember me?" Arnold asked.

"Sure," Truely said.

"Then you gon come get me?"

"Give me twenty minutes," Truely said. "Meet me out front. Silver Escalade. I don't want to have to try to park down there."

"All right then." Arnold hung up.

"Damn," Truely mumbled. "What the hell?"

*   *   *

FROM A DISTANCE Truely saw Arnold standing in front of the bus station with a couple of red suitcases on wheels that he recognized as Shauna's. Arnold looked smaller and younger than Truely remembered. He wasn't wearing a jacket and it was cold.

They shook hands and loaded the suitcases in the car. Truely felt like a crotchety old uncle as he slung the luggage inside. "Hope you got a jacket packed in here. It gets cold."

"Nice ride, man," was all Arnold said.

ONCE THEY WERE on their way Truely said, "Okay, why don't you tell me what the hell is going on."

"Suleeta said she gon call you and explain."

"Well, she didn't."

"You pissed, right?"

"Just tell me what you're doing here."

"Shauna got this unoccupied apartment, right? She paying rent on it and ain't nobody staying in it, right? So Suleeta, she think I ought to get out on my own, come up here and stay in Shauna's place. Shauna call this friend of hers and get me a job delivering office furniture. So then I'm set. Ain't nothing to keep me from coming up here."

"What about school?"

"I dropped out."

"That's stupid, man. You need to finish school. Suleeta shouldn't encourage you to quit school. What is she thinking?"

"Ima take the GED, man. No problem."

"Yeah, yeah. No problem."

"What you so mad about?"

"You're a kid. You need your education. You don't need to be up here moving furniture when you haven't even finished high school."

"Ima work it out, man."

"I bet."

"So Suleeta don't tell you nothing about me coming."

"Not a damn thing."

"You don't want to be bothered, man, you just let me out right here." Arnold reached for the door handle and tried to open the door in moving traffic, but Truely had the lock on.

"Don't be a smart-ass," Truely said. "You're just proving my point. You're not ready to be up here on your own like this."

"Sometimes you just got to go on and do things, man. Ready or not."

Doug had left a key for Arnold under the front doormat. It was a wonder a vagrant hadn't located it and made off with Shauna's valuables. Truely should have just dropped Arnold off out front and let it go at that, but curiosity or some worse urge made him want to go inside and see the apartment again. He wasn't sure why. It looked like Doug had gone in and made a half-hearted attempt to make Shauna's bed. Otherwise things were the same. Messy, as if someone had left in a hurry, which Shauna had.

"So this Shauna's place?" Arnold said.

"This is it," Truely echoed.

"It's all right." Arnold dropped his suitcase and walked over to the window to look out. "Little bit small."

"Beggars can't be choosers," Truely said.

"You calling me a beggar, man?"

"Just a saying. That's all."

"I ain't no beggar. I ain't even all that crazy about coming up here. It's Suleeta wanted me to come."

"Well, you're here now," Truely said.

Arnold walked over and opened the refrigerator. It was empty. Doug must have come in and cleaned it out for Shauna too. Truely wondered if Arnold had any spending money. That was what his daddy used to call it—spending money. The kid was probably hungry. There he was opening the kitchen cabinets probably looking for something to eat.

"Look man," Truely said. "You unpack your stuff. I'll go down the street to the store and get you some food. Not much on hand here."

When Truely came back carrying a couple of sacks of groceries Arnold had made himself at home. He was sitting on Shauna's white sofa, channel surfing. His suitcases remained where he'd left them, unopened just inside the door. Truely put the food away while Arnold paused to listen to Judge Judy scold a slump-shouldered defendant.

"Okay, man," Truely said. "I'm going to take off. You got what you need?"

"Sure," Arnold said. "Thanks for the food. You know."

"When do you start work?"

"I'm supposed to call when I get in. Scheduled to start on Monday."

"Okay then. Good luck."

As Truely left the apartment, Arnold walked over and stood in the doorway, calling after him. "You think me and you could maybe hang out sometime? I don't know. Get something to eat or something sometime?"

Truely looked back at him and shrugged. "Why not?"

On his ride home Truely resisted the urge to call Suleeta and ask her if she'd lost her mind. What the hell was she doing sending this kid up here like this? He had no business being out in the world on his own.

THE NEXT FEW DAYS Truely busied himself with work. *Not your daddy's desk.* That was his concept. Jaxon objected to the word *daddy. Not your father's office furniture,* he said. He was probably right. Funny how you downloaded a particular vocabulary in childhood—and it remained the preferred dialect of your interior life. To Truely *father* was another word for God, not for somebody's daddy. He had never had much interest in being a father. But he had always dreamed of being somebody's daddy. To this day it caught him by surprise when he realized that he had no children—no family. Besides, if you asked him, the Catholics had played havoc with the word *father*—all those perps and child-molesters parading around calling themselves fathers. Damn.

Most days after work Truely went to the gym. Sometimes he

and Jaxon continued their brainstorming there. Other days Truely worked out alone, in silence. Sweat was his antidepressant. He had learned that back when he played football in high school. The coach had worked them hard. At first they complained and hated it, some guys even threatening to quit. Then next thing they knew, they were looking forward to it, pushing themselves as far as they could go. Sweating in the cruel Mississippi sun. Some days he had come to practice upset, his trigger finger poised on anger aimed at Mrs. Seacrest. But by the time he left practice he was less angry. Sometimes all that sweating convinced him that she was just a sad person, doing her best to find a little happiness and make herself an actual life against some heavy odds—and briefly, he took a time-out from actively hating her. Sweat was as good for the brain as for the body. Even now nothing cleared his mind like doing reps until he dropped.

Another thing. He had begun to look around him at the gym and notice a couple of the women there. He supposed they had always been there, doing their squats and stretches, but he had not actually paused to notice them before. With Shauna on the other side of the world with Pablo—what the hell? He guessed he could notice anything he felt like noticing.

COURTNEY CALLED to say that she was coming into the city on Friday and wanted to spend the weekend if it was okay with Truely. "I need to get out of the house," she told him. "And I figure with Shauna gone, you know, you might not be too busy?"

What was he going to say? No, don't come? I got things to do, people to see? Not likely she would believe that. Besides, to his surprise, Truely had come to half enjoy spending time with Courtney. She wasn't as high-intensity as she had been when they were younger, when just breathing the air she breathed for any period of time, no matter how interesting, could wear him out completely.

"Wow. Looks like my dance card is empty," he said. "So come on. What exactly are we trying to prove here? That misery loves company?" He was trying to tease her, although it came across as slightly bitter.

"True. I'm not coming so we can be miserable. I'm coming so we won't be."

She was right. He loved her sometimes when she said things like this and he knew that she meant it wholeheartedly. "Good plan," he said.

"I've got an idea, True. You can say no if you want to."

"Sounds like trouble to me."

"You know how you used to love to fish? Well, what if Saturday we go someplace and do some fishing?"

"You're coming into the city so we can go fishing?" He laughed.

"Why not?"

"Since when do you like to fish?"

"I can fish, Truely. Did I grow up in Mississippi or didn't I? It's like riding a bicycle. Besides, I think we need to do some things you like to do, so that when I call to say I'm coming up for the weekend you won't start dreading to see me."

"So, it's sort of like a bribe then?"

"Sort of."

"Well, I like it. Sure. Fishing is good. We can go down to Jaxon's place. He's right on the lake down there. I'll call him."

"Great then. I'll bring the crickets and worms. You'll bait my hooks for me, right?"

"Very funny."

"And True, I've got a little news for you too. I've made a decision."

"What is it?"

"You have to wait until I see you. I'll explain everything."

"Should I go ahead and start worrying now?"

IT TOOK TRUELY one whole afternoon digging through a storage unit he kept over in South San Francisco to gather up his fishing stuff. He and Jesse had rented the space originally to keep their Christmas decorations and camping equipment and her overflow of school materials and furniture she had changed her mind about and Lord knows what all. She had gotten what she wanted out of there after they split. Since then it had become mostly wasted space where he slung stuff he wasn't sure he'd ever use again but wasn't ready to get rid of. He was struck suddenly by the fact that this shambles of a storage unit sort of told the story of his life.

He had snow skis and water skis and life vests and plastic coolers and new and old tents in a variety of sizes and conditions. He had waders and worn-out boots and cowboy hats and an assortment of sweat-dried ball and ski caps. He had unloaded shotguns from Mississippi that had never been fired in California, since he'd never been hunting a single time since his daddy died. He had two sets of golf clubs; one a bag full of banged-up, nicked, hodgepodge clubs that he still played his best golf with and felt a sentimental attachment to, and two, a new bag of shiny high-end clubs he'd paid a small fortune for but never used since they seemed too nice to use.

Truely had accumulated quite an arsenal of fishing gear over the years. He grabbed all the newfangled rods and reels and tackle he thought they'd need, then on second thought went back for a couple of old cane poles that had belonged to his daddy. He'd never known Courtney to use anything but a cane pole. Fishing gear was one area, maybe the only area, in which she had resisted enlightenment.

By Thursday afternoon he had his Escalade packed and ready to go. He liked to plan ahead. Jesse had taught him that. A good teacher always had to plan ahead. "You cannot stand in front of the room facing thirty second-graders saying to yourself, 'Okay, now what?' " she had told him.

WHEN HE CAME HOME from the gym on Friday afternoon, Truely found Arnold sitting on the stoop of his building, waiting. "Hey, man," he called out as Truely jogged up the sidewalk. "How's it going?"

It took a minute for it to register, who the guy was, his over-sized pants and sideways ball cap. He was wearing a Raiders sweatshirt.

"Arnold? What's going on?"

"I got off early today, walked over here. It ain't that far. Suleeta give me your address. Thought maybe me and you could hang out."

"How's the new job?"

"Makes you see why maybe going to school might not be so bad," he said. "Lifting that stuff all day. But it's okay. Like they say, beggars can't be choosers. Right?"

Truely smiled. It occurred to him that if he invited Arnold inside he might be starting something he wouldn't know how to stop. He didn't want to encourage Arnold to just show up when-ever he felt like it. He needed to learn to call first. But what was he going to do, go inside his place and leave the kid sitting out here like he was waiting to rob somebody?

"Come on up," Truely said. "I got to change clothes." He saw the look on Arnold's face too, the pure relief.

TRUELY WAS IN THE SHOWER when Courtney showed up and found Arnold in the loft, lounging on one of the sofas listening to Truely's iPod. She had tapped at the open door and called out, "Anybody home?" then proceeded inside to find Arnold, a total stranger, sprawled on the furniture, dressed for what she could only guess must be a drive-by shooting. She let out an involuntary shriek.

Arnold saw her then, snatched the headphones off his head, and jumped to his feet. He stood staring at her with what she would later describe to Truely as fear in his eyes. "He was as scared of me as I was of him," she would say.

"Who are you?" she demanded.

"You looking for Truely? He's in the shower."

"Who are you?" she repeated.

"Friend of Truely's. Arnold. I'm just waiting for him to get out the shower. We going to get some food or something."

"Arnold?" Courtney dropped the overnight bag she was carrying and set her purse down on a table. "From San Diego?"

"He told you about me?" He looked pleased, Courtney would say later.

"No. Suleeta told me."

"Yeah," he said. "That's me. Arnold."

"Well, hey there, Arnold." Courtney walked over with her hand out, church-style, like when you shake hands with a preacher after a sermon because you appreciate his efforts to help you along toward salvation. "I'm Courtney. Truely's big sister. I know I look a lot younger than he does...but, yes, I'm the firstborn." She smiled.

"Nice to meet you." Arnold shook her hand cautiously.

"You're cute," she said. "Suleeta didn't tell me what a nice-looking young man you were."

"She might not think so," he said. "Her son, Gordo, everybody say he's the good-looking one."

"Yes," she said. "I saw his picture. He's handsome too."

Arnold seemed at a loss for words.

"That's quite a getup you're wearing there," Courtney said.

Arnold glanced down at his clothes.

"You should take your hat off in the house," she said. "Didn't your mother ever tell you that?"

"No," he said, removing his Raiders cap.

"Are you like in a gang or something?" she asked in a deadpan voice.

"No. I'm not in no gang." He obviously didn't like the question.

"Why are you wearing all that gangster-looking stuff then? You trying to scare white people like me? Make me clutch my purse and run?"

"I'm just wearing what I'm wearing. Not trying to scare nobody."

"Oh, Arnold." She smiled and patted his arm. "We dress ourselves as a signal to others. You know that. There is always a message in what we wear."

"What the message you trying to put out?" he asked. "You got on all that black stuff, sort of tight."

"This?" She laughed. "Okay, I must be saying—yes, I'm getting older, but look how thin I am—and eat your heart out, ya'll." She flared her Southern accent. "Black makes women look slimmer, Arnold. You know that, right?"

"That ain't all you saying," Arnold insisted.

"Arnold, you're good. What else? Well...let's be honest, okay? I am saying yes, honey, I got money. I am a rich bitch. You would not believe what I dropped for this little sweater. It's Italian, you know. I am saying, whatever it is, ya'll, I can afford it."

"Yeah," Arnold said. "Now, that right there what you saying."

Courtney laughed.

"Lucky for you I ain't in no gang," he said, "cause you definitely saying come on over here and rob me. You out there on the streets begging for a crime."

Courtney seemed to take this as a compliment. She laughed. "I like you, Arnold. You're funny."

"Suleeta tell me Truely got a crazy sister."

"Suleeta said that?" Courtney feigned surprise.

"She said she like you. But she say you're a little bit crazy."

Truely stepped into the room in a towel. "Well," he said sarcastically, "looks like the gang's all here. I take it you two have met."

"She already give me a lecture," Arnold said.

"The first of many, Arnold. You can be sure of that." Truely walked over and kissed Courtney's cheek. "Hey, Court. How you doing?"

"A little outnumbered. But I'm up for the challenge. Suleeta told me Arnold was going to come up here to work. I forgot all about it."

"You knew Arnold was coming?"

"I meant to tell you," she said.

"Pretty big detail to just slip your mind like that, don't you think?"

"Sorry," she said. "Guess I was pretty distracted. Suleeta thought it would be good for Arnold to get a change of scenery, right? She wasn't sure she could convince him. But he's here now. Right, Arnold?"

"Looks like it," he said.

"A change of scenery?" Truely looked skeptical.

"Might be a little bit more to it than that," Arnold admitted.

While Truely dressed, Courtney played hostess, pouring wine for herself and a sports water for Arnold. "You guys decide what you want to eat," Truely called out to them.

"You like Thai?" Courtney asked Arnold.

"Never eat it before," Arnold said.

Courtney looked interested. "How about Indian?"

"No," he said.

"Chinese?"

"Yeah, I eat Chinese sometimes. Some egg rolls. Some spicy shrimp."

"You like it?" Courtney asked.

"It's okay."

"What do you like to eat?"

"I like a lot of stuff."

"Name some stuff."

"I like chicken. I like barbecue. I like pot roast. I like pork chops. I like meatloaf. I like hamburgers. And steaks."

Courtney laughed. "Lord. Are you sure you're not from Mississippi?"

"My grandmama come from Mississippi. Yazoo City."

"No way," Courtney said.

"Yeah. She real country."

"So that's where you learned food?"

"I don't know. They got regular food in Mississippi? I like regular food."

"How about ethnic foods? What's your stance on ethnic food?"

"I like Mexican food."

"Tacos?"

"Yeah, I like tacos."

When Truely came into the room dressed, his hair still wet, Courtney poured him a glass of wine. "Houston, we have a problem," she said.

Truely had obviously overheard their conversation. "No problem, Court. Our boy, Arnold, may have a Mississippi appetite, but
he's willing to try something new to please a lady. Isn't that right,
Arnold?"

"I guess so."

"They have a great Indian buffet down at the Embarcadero.
It's fabulous," Courtney said. "If you hate it, Arnold, we'll stop
and get you something else on the way home, okay?"

"Okay," he agreed.

"You might really like it. It's spicy. Do you like spicy?"

"I'll try it," he said without enthusiasm.

GOA HOUSE WAS CROWDED as always, but they got a table after
a short wait. As the three of them circled the buffet table Truely
noticed that Arnold had not served himself anything except rice.
"Don't recognize nothing else," Arnold said.

"Well." Truely began to point to the various dishes. "This is
chickpeas. I know that. It's good too. And this is spinach with
yogurt right here. It's good. And that is some kind of cabbage
with a curry powder on it. And that red meat is tandoori chicken.
This is lamb with some vegetables or something. Cauliflower I
think."

Arnold looked at him with an expression of betrayal.

"Just try it," he said. "It won't kill you."

Arnold tentatively took a tandoori drumstick.

"No guts, no glory," Courtney teased.

Indian music was playing and the lights were dim. They sat
down at their table and Courtney said, "I love Indian food. Try
this, Arnold." She handed him a piece of naan. "I know you'll like
this. Us Mississippi types—we like our starches."

Arnold tasted the bread, then tore a larger piece. "Pretty
good," he said.

"So, Arnold"—Courtney paused, bowed her head and asked
a silent blessing—"tell us about yourself."

"What you want to know?" He was barely nibbling at his tandoori chicken.

"I don't know. What were you doing this time last year?"

"Nothing."

"You had to be doing something, didn't you?"

"No," he said. "Wasn't doing nothing."

"He was going to high school down in San Diego," Truely said. "He quit to come up here."

"Really?" Courtney was interested.

"Truely act like quitting school about the same as shooting yourself in the head. But that school was no good. I wasn't learning nothing. I figured it would be easier to just come on up here and get my GED."

"Why up here though?" Courtney asked.

"Free place to stay—over at Shauna's. Job opportunity at the furniture company. Suleeta, she thought it do me good to get away from down there, get off on my own and see how I like it."

"So, how do you like it?"

"Not too much so far."

"What about your mother? What did she think about you leaving?"

"She don't care."

"Really?"

"Like I told Truely. My mama got some issues. Everybody got issues, right?"

"I know I do," Courtney said.

"What kind of issues you got?"

"Did Truely tell you my husband left me?"

"No." Arnold looked at Courtney with new interest. "Why he leave you?"

"Another woman," she said. "Younger. Got two little boys."

"You mad?" Arnold asked.

"I'm sort of torn between wanting to kill him and wanting to forgive him."

"You better forgive him then," Arnold advised.

Courtney laughed her deep, rich laugh. "Out of the mouth of babes." She patted Arnold's arm. "You're right, baby."

"You don't seem too miserable." Arnold looked at Truely. "She don't seem miserable, does she? Lots of women, when a man does them wrong, they act miserable."

"I have my moments," Courtney said. "Believe me."

"Must be a dumb man," Arnold said. "I don't see why he want to leave you."

"Isn't that the truth," Truely echoed.

"You two are sweet." Courtney leaned over and kissed Arnold's cheek.

"I guess I'm sort of like you, Arnold. Starting a new chapter — whether I want to or not. And, come to think about it, Truely is starting a new chapter too."

"If it's all the same to you two, you can leave me out of the true confessions here," Truely said.

"You mean because of Shauna?" Arnold asked.

"You know about that?" Courtney asked.

"I know she double-timing him with that guy Pablo."

"What? Guess that must make me the only one who didn't know." Truely forced a smile.

"Suleeta say you don't want to know. She say all you got to do is open your eyes and see the truth, but you're not ready. She tell me not to say nothing about it unless you do."

"Hmmm. I don't remember saying anything about it either." Truely tore a piece of naan from Arnold's grip. "And here you are talking about it."

"My bad," Arnold said.

"Yes, why don't we all just pretend that it never happened or that we don't know it ever happened or that Truely is the only person in the world with no issues," Courtney said. "Would that be better, True?"

"Suits me," he said.

WHILE TRUELY PAID THE BILL, Courtney and Arnold waited outside on the sidewalk in the cool air. "So you hated it didn't you." Courtney said. "The food?"

"Some of it taste all right," Arnold said. "I just don't like the looks of it."

"You're not eating the looks of it," Courtney said.

"It just don't appeal to me," Arnold said. "Everything mixed together."

"Fair enough." Courtney looped her arm though his. "We'll stop and get you a hamburger on the way home. A growing boy needs food."

THEY DROVE ACROSS TOWN to an In-N-Out to get Arnold a Double-Double — his favorite. Afterward, when Truely turned the car toward Shauna's place in Nob Hill to take Arnold home, he said, "No need to drive over to Shauna's, man. Why don't I just stay over there with ya'll tonight? That way you ain't got to go out your way and take me back."

"I don't mind." Truely was missing the point, his specialty.

"You got all them sofas," Arnold said. "I just sack out there with ya'll."

"We're not really set up for company," Truely explained.

"I won't be like company. I'll just sleep anywhere."

"We've got to be up real early in the morning to head down to the lake."

"We're going fishing," Courtney explained. "Truely loves to fish."

"I like to fish," Arnold said.

"Really?" Courtney seemed amused.

"Maybe I just stay with ya'll tonight and go fishing with you tomorrow."

"Wait a minute here." Truely laughed.

"Come on, True." Courtney nudged him. "Let him stay over. It'll be fun."

"Fun?"

"We'll have a pajama party."

"The hell we will."

"Let him stay. He can go fishing with us tomorrow. What will it hurt?"

"Yeah, man," Arnold echoed.

"The more the merrier, True. Right?"

"What is this? Two against one?" Truely turned the car back toward his apartment building. "Arnold, Courtney's got the guest bed. So that means you got to sleep on one of the small sofas with your feet hanging off."

"Okay by me."

THAT NIGHT, Courtney went to bed in her crisp white monogrammed pajamas, Arnold in a pair of borrowed athletic shorts and Truely in his standard sweats and T-shirt. Courtney had taken off her makeup, and barefaced she looked heartbreakingly vulnerable to Truely. She had gotten a glass of water at the kitchen sink and fumbled through an assortment of prescription bottles which she lined up on the counter. That unnerved him too. "What is all that?" he'd asked her.

"Sleeping pills," she said. "Now that I'm living alone, you know, I told you I get nervous out in the woods alone like that. Even when Myra stays — we both get nervous. We hear stuff. I don't know how to fall asleep anymore. These pills are my best shot at it."

"What about all that other stuff?" Truely asked.

"Let's see. This one prevents swelling. This little pill here is for pain. And this is hormone replacement. This one is a diuretic. This one is a beta blocker..."

"Damn, Court," Truely said.

"You not careful, you get hooked on that stuff," Arnold said. "I mean it."

"I appreciate you two being concerned," Courtney said. "It warms a girl's heart." She walked over and kissed them both good night. "It's not every night I have such interested observers of my bedtime ritual."

Before bed Truely turned the TV on and did his habitual channel surfing in search of Gordo. Of course he didn't explain. He didn't need to. The others seemed to understand that they needed to lie in the darkness with the TV flashing war news, the spoken words blurring into a somber hum. They needed to remember Gordo and pay their private tribute to him before allowing themselves to drift off to sleep.

Just minutes after she lay down in bed Courtney's medication must have kicked in, because despite her claims of insomnia, she was quickly asleep. Arnold was next to fade. Truely remained awake long into the night. Long after he turned the TV off he lay staring into the darkness, listening to the comforting sounds of city traffic outside, the serenade of sirens, the occasional shouts of obscenities and wails of drunken laughter. His mind was wandering. He looked across the room where Arnold was sleeping on his back with his arm slung over his face. He was a funny kid. He was annoying for sure. But there was something about him.

It wasn't that he was like guys Truely had known back in Hinds County. None of them had dreamed any dreams to amount to anything—including himself. They hadn't known they were allowed to. Some found out too late. Others never found out. Well, except for Mose. Mose had stood apart from the others all along, not just because of his God-given talent, but because he refused to yield to the reality that slapped him in the face every morning when he woke up poor and black in rural Mississippi.

But Arnold was not Mose. Not a country boy. Not a Southerner really. He was a hardcore urban guy who wanted a life he didn't have, never had had, couldn't really even define, and had no idea how to get. He wasn't ashamed to want more, to want better. His transparency was hard to witness. It was embarrassing sometimes. But maybe that was the endearing thing too. Here he was claiming he liked to fish, practically insisting on going with them to the lake in the morning—when Truely doubted the kid had ever been near a lake before, never mind ever baited a hook or gutted a fish.

TRUELY'S BUDDY JAXON owned a good stretch of land just off 280 which backed up to one beautiful lake. You had to park on a bluff and walk down a steep path to get to the lake. But it was worth the trek. It was Courtney's job to carry the sandwiches and snacks they'd bought. Cheese curls, fried pig skins and salted peanuts, just for old time's sake. "There's fish food"—Truely'd held up the boxed worms—"and then there's fishing food"—he waved a bag of pig skins. Courtney laughed. Arnold was not amused.

Truely and Arnold carried the fishing rods, the tackle box, a blanket, a couple of folding chairs, a cooler of ice, and the cane poles and worms Courtney insisted on bringing—but so far had refused to touch. "We don't really need these," Truely said. "I can show you how to use these rods, Court. Once you get the hang of it it's a hell of a lot easier. No worms involved."

"I hate those rods and reels, True," she'd said. "I like to fish the way we fished as kids, with cane poles we cut ourselves out of Daddy's bamboo thicket and worms we dug out of his worm bed."

"You're just an old-fashioned girl at heart, aren't you, Court?" Truely teased.

"Some things can't be improved upon, True."

"I'm surprised you don't object to killing these worms. They never hurt anybody. You could just as easily use these pretty little lifeless hand-tied lures. Look, I got some great ones. Works of art, right here. See? Feathers and everything."

"No," she said. "I just want to do it the old way."

"I get it," Truely teased. "You're thinking you're less likely to catch anything the old way—and you'd just as soon not catch anything. Am I right?"

She laughed. "You know that fishing was the original form of transcendental meditation, don't you, True? If you trace it all the way back to its origins, the art of meditation goes directly back to cane pole fishing. It's a little-known fact."

"No doubt," he said.

ARNOLD WAS RELATIVELY QUIET on the trek down to the water. He was loaded like a pack mule and traveled cautiously down the path. At one point he paused and looked around. "They got snakes out here?" he asked.

"Sure," Truely said. "Snakes live in the woods. This is the woods."

"What kind of snakes?"

"I don't know. Snake snakes. Not like back home though, where you can hardly make a move without stepping on a snake."

"Poisonous snakes?"

"I guess so. Don't hear much about them though. Back home everybody has a personal family catalog of venomous snake stories. But people in California don't seem to be that big on snake stories."

"Or maybe we just don't know the right people," Courtney spoke up.

"You ever been snakebit?" Arnold asked.

Truely laughed. "Hell yes," he said. "But not in a literal sense."

"So you saying no?"

"Yes, I'm saying no."

"You ever been down to Mississippi, Arnold?" Courtney was gripping a small tree branch as she navigated down the steep hillside. "Did you ever go down to Yazoo City to see your grandmother's family or anything?"

"No," he said. "All we ever did was talk about it. Sometimes my mama get mad at me and threaten to send me down there though. She'd say, 'You not careful, boy, I'll send you back down to Mississippi where they get that smart talk out your system in a hurry with a leather strap.'"

"Lo," Courtney said. "The lore continues…"

"My grandmama believed you got to beat the devil out of kids. She says the trouble with my mama is she didn't beat her enough when she was coming up."

"Or maybe she beat her too much," Courtney said.

"My grandmama think the kids in California are all messed up because their parents ain't tear up their behinds enough."

"You're killing me here, Arnold," Courtney said. "Mississippi child rearing is a thing of beauty, isn't it? Goes hand in hand with all those lynchings."

"My grandmama got some stories about that too."

"No wonder you've never been to Mississippi," Truely said.

"I don't really like the country that much."

"The country?"

"You know. Those country people down there."

"Like me and Courtney?"

"Not ya'll," he said. "Ya'll got some teeth in your head."

Truely laughed. "Damn, Arnold."

"You seen them people they show on TV. They backward and shit."

"Careful, man, you're talking about our homeland now."

"But you left from down there, right?"

"I guess we did," Truely said.

"Must be some reason why then."

"Must be," Truely said.

ARNOLD CAUGHT THE FIRST FISH of his life. It was a country thing to do, but he liked it anyway. "Got something," he yelled when he felt the tug on his line. "Got something. I got something!" He was bellowing.

"Reel it in, man," Truely said. "Not too fast now. Just steady. Steady."

They were fishing catch-and-release. The fish was too small to keep anyway. Truely showed him how to disengage the hook, a somewhat gory procedure with the startled fish gasping and flapping. Arnold had a moment of panic. "Damn thing going to die before I get this hook loose," he said.

"Yank it a little," Truely said. "You try to be gentle like that and he'll die of your good intentions."

"Right." Arnold yanked then. The hook was out.

"Now just throw him back in," Truely instructed.

Arnold stepped to the water's edge and released the fish like it was one of God's most fragile and sensitive creatures. The fish made a small splash and serpentined away.

"Good job," Truely said. "Now that fish will have a story to tell."

"Me and him both," Arnold said.

ARNOLD TOOK TO FISHING. Before the morning was over he'd caught twelve fish, unhooked them and set them free. He was into it. Truely had taken the occasional opportunity to point something out—proper wrist action when casting your line, ways to zigzag the rod to get a good hold on the fish as you reeled in your catch, spots in the lake where fish were likely to congregate unsuspecting, how to read the surface water. It was a satisfying morning.

Meanwhile Courtney had thrown a blanket underneath some trees so she would be out of the sun, which even after all these years still caused her to freckle and burn. First she had gotten Truely to bait her hooks and then she had propped up her cane poles in the soft bank of the lake where she could keep an eye on the corks, but not necessarily obsess over it. If she got a nibble that morning, she never knew it. Next she set up a little home base on the blanket that resembled a rustic tea party of sorts. She laid out their sandwiches and set out their bottled waters and opened the pig skins and cheese curls. To Courtney presentation counted, even in the woods. Only then, wearing her straw hat and sunglasses, did she lie back on the blanket and read her most recent self-help book, *Healing Your Life Through Prayer.*

When they finally paused to eat lunch Truely and Arnold sprawled on the blanket and in relative silence wolfed down their sandwiches and swigged their water and absentmindedly munched bags of fishing food. Fishing is no good at high noon. Even the fish are inclined toward an afternoon nap. "You guys want to pack up and head back—beat the traffic?" Truely asked. "Or we could just take it easy out here for a while, maybe get in another round in the late afternoon."

"Let's stay, man," Arnold spoke up.

"Suits me," Courtney said. "I'm just getting to the good part." She lifted her book to show them.

So the three of them lazed around on the blanket, with bellies full and minds wandering. Truely even managed to drift off for a while, something he had not done the night before.

At one point, after studying the title of Courtney's book, Arnold nudged her. "You religious or something?" he asked.

"I'm a Christian if that's what you're asking."

"Yeah, everybody say that. My grandmother say she a Christian. She go to church every time something go wrong—which is pretty regular. My mother—all the mess she stay in—and she still claim she a Christian. Now you got to go some to believe that, right? Even my old man—if ain't nobody shot him—I believe he try to say he a Christian too."

"Well maybe they are," Courtney said.

Arnold shook his head.

"What?" Courtney asked.

"Too easy."

"Does it need to be difficult?"

"Just me saying I believe in outer space don't make me a astronaut."

"What?"

"Just saying it don't make it so."

"What about you?" Courtney asked.

"I don't say it."

"So you're not saved?"

"I been to church. I walked the aisle that time with my grandmother."

"Really? What happened?"

"Nothing. I was just a kid."

"So you didn't give your life to Christ?"

"I don't think he want my life."

"So you don't think you were saved?"

"Don't seem like it to me."

Truely, who had overheard them while pretending to sleep, reared his head. "Think you two can save this theological discourse for later? I'm trying to count sheep here."

Arnold seemed embarrassed. He went silent.

"Never mind him, Arnold," Courtney instructed. "He hates to discuss religion."

"You got that right," Truely said.

"So, I guess he's just destined to burn in hell then," she said.

Truely picked up a sack of pig skins and threw it at her. She laughed and turned her head. Truely shook his bottle of sparkling water and sprayed her with it.

"Truely, don't!" she screamed. But it was too late. She was soaked. "I was teasing," she shouted. "Can't you take a joke?" She turned to Arnold. "The man has no sense of humor."

Watching without expression, Arnold rolled over as if planning to snooze himself. "Ya'll juvenile," he declared.

BY THE TIME they finally left the lake that day the sun was setting. Arnold and Truely had gone back at it for a second round. This time Arnold separated himself from Truely, staked out his own area of the lake, and quietly went about the business of fishing. When he caught something he always shouted to let them know. Otherwise it was a quiet afternoon.

Truely loved being outside this way, casting and reeling, catching and releasing, thinking and not thinking. He was relaxed for the first time in a long while. Even that work-related checklist that tended to crop up in his head whenever given the chance had vanished on this day.

Courtney finished her book and took a nap on the bank. When she awoke she began packing up the leftover food and gathering up the items they had brought. It was a signal to Truely and Arnold that their time was up. The three of them made the slow careful climb up the hillside, hauling all their belongings, which seemed twice as heavy as they had coming down the path that morning. They loaded the car and drove back to the city. Traffic wasn't too bad. Truely put the radio on. They drove home in near total silence — the good kind.

That night they all bunked at Truely's again. While Truely and Arnold unloaded the car, Courtney walked a couple of blocks toward Market Street to a Thai restaurant she loved and got them some takeout. She also picked up a Subway sandwich, just in case Arnold was not in an adventuresome mood cuisine-wise. That night they sat around and ate and watched TV and Courtney did a load of Truely's laundry even though he asked her — twice — not to. At one point Arnold's cell phone rang. It was the first time he had ever gotten a call in their presence. He fished in his baggy pants and retrieved the phone, then stepped out on the terrace and closed the doors to take the call.

"Who you guess that is?" Courtney asked Truely. She was folding his T-shirts with irritating precision.

"Don't know."

"You think it's his mother?"

"I doubt it."

"He says his mother has issues. What's he talking about?"

"Don't know."

"Does he have a girlfriend back home?"

"Don't know."

"What? Is there an echo in here?" Courtney asked.

ON SUNDAY MORNING Courtney tried to talk Truely and Arnold into going to church someplace in the city. There were no takers. Instead they lounged around most of the afternoon, snacking and watching the Raiders suffer another loss. In protest, Courtney sat out on the terrace and drank coffee and studied her Bible. In the late afternoon, for an early supper, she heated up the leftover Thai food. It brought on such protest from Arnold that she put it away and walked to the market for groceries. When she got back she made turkey sandwiches on focaccia with avocado, red onion and fresh spinach.

"What's this?" Arnold asked, lifting the bread to investigate.

"Don't ask questions." She slapped his hand good-naturedly. "Just eat it. It's good for you."

MONDAY MORNING they were all up early. The plan was for Truely to drop Arnold off at the furniture store on his way over to San Jose for a morning meeting. Since he didn't bring a change of clothes Arnold had had to wear some jeans and a slightly too big sweater of Truely's to work. He hardly looked like himself without his oversized clothes, which he wore like camouflage. To

NANCI KINCAID

compensate he tied a bandana on his head, which they had not seen him do before.

Courtney took it upon herself to pack Arnold a lunch. Peanut butter and jelly sandwiches and cookies. Like he was a little kid. Truely thought Arnold might balk—but no, he just opened the bag to make sure what it was and said thank you.

"Don't worry." Courtney smiled. "I wouldn't try to slip anything exotic in on you."

Courtney was planning to take off for home later after they left. She said she wanted to finish her second cup of coffee and wait out the morning traffic first. It was only after Truely had dropped Arnold off and was nearly halfway to San Jose that he realized Courtney had never told him her news. "I've made a decision," she'd said. He had forgotten all about it until now. "Wait until I see you," she'd said.

Damn. How could he forget to ask her about it?

~208~

Sixteen

TRUELY AND JAXON spent the afternoon in San Jose meeting
with manufacturing company representatives and furniture
designers. The eBay offices in San Jose had put in a substantial
order but wanted some modifications. The possibilities were
exciting. At the end of the day Jaxon's wife, Melissa, had called
to invite Truely for dinner. He accepted. It was always casual and
relaxing at Jaxon's place. His kids and their friends coming and
going. Dogs barking. Melissa working her kitchen magic. He went
happily.

When he arrived he saw that Melissa had invited a single friend
of hers to join them. Lanie was her name. She directed a nonprofit
medical endowment in the city. She was nice. She was attractive.
There was nothing wrong with her. And yet when Truely saw her
and understood Melissa's good—but misguided—intentions
the evening took on the proportions of climbing Mount Everest.
He felt instantly exhausted. He became subdued and managed
the basic courtesies just one level above rudeness. The others
immediately sensed his discomfort and a collective tension set in
that spoiled the evening. Immediately after an awkward, stained
dinner Truely made an excuse to leave early. He kissed Melissa,
shook Jaxon's hand and before he could say the required *nice to
meet you* to Lanie, she stood up and said, "I'll walk you out." He
wished she wouldn't, but he obliged her with a nod.

Immediately she began to apologize. "I'm so sorry you got
ambushed this way. Melissa thought we might like to meet each

other. You know how the happily married always want to heal us lonely single types out here." She laughed. "Melissa meant well."

"Don't apologize," Truely said. "I'm lousy at surprises. That's all."

"Melissa had told me so many great things about you. She and Jaxon both. I got caught up in *what if*, you know. But I have been in your position here tonight—and I know it's awful. I'm really sorry."

"Listen," he said. "I can see you're a great person. A guy would be lucky to have dinner with you. I don't mean to be an ass here. It's just that I don't have the social graces required these days."

"I understand," she said. "No hard feelings?"

"No hard feelings." He smiled. "If it's any consolation, I'll probably start regretting the missed opportunity before I even get home tonight."

"Good," she said. "I hope so."

He wasn't ten miles down the road before Jaxon called his cell. "Look man, I'm sorry. I didn't know Melissa was plotting. She feels terrible about it too. I just want you to know it won't happen again. That's a promise."

"Good," Truely said. "You guys put too many of Melissa's friends through a night like this, subjecting them to an ass like me, and you won't have any friends left."

Jaxon tried to laugh. Truely tried too. And they hung up.

As if Truely were not humiliated and miserable enough, when he got home, as he pulled his car into the underground parking lot of his building, he saw Arnold sitting on the sidewalk there, his girlie red borrowed suitcases by his side. He was clutching a large black trash bag in one hand. If he hadn't looked closely Truely might have mistaken him for one of the street people that frequented the neighborhood. Truely parked his car and made his way back up to street level. He was definitely not in the mood for this.

"What are you doing out here?" Truely did not disguise his irritation.

"I was scared maybe you went out of town or something" Arnold said.

"Answer the question."

"It's nerve-wracking out here, man. I was about to get scared."

"It's because you have no business sitting out on the street like this, not this time of night. What do you think you're doing?"

"I decided to come stay at your place."

"That's not a decision you make without asking me, Arnold. You don't just show up like this. What's wrong with Shauna's place?"

"I don't like it over there."

"What's not to like?"

"I don't know anybody over there. There's nobody to talk to."

"You know Doug, don't you?"

"His girlfriend always over there."

"So you just decide to move in here? Just like that?"

"I won't be no trouble."

"Arnold, I'm not set up for a roommate. I didn't even have a roommate in college. I like living alone."

"Maybe I can do some work around the place. Clean up, you know. Earn my keep."

"It's just not a good idea," Truely said.

"On a trial basis, man?" Arnold said. "If we try it awhile and it don't work out, then I move out."

"No, Arnold. I'm sorry."

"I'll won't bother you none. I'll keep quiet. I'll be neat and whatnot. Won't mess nothing up. You might get to like having me around."

"Yeah, and I might get to like a stick in the eye, but I doubt it."

"I ain't going back over there to Shauna's."

"Wasn't that the whole point of all this geographical up-heaval — for you to try being independent?"

"I ain't going back over there."

"Somebody needs to jerk a knot in you. You know that?"

"You?"

"It's crossed my mind."

"If it's because you might want to bring a lady over here and I'll be in the way—that's no problem. You bring a lady over here and I'll go down in the garage and sleep in the car."

"Arnold, where do you come up with this shit?"

"Look like you could use a little company yourself, man. Those ladies call you. I heard some those messages they leave. But I don't never hear you call them back."

"You ever heard of a hermit, Arnold? That's me. I'm a hermit. I like being a hermit, okay?"

"Okay then. I be a hermit with you. Me and you both be hermits."

Truely couldn't decide whether he wanted to laugh or to shake Arnold until his head rattled. But it had been a long day and he was more than dog tired. "Get your damn stuff," Truely said.

Arnold jumped to his feet and grabbed his trash bag and the handles of his suitcases and started wheeling before Truely could change his mind. "This work out," Arnold said. "Don't worry. You'll see."

"One wrong move and you're gone, you hear me?"

"I bet, after a while, you start to like having me around."

"This is only temporary. You understand?"

"Sure."

"As soon as we get you straightened out, you go back."

"What you mean straightened out?"

"Another thing. You're going to starve over here. You've seen my kitchen. What you think you're going to eat?"

"I don't know. We eat some more that damn Thai food, I guess."

WHILE ARNOLD SITUATED his stuff in a far corner of the loft, unpacking, piling his things on the floor, Truely went to take a hot shower. With any luck he might drown. He turned the water up as hot as it would go and stayed in it as long as he could stand it. The scalding felt almost good. It was like some fiery baptism by hot shower—he wanted to be renewed when he stepped out and dried off. He wanted to be new and improved—his mood at least. His skin was red as a lobster, almost blistered—but otherwise he was the same old jerk.

Truely began his nightly routine, sweats and T-shirt, channel surfing through the stations in search of news of the war. He was silent. Meanwhile across the way Arnold was practically humming as he organized his belongings, lining up everything along the wall, neatly. Even his toiletries he began to line up, toothpaste, aftershave, razor…

"You can put your stuff in that other bathroom," Truely said. "For now."

Arnold grabbed up his toiletries and carried them to the bathroom.

"There are some drawers in that cabinet under the window. Put your clothes in there. We don't need your underwear and sweatshirts and stuff laying all over the floor like that."

"All right then."

By the time Truely was ready to switch off the TV, let go of his war vigil, Arnold had put his clothes in the empty drawers, made himself a bed on the sofa, stripped down and gottcn in it. For a while the two of them lay in the darkness in a deafening silence. Finally Truely broke the spell and called out to him, "Arnold, I need this like I need a hole in the head. You know that, right?"

"Yeah," he said. "I know it."

Seventeen

COURTNEY TOOK THE NEWS that Arnold had become a squatter in Truely's loft in characteristic good spirits. "That's great, True. You can keep each other company. You spend too much time alone. It's not good for you."

"I like my time alone, Court," he countered. "You know that."

"Just because you like it doesn't mean it's good for you."

"Oh, man," Truely moaned.

COURTNEY CAME INTO THE CITY early on Thursday afternoon and waited with Truely for Arnold to get home from work. He had barely walked in the door and started his instinctive and determined search of the mostly empty refrigerator before she called out, "Okay, buddy-boy, look what I brought."

"Buddy-boy?" Arnold raised a leery eyebrow. Truely laughed at Arnold's wary expression.

"Okay then," she teased. "Dude. Check it out, dude."

Arnold rolled his eyes and looked at the stack of books she had set out on the kitchen counter. *The GED for Dummies, Basic History and Government of the United States, Math for Dummies, Passing the Test, English Grammar for Dummies,* and who knew what else.

"Looks like you got a bunch of books for a dummy," he said sarcastically. "I guess you think that's me."

"No," she said. "Books for a future high school grad. I'm going to tutor you. We'll start tonight, okay? I checked with the DOE and got a schedule of when they offer the GED test. Look. You might even graduate early. Who knows?"

Arnold looked where Truely was sitting working on his laptop by the open terrace door. "Man, I got to do this?"

"You can try telling her no," Truely said. "I've never had much luck with that approach myself."

"Oh, don't be a big baby," Courtney said. "This is going to be fun, Arnold. You're not scared of books are you? You know what they say—if you think education is a lot of trouble, try ignorance."

Truely winced. She was misquoting one of Jesse's favorite sayings. But the spirit of the message was intact—which wasn't always true when Courtney adopted a mantra.

"Look," Courtney said. "I sent off for some practice tests. Samples, you know. We can go over those until you get the hang of actual test-taking."

"I'm not too good at tests," he said.

"That's about to change," she said. "It's a learned talent, Arnold—test-taking. It comes from practice. First, we just demystify it, see?"

Arnold looked like a man caught in an ambush.

"Oh, Arnold honey," she said. "Don't look so gloomy. Fear no classroom. A brain is a terrible thing to waste. Open your oyster and discover your pearl. Smart is the new sexy."

"What she talking about?" He looked at Truely, desperate for rescue.

Truely smiled and shrugged his shoulders.

THAT NIGHT while Truely went to the gym, then to pick up takeout pizza to bring home, Courtney held Arnold captive at the kitchen bar, books spread out, papers in neat stacks. When he returned Truely found the two of them exactly as he had left them, Arnold slumped over a book with sharpened pencil in hand, Courtney beside him whispering quietly, urging him on.

They paused long enough to eat—Arnold was uncharacteristically quiet—then went back at it for a couple more hours. Truely felt trapped in his own home. He wanted to turn on the TV and watch a Thursday-night college football game, but he didn't dare.

It would disturb the prayer meeting going on in the kitchen. He didn't want to be held responsible for sabotaging Arnold's best shot at a high school diploma. Arnold sat with his back to Truely so Truely had no way of reading his face, measuring the degree of suffering going on. Truely picked up a book and pretended to read it. Minutes later he put the book down and reread the *Chronicle* sports page for the second time that day.

Just when it seemed Courtney had finally put an end to the academic misery and officially declared their study session over for the night, she surprised them with one more well-meaning torment. "Arnold," she said. "Instead of listening to your iPod all night, I was thinking, you know, maybe you could listen to these." She fished through her big leather bag and held up a fist-ful of CDs and a CD player. "Audiobooks," she said. "I got some of the classics. See? *The Scarlet Letter. The Autobiography of Malcolm X. The Red Badge of Courage. Beloved. Confessions of Nat Turner. The Color Purple. Huckleberry Finn. Their Eyes Were Watching God.* Look at these."

It was like she was suddenly speaking a foreign language, showing them something so strange and otherworldly that Truely froze in place, incredulous, just like Arnold. Truely knew Jaxon's wife, Melissa, liked to listen to books on tape while she carpooled their kids all over the place. He had seen the cassettes strewn all over her Suburban. Jaxon called it the lazy woman's way of reading a book. But damn. There was nothing about it that appealed to Truely, listening to somebody gab in your ear, droning on and on and on. He was ninety-nine percent sure Arnold felt the same.

In a sudden show of brotherhood, Truely said, "Damn, Court. How about he just rents the movie?"

"The movie is never as good as the book," she insisted. "I mean as long as you've got your ears plugged up with something anyway, you could just try listening to some literature, couldn't you?" She looked at Arnold in that certain hopeful way of hers and Truely knew there was no chance Arnold could refuse her. "It won't kill you," she said. "I promise."

Arnold looked doubtful.

"Here." She handed him *The Autobiography of Malcolm X.* "This is good. I've read it. I couldn't put it down. I mean it. It's a must-read."

Arnold took it as if she were handing him a grenade.

"Would it help if I told you it was full of sex and violence?" she asked.

Arnold looked like he was about to break into a sweat. Truely felt for the kid. Unlike Truely, he wasn't really used to being bossed around by a female type—at least not like this. Maybe if Court were his mother, or his wife, or even his girlfriend she could be forgiven for her devotion to trying to improve him. But damn, she was some middle-aged woman with no blood ties to him whose own life was falling apart as she set out to rescue Arnold from his ill-perceived destiny.

"Give me one of those damn things." Truely snatched up a random CD. *The Scarlet Letter.* "If we're trying to get intellectual around here I guess I can sign on—on an experimental-only basis. I read this book in school. Forgot most of it. But Court, now, if I hate this audiobooks thing then I reserve the right to remain reasonably ignorant and to enjoy my ignorance as I see fit."

"Agreed," she said. "What about you, Arnold?"

"I rather watch some TV. We already missed the game tonight."

"Weeknights only," Truely declared. Since when did he start making up rules? Rules were Courtney's great love. "Books on tape no more than four nights a week. That's it. After TV. Not instead of TV. I'm not giving up the news and sports. And it's voluntary too—books on tape. Not mandatory. Everybody got that?"

"I'll suffer with you guys, okay?" Courtney picked up *The Red Badge of Courage.* "We'll just all suffer together in the name of intellectual pursuit." She smiled.

It would not have surprised Truely if Arnold suddenly decided to move the ten or so blocks back to Shauna's place. He half expected him to sling his meager belongings into a pillowcase and bolt out of the loft in a hurry, never looking back. It fact, it actually crossed Truely's mind to do the same damn thing.

That night all three of them settled into their assigned beds, which was beginning to feel weird to Truely, the excessive togetherness of sleeping out in the open with people you should not be sleeping with, each of them wired to their book of choice more or less, forcing themselves to listen and see if they could learn anything from the classically renowned wordmasters. It made Truely think of when the doctors had hooked his daddy up to an IV and pumped nutrition into him, forcing him to stay alive a little longer in hopes that he would be the better for it. And maybe he was.

Also, for the first time since moving into his loft, Truely found himself contemplating the merits of walls. It wouldn't be too hard to install some strategically placed space dividers in his place, which was feeling less and less like his place. He thought of his mother's discomfort trying to sleep in all this lavish open space when she used to visit Jesse and him. She would have much preferred a small, simple, enclosed space all to herself. Now Truely understood her sentiments. Maybe he was getting old.

Within an hour after the lights were out, Truely noticed that Arnold had drifted off, his earphones still plugged in. When Arnold slept he usually lay on his back with the covers mostly kicked off and his arm slung over his forehead. Minutes after noticing Arnold's surrender, Truely was almost sound asleep too, when Courtney tiptoed across the dark room and poked Truely gently.

"Wake up," she whispered. "I want to talk to you."

Truely got that same little pang of alarm he used to get when Jesse said those same words. "What is it?" he muttered.

"Let's step out on the terrace," she said, "so we don't wake up Arnold."

Courtney led the way across the unlit room in her robe and bare feet. She almost silently opened the terrace door and stepped outside into the soft night air. Truely was right behind her in his Spartan T-shirt and matted hair. "What's up?" he asked her.

She turned to face him in the darkness. Behind her the jeweled city sparkled like an artificial galaxy of stars. "This is not a big deal really"—she paused—"but in the interest of this involuntary pursuit of self-improvement I've begun—I'm scheduled for another surgery. I wanted you to know." It was chilly out, but the panoramic night vista was beyond spectacular and distracting in its magnitude. Truely used to like to sit out here in a chaise lounge, all alone, and think his disjointed thoughts. That was before he'd had his solitude shattered by this houseful of technically uninvited guests.

"My God, Court. What's wrong?" The concern in his voice was as earnest as the alarm.

"Nothing," she said. "It's not an illness, True. It's a choice. Elective surgery, they call it—right?"

"For what?" he asked.

"A breast lift—if you must know. Maybe some liposuction too."

"Hell no, Courtney," he said. "Liposuction? Isn't that where they suck fat out of you? Damn, you don't have any fat. What on earth are you thinking?"

"The liposuction is still a maybe. But the breast lift—that's scheduled."

"Don't do it, Courtney. Damn. You don't need it. You don't need anything."

"I'm not seeking permission here," she said. "Or even approval. I'm just being honest—letting you know what's going on with me. I mean, True, you were so great when I got my face done."

"I don't remember having much choice. There you were stitched together like a damn baseball."

"I haven't had a minute's regret either, True. I'm glad I did it."

"But why not stop while you're ahead?"

"Just to keep my spirits up, I guess. No pun intended." She smiled. "Surgery is a way for me to be proactive, to take action, you know—actually do something with myself. You've heard of self-improvement, right? Everybody is in favor of self-improvement."

"You're starting to worry me, Court. You aren't turning into one of those people who's addicted to plastic surgery, are you? I saw an article in the *New York Times* about this woman who got addicted to surgery and turned herself into a total freak. No lie. She ended up looking exactly like a circus lion—like some kind of wild animal. It's not funny, Courtney. You can't just play around with your body—your health—like that."

"You're sweet, bro," she said.

"I'd like to try to talk you out of this," he said.

"I know."

"Any chance I could do it?"

"Probably not."

"You're scaring me a little, Court. This new avocation of yours—it's damn bloody. Don't you think?"

"I'm results oriented, True. I don't obsess on process. You know that. I remember when I was growing up in Hinds County and Mother thought women who colored their hair were straight-up harlots. Remember? Mother was full-out gray before she was forty. She looked a good ten years older than Daddy. But she would never stoop to hair dye—that was supposed to be some sort of moral victory."

"So you're trying to tell me that this breast lift is the new hair dye?"

"Something like that." She laughed.

The door to the terrace opened then. Arnold stood half asleep in the doorway, bare-chested in a pair of Truely's sweatpants and a nylon-looking knit cap on his head. In Mississippi they had grown used to seeing black boys with one of their mama's stockings cut and knotted and pulled down on their heads just this same way. "Y'all out here talking about me?" Arnold asked.

"No," Truely said matter-of-factly.

"You sure?"

"We're more than sure, Arnold. You can go back to bed now."

"Why you got to sneak out here and talk then? Unless you worried I might hear what you say."

"We're not sneaking," Courtney said. "We didn't want to wake you up."

"Y'all out here talking like this—that's what woke me up. I'm wide-awake now."

"Well, go back to bed. It's late."

"If you got something to say about me, then just go on and say it to my face. We don't have no secrets around here—right?"

"This might be a shock, Arnold," Truely said. "But Courtney and I have plenty to talk about that does not concern you. We actually had conversations before we ever knew you—before you were even born."

"If y'all ain't talking about me, then what are you talking about?"

"Oh good heavens," Courtney said. "I was explaining to True that I'm thinking about having some surgery."

Arnold paused and studied her a minute. "Female surgery?" he asked.

Courtney glanced at Truely. "That description is a little vague—but yes, I guess so."

"Yeah, my grandmama had that. So did Suleeta." Arnold closed the door to the terrace behind him and walked over to where the two of them stood with the city lights flickering behind them. "So you worried about this?" he asked Truely.

"He's trying to talk me out of it," Courtney answered.

"You better be careful," Arnold warned. "Some people go in the hospital, just something minor, and they die in there."

"Thank you for the uplifting thought, Arnold."

"If she got her mind made up, you can't stop her, man," he told Truely. "My grandmama was the same."

"I don't remember anybody asking for your opinion on this," Truely said. "And this is not an argument, Arnold. We don't need a referee."

"Well, I just tell Courtney what my mama used to tell me whenever I started wanting to do something real bad."

"What?"

"She'd say, 'If you got the money to pay for it, then you can do it. If you don't, you can't.' Of course she knew I never had no money—so I never could do the stuff I was talking about. She'd just say that because it made deciding easy."

"But Arnold, I do have the money," Courtney said.

"I know."

"So, what's your point?"

"So, you can do it then. Go on and do it. Get that surgery. You got the money."

"It's not just money we're talking about here," Truely said. "No need to take a chance with your body—unless maybe it's a matter of life and death."

"Maybe it seem like it to her," Arnold said.

"He doesn't approve," Courtney said to Arnold.

"You mize well sign on, man," Arnold told Truely. "I bet she got her reasons."

"Maybe I'm just afraid that Courtney is looking for excitement in all the wrong places. Wasn't there a song about that?"

"It's not about excitement, for heaven's sake, Truely. My life is changing whether I like it or not. It's beyond my control. So maybe it's time for me to make a change on my own terms—just because I want to. Improve something. A change for the better, you know."

"Change by scalpel, Courtney, is something different from enlightenment."

"Okay then," Arnold said. "I'll leave y'all to argue this out. It's damn cold out here. And I would appreciate it if you two don't come out here no more like this and close the door on me. I sort of panic when I think you out here whispering about me. Okay?"

"We'll remember that," Truely said.

"I'm getting back in the sack then," Arnold said. "But Ima leave this door right here cracked open. I sleep better like that."

"Good night," Courtney and Truely echoed.

Before Arnold made his exit from the terrace he paused. "Courtney, if you decide you having this female surgery, tell us what day. I'll take off from work. Me and Truely will go with you. Right, man? You can't go to the hospital by yourself these days. Isn't no telling what them doctors do to you if they know nobody's there watching out for you. They about killed my grandmama when she went in there. I ain't lying either."

"Good night, Arnold," Truely said.

"Night." He vanished into the dark house in search of the sofa where he had set up camp.

"WELL," Courtney said, "small secrets among friends, I guess."

"It'd be a lie if I said all this surgery of yours didn't worry me, Court."

"I know."

"Would you be doing this if Hastings hadn't left?"

"I don't know."

"You think you need to turn back the hand of time so you can catch another man or something?"

"Catch? Is that what women do? Catch men?"

"Bad choice of words. But you know what I mean."

"Would I like to turn back the hand of time? That's your question? Yes, I think I would. Wouldn't you?"

"I know you want me to say yes, Court."

"But your answer is no? You don't want a redo? Not even with Jesse?"

"I'd say no. I don't."

"Really? I'm not sure you're telling the truth, but if you are—well, good for you."

"I have no desire to go backwards, Courtney. Not for all the Mulligans in the world. Damn. I have enough trouble just trying to move forward."

"Yes," she said, "you do." She leaned toward him and kissed his cheek.

Eighteen

THE NEXT MORNING, after Arnold headed off for a day of moving furniture, Courtney talked Truely into going to the market with her. "I'm in the mood to cook," she explained. Since that seemed better than some of the moods she might have been in, Truely embraced it. He had actually never been a to-the-market sort of guy. Unlike some men in the city he didn't roam fresh produce aisles with wonder or lust, he didn't read ingredient lists in a state of euphoria, or marvel at culinary masterpieces behind glass, or long to sample the little morsels handed out on trembling toothpicks.

No. He had rarely ever had the urge to cook anything himself either. He could make pretty good sloppy joes. Less than five minutes start to finish. He could reheat takeout. He could date women who claimed they loved cooking for him and let them go at it. But Courtney's acquired notion that the market was as full of wonders as any notable museum was essentially lost on him. She made lists and went to the market like an adventurer. He was more of a grocery store guy. A quick run inside to grab something fast—preferably preprepared, maybe on occasion a couple of filets or some fresh Atlantic salmon. But more often a couple of Hungry Man prepackaged dinners he could nuke in the microwave and eat without pausing to notice.

On this day they went first to Whole Foods. On Fridays there was often a certain zoolike quality to it, which was why he'd become more of a Safeway aficionado. But today Courtney was on a culinary mission and he was her trusty sidekick. While she selected cuts of meats—grass fed, free range, from this or that so-called-local organic farm, flown in fresh, not frozen, and on and on—he was assigned to dessert duty. This came naturally to him—selecting desserts. You might even say he had a gift for it.

His favorite desserts were the cobblers his mother used to make with fresh blackberries he picked himself as a child—and later peaches from his daddy's own trees. She'd made them with Bisquick, he remembered that. Along with what might now be considered illegal amounts of butter and sugar. She also made a ferocious banana pudding with the Jell-O pudding packets, ripe bananas *about to go bad* as she used to say, and a box of humidity-impaired vanilla wafers. To this day he actually believed that banana pudding had medicinal powers. In all the years since, in which he'd had any number of elaborate, artistic desserts, at many of the finest restaurants in this and other cities, he had never had anything that measured up in his mind to those early love-inspired desserts served on his mother's mismatched, chipped dishes. Nothing had been as satisfying since—either to the palate or to his soul.

He wandered through the upscale-slash-alternative crowd to the bakery section of the market. He always had the feeling he was among a sea of people who had started out as hippies rebelling against their upscale families but ended up rich in spite of themselves—and Whole Foods was where they went to reconcile both conditions. It required some degree of schizophrenia to pay six dollars for twenty-three organically grown blackberries, didn't it? No lie. It was all very pseudointellectual to Truely—who was as guilty as anyone of overpaying for something that wasn't worth it, just because he could.

Maybe Courtney was right. Maybe it was almost as good as going to a museum. From the looks of things they had some version of nearly everything sweet. After studying the offerings in search of the familiar he made his thoughtful selections—a flourless chocolate tart, to his way of thinking just a more hip version of a huge brownie (Courtney loved chocolate. Jesse used to love it too. And so did Shauna. It seemed a guy couldn't go too far wrong with chocolate); a three-layer carrot cake with nuts and cream cheese icing (They had never eaten carrot cake when he was growing up. He didn't think it had ever occurred to his mother to make a cake out of a garden vegetable).

Lastly he selected a tasty-looking cherry cobbler in an aluminum tray. (They didn't have peach or blackberry.) The cherry cobbler claimed to contain freshly picked, locally grown cherries and probably had most of the same ingredients as the cobblers his mother used to make — sans the love. Warm it up, sling a little vanilla ice cream on top and you could almost transport yourself back to the age of innocence.

Truely presented his selections to Courtney, who not only approved, but expressed enthusiasm. "Yummy," was her exact word. Truely loaded the bakery items into the cart, which by now contained an assortment of fresh greens, fruits, raw vegetables, sacks of organic flour and brown rice, couscous, lamb, beef, fish and fowl wrapped in white papers, freshly baked whole-grain breads, olive oil, and bottles of good wine, along with all kinds of stuff he didn't really recognize, just Lord knows what all that Courtney had hand-selected.

What was it about being with a happy woman in a grocery store that was so satisfying? It was a feeling he vaguely recalled. He flashed back to Mississippi and the days of Saturday trips into Jackson, where he had wandered around the aisles of the worn and weary Winn-Dixie or Piggly Wiggly, trailing his mother, who took her own sweet time, thumping the watermelons, sampling the seedless grapes to be sure, handling the pole beans, green beans, butter beans, opening the cartons of eggs, checking for cracks or worse, often pausing to chat with other women who were also shopping in slow motion with their own ragged children trailing them. On those early occasions of accompanying his mother to do her grocery shopping he had had the feeling, oddly, that overall this was a pretty decent world to live in. Maybe he felt a little bit that way now.

After he and Courtney hauled the groceries out to the car Courtney wanted to make a quick stop at the Safeway for "a few

---

staples." That was what their mother used to say, "Anybody want to run to the store with me? I got to pick up a few staples." When they were little they always loved to go to the grocery store in hopes of putting a penny in the gumball machine, or getting a quarter ride on the bouncing horse out front.

At the Safeway, he and Courtney split up and hurried through the store with separate buggies (as they are called in Mississippi) grabbing such staples as Doritos, Cheez Whiz, Ritz crackers, onion soup mix, low-fat sour cream, fat-free cream cheese, frozen cookie dough, containers of fluorescent pimento cheese, Diet Coke, beer, Campbell's cream of mushroom soup, Velveeta, frozen hash browns, instant grits, chunky peanut butter and whatever else called to them of an essential or alluring nature.

When they got back to Truely's place he carried the bounty up to the loft and attempted to help Courtney put it away, but she shooed him off, waving her hand, saying, "You've helped enough. I'll put things away myself. That way I'll know where things are." He didn't argue with her. Instead he went to the area of the loft that had, by default, become his pseudo-office space. He had some calls to return. Some contract proposals to fax. A few notes to write by hand. He turned the TV on. He liked the twenty-four-hour news as a backdrop for his labors.

He had no trouble busying himself with work-related tasks, but his eye kept wandering to the kitchen, where Courtney was happily arranging food in the cabinets and the refrigerator. He watched her wash fresh vegetables and stack canned goods, sorted by category, all labels facing forward. He saw her sniffing the meager contents of his refrigerator and tossing most of it into the trash. If he wasn't crazy she was actually humming.

By midafternoon Courtney had floured and browned a rump roast, the sizzling pan steaming up the kitchen, searing in the juices of the meat—and releasing his repressed hunger. Truely watched her put the roast in the oven to slow cook. The aroma was familiar and totally intoxicating. He imagined himself drunk from simply breathing the air. He watched as she washed and chopped a pot of greens, chopped an onion, grated some cheese and was busy stirring some dry ingredients into a large mixing bowl. She moved from task to task with confidence and grace. She was quiet mostly, busy with her kitchen revelry, lost in her own thoughts. Just her presence alone brought Truely a long-absent sense of peace.

By THE TIME ARNOLD GOT HOME from work that afternoon, Courtney had set the table, put out a vase of cut flowers and lit some small candles. When he walked in Arnold looked momentarily lost. He actually glanced around with an expression of concern. "What's going on?" he asked.

"Dinner," Courtney said. "You like roast beef, don't you?"

"Court got the urge to cook," Truely explained. "Can't fight an urge like that."

"Look like Thanksgiving or something in here," he said, walking over toward the kitchen, dropping his backpack on a chair. "Man," he said. "Is that them little red potatoes?"

"It is," Courtney said.

He lifted the lid on a pot, the steamy vapor escaping in a fragrant cloud. "No way," he said. "Collards?"

"With fatback," she said. "And pepper sauce if you want it."

"What you got in here?" He opened the oven.

"Hot cornbread," she said. "Just like mama used to make."

"Whose mama?" he asked.

"Good point." She laughed.

"Man," he said. "This look good."

"It's ready," Courtney said. "Wash up and we'll eat early. I know you come home from work half starved. Thought it would be nice if you walked in to supper on the table."

"You got any grape jelly?" Arnold called as he took off his jacket and made his way to the back to wash his hands. "For that cornbread?"

Courtney went to the pantry which she had earlier arranged

like a display case and grabbed a small jar of jelly, but the lid was stuck. "Can you open this?" She handed it off to Truely.

While Courtney poured iced tea, Truely muscled off the lid to the jelly. When Arnold returned he had put on a clean T-shirt and maybe even splashed water on his face.

"You guys sit down," Courtney said. "I'll put the food on."

"This got anything to do with you getting that surgery?" Arnold asked as he pulled out his chair.

"Nothing whatsoever," she said.

"You sure?"

"I'm positive."

"Then what brought this on?" he asked, sitting down.

"I just wanted to do it," Courtney said.

"Anybody ever tell you you ask a lot of questions?" Truely said.

"Got to," he said. "If you the kind that got the need to know."

"Truely is not that kind," Courtney volunteered, kissing the top of his head.

WHEN THEY WERE ALL THREE SEATED AROUND the table there was a palpable sense of good-food anticipation, like a holiday excitement in the air. "This looks great," Truely said maybe three or four times in a row. This was one of those occasions when he thought to himself, Yes, of course, food is love. How had he managed to forget that? Courtney insisted they all join hands and bow their heads and ask grace. She wanted each of them to take a turn—aloud. Neither Truely nor Arnold was necessarily inclined to do this, but under the circumstances they did their best to oblige Courtney. She began by squeezing both their hands, saying, *"Dear Lord, my life is a mess as you know, but I also have an abundance of things to be grateful for—and two of them are sitting right here now. I thank you for my good brother, Truely, and my good friend Arnold. We all ask that you help us use our strength to your service."*

Arnold went next. *"We thank you for all this good food right here. We wish everybody could get a chance to eat like this. We thank Courtney for cooking all this too."*

And Truely chimed in afterward. *"Lord, make us ever mindful of our many blessings."*

Within minutes dishes and utensils were clanking in that naturally choreographed, musical sort of way. Ice was rattling in the glasses, wine was being poured for Courtney and Truely, roast was being sliced, gravy was being ladled, butter was being passed, vegetables were being peppered and the aroma of plenty was wafting throughout the room like an anesthetic.

"I didn't know you could cook," Arnold said to Courtney. "You never did tell me your sister could cook," he echoed to Truely.

"Now you know." Truely was dishing himself a helping of collard greens.

"You talented," he told Courtney. "My grandmama the only other woman I know who can cook like this. But she's getting old now. She ain't like to cook that much anymore. Plus she say groceries too high nowadays—she says it make you lose your appetite."

THEY WERE MIDWAY into second helpings when Arnold's cell phone rang. It had the effect of a fire alarm going off, not just because it was loud, but because it was so rare. Usually Arnold kept it on vibrate and went about conducting his cell phone life under the radar. Arnold fished in his pocket, silenced his phone and checked to see who was calling. No specific expression crossed his face. "Got to get this," was all he said. "Y'all go on and finish without me."

"Can't you call back later?" Truely asked, sounding oddly parental.

"This can't wait." He stood up and began walking toward the back of the loft and the small bathroom he had claimed as his own. He went inside and closed the door.

"Who do you think is calling him?" Courtney asked.

"Don't know."

"You sure he hasn't got a girlfriend?"

"Don't know."

"You've never asked him?"

"We try to operate on don't ask, don't tell around here."

"I bet," she said sarcastically.

"It's just a phone call, Court. Some nights he stays locked up in that bathroom talking on his cell phone until all hours."

"Really? The same guy that goes nuts if we close the terrace door to talk privately? The same guy who says, 'No secrets among friends'?"

"One and the same."

"You're not the least bit curious, True?"

"He'll tell me if he wants me to know."

"Maybe he would appreciate being asked," she said. "That ever occur to you?"

"Not really," he said. "But I'm sure you'd be happy to oblige him, right?"

"You might be surprised to know that I'm not a card-carrying member of the don't ask, don't tell club, True."

"Yeah," Truely teased. "I'm pretty sure they don't let girls in."

THEY FINISHED THEIR MEAL, had second glasses of red wine and relaxed, thinking that Arnold might return to finish his supper. When it seemed he wouldn't, Courtney made him a second plate of food and asked Truely to take it to him, which he did, tapping on the bathroom door, then jiggling the knob and looking inside. Arnold was sitting on the side of the tub, his head in his hands. It was like he hadn't heard Truely knock. When Truely spoke his name, Arnold jumped. He turned to face Truely and Truely saw that he was upset, maybe even close to breaking down. "Here." He handed him the plate of food. "Courtney sent this."

Arnold took the plate and mouthed, "Thanks, man."

"Everything okay?" Truely asked.

Arnold didn't answer. He didn't need to.

IT WAS LATE when Arnold finally came out of the bathroom. By then Truely and Courtney had put the food away, cleaned the kitchen and loaded the dishwasher. Truely was propped up in front of the TV in his nightly pose. Courtney was lining up and counting out her various medicines on the kitchen counter. This seemed to instantly annoy Arnold. "You still taking all them pills?" He sounded more than disapproving.

"Arnold, for heaven's sake, these are prescribed by my doctor. Maybe he knows what's good for me even better than you do. Could that be?"

"You don't seem sick to me. What you need all that medicine for?"

"So I don't *get* sick," she said. "It's like preventative medicine."

"That's bullshit," he said.

"Arnold." Courtney turned to glare at him. "What is wrong with you?"

"Drugs ruin your damn life. I don't care if you get them off the street or where. I know what I'm talking about too. You act the same as a junkie, counting all them pills. You act like you enjoy it."

"Lord, Arnold. Are you trying to pick a fight here?"

"No," he said.

"I don't think you want to get in a fight with me, son."

He looked like he was being called out of a dream. Like he was just beginning to remember where he was. His eyes were brimming, but he seemed to catch himself before he fell into his feelings full force. He walked over to the counter where Courtney stood in her monogrammed pajamas and robe. "You think I could have some that cherry cobbler?"

Courtney looked at him with obvious irritation. It took a moment for his change in demeanor to register. She swallowed her fistfuls of pills with a glass of tap water before answering him. "Sure," she said. "I'll heat it up for you. You want ice cream too?"

He nodded.

While she set out to fix his cobbler, she said, "You must have one heck of a cell phone bill. You were in that bathroom there almost two hours."

"I wasn't on the phone the whole time," he said.

"You talking to a girl?"

"Yes."

"What's her name?"

"She go by Vonnie."

"From home? San Diego?"

"Yes."

"Well, she must have a lot to say," Courtney tried to tease.

"She got lot of problems," he said.

"And you're trying to help her?"

"Naw. I ain't no help." His voice broke.

"I bet you are," she insisted. "Truely," she called across the room, "Arnold is having cobbler. You want some too?"

Truely got up and walked into the kitchen. "I'll pass on the cobbler," he said, opening the refrigerator and taking out the leftover collards. He dished some cold collards into a bowl, got a piece of cornbread and crumbled it into the bowl too, then sprinkled a generous amount of pepper sauce on top.

"You want me to heat that up for you?" Courtney asked.

"No," he said. "It's good cold."

"Don't look too good," Arnold commented.

How many years had it been since Truely had had a late-night bowl of cold greens? He smashed the cornbread into the pot liquor and let it soak up the flavor. It was something he had seen his daddy do a hundred times when he was a boy. Nights when his mother went to bed early his daddy would often fix himself a bowl of cold pot liquor and take the leftover biscuits or cornbread from supper and crumble them into it. More than a few nights his daddy sat alone outside on the back steps with a Tupperware bowl in his hand, sopping his bread into the pot liquor. On rare occasions young Truely might go out and sit beside him, maybe with a bowl of Neapolitan ice cream, which was practically the only kind of ice cream he could ever remember his mother buying. The two of them would sit silently, and stare at the stars or listen to the crickets singing their sad, sad song. It had never occurred to him then that maybe his daddy was just the slightest bit sad too.

"Here." Courtney set Arnold's cobbler on the table. "Sit right here."

He sat down and Truely pulled out a chair beside him. Courtney poured herself a small glass of port and sat down too. The TV was still jabbering across the room, the war in Iraq was still raging, Gordo was still wounded, life still hung in the balance there. But here, the three of them sat in the near darkness and shared the silence the same way Truely and his daddy once had.

When Arnold finished eating, he looked at Truely. "We still going fishing tomorrow?"

"I guess so. Want to see what we can do at San Pablo Reservoir."

"Count me out," Courtney said.

"Is it because you're mad at me?" Arnold asked.

"It's because I want to bake tomorrow. I'm thinking peanut butter cookies."

"She mad at me," Arnold said to Truely.

"If she was mad at you, Arnold, there'd be no doubt about it."

"I do think you need to learn to respect your elders," Courtney said.

"I know," he agreed. "Sorry."

"It's in the Bible, Arnold."

"I know," he said again.

THAT NIGHT, before he got in bed, in a welcomed attempt to be light, Arnold sorted through his tangle of bedcovers, saying, "Okay, where's my man, Malcolm?"

"It's not a books-on-tape night," Truely told him. "It's Friday."

"I know, but Red got me on pins and needles," he said sarcastically. "I got to see what the dude gon do next. And if he get too slow, then maybe he just help me get off to sleep."

Courtney looked at Truely across the dark room and gave him a weary thumbs-up.

Nineteen

THE NEXT MORNING Truely and Arnold were up predawn.
Truely had set his alarm for five a.m. and it had awakened
everybody. While he and Arnold threw on some jeans and flannel
shirts, Courtney got up just long enough to pack them a lunch:
roast beef sandwiches, pickles, and big slabs of carrot cake. They
were out the door and on their way well before sunup.

First thing, they stopped at the Circle K so Truely could get
some bad coffee. Arnold didn't actually drink coffee, but he got
some too since Truely did. He muffled the taste with milk and too
many packets of sugar to count. Truely offered him a doughnut,
but he declined, saying, "Too early to eat." They drove through
the sleeping city and across the Bay Bridge in near silence. It was
too early to try to talk too. The next stop was Dupree's Bait, a
hard-to-find, hole-in-the-wall bait shop, where the old guy running the place seemed to know Truely, calling him Mr. Noonan.
He was a black guy, looked to be a couple hundred years old,
sporting a shiny bald head with white cotton balls of hair around
his ears. He gave Arnold the once-over when they got out of the
car. "Who you got here?" he asked.

"This is my buddy Arnold," Truely said. "Taking him over to
San Pablo—see if we can get some trout to bite."

"Is that right?"

"Yeah. Arnold's grandmama comes from Mississippi too,"
Truely said. "Yazoo City."

"You don't say?"

"Dupree is from Mississippi," Truely explained to Arnold.

"They done run me out of down there long time ago." He chuckled. "There's some old ladies down there still got they hearts broke."

"You too old to start lying now, Dupree," Truely said.

"Boy, you still got people down there?"

"My family stay in San Diego," Arnold said. "I ain't country."

Dupree got a good laugh out of that. "Course you ain't. I can look at you and see you one them urban-nites." He snickered. "What bring you up here?"

"Got a job," he said.

"Where you stay at?"

"At his place." He nodded at Truely.

Dupree raised his eyebrows. "Well, I reckon you living high then."

Truely got a couple of boxes of worms out of the cooler. "You got any chicken livers today, Dupree?" he asked.

"You know I got chicken livers." Dupree walked slowly to a refrigerator in the back of his shed. "You ever know me not to have no livers?" He reached into the freezer compartment and pulled out a plastic baggie of frozen livers. In slow motion he set out to wrap the livers in some old newspaper. "Use these here and you might get you some them bottom-feeding catfish. They got some big ones can't nobody catch. Myself, I rather have a good catfish than a trout any day."

"Lots of folks might disagree with that," Truely said.

"If they do, it's cause they don't know how to cook no fish. You miscook a fish and it ain't worth nothing, don't matter what kind it is."

"You're right about that." Truely handed the bait to Arnold, who headed back to the car while Truely paid Dupree. Dupree took his time counting out the change. At one point he looked up at Truely and said, "If I was you, Mr. Noonan, I'd keep my eye on that boy out there. I wouldn't turn my back on him. Something about that boy don't seem right."

Truely was startled by the unsolicited comment. He tried to

laugh it off. "You're wrong, Dupree. He's a good kid. Just got a lot on his mind."

"That the part that worry me," Dupree said. "What he got on his mind."

When Truely got in the car, Arnold responded as if he had heard Dupree's remark, which of course was impossible since he had been waiting out in the car. "That old man talk too much," Arnold said, annoyed. "That how they do down in Mississippi?"

"Pretty much," Truely said.

WITHOUT COURTNEY ALONG, a fishing trip was a totally different experience. For one thing, there was no home base, no cooler of drinks with ice, or blankets lovingly arranged on the bank. Just two paper sacks of sandwiches—and the basic tools of the serious fisherman. They parked the car and walked a short path to the water's edge. At a distance were several other fishermen sitting in folding chairs, manning multiple stationary rods at a time. And out on the water were a few small rented rowboats occupied by slump-shouldered, sleepy-looking men in sun hats, drinking coffee from thermoses.

Almost immediately, Truely and Arnold split up and went in separate directions. They remained within sight of one another, but not within word range. Instantly Truely relaxed and went inward, which was one of the great benefits of fishing. He did some of his best thinking on the bank of a river, or in this case, a reservoir. They should be able to get in several good hours before the midday sun heated the surface of the water, driving the fish into hiding.

Truely watched Arnold at a distance. He saw him carefully skewer the chicken livers on his fly hook. He saw the way he nervously cast his line the first few times. It didn't take him long to become more confident and throw his line like the natural extension of his arm, the way Truely had shown him, smooth, easy, with nearly perfect aim. Arnold had found a shady spot and stood planted there. Twice Truely noticed him pull in fish.

The first small one he threw back. The second one, large enough to put up a decent fight, he kept in a mesh sack at the water's edge.

The pink light of sunrise had surrendered. It seemed it would be an overcast day, threatening rain—a perfect day in Truely's mind. He didn't know what it said about him that he loved the rain so much. Mornings when he awoke to the sound of pounding rain, while rare, made him instantly happy—always had. As a boy he had loved school days most too when rainstorms raged with lightning and thunder and the sort of downpour that forced an awe-inspired silence among otherwise rowdy kids. He had loved being in cozy, yellow-lit classrooms, with teachers who had seemed, on stormy days at least, to genuinely love their students.

He remembered certain rainy Sundays when he and Jesse would stay inside all day in their pajamas and watch sad movies and make crazy love and be, to his mind, nearly totally happy. Later she graded papers while he made sloppy joes, which they ate outside on the covered terrace with the windswept rain flying in all directions around them.

It was funny the way memory obliged the heart. His happy recollections were always afloat in his soupy subconscious where so many of his darker memories had sunk to the underbelly of his past and been as good as lost forever. But without conscious instruction, memory had edited and enlarged the finest moments of his life and stored them like masterpieces in the private gallery of his personal history. He assumed this must be true for most people—although by this point in his life he should have learned never, never to assume.

RENEWED BY SEVERAL HOURS of quiet and a contented day of catch-and-release, Truely walked toward the distant spot Arnold had claimed. "Ready to shut it down?" he called out. Arnold nodded and began to reel in his line. The two of them sat on bank's edge and ate the lunches Courtney had packed. Arnold started with his carrot cake, breaking off big chunks, popping them in his mouth. Truely unwrapped his roast beef sandwich, made from last night's leftovers. Courtney had slathered his with horse-radish just the way he liked it too. Nothing like hours of silence to work up a healthy appetite.

"How many fish you got there?" Truely asked, looking at the mesh net in the water at their feet.

"Three," Arnold said. "Me, you and Courtney. Thought we'd eat them tonight. Maybe Courtney'd cook them for us."

"You ever clean a fish?" Truely asked.

"I seen it done."

"We'll clean them when we get back to the car," Truely said. "Take them home ready for the skillet."

They loaded up their equipment and walked back to the car. Truely retrieved a warped board from the roadside brush. "Flat surface," he said. He laid the fish out and took a knife from his tackle box. "Remove the heads," he said. "Like this." He sliced off the head of the first fish just behind the smallest throbbing gill. "Then slice the belly open, like so." He showed Arnold how to gut the fish, slinging the innards into a leftover lunch sack since there were no cats nearby to dine on the guts. "Now all we got to do is get these scales off." He dug through the tackle box for the tool he needed. "You scrape in this direction—against the grain. See?" Truely could clean a fish with his eyes closed. He'd prob-ably cleaned close to a million of them in his lifetime. "Okay," he said. "You clean these two, man. On the way home we'll stop at Dupree's and get some ice to ice them down."

Arnold squatted down over the board where the two remain-ing fish were laid out. While he went to work cleaning them with the queasy stomach of a first timer, Truely loaded their stuff in the car.

"This right here about make you think you don't want to eat no fish," Arnold said.

AFTER THE FISH WERE CLEANED and iced and the two of them had washed up at Dupree's and were en route home, sus-pended somewhere midair on the Bay Bridge, the clouds above them bruised and swollen, threatening to unleash at the first clap of thunder, Arnold said, "Man, I appreciate how you don't never ask me no questions."

It was not a comment Truely was prepared for. "Should I be asking you questions?"

"I figure you don't like nobody asking you no questions, so then to prove it, you don't ask nobody any questions yourself."

This was a new version of an old complaint that had been lodged against Truely before, no less subtly. "Look, man," Truely said. "If you got something you want to tell me—I'm listening."

After a cautious pause Arnold said, "We got some problems."

"We? Who's we?"

"Me and Vonnie."

"Vonnie is the girl you talk to on the phone all the time?"

"Yeah."

"Your girlfriend?" Already Truely was imagining that maybe Arnold had gotten his girlfriend pregnant. He was trying to think what in the world you tell a young man in a situation like that.

"Naw. Vonnie is my sister, man. Her name is Vontell, but everybody call her Vonnie."

"Got it," Truely said.

"She been staying over at my grandmama's house."

"Yeah?"

"My mama's boyfriend, he run her out of my mama's house—same as he done me. So she been staying with my grandmama, but they don't get along that good."

"Is that the problem?"

"No, man. That ain't it."

"What is it then?"

Arnold sucked in a big breath and let it out slow, like a tire with a hidden puncture wound, a slow leak. "Remember I told you my mama have some issues."

"I remember."

"She got a drug problem, man. She been sick long as I can remember. Then she get this new boyfriend and he just make it worse. Vonnie can't stand to watch it and she can't do nothing to stop it either. So she go over to my grandmama's house and she gets to crying and everything, tells my grandmama what's going on over there. So then my grandmama call the police on them."

Truely didn't speak. He was listening.

"So the police come around there. They arrest my mama."

"Oh, man," Truely said.

"It ain't the first time," Arnold said. "Usually she get out in a few days. But not this time. They got her locked up for real. Look like she going to do big jail time."

Truely let out a long, low whistle. It was a habit of his when he was at a loss for actual words. It generally made his point.

"We was trying to get her boyfriend out of there. He's the one was running drugs out her house. She just do what he say. Not that she's no angel or nothing. Mama, she needs some help. But she's too stubborn. Now look like she's going to jail instead."

"I'm sorry," Truely said. "That's one hell of a mess you got there."

"Yeah."

"How can I help you? What can I do?"

"You know any lawyers in San Diego?"

"I can make some calls. Try to get a referral maybe. What else?"

"Maybe we don't tell Courtney about this?"

"Really?"

"I don't want her getting no low opinion of nobody. She liable to think she can set them straight or something. She be loading them up with them damn books on tape."

Truely laughed. "Hard to keep a secret from Courtney."

"You saying we got to tell her?"

"I'm saying it's up to you. You tell her when you're ready."

"All right, then."

They crept along in silence for a while. It looked like maybe there had been an accident up ahead on the bridge. A misty drizzle had begun and the bridge was slick with shine. Truely thought he could see flashing lights in the distance. Nothing to do but relax and wait it out. They were in no hurry. Truely was oddly satisfied to be sitting in the car with Arnold slumped in the seat beside him, the windshield fogged, their cleaned, iced fish in a cooler in the backseat. There was nowhere else he wished to be.

Arnold was full of emotion. Truely could feel the misery radiating off him. He put on the radio in hopes of distracting Arnold from the weight of his despair. There was not a lot that needed to be said. Being present—sometimes that was enough. Right?

Before they were back in the city the rain started, a genuine downpour. Truely turned on the wipers. They slapped at the windshield, again, again, again. But it was almost useless. The traffic had slowed to a crawl. The city was awash with gloom.

"One question," Truely said as they sat bumper to bumper in the clotted traffic, inching toward home in the rain. "Vonnie. How old is she?"

"Just turned fourteen," Arnold said.

WHEN THEY GOT HOME the house smelled like peanut butter cookies. That was the good news. The bad news was that Courtney had taken it upon herself to rearrange some of Truely's furniture, nothing drastic, just enough minor change to annoy him. "What do you think?" she asked when they came in.

"I liked it the way it was," Truely said flatly.

"Try it for one week. Okay? If you hate it we'll move it back."

"Whatever." Truely wanted to ignore the situation, not discuss it.

"What's in the bag?" Courtney asked Arnold.

"Trout," Arnold said. "You in the mood to fry some fish?"

The idea seemed to appeal to her. She went to the kitchen and began glancing through the cabinets. "Don't think we have enough cornmeal left," she said. "And no Crisco either—if you want Southern fried."

"I'll walk down to the store and get some," Arnold said.

"It's pouring rain."

"I don't care."

Truely suspected Arnold was telling the truth. He thought walking in the deluge might actually be therapeutic for Arnold. A moment of emotional camouflage. Already he marveled at

Arnold's ability to transform his mood to accommodate the company he was in. "I'll drive you," Truely said. "What else we need?"

"Maybe a head of cabbage," Courtney said. "If you want slaw."

They left for the short drive to the nearest small grocery, Korean run. It was a painless errand really. Truely handed Arnold twenty bucks and sat in his double-parked car while Arnold went inside and completed the errand.

When they got back to the loft, Courtney had moved each piece of rearranged furniture back to its original spot. Truely noticed instantly. "What?" he asked Courtney. "You have aesthetic second thoughts?"

"I saw the look on your face, True, when you came in and saw that something had changed. It was a look, you know. A certain look. We're just so different, you and me. On some level I like change—even terrible change like Hastings walking out—it startles me back into life, like a violent jolt, it inspires me to take action. I don't know. Even when I hate it, I like it. If I go too long with nothing changing I get worried—then what the heck, I change something myself."

"Like your face?" It was a mean-spirited remark. He wasn't sure where it came from exactly, but it was too late to censor himself.

She paused as if to let the remark register. "Yes," she said. "My face. My circle of friends. My habits."

"And?"

"And you don't."

"And—according to you—that's because?"

"Because you hate change, True. Big or small. For better or worse. You hate it. I'm not sure why."

"Do you think maybe you might be exaggerating—just slightly?"

"Lord knows I hope so," she said.

"Y'all stop fussing and let's fry this fish," Arnold said.

"We aren't fussing," Truely corrected. "Not really."

"Yes we are," Courtney said. "Don't lie to the boy."

While Courtney fried fish and made slaw with the attentive assistance of Arnold, Truely went across the room and turned on the TV. Texas was playing Oklahoma in the Red River Shootout this afternoon. It should be a gut grinder. It was end of the first quarter already and the score was 7-up. Truely loved a good defensive struggle. But the thing that was even more compelling was that Mose Jones was the color guy for the game. Truely wanted to plant himself on the sofa with a cold beer and watch the game. That was all. And when it was over he wanted to watch the next one, USC at Oregon, and the one after that, whatever it might be.

At one point Courtney glimpsed the TV and commented, "Wow, look at Mose. He hasn't changed a bit. He looks great, doesn't he?"

"You know Mose Jones, the sports guy?" Arnold asked her.

"Truely does," she said.

"For real?"

"We played ball together," Truely said.

"You played ball?" Arnold sounded incredulous.

"High school," Truely said. "Then Mose went on to play college. And pro ball. And the rest is history, as they say."

"You know him? I didn't think you know nobody like him."

"He's from Hinds County, Mississippi," Courtney remarked. "Hometown boy makes good."

"You should have married him then," Arnold said, "as long as you was marrying somebody. Forget that Hastings."

Courtney laughed. "He was a child at the time," she said. "A black child too. Back then, white girls didn't marry black boys."

"And now they do?" Arnold asked.

"Sometimes, I guess," she said. She paused a second. "And then they get the heck out of Dodge, pronto. They move to California, maybe," she teased.

"My mama say if I marry a white girl she disown me," Arnold volunteered. "She think people need to stay with their own. She never liked me staying at the Mackeys' either. She'd throw a fit, said I was acting ashamed to be black, like I was wishing I was white."

"Were you?" Courtney asked.

"No," Arnold said flatly. "Sometimes my mama just talk bull."

"Mose Jones was the coolest guy in Hinds County," Courtney said. "Still is, I guess. I mean, besides our boy Truely here."

"Very funny," Truely said.

"I got some new respect for y'all," Arnold teased. "You know somebody like Mose Jones." You could almost see it coming, the idea. "Let's call him up. You got his phone number?"

"He's working," Truely said. "He's not going to answer the phone."

"We'll just leave him a message then. Come on, man. Call him."

"Bring me my cell phone off the desk," Truely said.

Arnold got the phone. "I want to listen to his voice message."

Truely got Mose's machine, passed the phone to Arnold, who clearly got a kick out of hearing Mose's voice. "He sound just like on TV."

"Hey man," Truely said into the phone, "I'm sitting here with a couple of your big fans, Courtney Noonan, former queen of Hinds County, and Mr. Arnold Carter, our buddy from down in San Diego. We're watching you cover the Red River Shootout. Good job, man. I see you got a little Texas bias, but I'm okay with that. Let us know if you get up this way for a Pac-10 game. Don't be a stranger. Take care."

"Cool," Arnold said. "Maybe he'll call us back."

"Okay, do y'all mind?" Truely turned the TV volume up. "I'm trying to catch Mose's commentary over here. I'd appreciate it if you'd reduce your idle chatter to a bare minimum." The only interruption he was willing to tolerate was when Courtney handed him a plate of hot fried fish with hush puppies and slaw.

Except for a couple of times when Arnold got brief vibrating phone calls, which he took in the bathroom—a place he now referred to as his office ("I'll take this in my office," he'd say)—the three of them sprawled out on the sofa with their food in their laps and watched football like reasonably normal people on a fall Saturday night.

At one point Courtney said, "True, I almost forgot to tell you—a woman named Lanie called this afternoon. She said she got your home number from Jaxon. She wants to know if you can meet her for coffee. I told her, never mind coffee, you'd love to take her out to dinner and a wild night of dancing!"

He shot her a threatening look. "I assume you're kidding." He was totally unsure that she was.

"I told her you'd call her. Her number is on the counter."

More to his own surprise than anyone else's, Truely got up, got the number and walked out on the terrace and called her back. He wasn't sure what had come over him.

Twenty

I N THE COMING WEEK Truely made calls to firms of contract lawyers who had worked for Jaxon and him in the past and got the name of a good criminal lawyer in San Diego, who agreed, for the right price, to represent Arnold's mother. A steady round of phone calls ensued, the gist of which was that the police had a sound case against Arnold's mother. Her boyfriend was only one of several people prepared to testify to having bought drugs from Arnold's mother at her apartment.

They had grainy police video of undercover cops scoring drugs at the address. It had been on TV down there. You could see Arnold's mother standing just inside the doorway. You could see she was talking to people, even laughing sometimes. Despite the shadows you could see she was a businesswoman of sorts, stuffing bills in the pockets of her tight jeans. It was startling to Truely, who had requested and been sent the poor-quality copy of the video evidence. Arnold's mother looked for all the world like a kid herself. If he were guessing, just from seeing the video, Truely might think she wasn't much older than Arnold was. Arnold claimed she was actually thirty-two—which meant she was fifteen or so when he was born. On the video she had on what looked like a skin-tight sweater with no bra. Her bared midriff bulged over low-slung, pasted-on jeans.

Honest to goodness it disturbed Truely to see Arnold's mother dressed like one of the runaway teenagers he sometimes saw panhandling on the streets of San Francisco—bumming cigarettes or quarters, offering all manner of disease-bearing favors. "She's doing some real jail time," the lawyer had told Truely. "The only question that remains is—how much?"

Arnold took the news with relative calm.

"Not an easy thing to deal with," Truely had said to him at the time.

"Could be worse," he said. "News I dread is when they go on and tell me she's dead. Somebody shot her or she overdosed. The rest, I take it as it comes."

Truely put his hand on Arnold's shoulder, instinctively, just like his father used to do to him when there were no words suitable for the occasion.

"My grandmama say this might be the best thing could happen—jail." It was like Arnold was talking himself—not Truely—into believing this. "She say she gon sleep better knowing Mama is straightened out and eating regular and can't get her hands on no street drugs. Might be she come to her senses."

Earlier Truely had given Arnold the business card of his mother's new attorney. "In case you have any questions," he'd said. "You can call him."

"Mama never had a actual lawyer before," Arnold had said. "Just court appointed is all. Everybody know court appointed is no good."

"This guy will do what he can," Truely promised. "But he's not a miracle worker."

"No problem," Arnold said. "I don't believe in miracles."

DAYS LATER when Truely got Courtney's phone call, clearly a distress call, it was midafternoon and he was at the warehouse space over on Mariposa Street. "You have to come home," she told him. "I need you to be here when Arnold gets home from work. We have a serious problem, True. I mean it."

When Truely got back to the loft, Courtney was clearly agitated and upset. "First of all," she told Truely, "I was not snooping. Okay? I want that made clear."

What felt like fire flashed through Truely's belly. This wasn't going to be good. Already he knew that.

"I was doing some laundry, right?" Courtney continued. "The sheets off the beds, some towels—and so I looked in Arnold's suitcases while I was at it, in case he had some things that needed to be washed, right? It was a harmless gesture." She made her way across the loft and Truely followed her. "I opened this suitcase right here. It wasn't locked or anything. And I glanced around for dirty T-shirts or whatever. Then I see this knot of a flannel shirt, all tied up, right? Like this. See, right here?" She pointed at a wadded-up plaid shirt. "Pick it up, True. You'll see."

Truely reached down and grabbed the shirt. Courtney's dramatic ways of doing things sort of rubbed him wrong, but he had learned long ago that it was easier to go along with it than to resist. "Okay," he said, lifting the knotted shirt. Immediately he noticed that it was unusually heavy. He put the shirt down on the bed and began to unwrap it, loosen the knots Arnold had so carefully tied. Hidden inside the shirt was a sizable handgun. When Truely lifted the shirt the gun rolled out on the bed. "Damn," he said.

"It's a gun," Courtney declared, as if Truely didn't have sense enough to know it. "He's brought a gun into this house."

Twenty-one

WHEN ARNOLD CAME IN from his long day of delivering furniture he found Truely and Courtney waiting for him. Courtney had made a pot of coffee earlier and had a good caffeine buzz going in addition to her moral outrage. "What in the world can he be thinking?" All afternoon, while they paced and waited for Arnold to come home, she had spoken that rhetorical question into the surrounding quiet.

"Let me handle this," Truely told her repeatedly.

"Sure," she said.

"I mean it, Courtney. Leave this to me."

"I wouldn't dream of interfering." Courtney was seething. "You handle it, True. I want you to. Really. Knock yourself out."

BY THE TIME Arnold finally walked into the house Courtney's restraint was spent. Before Arnold could drop his jacket on the chair and take off his boots, she said, "You have some explaining to do, buddy-boy." She knew Arnold didn't like being called buddy-boy.

"What's up?" Arnold looked first at Courtney and then at Truely, immediately sensing the seriousness of the occasion. "What's wrong?"

"That's what we want to know." Truely lifted the handgun in the air so Arnold could see it. Then he laid it out on the kitchen counter. "What's this?"

Arnold looked at the gun for a minute as though he had no

idea what it was. His eyes were darting from Truely to Courtney. "A gun," he finally said.

"Yeah, I know it's a gun," Truely said. "But whose gun? And what is it doing in my house?"

"It's mine," Arnold said.

"What? Are you some kind of criminal?" Courtney snapped. "You about to rob somebody or shoot somebody? What do you need a gun for?"

"I don't have that gun to cause any trouble," Arnold said. "I just have it to keep myself out of trouble."

"Bull," Courtney blurted out.

"Court," Truely snapped, "let me handle this."

She pretended to zip her mouth closed. But her intent gaze was fixed on Arnold and it was already causing him to break into a sweat.

"You go through my stuff?" Arnold asked.

"Oh, that's priceless," Courtney said. "Yes, we're the bad guys here—we're the ones betraying the trust around here."

"Courtney, stop," Truely barked.

"Sorry." She rolled her eyes and zipped her lips again.

"Courtney was doing some laundry," Truely said. "She looked in your suitcases for any clothes that needed to be washed—trying to help you out, man. She found your gun wrapped in an old shirt."

"Now y'all think I'm a criminal?"

"We don't know," Truely said. "What should we think?"

"Where I come from everybody got a gun, man. Out here folks got they computers and Blackberries and shit, but back home we got guns. That's how it is."

"That's stupid," Courtney said. "I'm sorry, but it's totally stupid."

"You got guns," Arnold said to Truely in an accusatory tone. "I heard you talk about you've got them guns in storage. You tell them stories about when you used to go hunting—shot all them deer."

"You trying to tell me this handgun here is for shooting deer? Right here in downtown San Fran? Come on, man."

"I used to get scared when I was staying over at Shauna's by myself. I heard noises and stuff. They some strange people walking around over there. You seen them. So I needed that gun. Only way I get to sleep is knowing I got that gun."

"You don't bring a gun into another man's house and not clear it with him first," Truely said. "You understand that?"

"Sorry," Arnold said.

"You're too young to even have a gun in the first place. I know you don't have the right paperwork to own a gun," Courtney said. "How do we know you weren't going to get up in the night and shoot us both and make off with our credit cards or something?"

"That what you think?" Arnold looked insulted.

"Maybe you're not a bad person, Arnold. Maybe you're a good person with really bad judgment," Truely offered.

"So y'all gon throw me out now?" Arnold asked.

"Throw you out? If this was Mississippi we'd take you and wear your rear end out—talk about it later. You'd get a whuppin' to remember," Courtney said. "It scares me, Arnold. This sneaky side of you. I don't like it. It's creepy."

"So y'all gon kick me out?"

"There's an idea," Courtney said. "A young kid without a lick of good sense roaming the streets of San Francisco with nothing to his name but a handgun. Now there's a scenario for you."

"Where did you get this gun, Arnold?" Truely interrupted. "Tell me that."

"Do it really matter, man?"

"What? Did you steal it from somebody?"

"Naw, man. Not really."

"Not really?"

"I borrowed it, man."

"You borrowed it? With the permission of the owner? With the owner's blessing?"

"I was going to put it back before the owner missed it."

"I bet you were," Courtney snapped.

"Whose gun is this, Arnold? Say? Where'd you get it?"

"It used to be Gordo's. I borrowed it. He won't care. Ima put it back before Gordo gets back home."

"Why in the world does a boy like Gordo need a handgun?" Courtney asked.

"From here on out, this gun belongs to me," Truely said. "You understand me? I'm going to put it right over here, see?" He walked over to a wall of library shelves and placed the gun on the highest shelf. "You don't touch this gun without asking me first—and chances are ten to one I'm going to tell you no. You got that?"

Arnold nodded.

"Don't test me on this, Arnold," Truely said. "I mean it. We can all look over here anytime and see whether or not this gun is where it should be. If we ever look over here and see that this gun is gone—then that means you're as good as gone too, you understand me?"

Arnold nodded again.

"How do we know he's not going to get up in the middle of the night and shoot us both in our sleep?" Courtney said. "How are we supposed to trust him now?"

"You can trust me." Arnold was almost indignant.

"This changes some things, Arnold," Truely said. "You know that, right?"

"Yeah, I know that."

"If you're going to live here you got to tell the truth whether you think we'll like it or not. We stop trusting you and there's no way you can stay here. Is that clear?"

Arnold nodded.

"Anything else you want to say to Arnold, Courtney?" Truely asked.

Before she could answer, Arnold spoke up. "There's something I got to say." He paused then as if to collect his thoughts. "Since y'all already mad I might as well go on and tell you what I got to tell you—I hope you ain't going to take it wrong."

"Oh, shit," Courtney said. "What? You killed somebody? You stole a car? You robbed a bank?"

"It wasn't no bank," he said.

"Go ahead." Truely nodded for him to continue.

"Y'all know Vonnie been calling me. You know she got a lot of problems—with my mama and all. Now with my grandmama too. My grandmama got behind on her rent. Vonnie trying to get some money together—she calling and crying and begging me to send some money." Arnold paused.

"Go ahead," Truely said.

"So, I go in your wallet, man. I slip three hundred bucks out your wallet."

"You little thief," Courtney said.

"That ain't all," he said. "I got in Courtney's pocketbook too. Took two hundred dollars. I sent the money to Vonnie."

"I ought to wear you out," Courtney said. Truely couldn't help but remember that this was a phrase his mother used to use when he and Courtney did something wrong—when they deserved to be punished but most likely would not be.

"Thing is," Arnold said, "neither one of y'all ever notice you missing no money. You got so much loose money that if a couple hundred come up missing here and there you never even know it. It don't mean nothing to y'all—that little bit of money—but it make a big damn difference to Vonnie and my grandmama."

"You know that's not the point, right?" Truely asked.

"It's still stealing, Arnold, no matter what your reasons are."

"I know that," Arnold said. "It ain't like I steal on no regular basis. Just this once. This emergency."

"Did it ever occur to you to ask us?" Courtney said. "You think we're too mean to help you out? You think we're so coldhearted we'd just let your grandmother and Vonnie get put out on the street? Damn, Arnold. Is bad judgment the only judgment you've got? You just got your heart set on messing up your life, don't you?"

"No," he said.

"Why you confessing now?" Truely asked.

"I get scared you gon throw me out if you know. But now I worry you liable to find out," Arnold said. "I was planning to pay y'all back when I get my next check, you know. I give y'all two hundred every payday until we settle up."

"Yeah, right," Courtney said. "You know all the verses to that song, don't you?"

"You don't believe me?" Arnold said. "I swear. Soon as I get paid I was going to put that money back."

"Talk is cheap," Courtney said.

"Yeah," he said. "That's why I keep quiet about it."

"You got an excuse for everything, Arnold. I swear. It's not normal."

"Y'all always acting like I don't know how to act normal. Thing is, I am acting normal. Normal mean different things to different folks. Y'all think it's normal to drop two hundred bucks on some hamburgers at lunch at a fancy restaurant. Damn, that freak me out the first time I seen that. Me, I think it's normal to carry a concealed gun. When somebody draws a gun on you—then you need a gun to defend yourself. You don't have no gun, then people mess with you. They don't take you serious."

"Rules of the jungle?" Courtney said sarcastically. "Maybe that's how it works in the ghetto or whatever, Arnold. But this is not the ghetto. We don't play by those rules."

"Just because you don't like it, don't mean it ain't the truth."

Truely shook his head. "So how do we resolve this then?"

Arnold was quiet a minute, glancing at the gun up on the library shelf. "Maybe y'all give me another chance?"

"And what do you do to deserve another chance?" Truely asked.

"Whatever y'all want me to do."

"Well, if there was ever a boy who needed an education—it's you, Arnold." Courtney stepped up to her imaginary pulpit and started preaching her familiar sermon. "Damn if you don't need to learn some new ways of thinking, son. If you live here with Truely, you have got to educate yourself—get that GED. Maybe even go on to community college. Become a citizen of the world. Make something out of yourself. I'm going to insist even if Truely doesn't. Otherwise you might as well take that silly gun of yours and go back down to San Diego and be a foolish little gangster playing deadly games with the other foolish little gangsters. If you're lucky maybe you can end up spending the rest of your life locked up in prison somewhere, living out your life in a small cage with some child molester covered in tattoos. Now there's a great aspiration—that's a life well spent. It's just too ridiculous."

"Go on and load me up with them damn books on tape then. I listen to all of them if you want me to," Arnold said.

"Okay, guys." Truely waved his hand to get their attention. "I think we need to institute some basic rules around here. It's my house, so I guess I make the rules. Anybody object? No? Good. So listen up. You too, Court."

"You know I love rules." Courtney was totally serious.

"No guns," Truely began. "No activities involving guns. No hanging out with other guys who pack guns, deal in guns, think guns are normal or bring guns into this house. Period."

"Okay," Arnold said.

"Likewise, no drugs."

"Except all them drugs Courtney got," Arnold added.

"Okay. No *illegal* drugs," Truely amended. "No street drugs. No using. No selling. No hanging out with people who use or sell."

"Okay. What else, man?"

"When you go out, you let somebody know where you are. You leave a note, you leave a phone message. We do the same. You come in at a reasonable time—don't make people worry and wonder where you are. If it gets late, you call. We do the same."

"No problem," Arnold said. "It's not like I know nobody around here to hang out with anyway. It's not like I go nowhere except to work."

"It's a good thing too," Courtney said.

"Everybody contributes around here," Truely said. "Everybody helps out everybody else. Nobody complains."

"Say something about Arnold studying," Courtney said. "Make it a rule."

"You work toward the GED," Truely said. "You get your high school equivalency before the end of the year. No excuses. When the day comes we'll all celebrate—big-time. Maybe you can get Courtney off your back—but there's no guarantee, of course."

"This is not a boy who needs to be freed from expectation, Truely," Courtney insisted. "His expectations are so low now it's practically a crime by itself."

"Court," Truely snapped at her.

"Excuse me," she said, "for giving a damn."

"After you get your GED," Truely said, "then if you want to, you can get your driver's license. Maybe you can use that old truck of mine sitting idle downstairs in the parking garage—you know, help you come and go to school or work, one or the other."

"Truely," Courtney complained. "That's not a punishment. That's a reward. You're bribing him."

"I'm handling this my way," he said. "You ever hear of motivation, Court?"

"My God, Truely, the boy brings a gun into your house, steals money from you—and you want to motivate him? What's wrong with giving him a good old-fashioned ass-kicking, that's what he needs."

"Ignore her," Truely told Arnold. "She's having a Mississippi moment." He turned to Courtney. "Will you let me handle this, please?"

"Whatever," she shrugged. "But you're letting him get away with murder."

"This no kind of murder," Arnold corrected.

"If Truely'd ever pulled a stunt like this, our daddy would have skinned him alive," Courtney said. "He knows it too."

"This is not helping, Courtney," Truely said.

She pantomimed zipping her mouth closed again.

"Listen, man," Truely said to Arnold. "You got to think about your life here—decide what you want to do with it. Get started in that direction. You understand what I'm saying? You can't just live day to day waiting to see what happens, waiting to see what goes wrong next—then scrambling to survive whatever it is. That's not any way to live. That's miserable, Arnold. It's a waste too. You've got to *make* something good happen for yourself."

"I know."

"You don't just do what a bunch of fools do just because they do it—not unless you want to be a fool too. A man has got to have a plan, Arnold. Of his own. You need a plan. Get yourself a plan." Truely ran his hands through his hair in exasperation. He knew he was in over his head. "That's a new rule around here—everybody's got to have a plan."

"Okay then," Arnold said.

"I still say you're getting away with murder," Courtney said.

"You just gon stay mad at me no matter what I do?" Arnold asked Courtney. "You act like you gon hold a grudge."

"No holding grudges," Truely added.

"It's not a grudge," Courtney insisted. "I am crazy about Arnold—about who he can be. He knows that. He's got so much potential it makes me crazy. I just refuse to watch him make a mess of things and throw his life away."

"That's the way my old football coach used to talk," Arnold said.

"You should have listened to him," Courtney said.

IT TOOK SEVERAL DAYS for the high tension to dissipate. The gun sat up on the bookshelf in plain sight. Courtney watched Arnold like a hawk. He knew it too, which made him unnaturally quiet and cautious. Courtney made the three of them suppers as usual, meatloaf, barbecue chicken, pork chops. It was awkward to sit down together to eat. The food was good, but the conversation was strained. Truely gave up on trying to lead them out of their conversational quagmire.

One night when Courtney was serving them scoops of bread pudding she had bought at Whole Foods, she suddenly put her spoon down and leaned over Arnold, putting her arms around his neck. He jumped, like he was afraid she was going to hit him or choke him. "I'm only mad at you because I care," she said.

It was such a corny thing to say that Truely nearly laughed. "What the hell is this—a soap opera?"

But he saw that Arnold wasn't laughing. He was listening. "I'm treating you the same as if you were my own boy," Courtney said. "I would say to my own child everything that I am saying to you."

"Thank you," Arnold said, cautiously.

The spell was broken.

Twenty-two

OVER THE NEXT WEEKS Courtney intensified the torturous GED study sessions with Arnold as captive. Already it seemed he was complaining slightly less. The last few weeks instead of Courtney heading home to Saratoga on Monday mornings she had stayed on until Tuesday morning and then come back on Thursday afternoon. She was in the city with Truely and Arnold now more than she wasn't.

Arnold was orally answering questions that Courtney was calling out to him from a U.S. citizenship worksheet she got off the Internet. Arnold's listening comprehension was impressive. They were interrupted by the sound of the loft buzzer. "Oops, that must be your tutor." Courtney glanced at her watch.

Within a few minutes a tall, young black man stood at the door with shoulder-length dreads, a keen look in his eye and a gracious manner. "You must be Terrance." Courtney shook his hand. "I knew from your Web site you were smart, but I didn't know you'd be handsome too. Come in. Meet Arnold Carter, your student."

Terrance entered the room, looked around and walked toward the table where Arnold sat with his books and papers scattered about. Arnold stood up and looked Terrance over suspiciously. "You didn't tell me the dude was black," he said to Courtney.

She seemed startled. "Arnold, that's because I didn't know. His Web site is not racially specific. For heaven's sake, what difference does it make?"

"You don't fool me," he said. "I get what you doing here."

Terrance paused, unsure, and looked at Courtney for an explanation.

"What I'm doing is—I'm hiring you a math tutor. I forgot any math I ever learned. I was an art major, remember?"

"She put you up to this, man?" he asked Terrance.

"Up to what?"

"You coming over here to set an example—right? Show me an African American dude being a college man. College—that her thing. She want you to plant the education seed—like she says. I know how she do."

"Like the lady told you, I'm here to go over some algebra. That's all."

"Arnold, you're embarrassing yourself—and me too," Courtney said. "I told you I found Terrance online. He's a math major at City College. I e-mailed him. We set a time. He's here. And now you are acting a fool."

"When you talk about a math guy from City College I'm thinking some Asian dude. All them math guys over there are Asian."

"Arnold, stop it. Terrance is a math guy. And he's not Asian. Okay? Honestly." She shook her head to exaggerate her exasperation. "Ignore him," she instructed Terrance. "As I told you in my e-mail, Arnold is a smart guy who's afraid to be a smart guy. He'd rather be a dumb guy, right Arnold? Because, you know, the sky is the limit for a dumb guy. Everywhere you look you see dumb guys living the good life."

"I didn't say that," Arnold corrected. "I just say you don't have to get a degree to prove you're smart. Plenty of smart people never went to college."

"Oh, that's right," Courtney said. "College has ruined more lives than you can count, right? That degree, that meaningless piece of paper, is just destined to set you on the path to ruin. What do you think drove all those homeless folks to have to camp out on the street out there—it was that damn education that messed them up and caused their downward spiral, right Arnold?"

"Maybe I should leave," Terrance said.

"Absolutely not," Courtney said. "Arnold needs help with algebra—and you're here to help him."

"Maybe you two should work this out and call me later."

"It's worked out," Courtney insisted. "Arnold is taking the GED in a matter of weeks and we want him to ace it."

"She means *she* want me to ace it," Arnold said.

"See, Terrance," Courtney said sarcastically, "it's not just black people Arnold doesn't like—he doesn't like white people either. Nothing is a pain in the butt like a middle-aged white woman trying to interfere with a guy's fabulous, outstanding ghetto life. Us white women, we don't get it. We don't know shit. Right, Arnold? That's why Arnold doesn't really care about that silly GED—because it's just a stupid old white lady thing. Maybe he'll just fail altogether. That will show me, won't it? And get him off the hook."

"I ain't on no hook," Arnold said.

"Have you ever heard of self-fulfilling prophecy, Arnold?"

"What?"

"I bet Terrance has heard of it, haven't you, Terrance?"

"I've heard of it."

"See, Arnold?"

"Maybe Terrance here got that love of learning you talk about. And maybe I don't have it. You trying to make me a book guy. Maybe I ain't no book guy. That's all I'm saying."

"Bull," Courtney said. "You're just afraid if you ever find out that you're not stupid like you're hoping—if you find out you're really smart then maybe you'll have to do something about it. That scares the hell out of you."

"You don't know what scares me," Arnold said.

Terrance took a few steps backward as if he were leaving. "I'll come back some other time."

Courtney folded her arms and stared at Arnold. She didn't speak, just drilled him with her intense stare.

Arnold rolled his eyes. "No, man. Don't go. This none your doing."

Courtney continued to glare at Arnold, raising her eyebrows as a signal.

"Sorry about that, man." Arnold stuck out his hand. "I just wasn't expecting no brother. I didn't mean nothing by it."

"No problem."

"This the prison yard over here." He stepped to the table where he had been working and sat down. Terrance pulled out a chair and sat down across from him.

"One thing," Arnold said. "Don't think nothing about her saying you handsome. Courtney tell everybody they handsome."

While Terrance set out to work with his resistant student, Courtney busied herself making a pot of chili. When Truely got home she would tell him already she could see that they needed to change the location of these study sessions. She was going to suggest that next time Arnold meet Terrance at the City College library—or any other library. It couldn't hurt Arnold to get comfortable in a library—demystify the place. Truely had once tried to tell Courtney that these days if you had the Internet you might not need the library anymore—but she wasn't buying that.

By the time Truely came home Terrance was gone. Courtney related the afternoon's events to Truely, word for word. "Arnold thought it was a plot or something," she explained. "Can you believe that? He actually thinks I'm all about tricking him."

"Don't worry about it." Truely was distracted, his mind still on the latest collaboration he and Jaxon had had with their furniture designer. He'd brought home a fistful of revised sketches that he was anxious to study.

"I wish it were that simple, True. The truth is if I thought I could trick Arnold into things that are good for him, I would," she confessed.

"I guess he knows that," Truely said.

DESPITE HIS OCCASIONAL RESISTANCE Courtney went at Arnold's pursuit of the GED with the same exuberant dedication that she brought to nearly everything she did. Her secondary goal was to keep him motivated—materially speaking. She had taken a cue from Truely's attempts to bribe him with use of his truck. It became a point of pride with her. She set up a hierarchy of unabashed bribes. Phone cards, CDs, DVDs and the question-able audiobooks (those that earned her seal of approval only), iPod downloads, movie tickets, museum passes, shopping trips, and most recently, the two top-tier bribes—money to send home to Vonnie and his grandmother and a Sunday-afternoon Forty-niners game.

Littleton Properties had had a skybox at Candlestick Park for years which Hastings offered to his business associates and cli-ents as incentive or thanks. The first few years they'd owned the box Hastings and Courtney had rarely missed a game, and True-ly had been to his share too, but in more recent years they had only rarely ever gone to any games. Instead Hastings routinely offered the box to a long list of corporate people who doubled as enthusiastic football fans. Courtney had assumed Arnold might fall into the latter category. But she was only partly right.

"The Forty-niners?" he'd said hesitantly. "Y'all got a box at the Raiders' stadium?"

"No," she'd said. "Just the Forty-niners."

"Too bad," he'd complained.

"What?" Courtney asked. "You're too good for the Forty-niners?"

"No," he said. "But I been a Raider fan all my life. Down home people follow the Chargers—but not me. I always liked the Raiders."

Courtney checked the schedule and found the date the Raid-ers were playing the Forty-niners at Candlestick. She called Lit-tleton Properties and reserved the date so that Hastings wouldn't promise that particular game to anyone else. Arnold had to fin-ish a notebook of grammar exercises—and take a social studies comprehension essay test—before she was satisfied. But when all was said and done Truely thought Courtney was looking forward to the game almost as much as Arnold was. She had always been a reasonably enthusiastic—if uninformed—football fan.

DESPITE COURTNEY'S RAISED EYEBROW, Arnold dressed him-self in black Raiders garb, including a bunch of chains and a spiked dog collar he had bought from a street vendor. He tied a Raiders bandana around his head and another one around one ankle. He put in a rhinestone earring the size of a dime. He had his Raiders ball cap on sideways and his baggy pants hanging off his butt and just generally, to Truely's way of thinking, looked like a ghetto gangbanger on his way to exercising his right to poor judgment.

"Let me get this straight," Truely said. "You're going to a Forty-niner hospitality suite dressed like rabid Raider fan, no holds barred?"

"You got to be true to your team, man," Arnold said proudly. "I ain't gon leave no doubt who my homies are."

"I guess not. You look properly dressed for a good ass-kicking." Truely was wearing a Forty-niners T-shirt and a requisite ball cap. "On the other hand—we Forty-niner fans are all about subtlety."

"That mean boring?" Arnold asked.

THE THREE OF THEM had the luxury skybox all to themselves through the end of the first quarter. There was enough food and beverage to feed a small army, and they took turns hovering around the buffet table, loading and reloading their plates. The first quarter ended with a 6–3 score, Raiders ahead. Arnold was happy. "I ever tell you that I was a pretty good athlete back in high school?" he said. "For a while it looked like I had a shot at maybe playing college ball—if I could have got my grades together and whatnot. I had the dream back then, man."

"Seems like I heard something about that," Truely said. "What went wrong?"

"Me," he said. "I missed my chance. It got away from me."

"Too bad," Truely said.

"I still love the game though, man. I always be a fan. And that little bit of time when I was dreaming the dream, you know, that was the happiest I ever was."

Maybe it's time you get yourself a new dream then, Truely was just about to say, but he thought better of it. Arnold got enough advice Monday through Friday. He was going to let Sunday be his day of rest.

* * *

WHEN THE DOOR SWUNG OPEN, they barely noticed. A service
person coming to replenish ice maybe? But it was the voices of
kids that caught them off guard and caused them to turn around
and look. Two boys barreled into the skybox with abandon and
headed straight for the food table. When they saw Arnold standing there in his all-black attire and chains holding a plate full of
meatballs they froze. Right behind them, distracted by intense
conversation, came Hastings and Meghan. Courtney, despite her
usual composure, let out a small, involuntary gasp when she saw
them.

Truely turned just in time to see the startled look on Hastings'
face. Like a chain reaction, Hastings turned to face Meghan, to
reassure her maybe, but by then she had seen Arnold, and Truely
thought she actually looked slightly afraid.

It fell to Truely to break the ice. "Well," he said, "speak of the
devil." He was trying to be light, of course, since no one had mentioned Hastings' name all day. If anyone was aiming to represent
the devil it was most likely Arnold in his Raiders getup. Truely
walked over to shake Hastings' hand. "What's up?" he asked.
"This is a surprise. We weren't expecting to see you here today."

Hastings looked momentarily startled by the surroundings
and events. Meghan went silent and stood behind Hastings
almost as though she was trying to hide behind him.

Seeing the two of them so unexpectedly had silenced Courtney. It took a couple of moments for Courtney to find her voice.
"Hastings," she said. "I called your secretary at Littleton to book
the box for today. She told me you wouldn't be using it."

Hastings looked at her a full minute before responding. "She
didn't say you'd called."

"We can leave," Truely offered, "if there's been some kind of
mix-up."

"Now?" It was Arnold, registering modest complaint, still jab-
bing at meatballs with his toothpick.

"Who's this?" Hastings asked. Meghan's two boys were clearly
enthralled by this black guy in his gangster garb, wearing his sun-

glasses indoors. They stood staring at him with obvious interest and caution.

"This is Arnold." Courtney walked over and looped her arm through his.

Then she thought a second and revised. "Arnold Carter from San Diego."

As if on cue, Arnold stepped over to Hastings and stuck out his hand. "How you do, man?"

Hastings shook his hand mumbling, "Nice to meet you."

"You Courtney's husband?" Arnold asked the obvious.

"Soon to be ex-husband," Courtney clarified.

"This your girlfriend?" Arnold asked, referring to the stricken Meghan.

"This is Meghan Morehead." Hastings introduced her. She smiled awkwardly and nodded hello. "And these are her sons, Travis and Taylor. Say hello, guys," he instructed.

"Hello," the boys said in quiet unison.

"Y'all come in." Arnold suddenly and inappropriately assumed the role of host. "We got plenty of room in here and plenty of food too. I was wanting to meet Courtney's husband sometime."

"Soon to be ex-husband, Arnold," Courtney said again, trying to smile at Meghan. Then as an afterthought, she added, "Arnold's right. Hastings, you and Meghan come in and make yourselves comfortable. We might as well practice civility, right? People get divorced all the time. Doesn't mean we can't all be civil."

"What's that thing on your neck?" one of the boys asked Arnold.

"Dog collar," he said. "Spikes."

"Why you got on a dog collar?" he asked.

"I'm a Raider fan," he said. "You heard of the Raider Nation, haven't you? Why don't y'all get a plate and get you something to eat."

They looked at their mother, seeking the nod of her head, permission to go ahead. Instead she said, "We're not staying, boys. The box is already occupied."

Travis, the older boy, said, "They said we can stay. They don't care."

"We'll sit outside in the stands," Hastings announced. "It's a nice day to sit outside, guys."

"Why can't we just stay here?" Travis asked.

"Don't argue with Hastings, Travis," Meghan scolded.

The boy shrugged his shoulders and picked up a plate. His younger brother followed suit.

Hastings cleared his throat and turned to face Meghan. "Babe, why don't you take the boys and go ahead into the stands. I'll catch up with you in a few minutes."

Babe? Is that what Hastings called Meghan? Truely had never heard Hastings call Courtney *babe*. He resented it instinctively.

Meghan looked at Hastings with uncertainty, as though considering whether or not to do as he instructed.

"It's okay," he told her. "I need to talk to Courtney for a minute."

Clearly irritated, Meghan looked away from him then and did not make eye contact again as she rounded up the boys—but not before they each loaded a plate with chicken wings and a stack of brownies. "Right now, boys," she said, "I mean it. Let's go."

Courtney stood beside the door as they left. "I wish you'd reconsider," she told Meghan. "We'd be happy for you guys to stay."

"Maybe next time." Meghan was hurrying to leave, nudging the boys along.

After they made their exits Hastings stood awkwardly looking around the skybox in what almost seemed a mild state of confusion. He took off his glasses and cleaned them on a paper napkin, a gesture Truely recognized. It was what he thought of as Hastings' stalling-for-time routine.

It was Courtney who spoke up. "Meghan's boys are darling, Hastings."

"They're good kids," he agreed.

"Sorry if they're disappointed about not watching the game in the box."

"No," he said. "They'll have plenty of chances to do that."

"Can I get you a drink?" Truely asked him. "Diet Coke?"

"No." He glanced at Arnold, looked at him for more than a few seconds. "How did you say you guys met?" he asked.

"It's a long story." Courtney smiled at Arnold.

"I'd like to hear it," Hastings said. "Sometime."

"Arnold is working downtown. He's been staying at Truely's," she explained.

"Roommates," Truely said sarcastically.

"Your wife been torturing me — oops, I mean tutoring me," Arnold volunteered. "She trying to instill in me what she like to call *the love of learning*. Right, Courtney? If it don't kill me I might get to like it."

She chuckled. "Something like that."

"I see." Hastings looked at his watch, then put his hands in his pockets, decidedly uncomfortable. "Look, Courtney, you think we could talk a minute?"

"Now?" She seemed startled.

"Maybe outside? Could we step out into the hall for a minute?"

She looked at Truely and Arnold — as if seeking their permission.

"If y'all about to get into some drama, then yes, I wish you would step out into the hall there," Arnold said. "Me and Truely trying to watch the game in here. We got money riding on this game."

"A dollar," Truely clarified.

"It ain't about the money. It's about team pride," Arnold insisted.

"Okay, then," Courtney said. "I guess we could talk outside. Just for a minute."

Hastings looked relieved. He put his hand on Courtney's back the way he used to do when they were happily married and he escorted her through a doorway. "Good to see you, Truely," he said. "Nice to meet you, Andy."

"It's Arnold," Arnold said. "Arnold Carter," he repeated.

After Hastings and Courtney retreated to the hall, Arnold and

Truely took their food and sat in the leather swivel seats in front
of the glass wall overlooking the field. They turned their attention back to the game. Truely had a cold beer in his hand and
balanced hot dogs and pasta salad on his lap. The Forty-niners
were moving the ball. The O line was looking good.

"So that's Courtney's husband?" Arnold was dipping chicken
wings into ranch dressing.

"That's Hastings," Truely said.

"He don't look like I was expecting."

"Hastings is all right."

"Thought he might be better-looking. He's a little bit on the
thin side."

"He's a runner. Sort of a health freak."

"You like his girlfriend, that Meghan?"

"She seems all right."

"She got some good kids," Arnold offered.

"Yep. You going to use that napkin right there?"

Arnold handed the napkin to Truely. "She might be nice
enough," Arnold concluded. "But she's no Courtney though."

Truely agreed, as he shoveled the last bite of hot dog into his
mouth. "Only one of those."

Arnold was quiet for a while, distracted by a Raiders goal-line
stand, then he said, "What you guess make a man let go a woman
like Courtney—and then turn around and take up with a woman
like Meghan?"

"I couldn't tell you," Truely said.

"Shauna used to say she was the opposite of your wife. Said
you went from one extreme to the other like that."

Truely half-choked on his swig of beer. "Shauna said that?"

"She did. Is it true?"

Truely wiped his mouth. "Shauna wouldn't lie. But she might
exaggerate."

Arnold grinned.

The Raiders threw two incomplete passes and suffered a sack.
Special teams ran onto the field to punt. It wasn't looking good
for the Raiders offense.

"You guess Courtney was just too much for Hastings?" Arnold asked. "He's an older dude. You guess Hastings just got worn out?"
"Could be."
"Ask me, she could do a lot better anyway."
"I'm sure she'll be real happy to hear that," Truely said.

FROM WHERE THEY SAT in the skybox Truely and Arnold could see Meghan and her boys sitting out in the stands. More than a few times they saw Meghan stand up and look in the direction of the skyboxes, as if searching for Hastings. Courtney and Hastings stood talking in the hall for a long time. When Courtney didn't come back in a half hour, Arnold took it upon himself to walk out into the hall and look for her. Sure enough, she and Hastings were standing in a little huddle of their own, talking quietly. Courtney seemed mad, but obviously not mad enough to walk away and come back into the skybox and watch the game—which was what Arnold told Truely she should do.

When forty-five minutes had passed Truely saw Meghan dial her cell phone. Hastings shouldn't let her sit out there with her boys not knowing where he was or when he was coming to join them. It irked Truely on Meghan's behalf. This time he walked out into the hall, spotted Hastings, who seemed deep in explanatory mode, and called out. "Hastings, I think Meghan is looking for you. You need to answer your phone, man."

Hastings looked embarrassed. Immediately he fished in his pocket for his phone and checked his messages.

"Everything okay?" Truely asked Courtney.

"No," she said. "Of course not."

"There's a game going on in here," he said. "In case you're interested."

"You're right," she said. "I'm coming."

Truely waited in the hall while Courtney whispered something to Hastings, then turned and walked back to the skybox. "Sorry," she said.

From the box vantage point Truely saw Hastings make his way down the bleachers to where Meghan and the boys sat. Instead of looking annoyed when Hastings finally appeared, he thought Meghan looked relieved to see him. Hastings wove his way down the crowded row of people, sat next to Meghan and put his arm around her. She put her head on his shoulder for a few seconds. Then Hastings leaned forward and spoke to the boys, who smiled and nodded yes. In no time they had come to look like any happy family anywhere.

Courtney poured herself a glass of wine and sat in a swivel chair looking out over the crowd. "Who's winning?" Her indifference was unmistakable.

"What'd he want to talk to you about?" Arnold asked.

"Arnold?" Courtney said. "That's personal."

"You not going to tell us what he said?" He seemed incredulous.

"She's trying to tell us it's none of our business," Truely said.

"I make it my business," he said. "I want to know what the man said."

Courtney laughed. "Arnold, good heavens."

"I know you want to tell us," Arnold insisted.

"No, I don't," she insisted.

"Listen at that," he said to Truely. "Don't you hate it when a woman lie?"

They left midway through the fourth quarter because the score was 33–6 and it appeared the Raiders had no chance of making a comeback. Besides Truely wanted to try to beat the traffic. He had what Courtney referred to as traffic issues. He would admit it too. As they exited through the raucous crowd Arnold commented, "Check this out, man. Raiders celebrate better when they lose a damn game than the whiners do when they win one!"

"They're not celebrating," Truely said. "They're trick-or-treating!"

COURTNEY WAS QUIET, lost in her own thoughts. On the drive home she barely spoke a word. But the thing that surprised Truely most was her announcement when they got back to the loft that she was going to drive to Saratoga that night. She had never left for home on Sunday night.

"What about our study time?" Arnold asked. "You skipping out on me?"

"You said you finished Malcolm X," she said. "Start a new book on tape."

"Never thought you'd be letting me off the hook," Arnold said. "But I ain't complaining."

"What's the big hurry?" Truely asked. "What is there that can't wait until tomorrow?"

"I just need to check in with Myra. Lola is there for the weekend too. She goes back to school tomorrow. I want to see her before she goes."

"Naw," Arnold said. "This got to do with that Hastings, don't it?"

"No," she said. "I just need to go home and take care of some things."

"That's what I'm talking about. You taking care of Hastings."

"Arnold, you have some wild imagination." Courtney handed him her canvas bag. "Carry this down to the car for me, will you?"

"You got something up your sleeve." Arnold took the bag from her. "That's what my grandmama like to say. You ain't fooling us."

"Church." Courtney's voice sounded oddly emotional. "I haven't been to church in a while. Hastings and Meghan have been going to church nearly every Sunday and taking the boys with them — to my church — our church — Hastings and my church — but they never see me there because I haven't been going. I've been here instead — hanging out with the two of you."

"Why don't you just say so then?"

"Just for your information — both of you — there is more to Sundays than pro football or fishing," Courtney said.

"You can't go to church until next Sunday, Court — that's a week away. So how does your driving home tonight address any of this?" Truely asked.

"Maybe it doesn't."

"You're feeling guilty because you've been missing church? Is that it?"

"Among other things," she said.

Truely walked her down to her car. He wasn't sure what was bothering Courtney really. He assumed she would talk about it when she was ready—and not before. So for the time being, he let it go.

THAT NIGHT when Truely and Arnold were camped out as usual, the TV blaring precious little actual news of the war but lots of useless talk, talk, talk about it, Arnold spoke up, interrupting Truely's train of thought. "Courtney got a lot of secrets," he said.

"You think so?" Truely was only half listening.

"I know so, man. She got me in on a couple of her secrets."

"Is that right?"

"When she told you she took me down to San Jose—remember, she said she had to pick up a chair she got reupholstered, right? She act like she needed me to load it into the car for her, right?"

"I remember something about that."

"You know what else we done?"

"What?"

"We went out to Silver Creek golf course out there, right? She drove me by your wife's house out there."

"Just call her Jesse, Arnold. She hasn't been my wife in a long time."

"Right. Sorry. Okay, so we drive down to the clubhouse, where they were just winding up her kid's birthday party. Jesse, your former wife, I guess she invited Courtney, because she had a present for the kid. She had one for the new baby too. So it wasn't pure coincidence, us going by there."

This caught Truely off guard. So Jesse had had her baby. He'd lost track. And her oldest girl was over three now. That was easy enough to figure out. Courtney hadn't mentioned to him having seen Jesse or her children. Why would she omit something like that? "Go on," he said to Arnold.

"Well, they chat it up, man. Two women, you know. I just say hello and Courtney tell her I'm staying here with you. Then, you know, your wife ask Courtney about her divorce from Hastings and they go off on that subject."

"I bet," Truely said.

"She got cute kids," Arnold said. "The baby is happy for being so little. She never hardly cry."

Truely was more interested in this than he really wanted to be. "Jesse sends me a Christmas card," he said. "Usually a picture of her daughter—now it'll be both her daughters, I guess."

"She pretty nice seems like, your wife—I mean Jesse."

"How was she?" Why was Truely asking Arnold this? How would Arnold possibly know how Jesse was doing?

"You mean how do she look? She look pretty good—in a plain kind of way. She sort of pretty I guess."

"She's beautiful, Arnold," Truely corrected. "I guess you're too young to see that."

"I sort of see that, man," Arnold said. "But you know, Shauna, she's good-looking. Nothing plain about Shauna. She fix herself up a little more."

"Jesse doesn't need to fix herself up," Truely said.

"Okay then. I didn't know you still got a thing going on for your wife."

"What else?" It was pathetic, his sudden longing for information about Jesse and this life she was living without him.

"She invited us back over to her house after the birthday party. She got a big house, man. You seen it?"

"I bought it." Truely spoke before he could stop himself. Why did he say that? It wasn't true. Snoop.com bought it for her. Their division of common property bought it for her. She deserved it too. What was wrong with him?

"What?" Arnold asked.

"Nothing. Big house, you were saying."

"She got a pool. She got rooms everywhere you look. It's nice."

"Not nicer than this place?" he joked. "I know that can't be right."

"You want to hear this or not?" Arnold asked.

"Sure, go ahead."

"She asked Courtney lots of questions about you. How's True-ly doing? She know all about Shauna and Pablo. I guess Court-ney already told her that story. She say Shauna is a fool—so it's clear she don't have a high opinion of Shauna. Then she also said somebody named Melissa—who's Melissa?—tried to set you up with a new woman, but you didn't like her."

"That's not true. That's ridiculous."

"I think Courtney and Jesse talk on the phone sometimes or something. It wasn't like they're two strangers. On the way home Courtney tells me, 'No need to mention to Truely that we saw Jesse today. It would only upset him.'"

"She said that?"

"She said it."

"Do I look upset to you? I don't know what she's talking about."

"So now, see, she got me keeping one of her secrets."

"But you're not keeping it, are you? Because you're telling me right now."

"Seems like you should know. No secrets between friends, right? Besides you need to know I ain't the only one around here who don't tell everything I know. Courtney don't either."

"What is my sister up to now?" Truely wondered aloud.

"She got a lot of secrets, man. That's what I'm telling you."

"Women like secrets." Truely sounded almost bitter. "But I don't. Not mine. Not hers. Not anybody's."

"Me neither, man. My mama put me to the test on keeping her secrets until I finally had to quit it. She get me arrested trying to keep her secrets. So don't you tell me nothing you don't want Courtney to know, because I tell her the truth same as I do you."

"Good enough," Truely said.

Twenty-three

IT WOULD BE A LIE to say he was eagerly looking forward to it, but at least he wasn't actively dreading it. He'd gone to the gym earlier that afternoon, and when he got home Arnold was back from work, hunched over a stack of worksheets Courtney had left him, eating a bowl of cereal, the TV blaring the six o'clock news loud enough for the hard of hearing. Truely showered and dressed in jeans and a clean shirt. He was meeting Lanie at a coffee shop a few blocks away. A cup of coffee seemed pretty harmless.

On his way out the door he said, "Arnold, when you finish up there how about running the dishwasher, okay? And you got a load of wet towels in the washer. You need to run them though the washer again before you put them in the dryer — otherwise they'll smell."

"I got it," Arnold said. "Where you going?"

"Going out for a cup of coffee. Won't be too long."

"Oh," Arnold said. "With that lady that been calling you?"

"She called once. And yes. With her."

WHEN HE GOT TO THE COFFEE SHOP he found a couple of comfortable upholstered chairs by the front window. It occurred to him he might not remember what Lanie looked like, having only seen her that one time at Jaxon's house and having been so annoyed at the time he had barely even made eye contact. He picked up a crumpled *New York Times* somebody had left on the next table and began to scan it. He was absorbed in an article about the opium trade in Afghanistan when he heard his name spoken. He looked up and Lanie was standing there looking at him quizzically. "Is that you?"

"Afraid so." He stood up and smiled. She was smaller than he remembered, with medium-length straight brown hair and great skin. She looked like an East Coast woman to him, Ivy League maybe, but he couldn't say why for sure. Her energy maybe. She appeared to be a woman who managed to get a lot done every day—a quiet, go-getter type. Californians got things done too, but they just weren't in the same hurry to do it. He imagined himself jotted down on Lanie's to-do list. *Have coffee with that guy, Truely Noonan. See if he has rehabbed himself at all.*

"I'm glad you could come," she said. "I wasn't sure you would."

"Not every day a guy gets a do-over."

They ordered coffee. She drank regular coffee, medium. For some reason he liked that. In the chic San Francisco coffee culture, which had established an entire pretentious language for ordering something as simple as a cup of coffee, she simply wanted a regular, medium. Right off the bat that seemed pretty promising to Truely.

Lanie seemed relaxed which helped him relax too. She also seemed more devoted to being interested in him than in trying to be interesting herself. And yet, clearly she was interesting. She told him she had had a sister who died of a rare blood disease when she was a child. The death of her sister had left Lanie an only child—one who went to sleep every night with her dead sister's empty bed beside her own. She had had fabulous parents, she said. Nobody in the world ever had better parents. They lived in Phoenix now, retired. She loved them like crazy, she said. She had chosen to work in the medical world because of her sister—but she had never wanted to be a doctor or a nurse, so she made her contribution to the world of children's health with an MBA instead, raising big money for specific medical institutions and causes. It had evolved into a highly lucrative career—and yet, unlike so many people who had made good money, she said, she never felt she had sold out.

While they talked Truely began to unwind in a way he hadn't in a long time. He liked Lanie just enough to open up a little and answer the questions she asked. She wasn't trying to probe. She was just being a pleasant, thoughtful conversationalist. He sensed this and so he trusted her with some of the shabby details of his personal story. She knew his professional story already, partly from Jaxon and Melissa, but also because she had Googled him—which she readily admitted. Why hadn't he Googled her? It never even occurred to him. He wondered if she would be offended to know he hadn't bothered to Google her. Was going un-Googled an insult these days? He guessed that was another aspect of the new world of singles he found himself awkwardly navigating—or not navigating. It ranked right up there with ordering a cup of coffee using a string of five or six prescribed adjectives. When he wasn't looking, dating as he had once known it had become a far more elaborate game with a whole set of new rules—and he didn't really know what those rules were anymore. The whole prospect just made him feel tired. Besides, for all he really knew Lanie might just be working him for a sizable donation to the medical foundation she represented. And if she was—he would be happy to make one too. He could use the clarification.

The thing about Lanie that almost made him nervous was that she reminded him just slightly of Jesse. Not her looks, really. It was more that she had that same zeal to do good. That drive to leave her corner of the world a better place than she found it. He was attracted to people like that. Always had been.

Almost two hours to the minute after arriving at the coffee shop, Lanie began to check her watch, put on her sweater, gather her keys and sunglasses. She fished her wallet out of her purse. "I'll get this," she insisted. "My treat."

Back in Mississippi his daddy had taught him that a man never let a lady pay—and he had started out sharing that sentiment. But this was California. Sometimes here, the woman who issued the invitation picked up the tab. So he didn't argue.

Before they parted ways, Lanie said, "Thanks for coming.

You're a nice guy, Truely. Nice guys—well." She didn't finish her sentence. "This was fun," she said, "but I won't be calling you again. The ball is in your court now—or not. But don't worry. Either way, I'm fine with it."

What? Was she issuing him a disclaimer? *Either you do or you don't,* she was saying—*either way you don't have the power to hurt or disappoint me. I won't let you.*

"I understand." He helped her with her jacket and kissed her cheek. He didn't say *I'll call you*—he had no idea whether or not he ever would. "You take care," he said instead.

She waved as she left to walk to her car. He didn't see her to her car. It was clear she didn't expect him to. Instead he walked to a nearby Subway and bought a couple of sandwiches for a late supper for Arnold and himself, then headed home. His plan was to Google Lanie Brokaw first chance he got.

But when he arrived back at the loft he had a surprise waiting. Arnold had strung what Truely would later determine to be fishing line from several beams in the loft and he had pinned up, with old-fashioned wooden clothespins, white bedsheets which hung like a homemade tent apparatus in one center section of the loft. It took Truely a few seconds to comprehend what he was seeing.

"What you think?" Arnold asked him. "You like it?"

"What the hell is it?" Truely asked.

"I made myself a little room. For privacy. I wanted to hang blankets, so you couldn't see through so easy, but I didn't have no heavy enough rope. But this is pretty good. Now you don't have to be looking at me every minute. I can go in my room and sort of leave you alone."

"And vice versa, no doubt," Truely said. He didn't know whether to laugh or be irritated. "Good thing Shauna's not here," he found himself saying. "She would have a fit. She always says the space tells you what it needs—but I doubt she would believe it told you it needed sheets hanging everywhere."

"It like walls," Arnold defended himself. "Only temporary."

"I get it," Truely said.

"Look." Arnold demonstrated. "You can pull this one over, like this"—he gave it a gentle yank—"and it will open for watching TV and whatnot. But when I sleep, then"—he yanked it back—"I can close it up. See?"

"Genius," Truely said sarcastically.

"Courtney will hate it too, right?"

"Definitely."

"But she don't actually live here, right?"

"Technically speaking—no."

"And I do."

Truely half laughed. "It does seem that way."

"So you don't care then?"

"I'll reserve judgment," Truely said. "Let's go with it for tonight and see what we think in the morning. But I have to tell you right off the bat I'm not crazy about a circus tent in the middle of my house."

"Maybe you get used to it," Arnold suggested.

"You hungry?" Truely slung the Subway sack on the kitchen counter. "I brought some supper."

Arnold went to the kitchen to investigate. "So how was your coffee?"

"Fine."

"You like that lady?"

"She's nice."

ARNOLD HAD FALLEN ASLEEP ensconced in his makeshift tent, listening to an audiobook. Truely was drifting off with the TV still blabbing away—a habit hard for him to break. It was his longing for the human voice coupled with his innate ability not to listen that made this such an excellent sleep-inducing technique. He was almost asleep when the phone rang. Not his cell—or Arnold's. But the house telephone, which rarely ever rang. He untangled himself from the bedsheets and went to get the phone. "Truely Noonan," he mumbled.

"Truely? This Suleeta here."

"Suleeta?" The surprise in his voice appeared to wake Arnold. The sheet walls began to stir and shift.

"You said call you with the news, yes?"

"Of course."

"I tell Shauna to call you, but nobody can tell Shauna anything no more."

Truely would have to think about that remark later. "That's okay, Suleeta. I'm glad you're calling now."

"I think she never tell you when they bring Gordo to Washington, DC. They have him at Walter Reed for almost a month now. He's very serious. No visitors except family. Shelly and Trey, they drive me all the way to Baltimore to see him. It was a long trip—very terrible. Gordo suffering too much. He's not glad to see us. He tell us to go home. We just pray."

"Sorry, Suleeta. I know that's hard."

"Very terrible," she said again. "They bringing him to San Diego. We got the papers from the government. Shauna is upset. She don't want him to go to San Diego VA Hospital. She want him to go to San Antonio. She say San Antonio have much better rehabilitation. But Jerry and me, we think Gordo need to be close to home. He need his family."

"I see," Truely said.

"They fly him to the hospital here on Friday—on a U.S. military plane."

"That's good news then, I guess."

"Yes," she said. "Is Arnold still there with you?"

"He is. Just a minute." Truely covered the phone and said, "Arnold, get up, man. It's Suleeta. She wants to talk to you. She says they're bringing Gordo back to California."

Arnold was already awake. Some nights he liked to sleep with a wave cap or a nylon stocking on his head to keep his hair from going nappy, as he explained it. He stumbled to the phone wearing a pair of Truely's boxers and a ripped T-shirt. "Everything okay?" He whispered the question to Truely.

"Here, talk to her." Truely handed him the phone.

Arnold took the phone hesitantly, like someone who understood that the telephone was invented primarily for the purpose of delivering bad news. "Hello?" he said quietly.

Truely stood nearby but could not hear the conversation. He simply heard Arnold utter a series of single words, "Fine. Good. Yeah. Really? Okay. Sure. Yeah. All right. When? Yeah. Yeah. Maybe. Okay," and then Arnold handed the phone back to him. "She wants to talk to you."

"I tell Arnold that Gordo asked for him," Suleeta said. "He don't ask for nobody—but he asks for Arnold."

"Good," Truely said.

"Maybe you can bring Arnold back home then? Is it too much trouble?"

"We'll work it out," Truely said. "Sure."

"Also Truely…" Suleeta paused. "I'm sorry for your trouble with Shauna. Pablo too. I hope it don't turn you against the Mackey family."

It was an awkward subject. "No," he said. "Of course not."

"It might help Gordo to see Arnold. It might encourage him, yes?"

"Yes," he agreed.

"So you bring Arnold back home then?"

"Of course. We'll come whenever you say."

After Truely hung up he and Arnold were stunned into near silence. Arnold finally said, "We been waiting for Gordo to come home. Now here he come." He got a glass of water at the kitchen sink and went back into his tent, pulling the sheets closed.

Truely had no idea how long it took Arnold to go back to sleep, but in his case it was nearly morning before he was finally able to drift off.

THEY AWOKE to Truely's cell phone ringing. He slapped for it on the bedside table. "Damn," he whispered, knocking the phone to the floor. When he finally managed to grab and silence it, he barked into the receiver, "What?"

"Truely, it's Shauna."

He sat up in bed like a man jabbed with a cattle prod. "Hey," he managed to mumble.

"I'm sorry to call so early. Mama just told me she called you last night. I wish she hadn't done that, Truely. I specifically asked her not to."

He remained silent. He had no idea what to say. But the awkward silence only served to urge her on. "There is no need for you to get involved in our family issues, especially after—you know—what happened. I know I should have been the one to tell you about Pablo, Truely, and I was going to, but Mama beat me to it. She had no right to speak for me. And she has no right to pull you into this now." Shauna sounded genuinely distraught.

"I'm not pulled into it," he said flatly. "Suleeta thinks it would help Gordo to see Arnold. That's why she called."

"I disagree," Shauna said sternly.

"With what?" Truely was losing his way in the apparent antagonism of the conversation.

"I don't think it would be good for Gordo to see Arnold. I think Arnold is the last person in the world Gordo needs to see right now."

Truely was taken aback, unsure how to respond. "Why?" he asked.

"Mama has always had a soft spot for Arnold. But just because you have a rotten childhood doesn't mean you're a good person just waiting for a chance. That's what Mama thinks. But the truth is Arnold is trouble, Truely. Mama probably failed to mention all the trouble Arnold has caused us—well, caused Gordo. And therefore all of us. He's a little con man, Truely. In case you haven't figured that out."

Across the room, Arnold's tent was trembling and twisting. He stuck his head out from behind the sagging sheet. "Who is that?" he asked.

"Nobody," Truely answered. It was instinct on his part—to lie.

"Truely, are you listening?" Shauna asked.

"Sorry," he said. "Can you tell me the purpose of your call?" He was trying to sound businesslike because he knew Arnold was curious and listening hard.

"The purpose of my call"—Shauna sounded highly irritated by the way he had phrased the question—"is to tell you not to bring Arnold to San Diego. Mama should not have asked you to. It would be a mistake all around. So, if you really care about Gordo, then you'll just stay out of this. Believe me when I tell you the two of you showing up will only make matters worse."

"How is that possible?"

"There is history here, Truely. Did Arnold tell you he was arrested a couple of years back? That he went to juvenile detention?"

"He told me." But the truth was he had barely mentioned it—and Truely knew none of the details. He had never bothered to ask Arnold about it either.

"He stole money from Mackey's Construction, Truely, a sizable amount, and then lied about it. He tried to blame Gordo. But they had him on surveillance tape—it showed the whole thing. He didn't know Daddy had installed a video camera system on the property. If he'd been a little older he probably would have done prison time. Mama and Gordo forgave him—they always feel sorry for him. Poor Arnold. But Daddy and I never will. He's used this family enough—caused us enough heartache. And now thanks to Mama he's using you the same way."

"I'll have to get back to you on this." Truely sounded oddly detached, even to himself.

"You don't need to get back to me, Truely. You just need to tell Mama you're not coming and you're not bringing Arnold."

"I'll get back to you," he repeated. By this time Arnold was up and obviously listening while he looked through the refrigerator for something to call breakfast. "I'll call you later," Truely said again.

This time Shauna seemed to understand. "Is Arnold there with you? Is he listening?"

"Possibly."

"Truely, I don't care if he knows it's me. I don't care if he hears what I'm saying to you. It's all true. He knows it's true too."

"I see."

"I'm not trying to be hateful, Truely. I'm trying to be help-ful—to Gordo."

"I know you've been through a lot."

"You don't know," she said. "You don't. You have no idea."

"I'll have to call you back."

"Don't bother." She hung up the phone.

Truely let out a long involuntary whistle. "Whewwww," he said.

Arnold was standing at the kitchen counter, pouring Cheerios into a bowl. "Who was that?" he asked again.

"Nobody you know," Truely said. Lie number two.

"Even if I don't know them, I still want to know who was it."

"Why? What does it matter?"

"Because you lying. You don't want to tell me who it was—and that make me really need to know all the more."

"I don't ask you who it is every time your phone rings, do I?"

"You ain't me though. I got the need to know. I know it's some-body that knows me because I heard you say my name."

"Maybe you should become a lawyer," Truely said. "Or a damn detective."

"Maybe I will too, if I ever pass the GED Courtney so crazy about."

"Not if—*when*," Truely corrected. "It's a shame that the need to know is not the same as the love of learning."

"What?"

"Nothing."

"So just tell me then—who was it?"

This was why Truely hated secrets. They were like mosquitoes, swarming, swarming, circling your head, biting, just annoying the hell out of you. There was no way he could keep this secret for long. So why waste time trying? "It was Shauna," he said.

"I thought so." Arnold poured milk on his cereal. He grabbed a banana and was searching the drawer for a knife. "Shauna don't like me."

"I gathered that." If he was going with honesty—then by damn, he'd go with it. "You want to tell me why?"

"She thinks I stole some money from the Mackey business office."

"Did you?"

"Yes." He scooped a spoonful of cereal into his mouth.

"Then she thinks right?"

"She don't know the whole story. Wouldn't believe it if she knew."

"Did you try to tell her the whole story?"

"Part of it."

"Why just part of it? Why not all of it?"

"It make Gordo look bad."

"What are you saying, man?"

"I don't want to be talking about this," Arnold said. "Don't do no good to talk about it. It's done. I served my time in juvenile. Paid my dues like they said."

"What has Gordo got to do with this?"

"Gordo the best friend I ever had. Gordo try to look out for me when I was a messed-up kid running the streets. I owe Gordo big-time." Arnold was spooning cereal into his mouth as he talked.

"Okay," Truely said. "And what else?"

"Nothing else. That's all there is to say."

"What happened to no secrets among friends?" Truely asked.

"I got to get my shower and get out of here." Arnold turned up his cereal bowl and drank the last of the milk. "Ima be late, man."

"We're not through talking here, Arnold," Truely said. "You go ahead to your job. Just make sure you understand that this conversation is not over. We're going to finish this discussion right here. Count on it." His voice was stern in a way he didn't quite intend. It was the voice he sometimes used in a confrontational business setting. Jaxon referred to it as his take-no-prisoners tone. It was generally effective in the corporate world.

Arnold nodded and put his dishes in the dishwasher and went to the back bathroom, his office, to take a shower.

AFTER ARNOLD LEFT for the furniture warehouse, Truely called the attorney he had hired to defend Arnold's mother. As long as he was running a tab he might as well get some questions answered. "Look," Truely said when he got the guy on the phone, "as long as you're handling Keesha Carter's case, I'd like you to research her son's problems with the police. His name is Arnold Carter."

"DOB?" the attorney asked.

"Don't know," Truely said. "I think he's sixteen. Maybe seventeen. Some of his trouble involved Mackey's Construction — if that helps."

"I'll get his DOB from his mother," he said.

"Good. Maybe she can tell you Arnold's arrest history."

"Keesha Carter doesn't have a good relationship with the truth," he explained. "Besides, she lives her life like she never had any kids. She never mentions them. Her mother is the one who raised them."

"Ask his grandmother then," Truely suggested. "Maybe she knows."

"I'll get one of the clerks on this," he said. "I'll get back to you."

After Truely hung up the phone he had the feeling maybe he had taken the lid off something that was better left closed. On the other hand, one of the grave mistakes of his life was believing what people told him — because he usually wanted to. It was easier that way.

NEXT HE CALLED Shauna back. She answered the phone with the same abrupt tone she had used earlier. When she realized it was Truely she offered an explanation but not an apology. "I thought you were the Walter Reed medical officer calling back. He's been trying to avoid talking to me. He's a useless paper shuffler who calls himself a medical professional. He doesn't care what's best for Gordo—or anybody else. He's filling vacant slots. That's his job as he sees it, forcing square pegs into round holes. But that's a different battle."

"A different battle from this battle?" he asked.

"I've already made my feelings about Arnold clear," Shauna said.

"Funny, you never mentioned any of this to me before. You'd think maybe this might have come up at some point in the last few years, Shauna. I didn't ever hear Arnold's name spoken. And now it seems he's somehow at the center of this Mackey family crisis. I don't get it."

"I think we hoped Arnold was out of Gordo's life. He probably would be too, except that Mama keeps drawing him back in."

"She says Gordo is asking to see Arnold. That Arnold is the only person he's asked for."

"Good Lord, Truely. Gordo is not Gordo. He is not of sound mind. Do you understand what I'm saying here? He might just as well ask for Santa Claus or Satan or God knows who. Sometimes he makes no sense at all. Mama thinks she understands what he's saying, but she doesn't. She translates his jabber into requests that he isn't even capable of making."

Truely didn't respond.

After an awkward silence Shauna said, "Gordo might not even remember Arnold if he saw him. One minute he knows who he's talking to, the next he isn't sure. He's known Pablo most of his life, right? And sometimes now Pablo comes into his room and he has to introduce himself—like a total stranger, over and over, day after day. Gordo's memory comes and goes. You know how much Gordo weighs, Truely? A hundred and eighteen pounds. Less than I weigh. He's not himself. That's the point I'm trying to make."

"Look." Truely finally spoke. "I'm going to take Arnold down to San Diego when Suleeta calls. I promised her that. Once we get down there we'll decide whether or not it will be good for him to see Gordo. Okay? If we decide it's not the right thing, no problem, we'll leave and come back."

"I can't believe you're doing this, Truely. Is this your way of getting back at me? Is that it?"

"Come on, Shauna. I think you know me better than that. But maybe you don't."

"Please don't do this, Truely. Just stay out of it."

"Maybe you're right and Gordo doesn't know what he's asking for. I don't know. But if by some long shot he does—then I don't want to be the one who kept him from getting what he wanted. And besides..." Truely paused.

"Besides, what?" Shauna demanded.

"I don't know their history, granted. But I do know this—Arnold loves Gordo. I know that much."

Shauna's laugh was bitter and caustic. "God, Truely, you're such a fool."

"Yeah," he said. "I think that's been established."

DESPITE ALL THE DAMN DISTRACTIONS, this was going to be a good day. Nothing could ruin it. Truely had an afternoon meeting in San Jose. The latest prototype of their new product was being unveiled. Already it had been revised maybe a dozen times—including a new name. From Not Your Daddy's Desk, to Not Your Father's Work Space all the way to the Techno-Chair for a week or two. Now condensed to the tChair. Perfect. The renderings were pure space age, complete with red leather samples and imported Italian fabrics. The tempurpedic underpinnings conformed to your body shape, supported your lumbar region, and provided what was referred to as chiropractic comfort. The tChair rotated on a pedestal base. A twenty-two-inch computer screen tucked into the chair arm à la the tray table in the arm of an airline seat—along with a foldout lap keyboard. Movies, music, games, Internet, cell phone, whatever you needed, at your fingertips. The tChair leaned back into a reclining position for napping and included a sleek pull-down apparatus similar to what you saw on a baby stroller, so the occupant could sleep in privacy—with a fan to circulate and purify the air and provide the white noise of his choice—ocean waves, singing birds, quiet heartbeat. The tChair had push-button massage treatments, heat settings and vibration capabilities. Damn, Truely kept thinking, if only George Jetson could see this chair.

The exciting thing was that Truely and Jaxon were meeting with Global Airlines this afternoon—an emerging U.S.-China-owned company. They had invited them to the unveiling of the prototype tChair—and the implications were huge. Global Airlines was contemplating a savvy new fleet of business-class jets seating from 24 to 50 passengers on the commuter line and upwards of 100 to 300 on a new full-service line. They were doing a feasibility study on the possibility of using the tChair in place of the standard airline chair. There was a revolution at hand in the workplace—and if all went well, in the world of air travel too. And that might be just the beginning. It was invigorating for sure. Truely felt alive and totally competent in the work world. He was happiest when he was immersed in a go-for-broke project.

Courtney had teased him when he showed her the latest batch of sketches and enthusiastically described the chair's revised design and newest name. "The tChair? Would that be short for the Truely-Chair?" Now both she and Arnold fondly referred to the tChair as the Truely-Chair.

"How that Truely-Chair coming along?" Arnold asked from time to time.

ON HIS WAY over to San Jose he called Courtney to meet him for coffee. After her odd mood on Sunday he wanted to check and see how she was doing. She met him at a Starbucks on El Paseo. She arrived with a smile on her face, wearing jeans and a sequined T-shirt with the word Jose on it. She kissed him hello. "So today is the big day?"

"*One* of the big days," he corrected. "If things go well, there should be plenty of big days ahead." He handed her a cup of coffee. "I got you a low-fat latte, no kick."

They sat outside at a rickety bistro table. Traffic was lazy. The air was cool and crisp. "How's Arnold?" Courtney asked. Before he could respond she continued. "Have you noticed that about half the time Arnold wears your clothes, True? Your shirts and sweats. He even sleeps in your stuff."

"It's no problem." Truely had noticed, but had never minded.

"I'm thinking I'd like to take him shopping. Get him some new things. What do you think?"

"Suit yourself."

"Maybe I'll tie it into his GED thing." She sipped her coffee and made a face because it was too hot. "Arnold's smart, True. Really. He has some sort of reading thing, I think. He's a slow, deliberate reader. I'm no teacher, but I think he just hasn't read enough to be confident in his ability, you know? But his listening skills are off the chart. You tell him once — and he remembers. He knows it."

"He's no dummy," Truely agreed. "Although from what I gather he's done some pretty dumb shit in his past."

"Haven't we all?" Courtney mumbled.

"Looks like I'll be taking him down to San Diego pretty soon. Suleeta called. They're putting Gordo in a rehab hospital down there. And he's asking to see Arnold."

"That's great, isn't it?" She removed the lid from her coffee so it could cool.

"You'd think so, wouldn't you? But no."

"What do you mean?"

"Shauna called too. She doesn't want Arnold down there."

"You talked to Shauna?"

"More like she talked to me, I'd say. She made it clear Arnold was not welcome down there as far as she and Jerry are concerned. And Pablo too, I guess."

"Why not?"

"I've got a guy down in San Diego looking into that, checking out Arnold's arrest history. There was some trouble a while back. It seems he robbed the Mackeys. Did some time in juvenile. From what I gather it was not his first run-in with the law."

"Good Lord." Courtney blew into her coffee.

"I think there's more to the story. We're supposed to talk later. We'll see what Arnold has to say."

"Where is his mother, for heaven's sake?"

"That's another story, I'm afraid."

"What?" she asked.

"He wants to tell you himself. Next time you come up maybe."

"Lord, all this suspense and mystery."

"I know."

"So, little brother, how was talking to Shauna?"

"Okay."

"You feel anything—longing, regret, fury or anything?"

"Not really."

"Why do I bother asking?" she said. "You don't really miss her, do you?"

"How does a gentleman answer a question like that?" He was only half kidding. "I didn't bring enough to Shauna's party. I just never did. I can't say why. Suleeta was right, Shauna deserved somebody more...invested."

"And that would be Pablo?"

"Maybe. I hope so."

"Good grief, Truely."

"I know."

What Truely didn't say was that he missed the way Shauna had peopled his life for him. Holidays with her family. Outings with her clients and artsy friends. Weekends lazing around the loft, walking the dogs, cooking, watching TV. He wasn't sure what real contribution he had ever made to their relationship. The best he could figure it was as simple as willingness. He was willing. And for a while at least, she had seemed satisfied with that. Now that Shauna was gone, did he miss her? They had been more or less together for almost three years. He thought maybe what he really missed was the way she had kept him busy and not too bothered. Thanks to Shauna he'd been able to convince himself that he wasn't really lonely.

"Okay." Courtney interrupted his thoughts. "Do you want to hear about my conversation with Hastings?"

"Of course."

"In a nutshell, he's bought two sizable wooded lots less than a quarter mile from our present house—which will soon be my house, I guess. Or so he tells me. He and Meghan are building a place there. So—we'll all be neighbors. Nice, huh? He insists it's fundamentally a spec house that they *might* live in—*if* Meghan wants to—*if* it turns out as well as they expect, *if* things continue to move along the way it seems they are now."

"That's weird," Truely said. "You do know that's weird, right, Court? All the land in the Bay Area and he needs to be your neighbor—he and his girlfriend."

"I know," she said. "It's creepy and all that—but something is wrong with me, True, because I don't hate the idea."

"You will in time," he said. "You'll have no choice. It's twisted, that's why. What the hell is wrong with Hastings?"

"Is that a rhetorical question?" She smiled.

"Okay, what else?"

"Meghan and the boys have joined our church. I wasn't there the Sunday they joined. He thought somebody would tell me, but nobody did."

"Thus your meltdown last Sunday over missing church?"

"I guess. It's bad enough that I have to share Hastings with Meghan—but damn, do I have to share Jesus too?" She laughed unconvincingly.

"Hastings is a piece of work," Truely said. "Arnold thinks you can do better, by the way. He told me so."

"Sweet Arnold." Courtney smiled. "He's very sweet for a boy with criminal tendencies—isn't he?"

"So that's it for the Hastings report?" Truely checked his watch. He wanted to be at the Fairmont early, check to make sure everything was set up in the conference room and in good order.

~294~

He was meeting Jaxon and Melissa early to go over last-minute details.

"Well, there is one more thing, True. Bobby Gavin asked me out."

"What?"

"Bob Gavin. You know, he's been Hastings' good friend — maybe one of his best friends — for years. His wife died of uterine cancer a couple of years ago and he endowed a chair at Santa Clara in her honor — you know, Lillian Gavin Chair in Literature. We went to the ceremony. You played golf with him all those times at Cypress. Remember?"

"I know who Bobby Gavin is, for God's sake. Everybody knows who Bobby is."

"Then what's your question?"

"What is Bobby doing asking you out? Last I heard he was supposed to be Hastings' great buddy. Besides, as far as I know, you aren't divorced yet."

"Oh please." Courtney rolled her eyes.

"Really, Court. What are the rules these days? Best I can remember I didn't go out with any women until I had my official walking papers in my grubby little hands. What's the big hurry here?"

"You're teasing, right?"

"Not really."

"Lord, Truely. I'm not committing adultery. I'm going to dinner with an old friend. It's more than legal."

Truely's reaction had surprised him. He had spoken off the top of his head, without thinking. Courtney — Christian disciple, self-appointed spokeswoman for the moral police — did not need a lecture from the likes of him. That was for sure. You could count on Courtney to do the right thing. Even if she did the wrong thing, the style in which she did it made it seem like the right thing. "You're right," he said. "Of course."

"It's no big deal, True. Really."

"Does Hastings know?" he asked.

"If he doesn't" — she smiled — "he will."

ON TRUELY'S DRIVE HOME from San Jose that evening he was happy. The day had gone even better than expected, the meeting naturally propelling itself into late-afternoon drinks with the Global Airlines people and from there on to a lively dinner full of translated storytelling and laughter. Everyone had seemed caught up in the implications of a partnership. They were all high on the projections—even the numbers guys were signed on. It was stimulating and exciting. Melissa got teary at one point, so happy at the future prospects, so proud of Jaxon. It was a nearly perfect day.

There had been a time when Jesse had dreamed of having her own charter school. She had spent hours fantasizing about it and telling Truely how it would be operated—explaining the underlying philosophy that would make it maybe the best school in the world—or at least in the Bay Area. If this deal went through as it looked like it would, Truely would be in a position to fully finance a charter school, make Jesse's dream come true. But, of course, Jesse probably had a totally new dream by now. She was gone, after all. The charter school dream was gone with her. Truely was at peace with that. It just struck him that when it came to putting his money to good use she had always been the one with all the best ideas.

WHEN TRUELY GOT HOME Arnold was in his sheet tent talking on the phone. When he heard Truely come in the door, he poked his head out and gestured frantically to him. "Hold on a minute," he said, "Truely is just now coming in the door." He covered the receiver with his hand. "Man, guess who I been talking to here. Mose Jones. He's on the phone. For real."

Truely took the phone. "To what do I owe this honor?" he said.

"Whenever I start to need a shot of aggravation, then I just go on and call you," Mose said. But Mose was not one to call just for the sake of calling. He always had a reason for picking up the phone and Truely knew this. After covering the basics of civil discourse, catching up as is protocol, Mose got to the point—or in this case, points. "Three reasons for my call," he began. "One, I'm doing the Charger-Raider game in San Diego in a few weeks. I was thinking that afterward I might swing up there and see you. Talk a little business, maybe."

"What kind of business?" Truely was immediately interested.

"I'll explain when I see you," Mose said. "Got an idea I'd like to run by you."

"Come on then," Truely said. "We can always sling up a few more sheets."

"What?"

"We'll all look forward to it."

"I talked to your man Arnold. Nice kid."

"He's a fan for sure," Trucly said.

"It's done then," he said, "which leads me to the second reason for my call. Looks like you're going to be losing your renter down on the Hinds County place. Hinds County Organics hasn't exactly taken off like they were hoping. They'll be moving the farm to Baton Rouge at the end of the month—wanted to give you a heads-up."

"Good enough," Truely said.

"Which brings me to the real reason for my call," Mose said. "I wanted to let you know that Tay-Ann lost her husband."

Truely was totally disoriented. "Lost?" He had not seen or spoken to Tay-Ann since his mother was buried. Over the years he had gotten an occasional Christmas card from her with a family photo, but most years he hadn't.

"Heart attack," Mose said.

"I hate hearing that," Truely said.

"So you'll be in touch with Tay-Ann then?"

"Of course. I'll send something. You got funeral details?"

"The funeral is over, man. I was thinking maybe you could just pick up the phone and call her."

"She doesn't want to hear from me out of the blue," Truely said. "I haven't even seen her since my mother died."

"As I recall," Mose said, "Tay-Ann showed up at your mother's and your daddy's services. She didn't have to do that. I think you need to call her and offer your condolences. I think it's the least you can do, man — but maybe that's just me."

"Since when did you become Tay-Ann's front man?" Truely asked.

"Just because you stopped knowing her once you moved away doesn't mean I did. I see her at the Gem all the time. She's good people."

"I believe you," Truely said. "I'll call her if you think it will help. Not sure what I'll say. I never knew her husband. Don't even know his name."

"Raymond DeLease was his name. He was a good guy too. A hell of a good guy. He was only forty-four — and *wham*, out of nowhere, gone. Tay-Ann is struggling, True. She will be for a good while. Got two kids in high school. No warning. Ray was working late. Tay-Ann gets worried when Ray doesn't come home from the office and doesn't answer her calls. She's getting in her car to drive over to his office when the police come to the house — she sees them come up the drive and she just knows. The janitor found him slumped over his desk. Dead."

"That's bad," Truely said. "I'll call her. Give me her number."

"Just for old times' sake," Mose said.

"For old times' sake," Truely agreed.

"WHAT'S WRONG?" Arnold asked when Truely hung up the phone. "Somebody die?"

"The husband of an old friend."

"He get shot?"

"No, he didn't get shot."

"Car wreck?"

"No."

"Plane crash?"

"Plane crash? What is this—twenty questions? The man had a heart attack."

"Sorry," Arnold said.

It was obvious to Truely that Arnold didn't associate death with natural causes. He associated death with catastrophic events—something he knew a good bit more about.

Twenty-four

ON THE FOLLOWING SUNDAY, after church, Courtney drove into the city because her breast lift was scheduled for Tuesday morning. Despite his best efforts Truely had not been able to dissuade her. He wasn't happy about it either. It would not work for Arnold to go with them to the surgery center. In matters of her breasts Courtney preferred a modicum of privacy. Truely planned to drive her, wait for her to have the procedure and then drive her home to Saratoga, where Myra would look after her the best she could—with the help of Lola. In time, when Courtney was well enough, she would pick up where she left off, driving over to San Francisco, riding herd on Arnold, prodding him toward his high school equivalency, cooking enough food for an army. Her secret would be safe.

To be honest, Truely was worried about what she might decide to have done next. How many aging body parts did your average woman have? Even though Truely didn't believe in cosmetic surgery, he was committed to seeing Courtney through this reckless act of impaired judgment—in hopes that it would be her last.

COURTNEY WAS MAKING enchilada casserole while Truely and Arnold sat at the kitchen island and watched. Arnold had already told her about his in-person conversation with Mose Jones, which had led Truely to tell her about Tay-Ann's husband's untimely death. Truely had called Tay-Ann earlier, just as Mose thought he should, and she had seemed more than surprised to hear from him. When he expressed his condolences she became very emotional, actually sobbing into the phone. Truely had been at a loss then, not knowing what to say—and the conversation, however well meaning, quickly became unbearably awkward. He hardly remembered what he'd said to offer comfort except that he had found himself suggesting that she should think about bringing her kids and coming out to San Francisco for a little sightseeing—a healthy distraction. Maybe a change of scenery would help them all deal with their sorrow, he'd said—a break from seeing their husband/father everywhere they looked in Hinds County. None of them had ever been to California. He had just invited them because he was at a total loss to know what else to do.

ARNOLD'S PHONE HAD BEEN RINGING on and off all evening. Often he checked the caller's name and turned off the ringer, ignoring the call. "Who is that?" Courtney asked. "Vonnie?"

"I'll call her back later," he said. "We already talked three times today. She have her way, we just talk all day long. I'd never get nothing done."

So when his phone interrupted the evening once again, Arnold glanced at it, mumbled, "Who's this?" Truely could see him trying to decide whether or not to answer a call from an unknown caller. Already Truely had learned that Arnold had a certain fear of the phone to start with. He watched him waver before finally answering. "Who is it?" he barked.

The expression on his face totally changed. He stood up from the stool where he'd been seated and glanced at Truely and Courtney, then lowered his head the way he did when he was signaling them not to listen, knowing that they had no real choice but to listen after a signal like that. "I'll take this in my office," he said and hurried to the bathroom at the back of the loft.

He was gone barely a minute or two before he came back with a startled, nervous expression. "You ain't gon believe who that was," he began, shaking his head. "That was Gordo, man. Said he borrowed a phone from somebody at the VA Hospital. He didn't sound good. He sort of scare me the way he was talking. Said he needs to see me. Wants me to come down there to San Diego."

"When?" Truely asked.

"Now," Arnold said.

TRUELY HAD STEELED himself for this moment. He methodically called his secretary to reschedule his appointments. He called Suleeta to alert her that they would be coming down. She cried when she heard his voice on the phone. "Gracias, True," she said. "Gracias."

As they began to organize for the trip, Arnold raked through his pile of dirty clothes. "You think you can wash some of this stuff for me while I'm gone?" he asked Courtney.

"I'm going with you guys," she said.

"It's not necessary, Court," Truely told her. "We don't know what we'll find when we get there or how long we'll stay."

"I'm going," Courtney said. "Don't even try to talk me out of it."

Truely noticed when Courtney stepped out on the terrace and called her surgeon to postpone her procedure. She didn't think twice. She spent the rest of the night doing laundry so Truely and Arnold would have clean clothes to pack.

Arnold was totally distracted. "Gordo talking crazy," he said to no one in particular. "Ain't no telling what going on in his head."

They had planned to leave early the next morning for the long drive down to San Diego. But none of them could really sleep, so by four a.m. they were up and loading the car. Well before sunup Truely eased the loaded Escalade out of the underground garage. He was just about to pull out into the street when Arnold shouted, "Wait, man. I forgot something. I got to go back inside."

"Whatever it is, you don't need it." Truely sounded oddly like his own daddy, who used to hate to stop the car for any reason once he embarked on a trip of any minor description.

"Be right back." Arnold leaped from the car, leaving the door hanging open. "Wait right here." He bounded down to the garage elevator before they could stop him.

"What in the world?" Courtney said.

Minutes later Arnold returned, carrying his backpack, waving some audiobook CDs in his hand. "Don't want to go nowhere without Malcolm and them," he said sarcastically. "Courtney got me where I can't get to sleep without some time listening to one these fool CDs. She got me addicted or something." He slung the backpack on the floor of the backseat and climbed in. "Okay, man, we can hit the road now."

TRUELY'S PLAN was to take Highway 101 and then cut across to Fresno and pick up Highway 5. It would be a desolate trip through miles of agricultural terrain. Ordinarily Truely loved this drive, loved seeing the manicured farms, the crops, the migrant workers bent over in the fields, the gleaming machinery moving at caterpillar speed. The cotton, corn and soybean fields reminded him of the Mississippi fields from his childhood. He had grown up still seeing cotton picked by hand on the smaller farms—like the one where his daddy had been raised. More than once his daddy had taken Truely to the cotton fields to show him the right way to pick a boll. His daddy had been proud of his family's failed efforts to farm cotton. He always spoke of their moving off the farm with great regret and heartache. So whenever Truely drove to Fresno he thought of these moments with his daddy and took comfort in the memories.

But this night they traveled in darkness, balancing Styrofoam cups of bitter Circle K coffee. There was little to see except the intrusive headlights of the occasional passing car. Courtney rode shotgun, trying to manage the music—much of which she disapproved of. "Lord, True, where is your country music?" she asked. "What? No Alan Jackson CDs? No Vince Gill? No Garth Brooks? I could have sworn you were once a Mississippi boy."

"Maybe I've evolved—musically speaking," he said.

"Or not."

*   *   *

ARNOLD QUICKLY GAVE UP on them entirely in terms of musical possibilities and sprawled across the backseat plugged into his iPod, drinking his sugar/milk/splash-of-coffee concoction—not that he needed the caffeine since he was clearly too wound up to sleep.

They eventually stopped outside Fresno at an overlit Denny's for breakfast. It was Arnold's choice. It seemed he was a big fan of Denny's all-you-can-eat breakfast. The sun was coming up. Truely called and left a message to have his secretary make hotel reservations for Courtney and himself in San Diego. Courtney called Myra to explain her change in plans. No surgery after all. Arnold called Vonnie to say he would be coming home to San Diego—then walked outside the restaurant, paced up and down the sidewalk and whispered urgently into the phone.

Hours later they stopped again, outside LA, for gas and the stretching of legs. There was discussion of lunch—but no one was hungry. The nearer they got to their destination the more they lost their appetites. Truely pretended to need to make some business calls and wandered a good distance away from the others, totally out of earshot. Instead he called the San Diego attorney he had hired and tried to get an official handle on Arnold's police history. He was transferred to the law clerk who had researched *Carter, Arnold O.*

"The kid is no angel," the clerk said. "Earliest run-ins with the law when he was nine years old, running drugs for his mother's homegrown operation. Neighbors called the cops on him. He was brought in as a delinquent, let's see, six times. Reported to social services each time. No action taken—according to what I got here. Got a good bit of truancy reported too. Schools reported him truant—how many—eight separate times. A couple of runaways noted here. His grandmother reported him missing, let's see, four times. First serious legal trouble involved an older kid—name Gordon Gerald Mackey Jr., possession of narcotics with intent to sell. Charges dropped against Mackey. Then, let's see, eight months later, the Mackey's Construction theft."

So far none of this was much of a surprise to Truely. Arnold had alluded to it, even if he had been nonspecific.

"I spoke with Ms. Carter," the clerk said. "According to her, the aforementioned Gordon Mackey worked for her on the side. She set him up with weed or cocaine from her dealer—just a local neighborhood thug—and he sold it for her at local clubs, parking lots, places he knew there were plenty of upscale kids with money. Translation: white kids. On one occasion Mackey got in the wrong situation in the wrong neighborhood—got robbed of around eighteen hundred dollars in drug money. She claimed she came down hard on him. She had to have the money he owed her because her dealer had to have the money she owed him. People get shot for a lot less than eighteen hundred dollars, she said she told him. That same night he drove Arnold Carter out to Mackey's Construction Company and gave him the key to the main office—sent him in to take eighteen hundred dollars out of petty cash, which he did. Not four thousand—which was how much was available—but just the eighteen hundred Gordon Mackey needed. The kid was recorded entering the building on surveillance video. They got him going into the petty cash drawer too. I think you got a copy of that, right?

"Anyway, according to Ms. Carter, this Gordon Mackey had parked his car down the street from Mackey's Construction, out of surveillance camera range. There was no way to prove his involvement. He denied being involved. When Ms. Carter got wind of this she threatened to testify that Gordon Mackey was working for her—dealing drugs. She threatened to spill the beans about his having that eighteen hundred dollars ripped off. According to her, Gordon Mackey's father—Mr. Gerald Mackey—paid her off. Ten thousand dollars for her not to testify against the guy. Gordon Mackey goes free. Arnold Carter served eleven months in juvenile detention for the robbery. Lots of bad blood between the families since then, according to Ms. Carter. And, let's see here, yes, that looks like pretty much the bulk of it."

Truely thanked the clerk and went back to meet Courtney

and Arnold, who were waiting for him in the car. "You talking to somebody about the Truely-Chair?" Arnold asked.

"Something like that," Truely said.

At one point while they were en route, Arnold tried to call Gordo, but the cell phone Gordo had used earlier had been returned to its rightful owner, who claimed not to know anybody named Gordo.

"I GUESS we'll finally get to meet Vonnie," Courtney said.

"I guess," Arnold said. "You probably like her. She do all right in school. She sort of bookish."

"I like her already," Courtney said.

"Just because she the school type now don't mean you can mess with Vonnie. Don't nobody mess with Vonnie."

"Last thing on my mind," Courtney said.

"How about your grandmother?" Truely asked.

"You meet Vonnie, you most likely meet my grandmama. That's the way it usually work."

WHEN THEY FINALLY PULLED into the San Diego city limits they were all weary and worried about the events that lay in wait. Truely decided to go to the hotel first—check in, freshen up, call Suleeta again to let her know they had arrived—and get directions to the VA Hospital. Truely was nervous talking to Suleeta. He thought she sounded distant and slightly afraid—but maybe that was his imagination. Maybe he was the one slightly afraid.

They got oceanfront rooms on the twenty-second floor at the Hyatt. Truely noticed that once they had checked in Arnold got his suitcase out of the car same as they did and took it up and parked it in the middle of Truely's room—which was not something they had discussed. Truely had wrongly assumed that Arnold might want to stay with his sister and grandmother, consequently he had ended up with a room with one king-sized bed. "Call down there and tell them we need two beds up here," Arnold instructed. He appeared annoyed that Truely had not thought of this on his own. Truely called down and got reassigned to a room with two double beds—a room that adjoined Courtney's room. Arnold seemed relieved.

Courtney went to her room to shower and rest. She insisted on keeping the doors between her room and theirs wide open like she was their mother and they were a couple of kids in need of supervision. Arnold turned on the hotel room TV and was sitting on his bed changing channels at an annoying clip. It filled the room with a false sense of activity.

Truely felt obliged to call Shauna. Luckily for him she didn't answer and he was able to leave her a message without triggering an argument. Afterward he called downstairs to the hotel concierge to request a printout of directions to the VA Hospital.

Arnold showered and dressed in clean clothes—some his own, and some Truely's. Truely took time to shave. He was last to be ready. The three of them loaded into the Escalade again, travel weary, refreshed only slightly and full of apprehension. "You navigate." Truely handed Courtney the printed directions. She glanced at them and then handed them off to Arnold. "This is your town," she said. "You navigate." So Arnold moved into the front passenger seat to direct Truely—and Courtney got in the backseat and silently stared out the window. Truely looked over at Arnold and noticed beads of sweat had popped out on his forehead.

"Pull out and go right," Arnold instructed, robot-style.

The VA Hospital was a massive structure. The rehab facility was more obscure, relatively nondescript from the outside. It looked more like a corporate structure than part of a hospital. Maybe that was good. A small sign declared subtly: U.S. MILITARY. The parking lot was nearly full. It took them several orbits before they found a vacant spot.

As they entered the lobby Courtney broke the silence. "I'll stay in the waiting room with Suleeta," she said. "I don't know Gordo. No reason he'd want to meet me now."

At the information desk they got directions to Gordo's room—fifth floor, east wing. They rode up the elevator in perfect silence. When the elevator doors opened the first person they saw was Pablo. He looked totally confused, as if he didn't quite recognize them.

"Pablo." Truely put out his hand. "Truely Noonan." His name seemed to echo and bring Pablo reluctantly into the moment.

"Hey," he said passively.

"You remember Arnold Carter? And this is my sister, Courtney. We just drove down from the Bay Area. I left a message on Shauna's phone letting her know we were coming. I hope she got it."

"I don't know," Pablo said. "They're all down the hall in the waiting room. We've been here most of the day. Gordo is not transitioning well. I was just going for some coffee for the others."

Transitioning well? The phrase struck Truely. It was such medispeak, psychobabble. What would be the definition of *transitioning well*? And why would anybody expect that Gordo might *transition well*? It sounded oddly like Gordo had failed some sort of test.

"Do you want to go tell them we're here?" Truely asked. "Or should we just go ahead down there? I hate to surprise them if they're not expecting us."

Pablo seemed to consider the question. "Probably best if I give them a heads-up. Wait here. I'll come back for you." He turned and walked a short distance then turned down a hallway and disappeared.

"That was awkward." Courtney spoke the obvious. Truely knew she wasn't accustomed to feeling that her presence wasn't welcome.

Arnold had sweat underarm circles on his clean shirt— actually, on Truely's clean shirt. He had not spoken a single word since they had entered the building. Minutes passed before Pablo came back with Shauna. She looked exhausted and noticeably thinner than when Truely had last seen her. She had cut her hair and it had gone slightly wavy on her. Truely thought it softened her. She looked fragile, the dark circles under her eyes pronounced. Her face was bare and drawn.

"I never could talk sense to you, True, could I? You always won every argument, didn't you?"

Truely wasn't sure how to respond. Honest to God, he couldn't remember any argument they had ever had. That was partly what he had liked—that they'd never argued. They got along. Had he been wrong about that?

"Hey, Courtney," Shauna said coolly. "So, you came too?"

"I'm really sorry for all you've been through," Courtney said.

"How's Gordo doing?" Arnold spoke up.

"Not good," Shauna said.

"You gon let me see him?" Arnold asked.

"We can't stop you," Shauna said bitterly. "I wish we could. But this is a free country—or so I've been told. Gordo can see who he wants to see."

"Can I see him now?" Arnold asked.

"Jerry is with him," Pablo explained. "When Jerry comes out we're taking him to get some supper."

"I hope you can all be gone by the time we get back," Shauna said.

"Sure," Truely agreed.

Shauna looked them over with a glassy-eyed indifference. Was she just too tired for a fight? He could sense her seething anger. She seemed to aim it primarily at Arnold. "Look, Arnold," she said, "maybe I can't keep you from seeing Gordo. But I hope you have sense enough to stay away from me." Arnold didn't respond. Shauna turned to Truely then. "You're making a big mistake, True," she said. "But mistakes always were your strong suit." She turned and walked away.

Pablo followed. He looked at Truely apologetically, shrugging his shoulders slightly. "As soon as we get Jerry out of here, you can go back," he said.

Minutes later Pablo and Shauna escorted Jerry to the elevator. Jerry was barely recognizable, unshaven, with the same distant stare that Shauna had had earlier. It seemed to Truely that Jerry had aged significantly. He seemed to look right at the three of them and not see them. Truely didn't think Jerry was being rude nor driving home the message that they were not welcome. He didn't even think Jerry was angry in any overt sense. He simply seemed unable to recognize or acknowledge the people around him. When the elevator finally swallowed them relief set in.

"Okay. Here goes." Arnold led them down the hall toward room 515.

SULEETA WAS STANDING in the doorway of the waiting room. Her response was welcoming. "Arnold, niño." She put her arm around him. "You're here. Gordo will be glad." Then she embraced Courtney and Truely. "Hola, hola."

"How is he?" Truely asked.

"Gordo suffers. Besides his legs he has a head wound. You'll see. And they give him too much medicines—so he is not right. He is not Gordo. He don't want to see nobody—not his family, not his friends. He's not ready. You the one he wants." She looked at Arnold. "He ask for you."

Truely and Courtney sat in the waiting room with Suleeta while Arnold went in to see Gordo. He looked frightened to enter the room, but determined.

"You call out if you need us," Suleeta said. It was an ominous comment.

In Truely's effort to distract Suleeta he said, "We saw Shauna and Pablo at the elevator. And Jerry."

"Everybody upset," she said. "That's all."

A LONG, awkward hour passed before Suleeta looked at her watch and announced, "I'd better get Arnold out of Gordo's room before Jerry comes back. After his supper Shauna should take Jerry home to bed like I tell her—not bring him back up here. But she is worried Jerry will drink if he goes home. That's the only way he can ever sleep, you know. Drink himself to sleep." She left them and went to get Arnold.

When they returned to the waiting room Arnold was emotional. He didn't look any of them in the eye. His eyes were swollen and he was silent.

"It's not easy," Suleeta explained. "Gordo is not Gordo like he used to be. It's good to try anyway. You can come back tomorrow, right?" Suleeta was speaking to Arnold but looked to Truely to answer her.

"We'll come back," he said. "Sure."

ON THE WAY OUT to the car Arnold said, "I appreciate it if y'all don't ask me a bunch of questions."

"Can you tell us anything?" Truely asked.

"Gordo wish that suicide bomber just go on and finish the job. He wishing he was a dead man. He mean it too."

Courtney put her hand on Arnold's shoulder. "That's normal," she insisted. "He'll change his mind. You'll see."

THEY WOVE THROUGH the balmy city night on their way back to the Hyatt in total exhaustion. When they walked into the hotel lobby there was a slender young black girl waiting for Arnold. She was wearing jeans and a T-shirt and carrying a backpack with OLD NAVY stenciled across it. She jumped to her feet when they walked in. She waved and called out, "Arnold."

Arnold looked irritated. "I told you wait until I call you."

"I got a ride with L.J."

"L.J.? I told you stay away from L.J."

"It was just a ride," she said.

"Well, you can't be here," Arnold said. "I told you that."

The girl glanced at Courtney and Truely, who stood behind Arnold looking intensely curious. "Hey, y'all," she said. "I'm Vontell."

Arnold looked embarrassed. "She's not staying," he clarified.

"We've heard a lot about you." Truely was thinking that this habit of showing up someplace uninvited must run in the family.

Courtney hugged her. "Oh, honey, you look like your brother."

"Vonnie not supposed to be here," Arnold said. "She need to catch the bus back home."

"I wanted to see you," she whined. "Don't you want to see me?"

"You can't stay," Arnold repeated. "Not now."

"I won't be trouble," she insisted. "You over here in this nice hotel. Just let me stay here with you."

"I said wait until I call you. Why can't you do like I say? You got to get the bus."

"I'm not taking the bus." She folded her arms across her chest.

"Can we get Vonnie a cab?" Arnold asked Truely. "She need to get back home, man. She can't stay here."

"Sure," Truely said.

"I don't want no damn cab. Don't get me no cab," she instructed Truely.

"You going home," Arnold said. "Don't test me, Vonnie."

She began to cry then. "I don't see what it would hurt. You just selfish. Don't care about nobody but yourself."

"I got my reasons." Arnold waved to the doorman for a cab. "Ima call you," he said, "tell you when you can come back. Don't you come back until I say so."

"I hate you." Vonnie was crying into her hands now.

Arnold led Vonnie outside. Truely and Courtney followed behind them silently, like shadows. Arnold stepped over to a cab and opened the door for her. "Get in," he ordered. When she refused to budge, he grabbed her arm and yanked her over to the cab while she yelled, "Get your hands off me." People were turning to stare at them.

Truely and Courtney stepped back on instinct. Maybe they were just too tired to interfere. Maybe they had no real idea what to do.

When Arnold had more or less shoved the sobbing Vonnie into the cab he slammed the door closed and turned to Truely. "You got some money?"

Truely pulled out a fifty-dollar bill. "This enough?"

"You got another one of those?" he asked.

Truely handed him a hundred bucks and Arnold gave the money to Vonnie. "Stop crying," he said. "Here, take this." He shoved the money in her face. "Don't come back over here until I call you. I mean it, Vonnie."

Vonnie took the money. "I hate you," she repeated.

Arnold told the cab driver where to take Vonnie. "Don't let her get out nowhere else," he said. "I don't care if she beg you. Make sure you get her home."

As the cab pulled out into traffic Arnold stood and watched. Truely and Courtney were slightly stunned by the events. They waited for Arnold before going upstairs to their rooms. When the cab was out of sight and Arnold turned around they could see that he was nearly crying. "Lord, Arnold," Courtney whispered. Truely slung his arm around Arnold's shoulder and they walked to the elevator in silence.

Twenty-five

UPSTAIRS IN THEIR HOTEL ROOMS they began to get ready for bed without saying much. The TV was going in Truely's room with Arnold manning the remote—no station getting more than a two-second chance to interest him. Truely checked his messages—Mose Jones had left one. Two from Jaxon. One from a woman he didn't know. He nearly erased it before he realized it was Tay-Ann.

"Truely," she said, "I just want to thank you again for your condolence call. I'm sorry I went to pieces on you like that. I'm doing a lot better today. They say the loss gets a little easier each day that passes, so I'm trying to believe that. I just wanted to say, you know—thanks." And she had hung up.

He saved the message. He would need to listen to it again later when he was alone. He listened differently when he was alone than when he had his two self-appointed sidekicks surrounding him, listening to him listen.

Through the open adjoining door Truely could see Courtney unpacking her overnight bag, lining up her medications on the bathroom counter just like she did at home. He thought she was like a woman in a trance when she executed this ritual. He turned his head away, hating to watch her medicate herself night after night no matter her reasons. He sat down at the small desk and jotted down a few things he needed to take care of tomorrow. In recent years he had become a list maker just like his daddy used to be. Courtney got into the minibar and poured them each a large glass of unremarkable red wine and an apple juice for

Arnold. When she carried the drinks into their room she clicked the TV off—which had the effect of taking Arnold off a respirator. "Okay, y'all," she said. You could see the shine of her face where she had put on some slick night cream. She had also patted some white stuff under each of her renewed eyes. "Okay, baby boys," she said, "I've got an idea."

Arnold rolled his eyes, but looked interested.

"Can you stop what you're doing, True?" she asked. "Can you just give me a minute and hear me out." Courtney, although more or less the self-appointed ruler of their three-person world, rarely issued such a direct request.

Truely put down his pen and shoved the paper aside. "I'm all ears."

"Y'all come sit over here." Courtney patted the bed where she now sat propped up Indian-style. Courtney handed Truely his wine and he took a seat on the bed as instructed. He and Arnold looked at Courtney as if waiting for further orders. "Here's what we're going to do," she said. "You know how Arnold always says no secrets among friends, right? Well, that's bull, right? So we're going to go around—and we're each going to tell one secret. Like a confession, see? And it can't be a little insignificant secret neither. It's got to be something big. It's got to hurt you a little to tell it. You've got to be worried the others might get up and run from the room when you tell it. Right?"

"What the hell kind of game is that?" Truely asked.

"It's not a game. It's stopping the game playing, True, don't you see? It's about trust. And we've all got to do it."

"Lord, Courtney, where do you get off making up all these rules?"

"You saying you ain't going to do it?" Arnold asked him, in an almost accusatory tone.

"He'll do it," Courtney answered for him. "He'll hate it, but he'll do it."

"Excuse me," Truely snapped, "but I believe I can answer for myself."

"What you say then?" Arnold asked.

"Can you tell me why this is necessary, Court? You been read-ing some New Age book again or what?"

"It's not something I can explain to you," Courtney said. "I just know we have to do it. They say the truth will set you free. And it's time." Courtney had finished her glass of wine quickly—she had practically gulped it down. She got up and went for more. "Just a minute," she said. "Wait."

"What the hell is going on?" Truely asked Arnold while Court-ney was out of the room.

"You know how your cell phone message center get too full?" Arnold said. "You can't take in no new messages when your mes-sage center get full. You got to delete some crap, right? I guess it's like that."

"What if we don't actually have any big secrets?" Truely asked. "Then what?"

Courtney scowled at him. "So help me, Truely Noonan, if you try to go there I will have to personally kill you. Maybe you're going to act like you can't think of any big secrets you have, but I can think of several for you. You want me to take your turn and mine both?"

"I'd sure as hell love to know what you think my big secrets are."

"Y'all can fuss later," Arnold said. "We gon do this or not?"

"No guts no glory," Courtney said.

"Maybe we ought to give Courtney more than one run at it," Truely said sarcastically. "She's going to have trouble making her personal selection from among her long list of possibilities. Aren't you, big sister?"

"Go to hell," she said.

"Ya'll stop," Arnold said. "Y'all got to act right if we gon to do this."

"Okay." Courtney bounced down on the bed, sloshing Truely's wine nearly out of his glass. "Who goes first?"

"Truely got to go first," Arnold insisted.

"Me? Why me?"

"So you can't hear what me and Courtney say and then you back out."

"Damn," he said. "You two got a high opinion of me. I see that."

"Okay, bro, you're up." Courtney raised her glass as if to toast him. "Spill."

Maybe it was because he was exhausted or because he felt like he was being dared. Maybe it was because Courtney was right and the time had finally come. The chance to let go of what seemed to him the only real secret he'd ever managed to keep was just too compelling. Truely found himself opening his mouth, unsure what would come out. "Y'all want big? Is that right?"

"Biggest you got," Arnold said.

"Okay." He stood up and paced a little. He could not have explained why he was telling the truth like this now, saying what he had vowed never to say in his life, but he opened his mouth and it seemed the truth just worked its way out. "When I was in high school—Courtney had already moved out to California—Mose Jones and I took Mother's old station wagon and said we were going to a science fair or some such foolishness over in Louisiana. We really went down to New Orleans and got ourselves into some harmless little nothing trouble down there—but on the way back home we went through Meridian, Mississippi. Mose claimed he knew a girl over in Meridian, but of course when we got there he never could conjure her up—but that's beside the point."

Truely paused and looked at Arnold and Courtney. He had time to change his mind. He hadn't traveled the trail of truth so far he couldn't U-turn and come back to the safety of secret-keeping. Whether it was decision or instinct he wasn't sure, but he kept talking.

"We're driving by this run-down motel outside Meridian, right? One of those real tacky places. And it's late too. Damn late. It is maybe three o'clock in the morning. Mose is driving and I'm just looking out the window at all the nothing, right? Then I see it. Daddy's old truck. Courtney can tell you there wasn't but one truck in the world like it. He had these fish decals all over the back. He had this gun rack where he kept a little pickax and some rope and whatnot. He might just as well have had his name written out on the side of that truck."

Truely paused because remembering, when he let himself, slowed it all down. He remembered it just the way it had happened—and he felt just the way he had felt too. Like the ground they rode on came out from under them and they were free-falling, Mose and him, through a senseless world with nothing solid holding it together.

"Go on," Courtney said. "What?"

"Daddy's truck was parked outside motel room fourteen. I remember it like it was my birthday. Fourteen. Stop! I yell at Mose. That's my daddy's truck back there. You're crazy, man, Mose said. See Mose and Daddy, they never did get along that good. Mose didn't like to deal with anything concerning Daddy. We got to go back, I tell him. We got to. I'm jerking at the steering wheel. So we circle back—and there it is. I was not dreaming. Even Mose can see whose truck it is. He doesn't even try to talk me out of seeing what I see. We pull up in Mother's old station wagon and park right alongside Daddy's truck. Some kind of psychiatrist, he could probably make something big out of a moment like that—the family station wagon easing up beside the parked truck. There is not a light on anywhere except for the blink of the Vacancy sign at the front of the motel. It is a tacky motel too."

"You said that," Courtney told him.

"Right. So right off I know what is going on—my blood does—but I'm trying not to believe it. I'm saying hell no, not Daddy. Not the deacon of Hinds County Primitive Baptist—moral compass of our happy family. This ain't right. No way. It had never crossed my mind that Daddy was the sort to break one of the Ten Commandments. Wasn't he the one that hung that Ten Commandment plaque in the kitchen right over the door so you had to see it every time you came and went from the house? I'm thinking I will kill his sorry ass and stuff like that. You know, thoughts of a hotheaded sixteen-year-old kid." He glanced at Arnold. "Not every sixteen-year-old. Just myself, at sixteen. I jump out of the station wagon and run over there and pound on the door of number fourteen like a madman. Mose tries to stop me, to make me get back in the car, but he can't do it. I'm shouting, 'Daddy, I know you're in there! Come out here or I'll break this door down. I'll wake up everybody in this godforsaken hellhole.' That's how I was talking. That and worse. And finally, after I threaten him that I'll run through the motel room wall with Mother's station wagon if he doesn't open the door—he gives up, I guess. He knows I'm not going away quietly. I yell for him to call the cops—I beg him to. 'Call the damn cops,' I scream."

"Lord, Truely." Courtney seemed disbelieving.

"Do he come out?" Arnold asks.

"He comes out. Oh, he comes out. He sticks his head out the door like maybe he can talk some reason to me. He's slung on his pants and his unbuttoned shirt and patted down his hair and is trying to wave me to quiet down—like maybe he doesn't want to wake up the other so-called guests of this fine Southern establishment. So I seize the moment. I just bust inside the door—into his room. I'm swinging my fists at him and calling him every lowlife name I know. I guess I was trying to protect our mother's honor or something. That's how I was feeling. I catch him on the chin one good time. I was playing ball back then, working out a lot, and I was pretty strong for a kid. Besides I had waked him out of a contented sleep I guess. He was sort of in shock. I smacked him as hard as I could and he went to the ground. While he was trying to get up and go back at me—I looked over and saw what I was afraid I would see. A woman. I knew her too. She was a teacher at my school."

"Oh, my God," Courtney whispered.

"By now I am crying, swinging my fists. It was like I went crazy. Daddy couldn't get me off him, so Mose comes and he pulls us apart and he about has to beat the hell out of me himself just to get me to stop. He drags me back to the station wagon and sort of throws me in. He's pissed off that I made a scene like that—with him, a black guy, along—because you know, back then, if there was ever any trouble and a black guy was around? Anyway, now Mose is mad and half scared himself—out in the middle of nowhere at a white motel like that. He tries to slap some sense into me since talking sense won't work. I finally give up and stop fighting. I just lie back in the passenger seat of that station wagon like a dead man and we drive all the way back to Hinds County that night. Get there in the early morning. We don't speak a word either, not one. And then...after that..."

"What?" Arnold asked.

"Then after that—nothing was ever the same again."

"My God, True," Courtney whispered. "I never knew you got in a fight with Daddy."

"That's why they call them secrets," Truely said. "People don't know." He drank some of his wine. He couldn't believe he had just done what he had done. Carried a secret on his back for most of his life, then suddenly, because his troubled sister had insisted, had dared him, laid it down once and for all—right at her feet too. Hadn't he intended for her to never know? Wasn't that what he'd told himself all these years? He finished his wine and got more.

"Y'all's family messed up," Arnold said. "I never knew y'all's family was messed up."

"It's a family, isn't it?" Courtney said. "Or, it used to be a family."

"I always think y'all's family like some of those *Sound of Music* people. You ever see *The Sound of Music?* All them white people do is smile and sing. My grandmama love that movie."

"We tried to be *Sound of Music* people," Courtney said. "God knows."

"The point is I was a kid. I overreacted," Truely said. "It was like Mother and Daddy were always telling me the world was flat and then out of nowhere I see for myself that the world is round—just round and fragile as an inflatable beach ball—and spinning fast—and we're all about to fall off of it too. Like that."

Courtney did not ask him a million questions. Not like he expected. She was biding her time, he guessed. She leaned over and kissed his cheek. "Thanks, True," she said. "I appreciate your telling me that. I never knew you knew about Mrs. Seacrest. Mama swore she didn't think you knew—and never wanted you to."

"Mama? She knew?"

"She's the one that told me," Courtney said. "She made me promise not to tell you. She never wanted you to be disappointed in Daddy, you know?"

"So, all those years afterward?"

"I don't know," Courtney said. "I guess they worked it out."

"She forgave him?"

"Who knows?" Courtney said. "We'll have plenty to wonder about for the rest of our lives, right?"

"Can't put the genie back in the bottle," he said.

"Okay, then." Arnold shook his head. "Man, I didn't know Truely have it in him. A confession like that. Now that right there gon be damn hard to beat, but I believe I can beat it."

"Oh, so it's a contest," Truely said. "Now you tell me."

"It's not a contest," Courtney insisted.

Truely could feel her intent gaze on him, a softened version that he wasn't sure he liked.

"Here's what I got to say," Arnold began. "I won't try to turn it into no interesting story or none of that. It's just the facts and the facts ain't never been told until now."

"So shoot." Truely didn't know how appropriate his word choice was.

"I told y'all that I never much knew my old man, right? I told y'all that when I was a kid he got shot and I don't hardly remember nothing about him, right?"

"You told us," Truely said.

"I was maybe six or seven. Had just started going to school and stuff. Vonnie was maybe two or three is all. My old man and my mama, they're high, right? I mean, I didn't know to say that back then, I was just a kid and they were just them. But this one night they were fighting real bad. I used to wake up and wet the bed when they got started fighting. Then, along with the rest of it, my mama would go on and whip me for wetting the bed—so I was pretty much in for it, one way or another, every time they got a fight going. So it was mostly true when I said my old man got shot in a drug deal gone bad—but what I never did tell nobody was that my mama was the one that shot him."

"Good Lord, Arnold," Courtney said.

"You were a little kid. You sure you remember right?" Truely asked.

"I seen her do it. She pulled his gun out from the bedsheets where he kept it when he slept and he sees she's got it and he starts to back up like he might try to make a run out the door or something. She waves that gun around and yells all this shit I can't remember what and then she just aims right at him and pulls the trigger. Just like that. The sound of that bullet go through me, crashing into my chest. Seemed like she shot me the way my body got to jerking. My old man, he went down like a tree falling over, like on those TV shows, you know, where the guy just die before he hit the floor. He just go out right there with me and Vonnie watching. Me, I was crying and wetting my pants, but Vonnie, she was just quiet. All she does is start rocking back and forth sort of banging her head into the wall where they had fixed us a little bed over on the side of the floor. I go over and get her, you know. She just bucking back and forth like that. My old man is laying there and bleeding a lake of red blood all over the floor of the house. He don't even twitch."

"Arnold, baby." Courtney touched his arm. "Oh, baby."

"When the police come, then I hear Mama tell them that my old man's brother is the one done it. His brother live off in New Jersey or somewhere. Or maybe he don't even have no brother. She was convincing too. She about make me believe her myself and I saw with my own eyes what really happened. But I hear what she say to the cops and then when they ask me—I am a kid now—I just say what she say. 'His brother done it. His brother shot him dead.' I was shaking like I was shot too and the police lady wrap me up in a quilt because she cannot get me to quit shaking. But Vonnie, she never cries."

"That's bad," Truely said. "I'm sorry, man."

"Me too," Courtney said.

"So, listen y'all, I'm not saying my mama just go around killing people. Right? She killed my old man—and maybe she got reason to. Don't seem like nobody suffered his loss too much. So

I don't condemn her. Okay? My mama got issues, like I say. This just one more on the pile."

"You never told anybody until now?" Truely asked.

"I ain't going to the police or none of that. I am just telling you two and maybe somebody else if I want to. My grandmama the only other one that knows."

"You told your grandmother?"

"Naw, man. My mama told her. Back then my mama act proud of it. She know her own mother ain't going to turn her in. She just said to me — 'Arnold, your old man got what he had coming, and now I don't want you to ever say nothing about this again, you hear me?' I never did. I just thought about it some. But I never said nothing."

"Wow." Truely whistled.

"So that right there is one of my secrets." Arnold spoke as if he had just put money in the offering plate and was relieved to have had the spare change. There were so many layers to this kid. He was maybe seventeen and had lived more mess than any six adults Truely knew. What had kept him from getting a gun and following his mother's example — just shooting the hell out of people causing him problems? Exactly how many bullets would that take? Instead he was funny and friendly — and charmingly, annoyingly bold. It occurred to Truely that he might need to say some things to Arnold that he had not said. He might need to tell him that despite the messes he had gotten himself into he was a special kid. He had the makings of a good man too. A man with a good heart, which was what Truely had originally set out to be as well. He wasn't sure if he had fared as well as Arnold.

It was funny, because when Courtney suggested this round of true confessions Truely had been almost positive that Arnold's secret would have something to do with Gordo. He would have bet money on it. Maybe Gordo was only a few years older than Arnold, but if anybody asked Truely he would say that Gordo was not actually the big brother Arnold had always wished for, that instead, somehow more menacingly, Gordo had become Arnold's surrogate father figure. Something about that wasn't right.

"Gordo know anything about this?" Truely asked.

"Maybe Gordo think he know something. But he wasn't there, was he? Besides, Gordo ain't the kind to rat. He got that much of the old neighborhood in him."

"This is some damn game we're playing here," Truely remarked.

"It's not a game," Arnold and Courtney echoed.

"Okay, you're next," Arnold said to Courtney. "We saved the best for last."

"Lord." Courtney cleared her throat. "I was sure mine would be the best—or worst. Now I'm not so sure."

"It's not a contest, remember?" Truely said.

"Nobody gets shot in mine," she said. "Not like that."

"Are you apologizing?" Truely asked her.

Courtney scooted over and put her arm around Arnold. "Scoot in, Truely," she instructed. "I want us all to hold hands when I tell mine."

"No way," Truely said. "This is not church camp, Court. Next you'll want to sing 'Kumbaya' and make some beaded belts."

"Please, True," she said.

"Just do it, man," Arnold pleaded. "It won't kill you."

"It might," he said. "I swear the two of you—you could wear somebody out." Truely stretched his hands to clasp with theirs. Already they were sweaty.

"It's okay," Courtney said. "Mine won't take long."

"Okay, go," Truely ordered. "Let's get this last cow in the barn."

Courtney squeezed both their hands really tight and closed her eyes and said, "Well, okay. Here goes. When I came to California and met Hastings and all—well, he was my first love, right? I got pregnant. I was scared to death—all alone in California, trying to act like I was grown. All I could think was that the shame of it would kill Mother and Daddy if they knew, that I would just break their hearts and they could never forgive me. I was scared to tell Hastings too. I thought he would feel trapped if I told him. Poor Mississippi girl traps rich California boy—right? I thought maybe he would leave me. It was too soon—it was before he ever mentioned the first word about getting married. So I got the pregnancy taken care of. My boss at the gallery knew a doctor over in Chinatown. He drove me over there and waited for me. When I cried, he cried too. Nobody else knows."

"Court?" Truely said softly.

Courtney slowly opened her eyes. "Don't you see? I got rid of Hastings' and my baby because I thought the time wasn't right. I was stupid. Later, when the time was right, I never could get pregnant. God wouldn't forgive me. Even when Hastings and I both got saved and born again—no baby ever came. It's my fault. I always knew that. So now, when everybody thinks Hastings is a jerk for leaving me for a younger woman with kids—I know better. There's a terrible justice to it—and he doesn't really even know that."

"Court, you could have told me," Truely said. "I would have helped you."

"I didn't want to shame the family, True. I never wanted you all to know what a mess I was making of things."

"So that's why you ain't hate Hastings too much," Arnold spoke up. "Everybody wonder why you don't hate him."

"I hate myself more," she said.

"Damn." Arnold shook his head.

Twenty-six

FOR THE NEXT FEW DAYS the three of them developed a routine. Sleeping late, handling their respective business and phone calls at the hotel during the day, going to the gym or walking the waterfront, maybe watching a movie in the room, then, like clockwork, heading for the VA rehab between the hours of six and seven—while Jerry was whisked away to eat his supper and drown his sorrows. Shauna's sisters, Shelly and Becca, took turns coming to sit with Suleeta in the mornings—so Truely never crossed paths with either of them, which was fine with him.

Most evenings Courtney brought some small token gift or a special morsel for Suleeta. The two of them seemed to have forged a connection that escaped Truely. He found his time sitting in the waiting room just short of excruciating. When he could, he made excuses to walk the halls, go down to the car for something, call Mose Jones just to check in, maybe reread the newspaper in the dim light out on the front steps of the facility. This last was what he was doing when Shauna appeared holding a cup of hot coffee and sat down beside him.

"Hey," she said.

Truely was uneasy, ready for the ritualized rumble.

"Do you despise me, True?" she asked him.

"No," he answered.

"You wouldn't admit it if you did."

"Where's Pablo?" he asked.

"He's got Daddy. I needed a break. I saw you sitting out here."

"Gets a little claustrophobic in the waiting room with Courtney and Suleeta," Truely said. "Think I'm cramping their style. I don't have their flair for waiting."

"Tell me about it." She laughed. It was an actual laugh. This was the way he remembered Shauna—a woman more inclined to laugh it off than fight it out. She gripped her coffee with both hands and paused. "So did Mama tell you the news?"

"Which news?"

"I'm getting married."

"She didn't tell me. But congratulations."

"This spring," she said. "Pablo is sort of an action guy, you know. I like that about him. Less talk, more action."

"Unlike me. Is that your point?"

"The trouble with you, True, was that you didn't love me. I always knew that."

"And the trouble with you was what?" he asked.

"You want me to say I didn't love you either?" She tried to smile. "But Lord knows I wanted to, True. I tried my best. It sure would have simplified things."

"Maybe."

"We had everything it would have taken to have a decent life together—except..."

"Look, I'm sorry if my indecisive ways slowed you down, Shauna. I feel bad about that now—looking back. It's not like I had a plan or something—you know, to mess up your life."

"Pablo is jealous of you."

"Since when does the winner envy the loser?"

"Your success mostly. Pablo has never made any money—you know that. He's going to work for Daddy. I guess that doesn't surprise you. Shelly's and Becca's husbands already work for Mackey's Construction. Pablo will be a front office guy—do the job that Daddy should be doing, you know, if he were himself. Daddy is not fighting it either."

"Good."

"Did Mama tell you Daddy has moved out of their bedroom?"

"She didn't. I can't imagine why she would." He couldn't help but think that might be more the sort of thing she would be likely to tell Courtney.

"No surprise really," Shauna said. "Between Mama's candles blazing day and night and Daddy's drinking and stumbling—you know. It's no surprise."

"Sorry," Truely said.

"Plus she's got the dogs in there with her now. They sleep in her bed. Foxie and Fred are more important to Mama now than Daddy is. Not that I really blame her. So Daddy has moved into Gordo's room."

"Is that a good idea?" Truely asked.

"The worst," she said. "All Daddy's ideas are the worst these days." She touched Truely's arm. "Sort of like yours."

"I don't want to argue about Arnold," Truely said. "It's done now."

"You know his mother is in jail?"

"I know."

"Couldn't happen to a nicer woman," Shauna said. "She almost ruined Gordo's life. I don't guess Arnold told you about that?"

"Seems like—according to you—lots of folks are busy ruining Gordo's life."

"You mean besides the suicide bomber?" she said sarcastically.

"Besides the suicide bomber," he said. "The others."

"You don't believe me, do you?" Shauna laughed. "Of course you don't."

After Shauna left to go meet Pablo and Jerry, Truely sat a while longer on the front stoop of the building. He was amazed that a woman who had, until recently, been a central figure in his life could suddenly become such a peripheral person—like a face he remembered from a dream he had forgotten.

ON FRIDAY Courtney bowed out of their regular trip to the VA Hospital. Bob Gavin called her and was flying down in his private plane in hopes of taking her to dinner. "How can I say no?" she had asked Truely. When Truely and Arnold left the hotel she still had not returned from a hair appointment she'd made at the last minute to have her roots done. They were in the car and ready to go when Arnold realized he'd forgotten something—his cell phone maybe—and had to run back upstairs to get it. That put them slightly behind schedule. They rode across town without much conversation. Truely sensed that Arnold was anxious. His nerves tended to manifest in waves of sweat. Already his brow was damp and glistening. He kept rubbing his hands over his face.

"So, how are things going with Gordo?" Truely rarely got much real report from Arnold and he had still not seen Gordo himself—Gordo had refused. Truely decided not to take the rejection personally since, according to Suleeta, the list of willing but rejected visitors was long. "Gordo doing okay?"

"No, bad," Arnold said. "Real bad."

"Anything I can do?"

"Too late."

"What do you mean too late?"

"Everything already what it is."

BECAUSE COURTNEY WAS OTHERWISE OCCUPIED on this night, Truely sat in the waiting room keeping Suleeta company while Arnold went in to see Gordo. "I didn't know Courtney have a new boyfriend?" Suleeta said when he explained Courtney's absence.

"Just an old friend," Truely corrected. "That's all."

He was sure Suleeta was disappointed in him as a stand-in for Courtney. He tried to make a little conversation, but gave up quickly because Suleeta seemed too tired to talk. She sat in a chair and seemed to be dozing off. Truely was not good at waiting. He never had been. Waiting in a place called a waiting room seemed even more of a challenge. He had trouble even sitting in a chair for long. He found himself standing up and pacing back and forth, checking his watch every few minutes, looking out the window, changing the TV channel even though the volume didn't work and there was no sound at all. So when Arnold burst into the waiting room and announced, "Let's get out of here, man," Truely was grateful and more than ready to go. They kissed Suleeta's cheek brusquely and hurried down the hall to the elevator.

"I've had about enough of this place," Truely said.

"Me too." Arnold had sweat through his shirt. His upper lip was beaded with perspiration. He seemed ready to bolt into a full run. Truely scrambled to keep up with him. "What's the big hurry, man?"

They made it downstairs, through the lobby, across the parking lot, nearly out to the car, when Truely's cell phone rang. He patted his pockets to get the phone. Arnold suddenly turned, a really awful look on his face, and ran back toward the front door of the VA rehab center. "Man, this ain't right," he shouted. "I got to go back."

Truely was confused. He paused to take the call.

"Thank God I caught you." It was Courtney. "Something weird is going on, True."

"You're telling me." He watched as Arnold broke into a run and flew through the front doors of the building, nearly upending an exiting couple as he passed.

"When I got back to the hotel just now—I don't know." Courtney was speaking in a quick, breathless voice. "My medicines are gone, True. The painkillers. Every single pill out of every bottle. You know how I always have them sitting out on the bathroom counter? The bottles are all knocked over, empty. You don't guess...?"

"Damn." Truely hung up the phone and took off after Arnold. He felt the flutter of danger—like something swooping down on him. "Arnold," he shouted. "Wait." He ran through the front doors of the building, the doors clanging behind him. Arnold was nowhere in sight. A cluster of subdued people waited at the elevator, so Truely took the stairs, trying to bound them two at a time. "Arnold," he shouted again. "Arnold, hold up." Upstairs he could hear the stairwell door slam.

By the time he had made his way to the fifth floor Truely was winded and gasping. He ran down the hall toward Gordo's room, where angry shouts erupted. It sounded like Arnold and Gordo were going at each other. He recognized Jerry's voice too. "What the hell did you do? You goddamn punk!"

Inside Gordo's room he saw Arnold at Gordo's bedside, struggling to pry a fistful of pills from his determined grip. Gordo was fighting him hard, struggling to stuff the handful of pills into his mouth. Spilled on the bedcovers were more pills, some of which rolled to the floor and bounced in all directions.

"You little bastard." Jerry took an unsteady leap and pounced on Arnold, slugging him in the face and then on the side of his head, again, again. Arnold tried to cover his face with one arm while still struggling with Gordo, but Jerry was pounding him in such a drunken frenzy that he was forced to let go.

Gordo responded by letting out a primal scream unlike anything Truely had ever heard. It was not a cry of fear. It was not sadness or resignation. It was a warrior cry—fueled by rage. If designed to strike terror in the heart of an enemy—it succeeded. The hair on Truely's neck stood on end.

Arnold was clearly afraid to hit Jerry back. He was bent over, covering his head with his arms and just letting Jerry use him for a punching bag. It turned Truely's stomach seeing the old guy pound on Arnold that way, especially when Arnold was refusing to hit back. It was like Jerry had been waiting for this moment all his life, the chance to pummel Arnold or Truely—or somebody. And maybe Truely had been waiting too. "Let go," he snarled. "He's a kid. He's just a damn kid." Before Truely could think or reconsider he crossed the room and swung his fist at Jerry's bloodshot face, hit him in the jaw as hard as he could. He felt the bone snap. He heard the sickening sound. He had busted the old man's jawbone. Jerry shouted in pain and clutched his face and appeared ready to collapse. Truely barely caught him before he hit the floor.

Out of the corner of his eye Truely saw Arnold dive toward

Gordo's bed a second time and begin to wrestle him again. "Give it to me, man," Arnold was snarling. That was when Truely saw that Gordo had a gun in his hand. Fear flashed through his body, momentarily paralyzing him.

"He got a gun, man," Arnold yelled. The two of them were locked into a grisly struggle. The gun — Truely recognized it. It was the handgun he had taken from Arnold and placed on the library shelf. Damn. He started toward them in slow motion. He was yelling too, screaming, but had no idea what he was saying.

When the first shot was fired, it was terrifying enough. Arnold and Gordo both groaned as if they had been hit, but their struggle continued without pause. It was the second shot that caused Gordo to cry out and let go of the handgun. A spurt of blood splattered out over the bedsheets. "Goddamn you, man," Gordo snarled at Arnold. "You shot me."

Arnold stood holding the gun in his hand. His clothes were drenched with sweat. He was crying soundlessly, tears snaking down his face. "You a liar, man," he said. "I'm trying to keep you from shooting yourself. You talking about blowing your brains out, man. I ain't gon let you do it."

By now Suleeta and Shauna were in the room too, both yelling hysterically. "What's wrong? What's happening?"

"Goddamn Arnold shot me," Gordo said.

"He was trying to shoot hisself," Arnold insisted. He was nearly crying. "He planning on killing hisself tonight. I'm just trying to stop him."

Pablo rushed to help Jerry, who collapsed onto the floor, his hands clasped to his jaw. He and Shauna dragged Jerry a few steps to a chair and propped him in it. "What the hell?" Pablo asked.

"I think I broke his jaw," Truely said.

"Arnold gave Gordo that damn gun," Jerry said in garbled speech.

"Arnold?" Suleeta asked, disbelieving. "You brought that gun in here?"

"I came back to get it," Arnold said. Tears ran down his face. "I tried to take it away from him."

"What are you thinking, niño?" Suleeta asked.

"Gordo beg me." Arnold was crying now. "He say if I don't bring him a gun so he can blow his brains out—he get somebody else to do it. He mean it too. He says if I'm any kind of friend I'll help him go out so he won't have to keep on like this. I keep telling y'all he want to die. Don't nobody listen. I come back because I don't want you finding him in here with a bullet in his head."

Truely turned to face Gordo, his words firing like a second round of bullets. "You lousy jerk."

Two security officers came barging into the room then. One of them pulled an emergency lever on the wall. A sickening beeping alarm began. Suleeta was saying to them, "He been shot in the hand. See?" It was his hand with the missing fingers. She was trying to wrap Gordo's hand tightly in the bedsheet to stop the bleeding.

Two nurses ran into the room wide-eyed. "He's been shot," one of the security officers said. "His hand."

"Clear the room," a nurse ordered. "Get everybody out of here."

"You got to pump his stomach too. He eat some pills. See here?" Suleeta motioned to the pills in the bed. "Gordo swallow some those pills." She was like a broken record.

Shauna was oddly quiet. "I knew something like this would happen," she said to no one in particular.

Jerry clutched his jaw with one hand, pointing at Arnold with the other. "He brought drugs in here. Brought a gun too—with intent to kill."

"Gordo, you speak up for Arnold. You hear me, man?" Truely was shouting. "Don't you let him go down for you here."

The nurses pushed Truely back from the bed. "You need to leave, sir."

The security guards summoned the military police upstairs. Two more nurses came running, code blue–style. Gordo was yelling for people to get out, cursing them by name, starting with Truely. The nurses scurried around Gordo's bed, getting his vital signs, making arrangements for him to be taken downstairs

to have his hand treated and his stomach pumped, getting someone to come up and remove the spilled pills from his bed and
floor.

Suleeta kept saying, "Hurry. You got to hurry."

The security guards herded everyone down the hall into the
waiting room, where they would all be held and questioned.

IT TOOK THE SAN DIEGO POLICE more than thirty minutes to
arrive on the scene. It seems domestic dispute was not unheard of at
the VA Hospital. It was not generally thought to be an emergency.

By the time they arrived the waiting room had divided into the
Mackey family on one side and Truely and Arnold on the other.
Arnold stood unnaturally close to Truely. "They ain't going to
arrest me, are they, man?"

"They are if Jerry has his way."

"You ain't going to leave me up here, are you? You going to
stay with me, right?"

"I'm not going anywhere," Truely said.

"You believe me, don't you?" Arnold asked.

"You carry a gun in someplace and what do you think is
going to happen, man? You took that goddamn gun down from
the shelf, didn't you? I thought you gave me your word, man. I
thought your word was starting to mean something."

"It was stupid."

"You think?"

"I tried to come back and get it. Gordo got to tell them the
truth."

"The Gordo that loves you like a brother? The Gordo that's
always got your back? That Gordo?"

"We didn't come back up here he could be dead right now."

"Or you could be," Truely said.

"What's gon happen?"

"Nothing good."

In the end, after rounds of contradicting statements were

taken, the police handcuffed Arnold and led him away. The expression on Arnold's face as they led him downstairs to the patrol car was something Truely would never forget. There was a flicker of fear, but a larger look of resignation, as if the biggest mistake of Arnold's life was ever entertaining the notion that his life could go differently.

Twenty-seven

I T WAS THE WORST THANKSGIVING Truely could remember. Even worse than his first Thanksgiving after Jesse left, when for the life of him he struggled to recall what he had to be thankful for. Courtney had planned to have Thanksgiving at her place in Saratoga—invite her usual friends, maybe this new guy on the scene, Bob Gavin, and of course Arnold and Truely. She had asked Arnold if he wanted to invite Vonnie and his grandmother to come too—she and Truely would fly them up to Northern California if he liked—and Arnold had promised to think it over.

Now Arnold would be having his Thanksgiving dinner in the San Diego jail. Courtney canceled dinner at her house in Saratoga. Bob Gavin had convinced her to join him at his daughter's house in Palo Alto. She had three kids. It would be fun, he'd promised. Get her mind off her troubles. Courtney would be a Thanksgiving guest for the first time in years—maybe ever. They invited Truely to join them too, but he didn't have the stomach for it—new people, making nice when he wasn't feeling nice.

In the weeks since Arnold had been arrested Truely had established a routine for visiting him at the county jail. He went on Wednesdays and often Arnold's lawyer joined him. They had to go into the glass-cage visitor stall one at a time, but afterward they could compare notes and collaborate. Saturdays were reserved for Arnold's grandmother and Vonnie. Truely had kept his room at the Hyatt. He made sure he was around to pick up Arnold's grandmother and Vonnie to drive them to the jail on Saturdays. That way he could make sure they got there with no excuses.

On a whim the Saturday before, Truely had invited Arnold's grandmother and Vonnie to have Thanksgiving with him at the Hyatt. He wanted little more than the convenience of staying put, ordering room service. "Nothing fancy," he told them. "We'll have some turkey and dressing, watch a little football, just try to take it easy." To his surprise they accepted. He arranged to have a small dinner for three set up in his room, overlooking the vast Pacific Ocean. He knew Vonnie would like it, judging by her original longing to stay in the hotel with Arnold. He wasn't as sure about the grandmother, who had asked that he call her Coletta. Coletta Carter. She was young-looking for a grandmother—but old of spirit, Mississippi-style. Not the type to smile without good reason. Her life had been hard, and if you couldn't detect that for yourself then she would be more than glad to tell you about it. Truely got along with her okay.

He drove over to Bay Vista Apartments to pick them up late on Thanksgiving afternoon. They came out to the car looking dressed for church. Had you seen the two of them someplace far away from Bay Vista you would easily have thought they were living the middle-class life they aspired to. But the Bay Vista address gave them away. Truely actually felt conspicuous going into the neighborhood, a middle-aged white man driving an Escalade. "Call Vonnie's cell phone when you get here," Coletta had told him. "No need to park your car and walk up to the door." He understood what they were saying. And he obeyed.

They got in the car, Coletta in the front, Vonnie in the back. Truely noticed Vonnie waving to a group of older boys standing in front of the building, leaning against the wall. "Who's that?" Truely asked.

"Nobody," Vonnie said. "Just L.J."

"That boy be in jail before he turn twenty," Coletta said.

"Like Arnold?" Vonnie asked sarcastically.

"Arnold don't belong in jail," she said, "but L.J., he do."

"He's not as bad as she make out," Vonnie said. "He got redeeming qualities—she just don't like him."

Coletta laughed a harsh nasal laugh.

"This sort of crazy, huh?" Vonnie said. "Couple of weeks ago we didn't even know you. Now here we are having Thanksgiving at your hotel."

"I guess we can thank Arnold for that," Coletta said. "I wish he was going to be with us today. I hate to think of him over at that jail."

"You and that lawyer are going to get Arnold out of there, right?" Vonnie said to Truely. "He say you are."

"We're going to try," Truely said.

DINNER WENT PRETTY WELL. Coletta and Vonnie admired the view awhile, commented on the hotel furnishings, opened some of the dresser drawers to see what was inside. Truely and Coletta drank a glass of champagne. Vonnie had a sparkling water. As soon as the food was rolled in on a small table with white tablecloth and fresh flowers, they pulled up three chairs and sat down. Truely lit the small tea-light candles on the table.

Coletta said, "Okay, y'all, let's bow our heads and thank the Lord." She proceeded to launch into an elaborate impromptu prayer, ending with *"Forgive me for the ways I have failed my daughter, and now my grandson. They both locked up in jail and here I am sitting here about to eat a beautiful dinner. It ain't right, God. You know that better than anybody. Please act upon their hearts and deliver them from their hard-living ways. We thank Mr. Truely Noonan for his concern over Arnold and for hiring a good lawyer to help us. I thank you for my baby grandgirl, Vonnie here. Keep her out of trouble, Lord. I don't believe I could take no more bad news concerning my children or grandchildren. In Jesus' name we pray."*

"Amen," Truely said, relieved not to have been asked to add a verse of his own to Coletta's prayer. He looked up and noticed that Coletta had tears in her eyes. He saw that with the slightest encouragement she might lapse into a full-out crying jag—which he didn't feel prepared to deal with.

"This a lot of food for three people," Vonnie said, serving herself. "We going to have a bunch of leftovers."

Truely had overordered on purpose. As far as he was concerned leftovers were an important Thanksgiving tradition. He would have the leftover food packed up to go home with Coletta and Vonnie. He had learned that from Courtney. She always sent her guests home with beautifully wrapped leftovers.

Coletta said the food was plenty good—that she could have made better if she'd cooked it herself but the nice thing was not having to cook it herself. Vonnie ate with enthusiasm too, but she was small and had a small appetite. She lost interest in the food quickly and became more interested in the perks of the hotel room. She studied the minibar, exclaimed over the absurdity of the price list, went in the bathroom and marveled a little at all the stuff they were giving away free. She asked Truely, "Are you fixing to need this lotion right here? What about this bath gel? Do you want this shower cap or these emery boards?"

"Take what you want," Truely said. "I got what I need in my shaving kit." So Vonnie loaded the toiletry items into her backpack, along with the stationery in the desk drawer and the notepad and pen beside the phone.

After dinner they watched the first half of the USC–Notre Dame game. Coletta claimed to be a USC fan—but Truely wasn't convinced. She talked almost nonstop through the whole first half, barely watched a down. Vonnie pretended to pull for Notre Dame just to make it interesting, but she was mostly thumbing through magazines. At halftime USC was up by twenty-one points. There was not much hope for a comeback by the Irish, so Truely drove the two of them back to Bay Vista Apartments.

Before she got out of the car, Coletta shook Truely's hand and said, "You a white man, but you a good man. Makes me think maybe I was wrong to ever leave Mississippi. Me and Vonnie appreciate what you're trying to do for Arnold. Arnold is a good boy."

She got out of the car carrying the sack of leftovers and walked up to the door. Truely noticed that the same pack of boys were still standing around outside, leaning against the building like before, looking plenty rough and ready for any sort of trouble that might come their way. Did Arnold used to be one of those boys? he wondered. Did he used to spend his Thanksgiving Day leaning against a wall looking lost and bored with life?

The swarm of idle boys propped up against the decaying building at Bay Vista were nameless except for the one Vonnie called L.J. Boys without fathers and without futures, Truely assumed, who had accepted their deficits long ago and stopped complaining. They dressed in mostly black, aiming for invisibility he guessed, with those droopy, baggy pants all the better for hiding contraband. They wore fake diamond jewelry, same as Arnold, and exaggerated sportswear—Nike, Adidas, Reebok, Chargers, Raiders, Lakers, USC, ASU, SDS. If they really were athletes they might actually have futures—or at least shots at futures. But from all indications, these boys were not athletes. They were wearing costumes like kids at Halloween—who dressed up like Superman fully understanding that wearing the costume was as close as they would ever come to having the powers. Truely waited until he saw that Coletta and Vonnie were inside with their door closed and then he drove back to his hotel.

THE FIRST TIME Truely visited Arnold in jail it had not gone well. Arnold was scared. Truely could see the fear in his eyes and it made him mad. "Don't even think about feeling sorry for yourself," Truely began. "You put yourself right where you are. You and that damn gun of yours. I guess you could see that Court and I trusted you. We stopped checking the bookcase for your gun. How's that for stupid? If I'd known you had that gun with you on the drive down here I would have stopped the car and put you out on the side of the road and been done with it. All of it."

After a long moment of silence, Arnold found his voice. "I messed up, man. You was saying one thing. Gordo saying the other thing. I ain't sure who to listen to." Arnold was staring at his clasped hands. "I know Gordo is counting on me. At first, you know, I see why dying don't sound too bad to him. I see why putting an end to things seems like the right thing when he all busted to hell and his legs torn off. There was times I felt like maybe putting an end to it all myself and I never had no bomb blow me apart like that."

"Excuses," Truely said. "Your specialty."

"So, what? You hate me now? You think I get what's coming to me?"

"You keep on like you're going, man, and you're going to self-destruct. You're halfway there now. Look around you, man. Do you see where the hell you are? I'm not your old man, right? I know that, but if I were, first thing I would do is try to beat some sense into you—Mississippi-style. I should have lit into you that night at the VA Hospital."

"I wish you had of. I don't know what stopped you."

"Me either," Truely said.

"Then, after that, after you beat the hell out me, what you do?"

"If I was your old man I'd blame myself. Isn't that what parents always do? But I'm not your old man and I don't blame myself. I look at you and see a kid who was born into a mess and grew up in spite of the fact that he never got any basic instruction on how to be a decent human being. You figured it out yourself—sort of. Like you changed your mind and went back in there to get that gun away from Gordo. That's about the only part of this whole damn story I like."

"Me too."

"Here's the thing, Arnold. I don't know where the hell you came from or how you ended up in my life, living in my house, hanging sheets all over the place, but dammit, you did. And in spite of everything I was starting to get used to you being around. I'd come in the house looking for you. On Saturdays when all the college games were on I liked having you in there hollering, pulling for the wrong teams, eating me out of house and home. Courtney always trying to cook something just because she thinks

you'll like it. Goddammit. We aren't ready to give up on you yet.
Courtney tries to tell me you were sent into our lives for a reason.
But I think that's bullshit. I think somehow you just pushed your
way in—God knows why—but never mind, because you're here
now, your life all snarled together with ours, and now we can't
be happy if you aren't. Isn't that one hell of a note? We can't be
happy if you aren't."

Truely paused and ran his hands through his hair in a gesture
of aggravation. "And you can't be happy locked away in this pur-
gatory of a jail for doing something totally stupid, for your infuri-
ating lack of judgment—and so, dammit, we have no choice. We
have to do what we can. And we're going to."

Arnold was staring at his hands, his head bowed. "Thank you,
then."

Truely watched him for a minute. This was a posture he had
not seen in Arnold before, the slumped shoulders, the refusal to
make eye contact. It occurred to Truely that it was already happening, the defeat Arnold had somehow managed to outrun all
his life was settling in.

"Sit up, man. Hold your head up." Truely tried to speak without anger.

Arnold shifted in his seat. It was almost like he welcomed
some instructions, even of the simplest nature. He pressed his
shoulders back against his chair. He lifted his gaze and looked
Truely in the eye cautiously.

"Here's the thing," Truely said. "Over the years I've lost a lot of
people who meant something to me. They died, they left me, or
they stayed when I left, they grew up or grew old, they changed
their minds—whatever. I know you know what I'm talking about
here. You've been losing people all your life too—and you started
damn young. So this is the thing, Arnold. I don't know about you,
but I don't want to lose anybody else I care about. You understand me? Dammit, I can't afford it."

"Okay." Arnold looked at Truely, then cast his eyes down
again, his shoulders going limp again.

"Sit up straight, man. Don't slump."

Arnold straightened his shoulders and sat up in his chair.

"Damn if I understand all this." Truely laid his hands down on the tabletop. "Damn if any of this makes any sense to me."

"I know," Arnold said. "Me neither."

Twenty-eight

TRUELY GOT A FLIGHT out to San Francisco. Jaxon was picking him up at SFO and they had plans to brainstorm a second-round presentation they would be giving to the Global Air people. It would do Truely good to get his mind off the mess in San Diego. Whenever he closed his eyes he saw Arnold's nervous face behind the Plexiglas wall, holding the phone in his hand, saying, "Man, I was worried you wouldn't come."

He remembered the surge of emotion that had risen in him. "Arnold," he'd said. "You can count on me. Don't you know that by now? I'm not going to let you down."

Arnold had nearly cried then. And Truely had come damn close.

JAXON WAS GETTING GRAY. Truely guessed that if a guy had four kids, three of them girls, then yes, he was going to go gray fast. Melissa liked to tease him that he was getting distinguished—and Truely actually thought he was. He looked like a successful man, happy with his life, at peace with the world. "How's it going down there?" Jaxon slung Truely's bag in the car. "Anything we can do to help out? Really, man, all you got to do is ask. I know how much you care about that kid."

"Yeah," Truely said. "Arnold is the great irritant of my life— for sure. Funny, here he is locked up down in San Diego, caught up in one hell of a big mess—and yet if anybody asked me I'd say that if I ever had a son, you know—I'd want him to be like Arnold. Just like him."

"When you get this thing sorted out," Jaxon said, "you're going to need to bring your irritant around to Woodside to hang out with our four irritants. I think they'd hit it off." Jaxon slapped Truely's back affectionately. "If you ask me, Arnold has worked a miracle no one before him has been able to pull off—he's made Truely Noonan a family man."

"Who knew?" Truely said.

JAXON DROVE TRUELY to Mariposa Street and they talked business the whole time. They'd hired a guy to put together a flashy video of the new tChair. It would be their first time to see what he had come up with. Truely wanted some time to put his own thoughts together first. Jaxon counted on Truely to be the big-idea guy. Jaxon was the find-a-way-to-get-it-done guy. They were a great team that way.

"Listen, True," Jaxon said when he let Truely out at his place. "This is not a plot or anything. You know Melissa and Lanie are good friends. She's at the house a lot these days. Anyway, Melissa is coming into the city tonight to meet me for dinner. She's bringing Lanie. So that's your heads-up. No pressure. Are you in or out, buddy?"

"In." Truely's answer surprised him as much as it did Jaxon, who was clearly pleased.

TRUELY MADE HIS WAY UPSTAIRS in the clumsy industrial-style elevator, which was slow and noisy. He walked to his door and unlocked it, swung it wide open, slung his bag on the floor and looked head-on at the white sheet monstrosity precariously constructed in the middle of the space. Arnold's room.

He had made sure it was only temporary—like everything else in his life. Arnold never assumed anything beyond the moment. "Courtney will hate it too, right?" he'd said. Truely was surprised to feel so overcome at the sight of it. Arnold had claimed the heart of this space as his own—and, with or without Truely's cooperation, he had made it his home.

On the kitchen bar sat Arnold's *GED for Dummies* book and a stack of other books and papers Courtney had gathered to usher him into the world of high school graduates. His work boots were just inside the front door, his coat was slung over the back of a chair. Lord, Arnold. Arnold was everywhere. Truely walked over to Arnold's sheet-draped semi-bedroom and pulled a sheet open. On the sofa that he had converted into his bed lay a couple of audiobooks and a little notepad he carried in his coat pocket.

Truely sat down on the improvised bed. With the sheet pulled open he could see the city outside—vast and beautiful, but daunting and ominous too. He hoped Arnold had felt safe here, in this loft, sleeping in this homemade tent. He hadn't thought to wonder before. But now it seemed the most important thing of all—that Arnold had felt safe. "You ain't going to leave me up here, are you?" he had said shortly before the police arrived and took him off to jail.

Truely held his head in his hands. His instinct was to pray for Arnold, to call on God to do what he could not do himself—keep Arnold safe—but instead of prayer a backwash of regret overtook him.

LATER WHEN MELISSA AND LANIE CRASHED in on the tChair powwow down at the Mariposa Street warehouse, Truely and Jaxon realized that they had lost track of time—easy to do since they felt such passion for their project. Also Truely had welcomed the distraction from recent negative events and given in to it completely. They were both high on the plethora of business possibilities and it showed—a joyful sort of natural drunkenness.

When Melissa flicked the light switch on and off a few times to signal their arrival—and the imposed end of the workday—Truely looked up to see Lanie standing beside Melissa and he realized he was glad to see her. She, on the other hand, looked cautious and unsure whether or not she was equally glad. Why the hell hadn't he ever called her? Damn. He knew better.

Women liked to be called after spending time with a man. He knew that, didn't he? Would it kill him to play by the rules?

Melissa had made reservations at this new place called The Porch. It was Southern-based cuisine. She thought Truely might especially like it. And he did.

When Jaxon and Melissa saw old friends and were called away from the table, leaving Lanie and him alone for a few minutes, Truely said, "I'm glad you came tonight. It's good to see you."

"Thanks." She busied herself sipping her drink.

"I know I didn't call. I guess you think I'm a jerk."

"I don't guess it would surprise you to know that I have extremely low expectations—the lowest—where you're concerned?"

He laughed.

"Jaxon and Melissa are the ones who think you're such a great guy. Not me." She smiled and Truely appreciated the gesture.

"This is not an excuse," he said, "but I've been going through a pretty hard time with a kid that—"

"Arnold?" She spoke his name with such familiarity. "Melissa said he's your adopted son or something, right?"

"Not exactly. He's a kid who has gotten himself into a terrible mess. I've been staying down in San Diego recently. Fly back tomorrow actually. We're trying to see if we can get the charges dropped and get him released."

"He's in jail?" She was clearly interested.

"Illegal possession of a weapon. Drug possession with intent to distribute. Attempted murder. Whatever they can make stick."

"Good grief, Truely."

"He made a bad mistake in judgment. He's not a criminal. Far from it."

"Guess he's glad to have you in his corner."

"Maybe you'll meet him sometime. You'd love him."

"Well, clearly you do," she said.

AFTER DINNER Jaxon and Melissa needed to hurry home as usual. Their kids were too old for a babysitter, so instead there were dozens of cell phone calls going back and forth between

Melissa and the kids throughout dinner. "It's always like this," Jaxon said. "I don't know what makes us think we can go out like a couple of adults and have an adult dinner."

"When they're grown and gone we're going to miss all this," Melissa insisted, her hand over the mouth of the phone. "But we do need to go. The natives are getting restless."

"You guys go ahead," Truely volunteered. "We'll get a cab. I'll get Lanie home."

Melissa looked at Lanie with doubt. "You sure?" she asked.

"It's okay," Lanie said. "He's harmless."

Melissa looked very unsure about leaving Lanie with Truely, a man who had proven himself to be nothing more than a disappointment waiting to happen. She seemed unwilling to abandon her friend. Finally Jaxon grabbed Melissa's arm. "Let's go," he insisted. "While the house is still standing."

Once they were gone Truely said, "Look, why don't we get a cab over to my place. I'd like to show you something."

"Your etchings?" Lanie said.

It was the first time in a while Truely could remember laughing out loud.

Lanie seemed unsure whether this was a good idea. "I don't know," she said. "It's late."

"Afterward I'll deliver you home in a timely fashion. I promise."

"Okay," she acquiesced. "I'm half curious."

They cabbed over to Truely's building. Truely hoped he hadn't oversold the sight awaiting Lanie. Maybe not everyone would be intrigued by a homemade tent in the middle of an upscale loft. Maybe she would miss the point entirely and be bored. Truely actually felt nervous. He had not invited a woman to his place since he split with Shauna. That seemed now like a long, long time ago. Shauna had morphed into an unpleasant woman who could not be reasoned with, who was void of what Truely considered basic compassion for a kid like Arnold.

When they got inside the loft Lanie seemed to know instantly what she was there to see. "Wow. It's like the forts my sister and I used to make in our parents' living room when we were kids—only this one is clearly designed for an adult."

"Arnold made it," Truely said. "I just came home one night and there it was. 'For privacy,' he said. 'So you don't have to be looking at me every minute.' Truely felt his voice go soft—and so he went silent until he could get his volume back.

Lanie walked over to the sheet monstrosity. "Can I open it? Is it okay to look inside?"

"Sure." He was relieved that she was intrigued. He watched her gently tug one of the sheets open.

"What holds this up?" She looked overhead.

"Fishing line."

"Very clever."

"Yep."

"So Arnold slept in here?"

"He did."

"And these are his CDs here? These audiobooks?"

"He didn't select them, mind you. My sister, Courtney, sort of imposed them on him. Trying to get him ready to pass the GED. But he was game. He plugged in every night and listened to the damn things."

"Nice vibe here," Lanie said. "If you believe in vibes."

"I do," he said, surprising himself.

"So you're going to leave this up, this tent? Wait until he comes back?"

"You make it sound like I've got a vigil going here—or something."

"Don't you?"

"I don't know. I keep thinking I need to call an architect and get some walls put in this place—surprise him when he comes back with a real room, you know."

"God, you miss him a lot, don't you?"

Truely felt that sway of the earth beneath him which was usually what happened right before he lost his composure. He turned and walked toward the kitchen. "Can I get you a drink?" He swiped at his eyes with a napkin.

"I'll have what you're having," Lanie said.

"Lord knows, I didn't bring you over here to see what a big baby I am. I don't know what's wrong with me." He opened a bottle of red pinot and poured two glasses.

Lanie walked into the kitchen. "These belong to Arnold too?" She ran her fingers over Arnold's books and papers.

"He wasn't the greatest reader, you know. He struggled. But he's plenty smart. Courtney was determined that the more he read the more confident reader he would become. Seemed like it was working too. He improved a lot."

"Your sister sounds like quite a lady," Lanie said.

"The best," he said. "She's intense, you know, but she's all heart. She sent Arnold some books first thing—sent them to the jail. They allow him to have five at a time, paperbacks only, and they have to be sent directly from a publisher or bookstore. They're worried about contraband, right? She sent him *The Autobiography of Malcolm X*. He already listened to it on CD. Now she wants him to read it for himself because, you know, it's about the way going to prison transformed the guy. He went in a nobody—and came out a great leader."

"I hope it helps," Lanie said.

Truely handed her a glass of wine. His hand was trembling just slightly. Not enough for her to notice, he thought. He knew his eyes were glistening. He knew he was talking too much too, but he had wanted so much to talk to somebody about Arnold. And here was Lanie—willing to listen.

"I appreciate your coming tonight," he said again.

"It's been interesting." She smiled.

"I'm sorry if I've been hard to get along with."

"Doesn't matter," she said. "It really doesn't."

Truely wasn't sure how to understand her slight standoffishness. It occurred to him that he misunderstood her interest in him—in both degree and description. "Wait," he said. "Don't tell me. While I was busy being a pain in the ass, you met somebody else? Is that it?"

"Something like that," she said.

Truely felt more disappointed at the news than he would have expected. "Lucky guy," he said. "Good for you."

"I was going to mention it," she said, "but why? It's nothing serious yet, he's just a really nice guy. You've probably heard that really nice guys are pretty rare—especially for women my age."

"Like I said—lucky guy." Truely took Lanie's arm. "Come over here, I'll show you our view of the city from the terrace. It's the reason we bought this place to start with. Here"—he grabbed Arnold's jacket from the chair where he'd left it and draped it over her shoulders—"it's chilly out."

They sat on the unlit terrace for a long time, talking. Lanie asked him about Arnold's family and Truely found himself talking at length about Vonnie and Coletta. He told her about Vonnie crying when Arnold wouldn't let her stay at the hotel, about their odd Thanksgiving at the Hyatt, about their place at Bay Vista Apartments with the rough-looking boys lounging around out front. He even found himself talking a little about Arnold's mother—only maybe fifteen years old when Arnold was born. He did not tell Lanie the rest of it—his daddy getting shot, his mother now in jail. He reserved the telling of that story for Arnold. It would be his to tell—or not.

Truely was grateful that he was not alone staring at evidence of Arnold everywhere he looked. He appreciated Lanie being interested, asking questions and listening to his attempts to answer honestly.

He had not expected her to spend the night. It had gotten very late. They had moved inside and sat down briefly inside Arnold's sheet tent. Truely had kissed her. That was all. One kiss. They lay down on the sofa turned improvised bed, and with Truely's arm loosely draped over Lanie and a ragged quilt pulled over them, they slept.

SUNDAY NIGHT Mose Jones was doing the Raiders-Chargers game in San Diego. He and Truely had planned to get together the following day—and Truely was looking forward to it. He talked to Mose on the phone fairly often now, so Mose was reasonably updated on the bleak turn of events concerning Arnold, whom he had never even met.

Arnold's lawyer, a guy named Mike Wineberg, invited Truely and Mose to play eighteen holes at La Jolla Country Club. Over the last couple of months Truely had inadvertently gotten to know Mike pretty well, first by phone, and lately from their joint trips to visit Arnold at the jail. Mike's firm was doing its best for Arnold's mother, and more important, Mike was doing his best for Arnold. Truely figured it could only help to have Mose hear whatever Mike had to say about Arnold's situation. He trusted Mose with the information—all of it. He knew Mose loved golf too, so the day's venue was perfect. Mose wasn't a great golfer and that drove him crazy—made him more competitive than ever. They hadn't played a round together in a long time. It should be a good day.

Meanwhile Truely was sprawled across the hotel bed with a six-pack of cold beer and some room service—nachos, a burger with fries, some barbecue chicken wings. He was planning to watch the Chargers game, listen to Mose pontificate, and maybe even doze off a time or two if he was lucky.

Immediately when he'd returned to San Diego late Saturday he'd called Lanie to check in, just to say thanks and to show her that he wasn't quite as clueless as he appeared. It was a small thing—but he felt good about it.

Originally Courtney was supposed to come back to San Diego with him and they planned to watch tonight's game together. But she had a meeting scheduled on Monday with Hastings and their respective lawyers, who were trying to sort out the divorce agreement, so she postponed her return to the Hyatt until Tuesday. She had promised to take Vonnie shopping when she came back. Vonnie had called Truely twice already to make sure Courtney hadn't changed her mind.

Last thing Truely could remember it was the third quarter and the Chargers were ahead by a field goal. When he woke up the next morning the TV was still jabbering and his leftover room service food was sitting on the bedside table sort of fossilized. He showered and dressed for golf and drove over to pick up Mose at his hotel. They would meet Mike at the course. Tee time was nine.

The great thing about Mose was that he and Truely had established a friendship that stayed put no matter where either of them might wander, for how long, or with whom. When they were together they reverted mostly to their original boyhood selves—Mose Jones and Truely Noonan, two ordinary guys from Hinds County, Mississippi. Buddies. No amount of success or travel or enlightenment or new companions ever altered the basis of their connection—that they came of age together in a time and place where life seemed simple in spite of being very complicated—and they considered themselves to be the same, simple and also very complicated.

They hit a few high spots in the attempt to catch up on the drive out to the golf course. "Mike is a decent guy," Truely told Mose. "He's trying to get the charges dropped against Arnold."

"What are the chances?"

"If we can get Arnold's mother involved it might give us some leverage."

"His mother? Isn't she locked up too?"

"Jerry paid her for her silence in the past, but now maybe she needs to speak up. That's what Wineberg thinks."

"So we're talking a little blackmail here?"

"Arnold is naive. You wouldn't think a streetwise guy could be naive, would you? But he is. He loves Gordo, man. He would never do anything he thought would hurt Gordo. But Gordo convinced him he was going to kill himself—and if Arnold was a true friend he would help him go out on his own terms. He convinced Arnold that that was what a real friend would do. He knew Arnold had that gun. He figured Arnold could get the pills from his mother. He was going to try to load up on painkillers—then go out with a bullet to his head. One shot."

"That was pretty stupid, man. Naive or not. Arnold should know better."

"Damn stupid. But he realized that and in the end he stepped in and saved Gordo's life. That's what I'm saying. He loves Gordo."

"What is this Gordo guy like?"

"You want to know the truth? Gordo is a good guy. Not perfect—a little reckless and rambunctious for sure. I'd say he made a pretty good soldier. I always liked Gordo. Even though I'd like to get my hands on him right now and slap some sense into him. He's lost his way a little—the war, you know. All he's endured. His family drives him a little nuts—but whose doesn't?"

"I know what you're saying," Mose said. "We've taken on a couple of returning soldiers out at Jackson's Gem. Rehabbing with prosthesis—you know. Two guys lost legs. One woman lost her arm below the elbow. They're all doing pretty good, but it's damn hard."

They pulled up at La Jolla Country Club and unloaded their clubs. Mike was waiting for them. He brought another guy, an attorney from his firm, to be their fourth. The mood shifted immediately. That was the great thing about sports—in this case, golf. It demanded your full attention, your energy, your focus, your best effort, and if you weren't careful, in this case, your money too. It didn't really erase your problems—that wasn't the point. But it let you escape the weight of them for four hours or so, and that alone was worth a lot. Truely was happy to be on the golf course again. He felt his competitive side come forward. "Okay, Mose, we both know golf is not your real game. I'll give you two strokes a side."

"The hell you will," Mose said. "I don't need your damn strokes. I'll beat your ass straight up."

Truely laughed. This was the Mose he loved.

"Mike," Truely asked, "you up for a friendly wager?"

"Hundred dollars a side," Mike said. "Press when you're two down."

It was a beautiful day. The weather was perfect, cool and sunny. The course was immaculate, the ocean view stunning. Somewhere around the fifth hole Truely started wondering why he had never taken Arnold out for a game of golf. Did he think it wouldn't be the right game for a guy like Arnold? Did he think Arnold wasn't country club material? They could have gone over to Harding or Olympic anytime—he could have taught Arnold the game, at least given him a chance to like it. He was bothered by the missed opportunity—by a long list of missed opportunities. When Arnold got released Truely had a lot of making up to do.

Mose rode in the golf cart with Mike. It was clear they had a lot to say to each other and Truely hoped at least some of their conversation was in regard to Arnold's case. Mose didn't shy away from asking questions. What Mike had failed to mention was that he was a scratch golfer. After they finished their round the other three were forking over their money. Mike pocketed six hundred bucks before they even sat down in the club to have drinks and lunch.

"Whoa, I hope you're as good a lawyer as you are a golfer." Truely had just peeled off four fifties. "Matter of fact, man, I'm counting on it."

"Trust me." Mike laughed.

AFTER GOLF, Truely and Mose headed back down to the Hyatt to discuss business. Once before Mose had borrowed some start-up money from Truely, to expand Jackson's Gem to include a weight-loss facility and spa. He had paid him back in full within the following six years. But this proposal seemed something different.

They sat up in Truely's hotel room at the small table in front of the sliding doors to the terrace. Truely cracked the door to allow the air to stir.

"Okay," Mose said. "Here's the concept. I want you to hear me out before you ask questions—you good with that?"

"You talk, I'll listen."

"Jackson's Gem is thriving, right? I brought the financial statement to show you. We've grown steadily—have a staff of over forty now. We still specialize in rehabbing athletes—that's still our primary focus. Right now we're working with twenty-eight professional athletes involved in eleven sports. We've hired some of the best trainers in the profession—I brought their profiles. They're impressive. I guarantee you that.

"Right now our clients are housed independently at local hotels. That's become problematic. There's the issue of rental cars and having to eat at hotel restaurants that don't meet our dietary needs, just to name a few. So we'd like to build a first-class residential facility—along the lines of the finest resort hotel—to house our rehabbing athletes and other clients. Top of the line—all the way."

Truely listened while Mose outlined his concepts for the expanded spa and weight-loss program and the addition of a post-detox program for people who wanted to reestablish their physical health after leaving rehab. Mose talked about the clientele and the staff and his vision for the future. There was excitement in his voice. It was obvious that Mose loved the work he was doing in Mississippi. Truely liked hearing him talk about it too.

"So, this is it in a nutshell," Mose concluded. "We'd like to break ground on the new Jackson's Gem. I've located an ideal tract of land out in Hinds County—actually it's not all that far from your family's place out there. Eight miles maybe—toward town. We can get a good-sized acreage—eighty-seven acres to be exact. The price is right. We envision a first-rate resort-type residential facility which will include all the bells and whistles. I'll show you our first-round renderings. Snake Creek runs through the acreage too. Did I tell you that? It's a beautiful tract of land, Truely. I wish we could walk it together. I think you'd be impressed."

"Snake Creek?" Just the thought of his boyhood haunt made him smile.

"Our concept is a *luxury well-being resort*. The first of its kind in Mississippi—maybe in the whole Southeast. Look." Mose held out his arm. "I'm getting goosebumps just talking about this. I think we could create something unique and socially beneficial—something Jackson, Hinds County, and the state of Mississippi could be proud of! I'm here to ask for your help."

"Wow." Truely was imagining Gordo going down to Mississippi to Jackson's Gem, checking in for a summer of rehabbing. It wasn't a crazy idea.

"Wow? That's all you've got to say?"

"How can I help?"

"I want you to be a primary investor—serve on the board too. Here." Mose pulled a slip of paper from his case. "I've jotted down some proposed figures. Look this over. Let me know your thoughts. I know this thing is a go. If I weren't certain I wouldn't ask you to get in."

"If anybody can do it, man, it's you," Truely said.

"Let me show you this then." Mose reached into his case again. "This is a list I put together of potential investors. Look it over."

Truely glanced over the list. The names that jumped out at him were Hastings and Courtney, some high-profile Jackson folks, a handful of sports icons and a couple of entertainers from the music industry.

"One more thing, man. Did I tell you I'm trying to talk Tay-Ann into coming to work for me? She's thinking it over. I'm offering her double what they pay her out at the hospital."

"Great," Truely said.

"She needs a change after everything. Could use the money too. Seemed like a good idea."

"Speaking of good ideas," Truely said. "We get this mess with Gordo straightened out—then maybe we'll send him down to the Gem and let you rehab him. What do you think?"

"Done," Mose said.

"You been overachieving since we were kids," Truely said. "If I can help you get this thing off the ground, I'm in. Count on it."

They shook hands. "You won't be sorry," Mose said.

ON TUESDAY NIGHT Bobby Gavin flew Courtney back to San Diego in his private plane. She was in good spirits. Truely had expected her meeting with Hastings and his legal team to be disturbing to her, but that didn't seem to be the case. Or else she had made peace with the proceedings before arriving so as not to add her anxiety to his own. Truely was actually glad to see her, although he didn't really understand why she was staying down in San Diego. He had tried to tell her it wasn't necessary. She had only been able to get in to see Arnold one time so far. She took a backseat to Truely in this regard. Instead she spent time with Vonnie—actually quite a bit of time. Vonnie had taken to calling her regularly. She also drove Coletta to the grocery store now and then and once to the doctor to get her blood pressure checked. Otherwise she busied herself in her room, reading, making phone calls, doing yoga. She took long oceanfront walks most days. She worked out in the hotel gym, which was less than stellar to say the least. Lots of nights she and Truely had a light supper together and maybe watched some TV afterward. Truely kept her posted on the legal twists and turns of Arnold's case—which to his way of thinking were too few and far between. He was fairly discouraged.

One evening Courtney returned to the hotel with Vonnie in tow. Vonnie insisted she wanted to show Truely the items Courtney had bought her. "Wait," she told Truely, who was watching the six o'clock news in his room. "I'll call you when I'm ready." She proceeded to lay out her purchases, display-style, on Courtney's bed. There were basically two outfits made up of assorted pieces. Vonnie laid the pieces out with great care, including the belts, earrings, patterned tights, a pair of tall leather boots and the pair of Nikes she had chosen. Courtney had also bought her a purse—which she referred to as a pocketbook, like girls from Mississippi. "Wait until you see the pocketbook Courtney got me," she called out to Truely. "You gon love it!" When she was ready, she yelled again through the adjoining door. "Okay, then. You can come in here and see."

Truely went into Courtney's room, where she sat quietly in the reading chair, watching Vonnie delight in her new stuff. "Ta-da!" Vonnie yelled. "Courtney let me get all this," she said. "Nothing cheap neither. Everything nice."

Truely wasn't sure of the protocol in a situation like this. His experience with teenage girls had pretty much ended when he stopped being a teenage boy. "Nice," he said, but he could see that that was an inadequate response. "Actually," he said, "very cool stuff, Vonnie. Sweet. Totally. For sure."

Vonnie laughed. "You crazy," she said. "What you like best though? Pick out your favorite thing."

"These boots right here," Truely said, spontaneously. "I knew you was going to say that," Vonnie insisted.

"Courtney, what you like best?"

"Either your shirt right there"—Courtney pointed—"or your pocketbook."

"Yeah," Vonnie said. "Me too. I just like it all."

"Well, let's order some supper and get you fed," Courtney said. "Then we need to get you back home."

"Oh," Vonnie exclaimed. "Do I have to go home? Can't I just stay here with you? Just one night. I been wanting to stay in this hotel."

Courtney laughed. "Not on a school night," she said. "Maybe this weekend. We'll see what Coletta has to say."

"Maybe Friday night?" Vonnie asked.

"We'll see," Courtney said. That had been their mother's response of choice to the endless requests Courtney and Truely had made as kids. It struck Truely how Courtney might have mothered her children the same as their mother had mothered them—if she had been fortunate enough to have children. It was obvious that she enjoyed Vonnie.

"Vonnie, did you tell Truely why we went shopping for all this stuff?" Courtney asked.

"I got it right here." She dug through her Old Navy backpack and located a tattered brown envelope which she pulled out and handed to him. "My report card," she said.

Truely looked at it—all B's except one A in social studies and a C in PE.

"It's the honor roll," she said. "That C in PE don't count against you getting on the honor roll."

"A C in PE? How hard can PE be?" Truely asked.

"They take points off if you forget your gym clothes," Vonnie said. "Also they make you participate when it's your time of the month—even if you don't feel good."

"Truely, you sound like Daddy used to," Courtney said. "He always focused on the lowest grade instead of the highest." It was true too. Truely realized he was patterning after his daddy same as Courtney was their mother.

"Vonnie, this is a good report card," he said. "You should be proud of yourself. Keep up the good work."

"You're welcome," she said.

They ordered shrimp cocktail and chef salads and ate supper in Courtney's room. Twice Vonnie asked, "Y'all sure you don't want me to try on my outfits for you? You could see how they look on."

"We know they look great," Truely said.

"It wouldn't take but a few minutes," she insisted.

"No," Courtney said. "I can vouch for how great you looked in those outfits. Truely will just have to take my word, because we need to get you home. Coletta is going to worry. Did you call her?"

The three of them loaded into the Escalade with Vonnie's packages in tow. They drove her home and watched her run inside the apartment as if she didn't want anybody to see that she had sacks of pricey items in hand.

When she was safely inside and Truely was turning the Escalade around in the small drive, Courtney said, "That is a sweet girl right there, Truely. She is a ball of fire for sure. But she is just as sweet as she can be."

"Next thing you know you'll be saying, 'Bless her heart.'"

She laughed. "You can take the woman out of Mississippi..."

"But?"

"I have to say it, True. *Bless her heart!* There. I said it. Bless Vonnie's heart!"

"Atta girl." He laughed.

Twenty-nine

IT WAS LESS THAN TWO WEEKS until Christmas and True-ly was dreading it—even more than usual. Seeing the gaudy decorations all over the place in sunny San Diego was absolutely depressing. At least in San Francisco you could count on a chill in the air, some morning fog to stall traffic, maybe a little rain or an icy wind off the ocean. He and Courtney had agreed to spend Christmas Day at her place in Saratoga. Myra had already put up the decorations—tree and all. Lola would be coming to stay too. It would be a long shot better than going home to his loft in the city and staring at Arnold's drooping tent—or staying at the Hyatt ordering Christmas dinner from room service.

To Truely's dismay, Mike Wineberg's legal team had not come up with anything powerful enough to force Arnold's release. It bothered Truely. "Look man," he told Mike, "I want Arnold out of here—bad. You understand that, right?" Mike assured Truely he was doing all he could.

EVERY WEDNESDAY Truely went to the jail for regular visiting hours. He stood in the too-long, mostly female line of mothers, girlfriends, sisters, daughters and babies. Today he was one of only three men in the crowd. He went through security and the metal detector, showed his paperwork and ID, and took a seat in the waiting room, where he would busy himself people watch-ing until he was called. It could take as long as two hours to accomplish a fifteen-minute visit. But it was worth it to Truely.

Already he had learned to recognize members of certain families that he saw week after week. The jail visitors were primarily minority—and poor. A good portion of them seemed not to speak English. It was not Truely's world, this jail culture. There were children here week after week, sucking on pacifiers, bringing small toys to play with on the dirty floor, growing up visiting their fathers or their mother's latest boyfriends in jail week after week. It was as normal to them as going to church used to be to Truely and Courtney.

It appeared obvious to him that the other visitors in this tedious process knew he was an outsider. Some of them nodded to him in recognition. No one struck up a conversation though. Truely had to remind himself again and again not to stare at the others, not to eavesdrop, not to be mesmerized and off-put by the casual, almost cheerful way so many of these families approached incarceration.

When he eventually got in to see Arnold he had a flood of foreign emotion. Truely had never been a germaphobe—but good Lord, these foul visiting booths were daunting. Greasy, scratched glass, covered in handprints and dried liquid that could be spit or mucus or the remains of a rebuffed kiss or worse. When Truely picked up the phone the residue of human filth crossed his mind. Heaven only knows what sort of disease lurked on the receiver. But he barged ahead. If Arnold had to contend with these circumstances twenty-four hours a day, then maybe he could tolerate it for fifteen minutes once a week.

When Arnold was finally led into his side of the booth he nodded at Truely, but stopped short of his usual smile. Maybe it was Truely's imagination, but he thought Arnold looked like he was losing weight. He had told Truely that the food was bad—really disgusting—but it didn't matter, he had said, since he had no appetite anyway. Arnold was Truely's height, naturally muscular, but now he was looking slender, almost bony.

"Hey, man," Truely said. "How you doing?"

"I'm ready to get out of this place," Arnold said. "Look like Ima spend Christmas in here, don't it?"

"We're working on it, man," Truely said. "I hate like hell seeing you in here. Just hang on. Keep the faith."

"How's Courtney?" Arnold asked halfheartedly.

"She's good. She's been spending some time with Vonnie. Those two are a handful now. She's going to try to get in to see you Saturday when she brings Coletta and Vonnie over here."

"Courtney don't need to come over here," he said. "She's a lady that don't belong nowhere like this."

"She wants to see you," Truely said. "Can't stop Courtney when she makes up her mind. You know that."

Arnold smiled briefly.

"How is your book supply holding up?" Truely asked. "You need more books sent in?"

"Naw," he said. "I got plenty." Arnold ran his hand through his hair—an unfamiliar gesture. Ordinarily Arnold kept his hair fairly short and neat. Now and then he got a design shaved into the back of his scalp. He took pride in his appearance—ghetto-style or whatever. But now that he was in jail his hair was growing out, getting nappy, which Truely knew bothered Arnold. Arnold went to lengths to keep his hair from getting nappy. He'd slept in his wave cap most nights at Truely's place. Truely wondered if Arnold even had a pick—if they allowed hair picks in jail. How else could he pick his hair out so it wouldn't mat up and stay itchy?

"They let you get a haircut in there?" Truely asked.

"Yeah," Arnold said. "They skin you, man, bad. My cellmate come back bleeding where they cut a gash in his ear. I got my name on the waiting list though."

"It'll grow back," Truely said. "It's just hair."

Arnold ignored the remark. "Vonnie tell me Courtney buy her some new clothes."

"They've been doing some shopping, yes. They got Christmas presents hidden all over Courtney's hotel room. Those two got the holiday spirit even if the rest of us don't."

"Courtney don't need to do that. Vonnie got a way of, you know, you give her a inch and she take a mile."

"Don't worry," Truely said. "Courtney is enjoying it more than Vonnie. Believe me. Courtney always overdoes the holidays. She's known for it. She's not being taken advantage of, if that's what you think. Nobody takes advantage of Courtney."

Arnold smiled. "How her new boyfriend doing?"

"He's got her flying around in his private plane. He likes her. That's for sure. To be honest, I haven't seen that much of him."

"Courtney had her female surgery yet?"

"Not yet."

"Maybe we talked her out of it."

"Maybe."

"But I doubt it though," Arnold said.

"Yeah, me too," Truely agreed.

There was an awkward pause between them, while they scanned for a new topic. Arnold scratched his scalp and shifted slightly in his seat. "I saw that Raider game with Mose Jones doing color," he said. "You see it?"

"Yeah, I saw it. I spent some time with Mose when he was in town," Truely said. "He's breaking ground on a first-class new health facility down in Mississippi. He rehabs athletes. NFL guys mostly. They come from everywhere. I told you that, right? He's branching out now, expanding to include residential capacity. He's building it out close to where Courtney and I grew up. Matter of fact, I'm going in on it with him. I'll be a partner."

"You putting up money?"

"Yeah, I'm investing," Truely said.

"How much?" Arnold asked.

Truely laughed. "A lot." He expounded on the details of Mose's concept — as Mose had relayed them to him. "A residential fitness and wellness center," he said, "like a first-rate resort with healing powers." Arnold listened distractedly, asking few questions, fidgeting in his chair.

So Truely tried moving on to another subject. "Played golf with Mose when he was in town too," Truely said. "Your attorney, Mike, played with us. Went over to La Jolla. Mike swept us too. We're demanding a rematch when Mose comes back. Matter of fact, I'm thinking when we get you out of here I'm going to take you out for a couple of rounds of golf. See if you like it. If you do, we'll get you set up with some clubs and some lessons. Golf is a good game. Character building and can drive you damn crazy too. You might like it."

"I give it a try," Arnold said.

"Mike told me he's got an appointment to see you this afternoon. That right?"

"That's what I hear." Arnold looked down at his folded hands.

"Look, Arnold," Truely said. "I can see your spirits are down, man. This is damn awkward trying to talk to you when you're in a Plexiglas cage coated in Lord knows what kind of germs and bacteria and human drivel. I mean, I hate seeing you in that damn box. I know it's tough. But listen to me, you're tough too. You know why? Because you have to be. No choice. You can tolerate whatever you have to tolerate until we can get you released. You got to make the best of it, man. Read books. Keep a journal—that's Courtney's idea. Watch damn TV. Think your thoughts, dream your dreams. Make your plans. I don't know. You can't collapse under the pressure. You hear what I'm saying?"

"I talked to Gordo," Arnold said.

"What?"

"Gordo. I talked to him."

"When?"

"Twice—this week."

"How the heck did you talk to Gordo?"

"I called Suleeta. She give the phone to Gordo."

"What did you say to him?"

"I tell him I need his help."

"What did he say?"

"I believe he gon help me."

"He said that?"

"He say something like that."

WHEN TRUELY'S TIME WAS UP the guard signaled him to leave. Truely put his hand up against the glass and Arnold placed his hand against it—sort of a subdued high five. Truely had seen people do that in movies and thought it was corny. Now he saw that it was pure human instinct. You needed to touch a person who was in bad trouble. And they needed to be touched too. Each visit to Arnold, Truely saw his subtle decline. His appearance, his voice, his energy, his spirits, his hope—all on the downslide.

WHEN TRUELY GOT BACK to the hotel he tried to call Lanie. He felt like talking to somebody about his visit to Arnold. He hoped she would want to listen. Maybe she would say something he needed to hear. But he only got her voice mail. "Hey, Lanie," he said. "Happy holidays. Hope things are going well with you. We're still down here in So Cal. No change. You take care and I'll be in touch later." He hung up the phone and wondered if she would call him back.

DURING THESE WEEKS Truely started making a list. It was mostly a doodle at first, but morphed itself into a list. The things he would do or have Arnold do when Arnold got released. It just began to create itself—the list. He labeled it *To Do When Arnold Gets Out.*

> *Season tickets to Raiders?*
> *Introduce Jaxon's kids. Lanie?*
> *Play golf?*
> *Help situate Vonnie and Coletta—better place?*
> *Driver's license?*
> *Truck in garage?*
> *Travel someplace. Where?*
> *Consider selling loft. Bigger place? Walls?*
> *Part-time job at tChair?*
> *Start savings account. Start investing.*
> *Get a dog? Maybe.*
> *Summer trip to Mississippi.*
> *Introduce Mose, Fontaine, Tay-Ann.*
> *Visit the cemetery in Hinds County.*

At some point Courtney found his list sitting on his bedside table and in the margins she penciled in a little column of her own.

> *Get Arnold baptized.*
> *Find a SF home church — start going!*
> *Bible on tape? (Read New Testament first.)*
> *Personalized Bible for Arnold — and Vonnie too?*
> *GED. No excuses. (Seriously, True.)*
> *Doctor — post-jail checkup?*
> *Dentist?*
> *Hire Terrance as full-time tutor?*
> *City College? Start with one class. See what happens.*
> *Take some photos — because we don't have any.*

ON SATURDAY while Courtney was at the jail with Coletta and Vonnie, Truely was working on his computer, reviewing some correspondence and revised renderings. He was pleasantly distracted when the phone rang. He answered it absentmindedly. "Truely Noonan here."

"Truely? It's Shauna." Her voice was strained.

It occurred to him he misheard her or that somebody was playing a joke on him. "Shauna?"

"It's me," she said. "You heard right."

"This is a surprise," he said. "What's up?"

"There are some things I need to tell you, Truely."

"Go ahead then." He was instantly tense.

"Well," she said. "First of all, I know you think you broke Daddy's jaw."

"I was hoping."

"You didn't. Daddy has a dental partial that he always wears. You hit him so hard it snapped in two. As drunk as he was it's amazing he didn't choke on it. It could have been a serious injury, Truely. It sliced into his gum. That was all the blood. I just wanted you to know."

"Well, I'm glad it wasn't as bad as I thought. Or maybe I'm

not—since as far as I can tell Jerry needed the hell smacked out of him. So I'll have to think about that. But thanks for the truth."

"He thinks you should pay to have his partial fixed."

Truely laughed. "I swear, Jerry's a piece of work."

"He wanted me to tell you."

"And you did. You're a good daughter, Shauna."

"Sarcasm doesn't become you, Truely."

"Anything else?" he asked.

"Yes, there's something else."

"Let's hear it then."

"Since the night Arnold shot Gordo—"

"You mean the night Gordo shot himself—in the hand," Truely corrected. "Which is a hell of a lot better than shooting himself in the head—don't you think?—which is what would have happened if Arnold hadn't stopped him."

"Since that night," Shauna continued, "Gordo has been in detox. Just like the family had been saying, he'd developed a serious drug dependency. Not just the stuff they were overprescribing for him—but street stuff too. They've got lots of vets in here struggling with street drugs. It's no wonder, really. Anyway, he's off nearly everything now except his antibiotics and his pain meds. He has to ask for meds now. The nurse has to administer anything he takes for pain. They do random drug tests too. They've assigned him a psychiatrist. He's beginning to cooperate with her. So, you know, Gordo is a lot better now, True. He's getting back to his old self."

"Well, that's good then. I'm glad to hear it. Seriously."

"Which leads me to one last thing."

"What is it?"

"Gordo asked me to call you."

"Really?"

"He wants to see you."

"Damn."

"I know."

"You mean it?"

"He wants you to come over to the VA tonight if you can."

THAT AFTERNOON when Courtney got back to the hotel after a day at the jail with Coletta and Vonnie, Truely told her about Shauna's phone call. She was worried. First she imagined that Gordo still had Arnold's gun and might just shoot Truely on sight. Next she imagined that the Mackeys had planned a family ambush, that they would gang up on Truely, hold him against his will, make him sign a false confession or a blank check or something. She didn't think he should go alone. She wanted him to call Mike Wineberg, but Truely refused. She volunteered to go with him herself, but he wouldn't hear of it. So she made him promise that he would call her the minute he got there and again the minute he left so she would not just sit in front of the jabbering TV and worry herself sick.

Truely drove to the VA Hospital exactly as he had done dozens of times before. He circled the parking lot in search of a vacant spot—part of the well-rehearsed ritual. He had no idea who would be in room 515 waiting for him. Would Gordo be alone? Would Shauna be there? If she was, then Pablo would be there too, no doubt. What about Jerry? He found himself actually hoping that Suleeta was there. Suleeta was the one who had put Arnold through to Gordo and he appreciated that. He appreciated Suleeta.

Truely made his way into the VA rehab center and retraced the steps of his earlier visits. When he reached the fifth floor and walked by the waiting room he glanced inside. No Mackeys were there. He went the short distance to Gordo's room, tapped on the door.

"Come on in," Gordo called out as Truely pushed the door open.

Gordo was dressed in shorts and a Chargers T-shirt, sitting in a chair. Truely was startled to see Gordo upright. On instinct he glanced immediately at the stump where Gordo's foot was miss-ing. It was a hideous-looking wound even these months later, bandaged loosely in a gooey saturated gauze. Gordo was wearing a baggy pair of athletic shorts so Truely couldn't see the other stump where he had lost his leg midthigh.

The last time he had seen Gordo—the night he was planning to kill himself—Gordo had been wearing a hospital gown, lying awkwardly in a tangle of bedsheets, propped low against a messy stack of wrinkled, stained pillows. He had been pale and hostile and so angry it was chilling.

"Whoa, man," Truely said. "Look at you."

"Six-million-dollar man. You ever used to watch that show?"

"Sure," Truely said.

"Soon as I get these stumps coarsened—you know, get the scar tissue built up—then they say I'll get some prostheses made. Not those old-time fake legs, you know. Steel appendages. They're saying in time I'll be able to walk—maybe even run. That's a long way off, of course. But what the hell? It's not like I got a busy schedule or anything. Nothing for anybody to do around here but concentrate on getting yourself back together."

"Suleeta must be happy," Truely said. "She ever show you that photo of President Bush running alongside a soldier from Iraq? He had metal attachments like the ones you're talking about—and he was running at a good clip too."

"Yeah, Mama showed me that picture. What? A thousand times."

"Speaking of Suleeta, where is she, man? I never came up here when she wasn't across the hall in the waiting room. Where are all the Mackeys tonight?"

"Home," he said. "They were about to smother me up here. Mama always watching me with those sad eyes of hers. And Daddy—he's just trying to drink his way through the pain—his pain. Shelly and Becca, they act half scared of me now. Shauna, she's mad all the time. She didn't used to be like that. It was a lot, you know? Too much. But you get in this detox program and your family has to agree to stay away while you go through the worst of it. They have to sign a paper. No exceptions. Now they don't come up here unless they call first. My psychiatrist asks me if I want to see them — I can say yes or no. Mostly I say no."

"Got it," Truely said.

"You want to see something?" Gordo asked.

"Sure," Truely said. "I guess so."

"See that chair over by the door? You think you can get it and open it up and roll it over here?"

"Sure." Truely walked over to the doorway and got the collapsed wheelchair and snapped it open.

"Push down on that back part," Gordo instructed. "That locks it open."

Truely did as he said and rolled the chair over to where Gordo sat.

"Okay, man." Gordo was animated in a way Truely hadn't expected. "You got to step over here in front of me and put your arms around me like you're about to kiss me on the mouth, right? Put your arms under my arms, yeah, like that. Now lift, man. Lift. I'm heavy. But not as heavy as I used to be. Just try to lift me up, man. Yeah, yeah. Like that. Then just sort of move me over this way, a little more, a little more, and help me down into that chair. Okay, okay," he said. "Good."

Truely was sweating by the time he had lifted Gordo, who was wrong — he was not heavy at all. Truely was able to lift him and move him over to the chair without much physical strain — but with great nervous tension. Gordo wrapped his arms around Truely's neck and held tight. Truely felt Gordo's muscles flex. He could smell the anxiety on Gordo's pungent skin — and his own.

"Probably don't seem like much. A man sitting in a chair," Gordo said. "But it's a big damn deal. Watch this."

Truely stepped back and Gordo propelled the chair forward, slowly at first, then faster, turning in a sharp circle and stopping suddenly before he crashed into the side of the bed. "Hold that door open and I'll take it up the hall a time or two."

Truely obliged, held the door ajar and watched Gordo navigate out into the hall. He was slightly clumsy, but determined. He made a sharp right and barreled up the deserted hall, turning just before he hit the distant closed doors. Then he made his way back, fast, his arm muscles bulging as he deftly turned the chair's wheels. Beads of sweat broke out on his forehead. He looked almost happy. "Pretty damn good, huh?" He eased the chair back to room 515.

"Glad to see it, man," Truely said. "I mean it."

"Like a freakin' kid with his first bike," Gordo said.

Truely held the door open while Gordo rolled the chair back into his room and stopped in front of the high mechanical bed. "Sit down, why don't you, man." He motioned to a couple of chairs against the wall. "Let's get real here, Truely, okay? I got some things to say." Gordo was badly winded.

Truely took a seat in a plastic chair.

Gordo wiped his glistening face with the tail of his T-shirt. "First of all," he said, "before all this shit happened, you know—I want you to know something. I was a damn good soldier. I know I was a kitchen guy—but I was still a good soldier. You can ask anybody in my unit. I didn't get messed up, my attitude screwed up, not with drugs or anything else, until after the blast—the bomb. I want you to know that—because it matters."

"I never doubted it," Truely said.

"Look, man. I'm not sure I like you much. That's no news flash. I think you did my sister wrong and she didn't deserve it. She spent a lot of years thinking she was going to marry you. I always knew that wasn't going to happen. And you knew it too, but you just let her keep on hoping like that."

"That's not how it was."

"That's how I see it. So when I come back here in this kind of shape"—he motioned down his body—"and I realize there is probably no woman on earth who'll ever have me, that I may never have any kids or a family of my own...I mean—it was damn scary. I never knew I wanted that—a wife and kids—until I saw how unlikely it was. And then *you* come around—you, like some cowardly son of a bitch—who could have it all if you weren't too damn afraid to make a commitment. I hated you for that, man. Yeah, I know Shauna has got Pablo now—and Pablo is a good guy. But he wasn't the one she expected to end up with. He is second prize and he knows it too."

"I'm telling you, man. It's not like that."

Gordo waved his hand, as if to say he didn't want to listen to any excuses. "Don't matter," he said. "Here's the thing. My psychiatrist—Dr. Romelli—she's a woman. She got me thinking about some things, you know. Do I want to spend the rest of my life being mad about something I can't change? The past is the past, but you know, you can get stuck there, just simmer the rest of your life in the events of the past—which was what I was set on doing before she started working with me. She said, 'I'm not as interested, Gordo, in who you used to be before you were changed by that bomb'—that's her word, *changed*." Gordo was imitating her female voice. " 'The guy you used to be before all this happened is gone. What I want to know is—who do you want to be now? Who do you want to be in the future? How are you going to reinvent yourself?'

"I tell you what, man. If she'd been a man I would have been pissed off. I would have smacked her with my shot-up hand—missing digits and everything." Gordo lifted his nubbed hand. "But she was a woman, so I just sat there and listened to her—not saying nothing. She asked me those same questions every day, over and over. 'Who do you want to be, Gordo?' It was like she was waiting for me to come up with a decent answer. At first I thought I'd prove my point by just keeping quiet—you know, refusing to talk to her. Truth was, I just wanted to be the same guy I used to be before everything. I didn't want to be anybody new. 'That's not one of your choices,' she'd tell me. You know how shrinks talk. 'Make another choice, Gordo.' After a while, I guess she wore me down. I started talking—whether I wanted to or not. Because damn if she didn't start to make some sense."

"Good." Truely was nervous and he wasn't sure why.

"It probably wouldn't hurt you to listen to what my psychiatrist got to say, man. My sister says you need a psychiatrist as bad as anybody does. According to Shauna you're stuck in the past yourself. She says you're dedicated to being miserable forever because your wife left you—what—five years ago?"

"Four," Truely corrected.

"She says you don't have no plans to ever get over it. Is that right?"

"I don't know. I'm not sure what my plans are." Truely didn't like the turn the conversation was taking.

"You know what the key to happiness is, man?" Gordo massaged his stump as he spoke. "This is what Dr. Romelli says."

"What?"

"You tell me, man. What do you think?"

"I don't know," Truely said. "What? Be true to yourself or something?"

"Hell no, man. That's most definitely not it. Far from it."

"You tell me then," Truely said. "What?"

"It's easy, man. Too simple, really. That's why so many people can't figure it out. This is it—*Help somebody.*"

"Help somebody. That's it?"

"Doc says when you can't help yourself—then help somebody else. See? It's supposed to boomerang back to you, I guess."

"Not a bad theory," Truely said without enthusiasm.

"Look man, maybe it works like this. If you need help—then you help somebody. If you need forgiveness—then you forgive somebody. If you need love—then you love somebody. See? Maybe it's that simple."

"Maybe."

"Dr. Romelli swears it works, man. That's all I know."

"So you're going to try that approach. Is that what you're saying?"

"What have I got to lose? That's how I look at it."

"Good point."

"Beats shooting myself in the head, don't it?" Gordo tried to laugh.

"No question," Truely agreed.

"Right now, I need help. So maybe I get it by helping some-body else out there who needs help too."

"Like Arnold maybe?" Truely sounded more hopeful than he meant to.

"Yeah, Arnold. Can you hand me a glass of that water over there?" Gordo nodded toward a tray on a table by his bed. Truely saw that the exertion earlier had caused Gordo to break out into a full sweat. He walked over and poured Gordo a glass of water and handed it to him.

"Arnold claims you're not the ass I think you are."

"I'd say maybe you ought to listen to Arnold."

"My old man is set on Arnold doing jail time. He's hard-core. Everybody knows that. He wants somebody to suffer like he suffers. Every time he looks at me he has to turn his face away because he can't stand to see what he sees. He needs somebody to blame. Not just President Bush. Man, he doesn't even know the president. What does President Bush care what he thinks any-way? What can he do to President Bush? 'If you want to blame somebody, Daddy,' I tell him, 'why don't you blame that suicide bomber?' I ask him that all the time. But hell no, he wants to blame somebody in the here and now, somebody he can watch suffer. So he's set on blaming Arnold."

"Jerry's hurting bad," Truely said.

"Arnold has always been Daddy's scapegoat—since we were kids. Back then I let Arnold deal with Daddy's bullshit—because that way I didn't have to."

"You were a kid then."

"And now I'm not a kid," Gordo said. "So who do I want to be now? See? That's Dr. Romelli's question again—right there. 'You don't have to let your father decide who you are, Gordo,' she tells me. 'You can decide for yourself.'"

"She's right," Truely said.

"Daddy ain't buying Dr. Romelli's theory *help somebody*." He laughed. "No way. He believes in *hurt somebody*—bad. He thinks if you can't find relief at the bottom of a bottle, then there's nothing else to do but get even. I watch Daddy, the way he's handled this mess—or not handled it—made it worse—and I see how I was dealing with things the same damn way. Runs in the family, I guess. I get scared I could end up the same as him if I'm not careful. Man—then I *would* need to shoot myself," Gordo joked.

"My wife used to say, 'True, you're your father's son—you're not your father.'"

"Yeah," Gordo said. "Sounds like Dr. Romelli. 'This is not about your father, Gordo,' she says. 'This is about you.'"

"And Arnold too," Truely reminded him.

Gordo looked down at his damaged hand, tried to stretch the two remaining fingers. He began to pick at the stitches or maybe it was a scab that had crusted there. "Me and Arnold been through more shit than anybody will ever know," Gordo said. "Arnold is my man. Been my man since he was a little kid running wild in the street. He had that mess of a family—him and Vonnie. Everybody's got a mess of a family—but Arnold and them, they kicked it up a notch, you know? When things got too bad, Arnold used to come to our house and Mama'd take him in, let him sleep in my room in the other bed. He liked that. Next thing you know he was acting like that was his bed. He kept some clothes under the bed in a grocery sack. Lord, you ever try to go to sleep with Arnold in your room?" Gordo laughed and looked up from where he was picking at his hand. "That boy could talk now. He'd ask a million questions. 'Gordo, you think God really see what everybody do down here? You think God all the time watching folks like they say?' Oh, man."

This was easy for Truely to imagine.

"When I didn't think I could trust anybody else I knew I could trust Arnold." Gordo paused and went at a stitch with his teeth, pulling it loose. He was not self-conscious. "The war changed me in a lot of ways—but I can't let it change that."

"What are you saying?" Truely asked.

"Arnold risked a lot to save me from my own stupid self. Now I need to return the favor."

"What are you saying?" Truely asked again.

"I won't testify against Arnold."

Truely lowered his head into his hands.

"There is no case without my testimony," Gordo continued. "I told my old man I want the charges dropped. I'm telling you—and I want you to tell that Wineberg guy, Arnold's lawyer."

Truely found himself unable to speak. He nodded instead.

IT WOULD BE HARD to say how long the two of them sat there in silence, Gordo seeming to concentrate on his mangled hand, biting some of his stitches loose, spitting them out. Truely sat with his head in his hands, almost afraid to lift his face and look Gordo in the eye—for fear he had somehow misunderstood him.

When Truely finally looked up, Gordo said, "Aren't you going to ask me what's the catch?"

Truely's heart sank. "The catch?"

"Arnold's got some ideas. Right? First he was saying he wants to be my caretaker—bring me my food, get me in and out of the bath, run errands, whatever I need. See? But, God knows, I don't want any situation like that. I told him so."

Truely was practically holding his breath. He wasn't sure why.

"So then Arnold tells me you're friends with Mose Jones. That right?"

"That's right."

"He says Mose is rehabbing some vets down in Mississippi."

"Yes."

"Arnold made me some promises that I might like to pursue."

"What kind of promises exactly?"

"They involve you."

"Me? It's done then, man. Whatever it is."

"I don't want you to agree to anything when you don't know what it is."

"Okay. Maybe you can lay it out for me then."

"That's part of the reason why I called you over here," Gordo said. "I want your word on a couple of things."

"I'm listening."

WHEN TRUELY LEFT the VA Hospital he was hopeful for the first time in a long while. He'd forgotten how it felt to be hopeful. He realized he was holding his breath still. *Breathe,* he reminded himself. He called Courtney like he'd promised. She was waiting by the phone. She begged for details, which Truely promised to deliver when he got back to the hotel. Next he called Mike Wineberg. Mike promised to contact Gordo himself, get the ball rolling uphill, so to speak.

What surprised Truely was what he did next. He did it fast, before he could think too much about it. He called Lanie's cell phone. When she answered Truely felt as nervous as an untested teenager. "Lanie, this is Truely Noonan."

"Hi." She sounded surprised.

"It's looking like maybe we've got the break we've needed," he said. "I wanted you to know."

"That's wonderful." Her voice was formal.

"Have you got a minute?" Truely sensed her uneasiness.

"Actually," she said, "I have a friend here. We were just on our way to dinner."

"Of course," Truely said. "Bad timing."

"We have a reservation. We're already late."

"I understand."

"I'm happy to hear there's good news, Truely. I hope everything works out."

"Thanks."

"I wish I had time to talk. Maybe we'll talk later?"

"Sure."

"Okay. Thanks for calling."

"Enjoy your dinner," he said.

Truely hung up. Disappointment swept over him. It registered in a way it often failed to, as happens when a man has long lived with minor disappointment and become essentially immune to it. But he wasn't going to let anything dampen his spirits on this occasion. Arnold would be a free man. That was what mattered.

WORD SPREAD QUICKLY that charges against Arnold would be dropped. But the legal process was painfully slow. According to Mike Wineberg it would be the end of January before the paperwork was in place and the charges were officially dismissed. There was nothing to do but wait.

Thirty

CHRISTMAS WAS COMPLETELY DWARFED by the anticipation of Arnold's release. The holidays came and went in a relative blur. Truely agreed to have Christmas Eve dinner with Jaxon and Melissa and their kids and friends at their Woodside place. They had warned him in advance, of course, that Lanie would be coming. He'd been happy to hear it. Then they had also warned him that she would be bringing her new boyfriend—a doctor she had met in her fund-raising efforts.

As it turned out he was an all right guy, nice enough, considerably older than Lanie. Truely was appropriately pleasant. He found himself watching Lanie on and off all evening. Melissa had seated him at the opposite end of the dinner table from Lanie, which was a letdown. But it gave him a good vantage point to observe her with her new man. He was ashamed to be so interested. As for Lanie—she was cordial but cool toward Truely. It bothered him.

What no one could predict was that the following day Lanie and her new man would fly together to Phoenix, to Lanie's parents' house, and the new man, the doctor, would produce a sizable diamond on bended knee and ask her to marry him—and she would cry and say yes. How could anyone have known? Truely felt the slightest twinge at the sudden loss of possibilities when he heard the news. Jaxon was the one to call and tell him. Evidently Lanie had called Melissa from Arizona to share the great excitement.

"Good news, buddy," Jaxon told Truely. "You escaped another

close call. Another clean getaway for Truely Noonan." They had an awkward chuckle over it.

"Moving kind of fast, aren't they?" Truely said. "What's the big hurry?"

"Spoken like a true romantic," Jaxon said. "Look, Lanie is nearly a forty-year-old woman. The way she sees it, this has been a long damn time in coming. Things can't move too fast to suit her. She's past ready."

"I never got that impression," Truely said.

"Of course you didn't." Jaxon laughed. "How many times did you see the woman? Three?"

"It wouldn't surprise me if she thinks this over and has a change of heart."

"What are you talking about?"

"Women change their minds all the time, Jax."

"What planet are you on, man? Lanie is not changing her mind. She's waited too long."

"Maybe," Truely said.

"Not maybe," Jaxon insisted.

"Give Lanie my best wishes then," Truely said. "I wish her all the happiness in the world."

"Of course you do," Jaxon had said sarcastically.

"You'll tell her for me?"

"Tell her yourself."

TRUELY SPENT CHRISTMAS DAY at Courtney's house in Saratoga. Myra and Lola were there as always, and Bobby Gavin and his daughters and their husbands and kids and the usual culprits among Courtney's longtime California friends. It was very nice, of course. The food was perfect. The house was beautiful. The people were all pleasant. But oddly, Truely felt Hastings' absence acutely and could only imagine how strongly Courtney felt it.

Bob Gavin stepped forward in his mild, good-natured way to fill the gap, along with the added energy and enthusiasm of his lively, attractive, well-mannered family. It helped. Bobby carved the turkey with the polish of a practiced host, made the first round of gracious toasts, hosted the dinner every bit as well as Hastings ever had—only he wasn't Hastings and that was the glaring thing.

At one point, after dinner, when Truely had wandered into the den, still his favorite room in Courtney's house, with all the now obsolete family photos on the shelves—Bobby Gavin followed him, bringing him a glass of eggnog. "Here you go," he said. "'Tis the season."

Truely took the drink and sipped it, not mentioning that he didn't really like eggnog. "I tried to talk Courtney out of doing Christmas dinner this year," Bobby said. "I wanted to take everybody to the club instead. But she insisted. Your sister is a force to be reckoned with when she makes up her mind."

"That she is," Truely said.

"You know she was a great friend to my late wife, Lillian."

"I remember that," Truely said.

"Two very different women," Bobby said. "Lillian was a quiet woman who loved books and music. Every year she knit a sweater for every member of the family. It took her all year. She always liked to refer to herself as a *mousewife*. She thought she was a wallflower, but she wasn't. She was a really beautiful person. She was just a homebody, you know. But, man, she loved Courtney. They were in book club together for a while, you know. Lillian would come home talking about what Courtney Littleton had to say about this or that. They hit it off. In the last months of Lillian's life Courtney used to come over to the house and just sit in Lillian's room while she slept. She'd bring a book and read—not try to talk or do anything, really. Just be there. That was enough too. Courtney was one of the few people outside the family that Lillian wanted to see right up until the end."

"Guess it's been really hard, losing your wife."

"It was hell at first. Even though I saw it coming—I was lost. Couldn't sleep. Couldn't eat. But my girls—you know—they sort of guided me through the grief. Three daughters. A guy doesn't have much chance to go under with three women on board."

"They're lovely," Truely said, "your daughters."

"I'm a lucky man," Bobby said. "Double lucky—now that Courtney has come into my life. All the years she was married to Hastings, you know, I always thought she stood apart. She was special. I thought Hastings was one of the luckiest guys around."

"And now what do you think?"

"About Hastings?" Bobby chuckled. "Look, Hastings is all right. I don't judge him harshly. You live as long as I have and you learn not to judge people. Most people are doing the best they can. Besides, if Hastings was smart enough to hang on to Courtney—then I wouldn't be here with her today. His foolishness is my good fortune. And I'd hate to miss out on this."

Truely really had no idea what Courtney was feeling about Bobby Gavin. She seemed to like him. She spoke fondly of him. She loved his grandchildren and was always happy to have them galloping through her house—the more rambunctious the better. "Just because I never was a mother," she told Truely, "doesn't mean I can't be a doting grandmother. Right?"

She had the talent for it—if that was what it was, talent. Truely had seen that himself when he had watched Courtney with Arnold. She was maybe the most overbearing mother Arnold had ever really had. For better or worse.

Later when Truely was in the kitchen talking with Myra, she said, "Mr. Bobby Gavin is good for Courtney. You ask me, he can do anything Hastings can do, plus some."

"You think so?" Truely asked.

"He bring these nice children and grandchildren into Courtney's life. Do Hastings do that?"

"No," Truely admitted.

"And he got that airplane. He fly her all over the place. Do Hastings own his own plane?"

"No," Truely said.

"So, see there. That's what I mean."

Courtney had tried to invite Coletta and Vonnie for Christmas dinner too, and as was predictable Vonnie begged to come, but Coletta refused. She insisted that her sister was coming from El Cajon with her kids and stepkids and all their kids and they were going to cook all day. They would need Vonnie's help, she insisted. And so Coletta declined the invitation.

Vonnie was sorely disappointed and let it be known. "Grandmama is just worried because she don't like to mix it up with too many white people at one time. White people make her nervous. Even y'all do. Plus she don't want to fly on any little airplane either."

"We understand that," Truely reassured her.

"But just because she never want to do nothing—do that mean I never get to do nothing either?"

"Of course not," Courtney had said. Truely was pretty sure Courtney had comforted Vonnie with some promises, but he didn't know what they were.

IT WAS THE FIRST YEAR Truely had been a lax gift giver. His obsession with Arnold and his circumstances had so overtaken him that he had done virtually no Christmas shopping and in the end had given cash stuffed into envelopes as a last resort. By all accounts it was tacky, but no one complained, of course.

The highlight of Christmas dinner, as Truely saw it, was when Bobby Gavin raised a glass and said, "Let's all remember a special young man today. Courtney's and Truely's young friend Arnold Carter, who is spending this day in anything but joyful circumstances. Let's offer a prayer for Arnold's speedy release back into the lives of the people who love him."

They all lifted their glasses then, all those good people who did not know Arnold, but by now knew of him. Truely had seen that Courtney, upon witnessing all the collective goodwill, had tears in her eyes. She dabbed at them with her cocktail napkin. Truely understood that her tears were for Arnold of course—but also, no doubt, to some extent for Hastings too.

Truely flew back to San Diego the next morning and continued his vigil at the Hyatt. The waiting was grueling. According to Mike, Arnold's release papers were being processed—a slow, tedious tangle of red tape. One afternoon while Truely was distracting himself with some tChair promo material, the phone rang. It was Arnold. "Is Courtney around?" he asked.

"She's still up in Saratoga," Truely said. "Be back tomorrow. Anything I can do for you?"

"They telling me you can bring me some street clothes, you know, for when I get out."

"Sure," Truely said.

"I was thinking maybe Courtney could get me some clothes together. I don't want none that old stuff I wore in here. I'm needing to start out new."

"I see."

"You think she put me some clothes together? They got a jail Web site that lays out what you can bring in. She could read it."

"Of course."

"I pay her back when I get back to work, get my money right. Tell her that, okay?"

"I'll tell her. Courtney would love to do a *GQ* number on you—no question."

"Well, thanks then, man."

"Sure."

"And Truely? One more thing."

"Yeah?"

"Do you think she get me some shoes, eleven-D? I been wearing that old pair of yours—remember? They never did fit me right."

"Courtney will get you set up, man. You can count on it."

"Good then," Arnold said. "And you can tell her I finished all these books she sent in here."

"Really?"

"Wasn't nothing else to do."

"I'll tell her. She'll be glad."

"And Truely, thank you, man. For—you know—everything."

"Time and money well spent," Truely said.

"You mean that, man?"

"I mean it."

THE DAY ARNOLD WALKED OUT of San Diego jail a free man his hair was shaved so close he was nearly bald and he was wearing expensive new clothes that Courtney had selected for him, using the jail Web site as her fashion guide. They looked a little big on him, but it didn't matter. He had on pricey new shoes and a leather jacket and a new wristwatch and everything. Truely, Courtney, Coletta and Vonnie were all waiting outside for him. Arnold had lost maybe fifteen pounds and was looking drawn—but he smiled his best smile when he saw them all standing on the sidewalk waving and calling his name. The tears came then. Everybody got a good cry out of seeing Arnold walk outside the jail into the sunny world where they stood together on the sidewalk, ready to welcome him. Truely realized clearly now how absolutely terrified he had been that this day might never come. Seeing Arnold get his second chance was enough to nearly break him down.

The idea was to whisk Arnold away to a fabulous dinner to celebrate his release. Courtney had made a first-class reservation down in the Gas Light District, but right away Arnold nixed that. All he wanted was an In-N-Out burger. So they changed the plan and all loaded up and drove to the In-N-Out and ate themselves nearly sick. They toasted Arnold with milkshakes. They were a little loud and emotional and the other In-N-Out diners definitely noticed the unusual group of celebrants who hugged Arnold and hugged him again and again.

"It his birthday?" somebody asked.

"In a way it is," Truely answered. Courtney and Coletta kissed him every time they could. Even Vonnie was adoring.

The holiday season had come and gone virtually unnoticed. It wasn't until now that Arnold was back among them that they finally experienced the true meaning of peace on earth and goodwill toward men. Truely got bold and tried to express that with his chocolate shake lifted high, but got choked up and lost his voice. His gratitude nearly overtook him in the form of raw emotion. The others almost cried too, as if on cue—and then they all laughed. He realized that words were inadequate to express what all of them were experiencing. One life saved. The resurgence of collective possibility.

Somewhere between Arnold's third Double-Double and second large fries he leaned over, put his arm around Truely's shoulders and asked, "So, when me and you going home, man?"

ACKNOWLEDGMENTS

As ALWAYS I want to thank Betsy Lerner for her wise counsel and encouragement. My thanks too to Judy Clain, my editor, and her assistant, Nathan Rostron, for their valuable help with this book. Special thanks to Arnold Carter, who forced his way into this story when I had other ideas. My deep appreciation to the young men whom I have witnessed overcoming accidents of birth, catastrophes of circumstance, and the relentless prophecies of doom. I marvel. I celebrate. To Dimitrous, who helped me with place names. To Southerners outside the South, who never forget where they come from — or why they left. To the No-Pressure Book Club of Austin, Texas, who helped me see the novel inside a short story. To Dick Tomey, my true companion. And to Caid, Coby and Carleigh Bergthold and Taylor and Ryan Tomey, who make this world a better place — and keep the rest of us trying.

ABOUT THE AUTHOR

NANCI KINCAID is the author of *Crossing Blood, Balls, Pretending the Bed Is a Raft* (made into the feature film *My Life Without Me*), *Verbena*, and *As Hot As It Was You Ought to Thank Me*. She divides her time between San Jose, California, and Honolulu.